SHADOW KILL

Also by Chris Ryan

CHRIS RYAN

SHADOW KILL

CORONET

First published in Great Britain in 2017 by Coronet
An imprint of Hodder & Stoughton
An Hachette UK company

First published in paperback in 2017

1

B Format Paperback ISBN: 978 1 444 78376 6
A Format Paperback ISBN: 978 1 473 64323 9
Ebook ISBN: 978 1 444 78375 9

Typeset in Bembo Std by Hewer Text UK Ltd, Edinburgh
Printed and bound by Clays Ltd, St Ives plc

Hodder & Stoughton policy is to use papers that are natural, renewable
and recyclable products and made from wood grown in sustainable
forests. The logging and manufacturing processes are expected to
conform to the environmental regulations of the country of origin.

Hodder & Stoughton Ltd
Carmelite House
50 Victoria Embankment
London EC4Y 0DZ

www.hodder.co.uk

ONE

Freetown, Sierra Leone.
Thursday 4 May 2000. 1428 hours.
Ronald Montague Soames, KBE, DSO, MC, was bricking it. It was an unfamiliar feeling for the former commanding officer of 22 SAS. You didn't spend two years running the Regiment and three years as Director Special Forces without growing brass balls. And Soames liked to think he had a bigger pair on him than most. But the stakes were higher today. Much higher. As he sat at his polished walnut desk counting down the seconds, Soames noticed his left hand twitching with anxiety. He swallowed hard and checked his Blancpain Fifty Fathoms for maybe the hundredth time in the past few minutes. Two minutes until the meeting. Not long to go now.

His office was located on the first floor of a two-storey colonial house on the Spur Road, pissing distance from the British High Commission. A worn leather chair faced the desk, and a tacky Victorian painting of a nude courtesan reclining on a chair hung from the wall. Cables snaked along the floor leading to a Psion laptop, a fax machine, a telephone and a printer. In one corner there was an old HF radio set. An overworked fan whirred noisily above, fighting a losing war against the thick forty-degree heat. The faded brass lettering on the office door was visible on the reverse side of the dirty glass. RONALD M. SOAMES, the lettering read. DIRECTOR, JANUS INTERNATIONAL. From his office window Soames could see a chaotic sprawl of shanty huts and decrepit colonial buildings stretching all the way to the ocean, capped by a blanket of leaden clouds the colour of filthy rags. The office wasn't much to look at, and neither was the view. But then, no one came to Sierra Leone to admire the scenery. They came for the same reason that had first brought Soames here eighteen months earlier.

Diamonds.

The east of the country was overflowing with them. Especially around Kono. The diamonds there were close to the surface. Something to do with alluvial soil deposits. Which meant you didn't need heavy, expensive machinery to drill down to the diamonds. You just needed a few guys with shovels, and sieves for panning. It was cheap work. Low overheads. Big profits. But it also meant everyone was competing for a slice of the action. And whoever controlled the mines, controlled Sierra Leone. It was like the Gold Rush, the oil boom and the Colombian drug trade all rolled into one. No government could run the country without controlling the diamond mines, and the place was awash with private military companies. Which is where Ronald Soames came in.

His PMC had been awarded a contract to provide security for the biggest diamond mine in Kono. It should have been a straightforward gig. The rebel fighters in the Revolutionary United Front were poorly armed, shoddily trained and undisciplined. They stood no chance against the fifty or so ex-Blades, former South African Recces and local guards on Janus's payroll. Plus the country's president had the backing of the Yanks as well as the Brits. Which meant he stood a better chance than most of clinging on to power. But recently things had started going south, big time. The rebels began making inroads in the south of the country. The president had panicked and legged it across the border to Conakry, Guinea. His supporters had quickly melted away. The money had started to dry up. All of a sudden, protecting the diamond mines in Kono didn't seem quite so straightforward or lucrative.

All of which worried Soames. He wasn't getting much sleep, and he was drinking more than normal. The stress of the situation, getting under his skin like a surgical knife. But in those darker moments Soames liked to remind himself that he also had his own operation. A nice little earner on the side. He liked to think of it as a sort of insurance policy. A way of protecting his interests in Sierra Leone. It was his secret. No one else associated with Janus International knew about his operation, and Soames preferred to keep it that way. He had a reputation to protect, after all. He was a respected fixer inside Whitehall, the go-to man for the Establishment and several key ministers. Play his cards right, and a year from now, at the age of fifty-three, he could be more powerful than ever. He'd have a direct line to the next Prime Minister, and maybe even a seat in the House of Lords.

For eighteen months, Soames had managed to keep his activities hidden from the authorities. No one had suspected a damn thing. There were rumours, of course. But in a festering shithole like Sierra Leone there were always rumours. No one paid them any notice. No one had anything on Soames that could damage him. He was practically untouchable.

Until a week ago, when the Russian had reached out to him.

Told him he knew what Soames was up to in Sierra Leone.

Claimed he had evidence. Witnesses. Proof.

Threatened to ruin Soames unless he handed over the spoils.

Gave him seven days to decide.

Soames had spent the past week weighing up his options. He'd thought about calling in a few favours back home. He had plenty of friends in high places. He was one of the most decorated officers in the British Army, a recipient of the Military Cross for his actions in Belfast, and on first-name terms with the Queen. People owed him, especially since Soames had cleaned up many of their own problems in the past. But he realised he couldn't ask for their help this time. On the sixth evening, Soames made up his mind. He wasn't going to be pushed around by this Russian bastard. He would do what he did best.

Fix the problem himself.

The Russian arrived sixty seconds later. Soames heard the screech of the guy's Mercedes pulling up just inside the gate, followed by the suck and thud of a car door opening and shutting. Maybe thirty seconds passed. Then the houseboy appeared at the office door and rapped twice. Soames closed his eyes. Took in a deep breath, and exhaled. Then he popped open his eyes and called for the Russian to enter.

Viktor Agron strode powerfully into the office, like he owned the fucking place. The guy looked like a football hooligan who'd landed a job at Bear Stearns. He was big and muscular and shaven-headed, with a tattoo on his thick neck showing a wolf's head baring its teeth. The kind of tattoo you got when you joined a Russian biker gang. The guy must have weighed north of a hundred and fifty kilos, Soames figured. His massive frame was crammed into a plain two-piece suit and white shirt with the collar button popped, and an arrogant smirk ran across his lips, like the quick stroke of a knife. He had a Breitling watch clamped around his left wrist like an oversized silver handcuff.

Soames nodded at the houseboy. 'Leave us, Vandi.'

Vandi bowed and turned to leave. Agron waited until the houseboy had closed the door behind him. Then he swaggered over to the chair opposite Soames and sat down, manspreading his legs. A tense silence lingered in the air. Like meat from a butcher's hook.

'I'm surprised you're still here, Ronald,' Agron said.

He spoke in a thick, slow tone of voice that sounded like wading through mud. Soames made a sound deep in his throat and shrugged.

'You thought I'd run?'

'It crossed my mind,' the Russian replied. 'Haven't you heard the reports on the radio? The rebels are fifty kilometres from Freetown now. If they take the city, we both know what will happen to you.'

'The rebels won't make it this far. They never do.'

'You'd better hope you're right.' Agron flashed a shit-eating grin. 'You're one of President Fofana's closest advisers, after all. I doubt they'd show someone in your position any mercy.'

Soames glared at the Russian. 'You came alone, I trust?'

'As agreed. But I wouldn't get any clever ideas. My people are everywhere. We have this place surrounded.'

Soames cleared his throat and said, 'I've been thinking about your offer.'

Agron smiled. 'Hand over your little business operation in Kono, and in return we'll keep it a secret between us. No one else ever has to know. Those were the terms, I believe. More than reasonable. Well? Have you made a decision?'

Soames hesitated. His mouth was suddenly very dry. 'My answer is no. We don't have a deal.'

Agron furrowed his brow. He looked pissed off. He remained silent for what felt like a long time, but was probably no more than two or three seconds.

'That's disappointing,' the Russian said at last. 'Extremely disappointing. But I had a feeling you'd say that.' He sighed. 'In that case, you leave me no choice. We'll have to do things the hard way.'

Soames let out a snort. 'Is that supposed to be a threat?'

Agron shrugged and held out his palms, like he had a bag of coins in each hand and was trying to decide which one was the heaviest. 'Not a threat, Ronald. I'm just laying out the bare facts. We made you a fair offer. Actually more than fair. You foolishly refused it. Since you have no intention of giving me what we want, I'm going to have to take it from you by force.'

'I'd like to see you try.'

A smile crept out of the corner of Agron's mouth. 'Actually, we already are.'

'What's that supposed to mean?' Soames demanded.

'At this very moment, friends of mine are on their way to the border. The kind of friends you don't mess with. They have orders to take everything from you. The entire business.' The Russian sat back and folded his arms across his chest, pleased with himself. 'We're going to clean you out.'

The news hit Soames like a fist. He clamped his jaw shut and stared at the Russian.

'Bullshit. You don't know where to look.'

'Maybe not,' Agron replied, shrugging. 'But you're going to tell us.'

'And why the hell would I do that?'

Agron's smile widened. 'Because otherwise I'm going to put a call in to the British High Commissioner and tell him everything we know. Give him all the evidence. Every last little bit. What we know is enough to sink your career, once word gets back to London. You'll be finished.'

Fear crawled up Soames's spine, chilling the nape of his neck. He shook his head. 'No.'

'The ball is still in your court,' said Agron. 'Hand over your business and the high commissioner won't find out what you've been doing. You can still save your own skin.'

'Fuck you,' Soames snapped.

The Russian chuckled. 'No, Ronald. It is you who is fucked. Supremely fucked, in fact. Like the whores in this town, no?' He winked at Soames. 'You know what you must do. Give us what we want. It's your only way out.'

The voice at the back of Soames's head said: *You can make this problem go away.*

You know what you have to do.

Soames sighed and nodded briskly at the Russian. 'If we're going to negotiate, then at least let's be civilised about it. How about something to drink? I have a bottle of Grey Goose somewhere.'

Agron's eyes lit up. 'Now you're speaking my language. Do you have any idea how hard it is to find good vodka in this fucking country?'

Soames smiled as he slid out from behind his desk. He paced over to the drinks cabinet in the far corner of the office. He kept a ready supply of spirits in the office in case of an emergency. In Sierra Leone, bribery was a way of life. Police officers, soldiers, government lackeys: they all had to be bought off before anything could get done. Some people paid with American dollars or the local currency. Others used cigarettes. Soames preferred to buy people off with bottles of Chivas Regal and Laphroaig. He reached for the bottle of Grey Goose. Next to it was an industrial-strength plastic cable-tie formed into a wide loop roughly the circumference of a human neck. It was the kind of thing you use to bind together a bunch of electrical wires. Soames had purchased a pack of cable-ties a few weeks earlier, intending to clean up the spaghetti network of wires that crisscrossed the office floor. But he'd never got around to the job. Now the cable-tie was going to come in handy.

He paused and glanced past his shoulder, making sure Agron still had his back turned to him. The guy was glancing down at his Breitling, as if he was in a big hurry to be somewhere else. Breathing hard, Soames reached out and grabbed the bottle of Grey Goose by the neck. He snatched up the length of cable-tie with his free hand. Then he turned and paced slowly over to Agron until he was standing directly behind the guy, throwing shadows over his back.

The Russian half-turned in his chair. Looked up at Soames. Saw the bottle. Saw the cable-tie. Screwed up his face.

'What the fuck do you—'

He didn't get a chance to finish the sentence. In a blur of movement Soames swung his left arm back and brought the vodka bottle crashing against the side of Agron's skull. The bottle made a satisfying metallic clink as it thunked against hard bone. Like an aluminium bat smashing a baseball out of the park. Agron made a dull sound in his throat and spilled out of the chair. His flailing arms scattered papers everywhere as he crashed to the ground, his head smacking against the tiled floor. Soames was on top of him in a flash. He worked fast, taking the looped end of the cable-tie and pulling it down over Agron's head as the guy lay writhing on his front. Then he took the other end of the cable and pulled it as tight as it would go. The cable-tie made a rasping sound as it fastened around Agron's neck, constricting his airway.

Soames crouched over Agron as the guy struggled to breathe. The Russian managed to haul himself to his knees, groaning and gasping for air. His eyes bulged until they were the size of saucepans. He lifted his hands to his neck and tried digging his fingers under the cable-tie in a desperate effort to prise it free. But the tie was pulled tight. The plastic started cuting into the thick folds of his flesh. Like wire through a block of cheese. No way to loosen it. No way at all.

Agron took a long time to die. His face shaded red. Then purple. Then blue. He collapsed to the floor, his fingers still clawing at the cable-tie. Snot bubbled under his flared nostrils. He made a desperate rasping sound deep in his throat as the fight began to seep out of him. His black leather shoes scraped against the floor in his death throes, leaving scuff marks on the polished tiles. A jagged row of black lines. Like a prisoner marking off days on a cell wall.

Twenty seconds later, Agron stopped breathing.

Soames waited a few beats. A thick stench of piss and shit slowly filled the air from where the Russian had voided his bowels in the last few seconds of his life. Fighting his gag reflex, Soames dropped to one knee and felt for a pulse. Nothing. Soames felt no remorse. As far as he was concerned, the Russian had it coming. The guy had signed his death warrant the moment he'd tried to blackmail Soames.

Well, fuck him.

Now what? Soames asked himself.

Get rid of him.

Then get to Kono. Before the Russians get there and rob me.

The first part of the plan was easy enough. He knew how to make Agron disappear. Strip the guy of his wallet, watch and clothes. Drag the body outside, shove him in the back of the Land Rover. There was a two-metre-high wall enclosing the property, high enough that none of his neighbours would be able to see him taking the body out into the front yard. Then Soames would drive out of the city and dump Agron on the side of the road somewhere outside Makeni. It would take days before the authorities discovered the body. Even then, they would simply assume that the guy had been killed in a roadside ambush. A classic case of wrong place, wrong time. The roads outside Freetown were heaving with armed rebels hopped up on ganja and poyo, the local brew. Westerners were forever getting attacked.

By the time Agron's body was found Soames would have reached Kono, cleaned the place out and covered his tracks. Twenty-four hours from now he could be out of the country, relaxing with a cool beer in Cape Town. He reached over to remove the guy's Breitling and froze.

A thin wire was sticking out of the side of the watch, no thicker than a strand of human hair and alternately coloured red and white. The striped wire ran from just above the Breitling crowns and snaked under the Russian's jacket sleeve. Which is why Soames hadn't seen it before now. Agron had kept it hidden from view. But as soon as Soames set eyes on the wire, he knew exactly what he was looking at. *A locator beacon*. He'd seen them before. The antenna transmitted a signal location on a specific frequency, picked up by whoever was monitoring activity on the other end.

My people are everywhere, Agron had said. *We have this place surrounded*.

The door flung open. Soames looked up. Vandi stood in the doorway, his skinny features stitched with anxiety. For a moment the houseboy didn't say a word. He glanced over at the dead body and stiffened. Then he lifted his terrified gaze back to Soames and pointed frantically towards the window.

'Men coming, Mister Ronald,' Vandi exclaimed. 'Look!'

Soames moved past the kid and rushed over to the window overlooking the front of the property. A pair of white Toyota Corollas were racing through the main gate twenty-five metres away, steering past the derelict garden. They skidded to a halt directly outside the house, ten metres away from the old Land Rover 110 Soames used to tool around the city. In the next instant the passenger doors on both Corollas flung open and four guys debussed, two from each vehicle. All four were decked out in safari gear and designer shades. And they were all brandishing stubby-looking pistols. PSM semi-automatics, Soames realised. Soviet-designed pieces, popular with the KGB back in the day, chambered for the 5.45x18mm round. One of those dependable Russian firearms that never went out of fashion in the Third

World. The four gunmen barrelled towards the main door fifteen metres away. Soames looked on for a cold beat.

Shit.

The Russian's friends, he realised.

They're coming for me.

There was no time to lose. He spun away from the window, his mind racing ahead. He had eight or nine seconds before the gunmen came bursting into the office. The lizard part of his brain kicked into gear. Told him to forget about hiding the dead body. There was no time to cover his tracks. He had to get out of the house, right this fucking instant. But how? The front door was out of the question, clearly. He could try bolting up the stairs and hiding in the roof. But the gunmen already knew where to look for him. It would only be a matter of time before they discovered his hiding place.

No, Soames told himself. There's only one thing for it.

He sprang into action. Sprinted past the desk and the dead Russian. Vandi thrust out his arms, pleading with his master to let him tag along. Soames shoved the kid aside, yelling at him to get out of his way. He ran towards the balcony at the far end of the office, his heart beating fast inside his chest. Behind him a chorus of angry shouts echoed in the stairwell, interspersed with the pounding of heavy boots on the treads. The voices were getting louder. The gunmen were closing in. Six seconds until they barged into the office, Soames figured.

Five.

On four seconds he hit the balcony door. Soames ripped it open and stepped out onto the balcony. The heat closed in on him. He leaned over the ledge and looked down. The balcony overlooked a garden at the rear of the property, littered with weeds and rusted bits of garden furniture, and surrounded by a crumbling brick wall topped with razor wire to keep the local criminals out. Beyond the wall Soames could just about see a maze of dilapidated huts in the nearby slum, their corrugated tin roofs gleaming like loose change under the dull glow of the sun. There, if anywhere, he might hope to lose his pursuers.

Three seconds to go. Soames gripped the ledge with both hands and swung his left leg over the railing. There was a drop of seven metres from the balcony to the ground below. High enough to hurt like fuck, but low enough to risk jumping down. He started to bring his right leg over the railing, holding onto the ledge with both hands. To his left he glimpsed Vandi diving inside the rickety wardrobe in a futile attempt to hide from the gunmen. Soames could hear voices on the other side of the door now. The Russians were almost at the office door. Soames took a breath. Then he swung his right leg over, releasing his grip just as the gunmen kicked in the door and came storming into the room.

He fell hard, landing on his side on the parched dry ground. It was like being thrown into the path of an onrushing truck. A jarring pain exploded in his shoulder and shot up into his skull. Soames felt something crack in his upper chest, like a branch snapping in half. His jaw ached. His legs felt as if someone had dropped a stack of breeze blocks on them. He lay on the ground for a moment, badly winded. Then the voice inside his head screamed at him.

Get up.

Keep fucking moving.

Soames forced himself to his feet, wincing with pain. It hurt to breathe, it hurt to move. A sharp pain sparked up inside his chest and he wondered if he'd broken a rib. He forced himself to push through it. Shoved it aside and moved on, stumbling through the weeds as he headed for the eastern side of the house ten metres away. His only hope of escape was to tack down the side path leading to the front of the house, get to the Landy and speed out of the main gate before the gunmen could figure out what the fuck was going on. It wasn't much of a plan, he knew. But it was either that or surrender. And if the gunmen arrested him, he was as good as dead.

Then Soames heard a shout at his six o'clock. He glanced past his shoulder and spotted one of the gunmen rushing onto the balcony. The guy pointed at Soames, then hollered at his muckers behind him in the office. Then he brought his PSM to bear.

Soames stood frozen to the spot for a split-second. The PSM muzzle flashed. Dirt fizzed up in the air half a metre behind Soames as the bullet struck the ground. The gunmen readjusted his aim. The other voices grew louder as the rest of the gunmen rushed towards the balcony. Soames quickly unfroze. He turned and ran on as the Russian fired again. He heard another pistol crack behind him, the thud of the bullet thumping into the hot, dry earth. Soames ran faster.

In the next instant he hit the corner, then hurried down the rubbish-strewn path leading towards the front of the house. He could see the Land Rover parked up ahead in the middle of the drive, twenty metres away. Not far to go now, he told himself. His heart was beating so fast he could feel it thumping inside his throat. The pain in his chest dialled down to a faint ache. Fear and adrenaline flooded into his bloodstream, temporarily numbing the pain. Ten metres to the driveway. Fifteen metres to the Land Rover.

Almost there.

Don't give up now.

The Land Rover was parked side-on in front of the house, with the driver's side door located on the far side of the wagon from the entrance. Soames rushed past the front of the house and reached the Land Rover in half a dozen ragged strides. He swept around to the side door, gasping for breath as he frantically dug his keys out of his cargo trouser pocket. Then he yanked open the door and dived behind the steering wheel as footsteps sounded from the front entrance to the house. Soames shoved the key into the ignition and cranked the engine. The Landy sputtered into life. He glanced across at the side window to his right and saw two of the gunmen surging out of the front door, their semi-automatic pistols raised. The other two gunmen were three metres further back and hurrying forward to join their mates. The two nearest gunmen were less than twelve metres from the Landy. Which put them well within the PSM's maximum effective range.

Fucking move, Soames told himself.

The two nearest gunmen fired. Their muzzles flashed, and a pair of cracks rumbled across the driveway. Soames ducked his head below the dash as the rounds hammered against the side of the Landy, pinballing through the chassis and shredding metal. He stayed low as four more bullets whipped across the driveway and hammered against the side of the wagon. A fifth round smashed like a fist through the passenger side window, shattering the glass and spilling hundreds of fragments across the seat opposite Soames.

There was a momentary lull in the shooting. The gunmen must be zeroing in their aim, Soames figured. Adrenaline took over. He shunted the Landy into first gear and put his foot to the gas pedal. The Landy growled, then accelerated towards the main gate fifteen metres away at the far end of the driveway. Putting distance between himself and the four gunmen. Soames glanced up at the rearview. The four gunmen were at his six o'clock now. Twelve metres behind him.

Now fourteen metres behind. Now sixteen.

Eleven metres to the main gate, thought Soames.

Ten metres.

Nine.

The Landy rocketed towards the gate. Eight metres to go now. Behind Soames, the four gunmen started pissing bullets at the Landy. Most of the rounds were wildly off target. A trio of bullets slapped into the brick wall either side of the gate, tearing out chunks of mortar and spitting hot dust into the air. One of the rounds thumped into the front passenger seat. Another zipped through the hole in the rear windscreen and narrowly whistled past Soames's head, spidercracking the front windscreen. For a terrifying moment Soames thought he was going to die. He kept going. The gunmen were running across the driveway, chasing after the Landy. But they were losing ground. The gap between the shooters and Soames was twenty metres. Six metres to the gate. He started to believe he was going to make it.

I'm going to give these Russian bastards the slip.

He was five metres from the entrance when he glimpsed a blur of movement in his peripheral vision. A third Toyota Corolla came hurtling down the Spur Road towards the front of the open gate. Same model and colour as the two vehicles parked in front of the house, Soames realised. Two white guys sat in the front seats, decked out in the same clothes as the four Russian gunmen. He instantly grasped who they were. *Backup.* The Russians must have kept a third team stationed outside the house, in case Soames tried to make a run for it. Now the guys in the third Corolla were moving forward to block him off in front of the gate, cutting off his only escape route and trapping him inside the grounds of the house.

The Corolla screeched to a halt in front of the gates. Directly in front of the Land Rover. Soames floored the gas, aiming straight for the Corolla. The Landy engine roared throatily. The needle on the speedometer climbed fast. There was a violent crunch and shudder as the Landy smashed into the front end of the smaller car. The Corolla's front wheels briefly lifted as the Land Rover rammed past the vehicle, the force of the impact crumpling the bonnet and punching out the headlamps. The Landy swept past the Corolla then bolted out through the gate, lurching onto the main road. Soames hit the brakes and wrenched the steering wheel hard to the right, narrowly avoiding a row of battered old motors parked on the opposite side of the road. He felt the full weight of the wagon pulling to the right, the tyres shrieking, the frame juddering. The Land Rover swerved away from the line of parked cars and straightened out, pointing north on the Spur Road.

Soames glanced across at his three o'clock and saw the damaged Corolla resting next to the main gate. The front end of the motor looked like a beer can somebody had crushed. Smoke fluted up from the engine. Glass was strewn across the ground in front of the motor. Behind the Corolla Soames caught sight of the four Russian gunmen as they raced towards the gate. Two of the Russians headed for one of the Corollas parked in the driveway. The other two sprinted forward and swept around the smashed-up Corolla, their PSMs raised at the Land Rover as they prepared to blast up the wagon.

Soames didn't fuck about. He mashed the pedal. The Landy fishtailed as it pulled away from the house, quickly picking up speed. Soames heard the crackle of gunfire to his rear as the two gunmen ran into the street and loosed off half a dozen rounds at the departing wagon. The bullets hammered against the back of the Landy, ricocheting off the bodywork. Soames kept flooring it, burning rubber as he put more distance between himself and the Russians. The speedometer needle climbed above fifty miles per. One of the gunmen unloaded another three-round burst. Soames didn't see where the bullets landed. Didn't care. He kept the Landy pointed north, leaving the shooters in his wake. The gunmen were a hundred and fifty metres behind him now. The needle soared past the sixty mark. Two hundred metres. He saw one of the Corollas pulling out into the main road, tyres screeching as it swerved past the damaged car. The two gunmen in the road lowered their weapons and dived into the back seats of the Corolla. A second later the vehicle rocketed forward, giving chase.

Soames kept his foot to the gas, driving as hard as he dared. The Corolla was a speck in the rearview, but the gap was steadily closing and Soames knew he had to get off the main road before the Russians caught up with him. After two hundred metres he passed the Mamba Point Guest House and hung a hard right, turning off the main street. The road suddenly degraded. A rancid stench filled the Land Rover – garbage rotting in the tropical heat. The wagon rocked as it bounced over deep potholes. Heaps of rotting vegetables and rubbish lined both sides of the road. Everything here was brown. The homes, the road. The people.

He made a series of quick turns through the backstreets. His eyes locked on the rearview mirror, looking for any sign of the enemy. Nothing. Soames figured he had lost the Russians. But he didn't want to take any chances. He took another sharp turn and then pulled over next to a line of corrugated tin shacks. He killed the engine. Booted open the door and jumped out of the bullet-riddled wagon.

I've got to ditch the vehicle. The Land Rover was hot, Soames knew. And there weren't many 110 Defenders inside the city.

Driving it around would make him stand out like a sore thumb. No. He would have to continue his journey on foot. He hurried down the street, ignoring the hostile looks from the locals, constantly glancing over his shoulder to make sure the Russians hadn't followed him. The heat was unbearable. Like being smothered with a hot towel. Sweat pasted his shirt to his back and dripped into his eyes. His mouth tasted dry. His body cried out for a brief rest, just to catch his breath. But he didn't stop. He knew he had to keep going.

I might have lost the Russians, Soames thought. *But my troubles are only just beginning*. For a start he'd had to leave a dead body in his office. Now the Russian security services were on his case. And they weren't the kind of people who would let him get away with killing one of their own. They would hunt for Soames in force, and they wouldn't stop until they found him. Which meant that right now, he was the most wanted man in Sierra Leone. He had no passport, no money, no gun. He'd had to abandon everything in the office when Viktor Agron's friends showed up.

Soames knew he would have to get to Kono. Before the Russians found out where he'd hidden everything, and robbed him blind. Which would be difficult enough in ordinary circumstances. But now he was a wanted man, in the most dangerous city on earth. There were about a dozen checkpoints and two hundred miles of rebel-held territory between Freetown and the diamond mine at Kono. He couldn't head there anytime soon. It was too dangerous. There were too many people looking for him. The whole city was on the cusp of a rebel coup. No, Soames told himself. Kono would have to wait.

First of all, he had to find a friend.

Sixteen hours later, John Porter's pager buzzed.

TWO

London, England.
Friday 5 May 2000. 0402 hours.
Six thousand miles away, John Porter sat inside the back of the Ford Transit and tried not to think about the pounding inside his head.

The Transit 350 rolled at a steady fifteen miles per down Stradbrooke Road, a stretch of neglected terrace houses just off the tatty Tottenham High Road. There were eight guys in the back of the van. Porter and his mucker John Bald, plus half a dozen officers from SO19, the Met's specialist firearms unit. The SO19 guys looked like they were about to re-enact Princes Gate. They were decked out in flame-retardant assault suits, body armour and ballistic helmets, and they carried Heckler & Koch MP5 carbines chambered with hollow-point nine-milli Parabellum. They rode in silence in the back of the Transit, counting down the seconds until the start of the op. Bald and Porter were dressed in cheap civvies, their Kevlar vests disguised under their sweatshirts, their police-issue Glock 17 semi-automatics holstered around their waists. Bald also wore a Petzl tactical head torch that transmitted a small beam of red light.

Less than a minute to go until the op began, and all Porter could think about was how long it had been since he'd had a drink.

Six hours since my last drop and I'm bloody gasping.

Porter felt like shit. His head was throbbing, his mouth tasted like someone had just emptied an ashtray into it, and he had a bad case of the shakes. Nausea rose in his throat as the Transit jounced over a pothole in the road and closed in on the target.

'Thirty seconds, lads,' said Dave Kemper, a thickset SO19 officer with a harsh Essex accent. 'Get ready. And remember, as soon as we're out of that door, we go silent.'

Their destination was a three-storey townhouse set a hundred metres down Stradbrooke Road, directly opposite a DIY superstore. According to intel, the leaders of one of Europe's most feared drug smuggling networks were currently holed up inside the townhouse. Sami Hoda and his brothers Berat and Bekim had risen to become the biggest distributors of cocaine and heroin in the south of England. The brothers used a Lithuanian food import business as a front to bring their product into the UK, smuggling the drugs inside the panelling of lorries belonging to the company. Once across the border the drugs were unpacked at a warehouse before being distributed across London in company-branded delivery vans. From there the drugs were diluted down and sold on to dealers on a consignment basis. These dealers then pushed the product on the streets of some of the most deprived estates in the country. The Hoda brothers had maimed, tortured and murdered their business rivals and made tens of millions in profit from getting people hooked on scag.

Now they were about to go down, big time.

Scotland Yard had been running surveillance on the Albanians for the past few months, gathering evidence until they had enough to put Sami Hoda and his crew away for life. Two days ago, they got a lucky break. One of the Hoda brothers' associates had tortured a dealer they suspected of skimming off a slice of the profits, and left him for dead. But the dealer survived. He spilled his guts to the cops and led them to a lock-up in Hackney registered in the name of Berat Hoda. The cops executed a warrant and discovered bank safes inside the lock-up filled with a hundred kilos of cocaine, fifty kilos of heroin, cutting agents and half a million quid in cash. Now they were moving in on the brothers before they found out about the garage raid and skipped town.

Surveillance teams had been observing the house for the past twenty-four hours, getting a mark-one eyeball on the targets and noting their movements. The plan was for a multi-floor assault on the property, with three teams moving into position silently before making a hard arrest. From start to finish the op would take sixty seconds.

There were good reasons for going stealthy. The Albanians were believed to have access to some heavy-duty weaponry and the planners at Scotland Yard didn't want to take any chances. If everything went to plan, Sami Hoda and his mates would all be wearing silver bracelets before they could get a chance to fight back.

Which is where Bald and Porter came in.

Thirteen months ago the two Regiment men had succeeded in taking down a Serbian war criminal who'd masterminded an attack on SAS Selection. Now they were working for MI5 and MI6 full-time on a joint retainer basis, running surveillance ops and snatching targets off the streets and taking orders from a greasy pole-climber in a Savile Row suit called Clarence Hawkridge. The guy ran the Counter-terrorism desk over at Thames House, and he was a first-class prick. Twelve hours ago, Hawkridge had learned about the op to arrest the Hoda clan.

Eleven hours ago, Hawkridge had reached out to Bald and Porter.

Unbeknown to the Met, Sami Hoda had been double-dealing with the Firm for the last two years, supplying MI5 with int on the big hitters in the drugs business, in exchange for protection. It was an arrangement both parties were happy to make. The Firm got intelligence on some of the most wanted crime bosses in the country, and Sami Hoda got to stay out of trouble. But if the police took Sami Hoda into custody and he spilled his guts, the whole operation would be blown apart.

'If that happens, chaps, heads will roll,' Hawkridge had informed them at the briefing the previous evening. 'The media would have a field day if they learned that Five had been helping a bunch of sadistic Albanian criminals to stay out of trouble. We can't let that happen, obviously.'

'What's the plan?' Bald had asked.

'There's only one solution,' Hawkridge replied in his silvery smooth voice. 'Sami Hoda has to go. Permanently.'

Bald and Porter had been placed on the team to make sure that Sami Hoda went down. Now the seconds were ticking down until the op kicked off, and Porter was suffering the effects of the hangover from hell.

'Ready for this, mate?' asked Bald.

Porter nodded. 'I'm fine, Jock.'

Bald arched an eyebrow. 'You sure about that? Christ, fucking look at you. You're shaking like a dog shitting razor blades.'

'It's nothing,' Porter growled.

But the truth was, he was a long way from fine. A long fucking way. Porter had managed to avoid the drink after transferring from Hereford to the British secret services. Staying off the booze had been a condition of his continued employment with the Firm. But then Diana had served him with the divorce papers. They had been living separately for a couple of years by that point and the divorce didn't come as a major shock. The real bombshell was in the small print. Diana wanted full custody of their daughter Sandy. The judge agreed. Said Porter didn't provide a stable home environment. Now he was only allowed to visit Sandy once a month for an hour, with a social worker present at all times. Just like that, Porter's world fell apart. First his life in the Regiment had been taken away from him. Then the courts had taken his daughter away from him too.

When you're a hardened alcoholic, all you need is an excuse. And I've got plenty of them, thought Porter. He started sneaking in a few crafty cans after the gym each day. One or two beers quickly became a dozen. Soon he was hitting the bottle. A few slugs of Bushmills in the morning to loosen himself up. Then he'd finish the bottle in the evening and wash it down with several tinnies. Porter knew he had a problem, but he tried to keep it a secret from Bald and his handlers at the Firm. He steered clear of the few off-licences close to his flat and bought most of his drinks from a Turkish supermarket in Kentish Town, always paying in cash and dumping the empty bottles in a bin a few streets away from where he lived. If he needed a drink on the job he'd fill a plastic water bottle with vodka and help himself to the occasional sip. But in spite of his best efforts, Porter knew Bald could see right through him. He was sure of it.

You can hide the smell on your breath and the empty bottles in the rubbish. But no matter how well you cover your tracks, you can't hide that glazed look in your eyes.

The pounding inside Porter's head grew louder. His right hand trembled. He was sweating hard under his layers. Jesus, he needed a drink.

Just get through this op. Then you can get back on it. All you've got to do is get through the next few minutes without being killed.

Suddenly the Transit slowed to a crawl. The driver shouted at the guys in the back. That was the signal for the team to debus. Kemper reached forward and grabbed the sliding door handle, then yanked it open. Porter and Bald jumped down from the van to the rain-slicked tarmac. The SO19 guys quickly followed. As soon as the last guy had debussed Kemper pulled the door shut and banged his fist on the side of the Transit. Then the driver pulled away, accelerating east down the street for fifty metres before hanging a left into the DIY store car park. The Transit was a vital part of the team's cover. Anyone observing the scene would have assumed that the driver was a tradesman pulling in early doors to the local DIY joint. It meant the team could make their approach without arousing the suspicion of anyone bottled up inside the townhouse.

'Fucking move it,' Bald said.

The two Blades led the way across the road towards the town-house, twelve metres away. The street was eerily quiet. A cordon had been set up at either end of the road to cut off traffic, and in the distance Porter could see a bunch of police cars and ambu-lances parked beyond the tape. On the left side of the road stood the DIY store, surrounded by an ocean of concrete. Opposite the store there was a long row of grimy three-storey townhouses, with a parade of shuttered shops further along. The townhouse belonging to the Hoda brothers stood at the end of the terrace. Porter and Bald moved towards the house, their Timberlands pounding against the wet concrete. All the lights in the townhouse were turned off, Porter noted. Dirty white curtains had been pulled across the ground-floor windows. The place looked dead.

Two metres from the porch now. Dave Kemper threw up a hand and ordered his team to a halt. He pointed to Bald and Porter.

'All yours, fellas,' he whispered.

The SO19 guys hung back while Bald edged through the gate and crept towards the front door, with Porter close behind. The two Hereford men were the entry team on this op. Which meant they were in charge of picking the lock on the front door and leading the rest of the guys into the stronghold. Once inside, the six SO19 guys would divide into two three-man teams and move into position on the ground and first floors. Bald and Porter would head to the second floor. As soon as everyone was in place they would rush into the rooms, disarm the suspects and drag them away to the reception team waiting outside the police cordon. The intelligence briefing stated that Sami Hoda's bedroom was on the second floor. Which meant that Bald and Porter would come crashing through his door at the exact moment the SO19 guys were busy sweeping through the lower floors. They would have around fifteen seconds to drop Sami Hoda before the cops came charging up the stairs.

Porter crouched beside the wall next to the door, his right hand resting on his Glock holster while Bald dropped to one knee beside the front door and angled his head so that the Petzl tactical light was directed at the lock, washing it in a bright red glow. Then he retrieved a standard lock-picking kit from his jeans pocket and set to work. The previous day one of the guys on the surveillance team had taken a photo of the lock using a long-range camera lens, so Bald and Porter knew exactly what type of lock they were dealing with. It was a pin tumbler mechanism, a common lock on older houses. Easy enough to break, for a Blade. The Regiment had its own lock-picking wing. Its guys were often called out by the Met to crack open various doors and lock-ups.

Bald took out the tension wrench and a titanium pick rake from his kit. He slid the tension wrench into the key hole and applied pressure to the wrench, bending it slightly to force the driver pins inside the lock to rise above the shear line. Then he inserted the pick rake into the top of the lock and started jamming the rake back and forth repeatedly into the keyhole.

'Hurry up, Jock,' Porter said under his breath as he scanned the street.

'Doing the best I fucking can, mate.'

'Just imagine there's a pair of tits on the other side.'

Bald glared at his mucker. He worked the lock some more, scrubbing the rake back and forth until all the pins were set in a line. After a few more twists there was a distinct, soft click as the plug fully rotated and the lock released.

'We're in,' Porter whispered over the comms mike.

Bald slowly pushed the door open, careful not to make any noise. Then he edged stealthily into the hallway. Porter shadowed him, drawing his Glock 17 and scanning the scene in front of him, his ears pricked as he listened for any sound coming from within the house. The place reeked of ganja and sweat. There were takeaway cartons and beer cans all over the place. Porter stilled his breath and stepped deeper into the hallway, eyes gradually adjusting to the half-light. Two metres ahead of him he could see the staircase leading up to the upper floors. The hallway carried on past the stairs into the back of the house. Porter stopped at the foot of the stairs, looked past his shoulder and indicated to Bald: *This way.* Bald nodded. Behind him, Dave Kemper motioned for the first three-man team to enter the house.

Porter turned and crept up the stairs, gritting his teeth against the monstrous hangover brewing inside his skull. The treads groaned under his weight. Halfway up he stopped momentarily to glance down at the front door, checking on the other teams.

Kemper was leading the ground-floor team towards the bedrooms at the rear of the property. MP5 carbine stocks tucked tight to each man's shoulder, torch attachments burning on the fore grips. A few steps behind them the second three-man SO19 team was moving into the hallway, six metres behind Bald. Porter faced ahead and continued up the stairs. Another two steps and he hit the first-floor landing. He traced the Glock across his line of sight, searching for the slightest movement.

Nothing.

Clear.

One floor down. One floor to go.

Porter and Bald inched across the landing and headed for the second flight of stairs, watching their step and taking care to avoid brushing against the crap strewn all over the place. The Hoda brothers might be multi-millionaires, thought Porter, but they lived like scum. Everywhere he looked he saw piles of rubbish, rotting chicken wings and pizza slices, ashtrays overflowing with cigarette butts. In another couple of strides he reached the stairs and climbed towards the bedroom on the top floor. Bald at his six o'clock, the second three-man SO19 on the first-floor landing and moving towards the first closed door.

In his earpiece Porter heard Kemper saying, 'Team One ready.'

Porter and Bald were four steps away from the second-floor landing now. A second voice crackled in his ear. Officer Steve Crabb. The leader of the team covering the first floor. 'Team Two ready.'

In the next moment Porter hit the landing. He moved towards the bedroom door and pushed himself against the wall to the left. Bald stopped by the wall on the other side of the door. Both had their weapons drawn.

'Team Three ready,' said Porter.

There was a long pause of silence. Two seconds, maybe three. Porter blocked out the pounding headache and tightened his fingers around the Glock 17's polymer grip. Kemper came back on the comms. 'Stand by ... stand by ... go!'

Downstairs, everything went real noisy, real fucking quick. The dead stillness was broken as the two SO19 teams crashed into the rooms on the lower floors. Through his earpiece Porter could hear the sharp crack of doors being kicked in, followed by several angry shouts, Dave Kemper yelling at someone to stand still, Steve Crabb shouting: 'Armed police!'

As it swung open Porter charged through the door ahead of Bald, his index finger tense on the Glock trigger as he swept his weapon in a broad arc from left to right, eyes scanning the room for any sign of Sami Hoda.

The room was four metres by four. A street lamp burned outside the window, throwing murky orange light over the interior. There was a TV in one corner of the room with a stack of DVDs and a PlayStation next to it. Bottle of Stolichnaya vodka on the coffee table, plus a couple of joints and a few cans of Tyskie lager. Clothes spilled out of a bin bag stashed in the opposite corner. The bed against the back wall had the sheets pulled back, revealing a stained mattress. The decor was somewhere between student digs and crack den. Whatever Sami Hoda was spending his wonga on, it wasn't home furnishings.

Sami Hoda stood next to the bed, dressed in a vest and a pair of boxers. He had a dazed look in his eyes. The guy stared at Porter, a look of confusion playing out on his acne-riddled face. By now Bald had pushed through the doorway. He stood at Porter's shoulder, his Glock trained on the Albanian.

'Police, police!' Porter shouted, loud enough that the guys on the other assault teams would pick up his voice over the comms. 'Stand still! Stand still!'

Sami Hoda did as he was told. His eyes darting between Bald and Porter. Through his earpiece Porter could hear one of the suspects shouting at the cops in his guttural foreign tongue. Another twenty seconds, he figured, and the other two teams would have their targets secured.

Porter nodded at Bald. The Jock nodded back. *Let's do this.*

Porter holstered his Glock and rushed over to Sami Hoda. Bald stood just inside the doorway, keeping the business end of his pistol aimed at the Albanian. Hoda kept looking from Bald to Porter and shaking his head. Like maybe if he shook his head enough times, his problems would magically disappear.

'You can't fucking do this,' he said. 'This is a big mistake.'

Porter ignored him. He brushed past the Albanian and dropped down beside the bed. According to the Firm's briefing, the guy kept an illegal weapon in a shoebox underneath the bed. Porter thrust an arm under the bed and found a shoebox shoved way back. He grabbed it, pulled it out and lifted the lid. Nestled inside was a stainless-steel pistol that Porter recognised as an old Czech CZ 75 semi-automatic. Nine-millimetre, twelve-round mag, hammer-forged barrel. Solid but unspectacular. As you might expect from the nation that designed the Skoda. He tugged back the slider, saw a round glinting dully in the chamber. Then he shot to his feet and turned to face the target.

Sami Hoda glanced over his shoulder at Porter. He caught sight of the CZ 75 in Porter's grip and his eyes went so wide they looked as if they might pop out of his skull. 'That's not mine. I don't know how that shit got there.'

'Hands behind your back,' Bald demanded.

The guy stopped protesting and fell silent. He sighed and faced forward, presenting his wrists to Porter. Like this was no big deal. Like he figured that in a couple of hours he'd get on the blower to his source at MI5 and walk away free.

He figured wrong.

Porter manoeuvred so that he was standing just behind and to the right of the Albanian. He flipped up the safety lever on the side of the CZ 75 receiver with his thumb and raised the weapon. Lined up the wall half a metre to the right of Bald between the front post and rear notch sights. Relaxed his forearm, tensed his shoulder muscles.

Squeezed the trigger twice.

The room lit up. The CZ barked. The muzzle flashed. Two rounds exploded out of the pistol snout. The sound was deafening. Porter felt the CZ recoil in his grip as he fired. The first bullet struck the wall roughly twelve inches to the right of Bald, embedding itself in the brickwork. The second round hit the doorframe less than six inches from Bald and tore a chunk out of the wooden frame, showering him in needle-like splinters. Bald instinctively flinched. It took him half a second to shift his firing stance. Then he lined up Sami Hoda's head between the sights on his Glock. Porter jumped back from the guy, stepping out of the killing zone.

The Albanian's eyes went wide. He had just enough time to realise what was happening. He raised a hand at Bald.

'No, fuck, don't—'

Bald pulled the trigger, emptying two rounds into the Albanian. The nine-millis thudded into the guy's skull, severing the plumbing in the front of his brain. His neck jerked back and he fell away, his arms pinwheeling. Like someone had just cut his strings. The guy was dead before he hit the floor. He slumped back against the wall, his jaw slack, the hot stink of blood filling the air.

Porter stared at the two bullet holes in the wall to Bald's right. Firing Sami Hoda's gun had been necessary to make his death look like a justifiable killing. Which meant Porter had needed to shoot a couple of rounds close enough to Bald to make it look as if Hoda had been aiming at him. But Porter had got his angles wrong and almost ended up taking off Bald's head in the process.

Christ, he thought. Maybe I am losing it.

I almost slotted my mucker.

Voices sparked up in the earpiece. More than one of them. Kemper and Crabb and a bunch of the other officers, responding to the gunshots on the second floor, wondering what the fuck was going on. Porter and Bald had a few seconds until the SO19 crew came storming up the stairs. Porter snapped out of his stupor, dropped down beside the slotted Albanian and quickly started wiping down the CZ 75 with his sweatshirt. He could hear the loud thud of footsteps pounding up the stairs. He had a few seconds until the cops hit the second floor.

'Fucking hurry,' Bald said.

Porter placed the Czech semi-automatic in Sami Hoda's right hand and clamped his chubby fingers around the grip.

Then he bolted to his feet and rushed past Bald into the hallway, digging his Glock 17 out of his holster. Swung around so that he was standing outside the door, with Bald a couple of steps inside the room. Kemper came vaulting up the stairs with Crabb and another officer hard on his heels. He flashed a look at Porter then stopped in the doorway and glanced inside the bedroom. Saw Sami Hoda lying against the wall, blood disgorging from the holes in his skull and slickening his front. Bald stood over the dead Albanian, gripping his Glock 17 and shaking his head.

'Oh Jesus,' said Bald. 'Fucking hell, I've killed a guy.'

Kemper shaded white. 'What happened?'

'He didn't give me any choice,' Bald said, turning to face Kemper and pretending to look anxious. 'Bastard pulled a weapon on us.'

'It's true,' Porter added. 'We entered the room to arrest the target and shouted for him to put his hands up, just like we'd been told. The fucker drew his weapon and let off a couple of rounds. That's when we engaged.'

'The suspect fired his weapon?' Kemper asked, working his face into a deep frown.

'Aye,' Porter replied. 'Two shots.' He pointed with his head at the bullet holes lodged in the wall and doorframe. 'You'll find the slugs in there.'

Kemper cocked his head at Porter. 'Where were you when this happened?'

'Outside the room, covering Jock.'

'Shit,' Kemper muttered.

'I can't believe I fucking killed him,' Bald said, fixing his eyes on the slotted Albanian.

Kemper turned to Officer Crabb. 'Cordon the area off. Clear everyone out and get the SOCOs down here asap. I want fingerprints, blood splatter, the lot. No one's to touch or move a fucking thing. Right now this house is a crime scene. Got it?'

'Yes, chief.'

'And for Chrissakes keep the press away from here.'

Crabb nodded, turned and marched down the stairs with the other SO19 officer. Kemper watched them leave. Then he turned towards Bald and sucked the air between his teeth. 'I'll have to get on the blower and notify the PCA about this. We're legally required to report every police shooting to them. They'll be wanting a word with the two of you at the debrief, no doubt.' Bald opened his mouth to speak but Kemper cut him off. 'Look, fellas. I know you were bang within your rights to engage the shooter, but we've got to do things by the book here. You understand.'

Bald and Porter exchanged a look. Porter looked back to Kemper. Nodded. 'We'll answer any questions they have.'

Kemper nodded and cleared his throat. 'Right, then. You'd better make your way down to the cordon. An investigator will be waiting there to take both your statements.'

Porter headed downstairs with Bald. They made their way down to the ground floor hallway and stepped out into the street. The noise of the assault had stirred the locals out of their sleep. Lights were switching on up and down the street. A few residents stood outside their front doors, rubbernecking the scene. The reception area downstream from the townhouse was buzzing with activity. A trio of police officers were processing the Albanians while another cop read them their rights. Police dog handlers remained close by in case any of the Albanians tried to make a run for it. A paramedic team was busy lowering a stretcher from the back of an ambo. Bit late for that, thought Porter. He grinned at Bald.

'You should give yourself an Oscar,' he said. 'You almost had me fooled back there, Jock. Looks like Kemper bought it.'

'Yeah, well.' Bald shrugged. 'We nearly screwed up the op, thanks to you.'

'The fuck's that supposed to mean?'

Bald rounded on Porter. His face was twitching with anger. 'You almost clipped me back there, pal. That second round was a cunt hair away from my face. Another inch or so and it would have been me lying on the carpet with the hole in my head.'

Porter clenched his jaws and met Bald's piercing stare. 'It was an accident. The pistol must have been dodgy. Christ, you know what those old CZs are like. They're dodgier than a two-bob watch.'

Bald shook his head. 'The gun wasn't the problem, mate. You are.'

'It was an honest mistake, that's all,' Porter said. He could feel the hangover returning. A dull pain throbbed inside his skull.

'Bollocks.' Bald stepped into Porter's face and glowered at his mucker. 'You'd better sort yourself out. Because the next time you almost clip me, I'll drop you. And mark my words, I won't fucking miss.'

THREE

The questioning took forty-nine long minutes. Bald and Porter had been taken to a dreary glass-fronted office block on High Holborn, opposite a row of tatty souvenir shops and grubby boozers. They were shown into a bland interview room with a two-way mirror, and found a guy in a sharkskin suit waiting for them inside. He introduced himself as Charles Capewell QC, and explained that he was one of the Firm's legal advisers, and that he had been brought in to advise Bald and Porter during the inter-rogation. If either of them was asked a question that might incriminate them, Capewell said, he would step in and cut the interview short. Bald and Porter both nodded. They had done this before. They knew the drill.

After a while a pair of investigators stepped into the room and introduced themselves. A guy called Westwood and a guy called Steer. They were both former police officers, and they both looked the part. Weary look in the eyes, beer bellies that threat-ened to burst out of their crumpled white shirts. They sat down opposite Bald and Porter and Capewell and said they had a few questions. They were broadly sympathetic, Westwood explained. They still had friends on the force. They knew how these things worked. They listened patiently as Bald and Porter walked them through the shooting. First Bald, then Porter. Then they walked them through it again. The investigators took notes, asked a few questions and didn't press too hard. As if they were going through the motions. Every so often, Capewell intervened and told them in a firm but polite voice that his clients would not be answering a particular question. When they were finished, Westwood said Bald and Porter were free to leave. He said they would have to interview Kemper and the other officers after the debrief. Steer added that if they had any more questions, they would be in touch. He thanked Bald and Porter for their time. Capewell made his excuses and left.

Two minutes after they left the building, Porter's pager buzzed.

Both he and Bald carried MoD-issued Motorola pagers clipped to their belts. It allowed their handler to contact them at any time, day or night. The pagers received two test messages a day. One at seven o'clock in the morning, and another at seven o'clock at night. As soon as they received the test messages, the guys had to check in on the secure line at Thames House. So when Porter's pager buzzed, he figured it was the first test message of the day coming through. Then he glanced at his G-Shock. 0620 hours. Too early for the test message. Which meant that someone at the Firm was reaching out to him.

He unclipped the pager from his belt and squinted at the tiny luminous screen. Messages sent from the Firm were in the form of a three-digit code. The different numbers corresponded to different instructions that Bald and Porter had committed to memory when they had transferred from Hereford. The number 555, for example, told them to check in with Thames House as soon as possible. Whereas 111 told the guys to drop everything and get over to the safehouse immediately. A 111 was the most urgent type of message that the Blades could receive.

Porter stopped. He stared at the pager.

The message on the screen read 111.

Sixty seconds later, they were hailing a black cab.

The safehouse was off Edgware Road. Less than three miles away, but a forty-minute journey, even at six-thirty in the morning. The pavements were mostly empty except for a few joggers and shift workers, but the roads were clogged with early-morning traffic. Delivery trucks, white vans, taxis, buses, cyclists. The speed of the traffic was somewhere between standstill and slow crawl. The taxi driver shuttled north on Southampton Row, passed Russell Square tube station, and then hooked a left and crawled along the Euston Road. Everywhere Porter looked the skyline was dominated by industrial cranes and the skeletal outlines of half-finished skyscrapers and high-rise apartment blocks. The city transforming. *It's come a long way since I grew up in Bethnal Green*, Porter thought. *Give it another ten years and I'll hardly recognise the place.*

They headed east on the Euston Road for a mile and a half. Past the steel-and-glass buildings around Great Portland Street, and the crowds of tourists around Baker Street, and the multi-million-pound houses lining Regent's Park. The driver inched through Marylebone and then angled left after Westminster Magistrates' Court. Rolled down Old Marylebone Road for a couple of hundred metres. Crossed the Edgware Road, past the shisha bars and Turkish coffee shops and greasy Lebanese restaurants. Headed down Sussex Gardens and took the first right onto Sale Place. After fifty metres the driver eased off the gas and pulled over. Porter handed him a twenty and got a handful of pocket shrapnel in change. Then he climbed out of the cab with Bald and the two of them waited until the taxi had pulled out and disappeared from view. They walked north on Sale for forty metres, then hung a left onto Star Street.

The safehouse was set midway down a row of discreet white-washed terraces. It looked like any other house on the street, with its small tiled porch and wrought-iron fence overlooking the basement. The only difference was that the curtains had been pulled across all the windows. From the outside the place looked neat, tidy. Anonymous. The kind of place that wouldn't attract attention. Which made it the perfect location for a safehouse. Bald fished a set of keys out of his jeans pocket, unlocked the door and stepped into into the hallway.

Bald stopped in his tracks, and listened.

'Alarm's been disabled,' he said.

Porter nodded. *We're not the first ones here, then.*

They headed down the hallway and made for the stairs. The place was modern but sparsely furnished. Like an Ikea showroom, five minutes after the clearance sale had ended. Porter followed Bald down the stairs into the basement. They paced down a short corridor and made for the heavy-duty door at the far end. A pair of flunkies in shiny suits stood either side of the door. One of the suits spoke into his microphone while the other pulled open the door. Then the flunkies stepped aside and Bald and Porter entered.

The briefing room looked like a recording studio, minus the music equipment. The walls and ceilings were lined with egg-box-shaped foam that was specially designed to absorb any sound. Which meant that conversations that took place inside the room would not transmit to anyone potentially listening in from the outside. There were no windows inside the basement and the only light came from a couple of tall halogen lamps burning in separate corners of the room. An American Security safe the size of a Smeg fridge stood against the far wall, the kind of thing a Texas gun fanatic might stash his assault rifles in. There was a plain metal desk in the middle of the room with a Cisco phone on it hooked up to a secure line, and four metal chairs. Porter knew the layout of the basement room like the back of his hand. He'd been in this place more times than he cared to remember over the last year. The Firm had dozens of safehouses just like this one, scattered across the capital.

He turned his attention to the two figures in the middle of the room. Clarence Hawkridge stood leaning against the edge of the desk, his arms folded across his front while he tapped a black leather brogue against the floor. A woman Porter didn't recognise sat at one of the chairs behind the metal desk, her hands resting on top of a pile of bulky manila folders. She wore a black pencil skirt and a dark-grey ponte jacket over a long-sleeve blouse. The corporate look. Porter guessed she was in her late thirties or early forties, but the lines on her face made her look ten years older. She had streaks of grey in her mid-length hair, and bloodshot eyes and heavy lines etched across her brow.

Hawkridge straightened up and glanced impatiently at his watch. 'You chaps took your time getting here.'

'Traffic,' said Bald with a shrug. 'Anyway, we were busy cleaning up your mess.'

Hawkridge cocked his chin at Porter. 'Well? Was it a clean job?'

Porter glanced over at Bald. The Jock shot him a funny look. He turned back to Hawkridge and nodded stiffly. 'It went down just the way we discussed. As far as the cops are concerned it was a justifiable shooting. We had to give a statement to the PCA, but there might be some follow-up involved.'

Hawkridge smiled and gave a dismissive wave of his hand. Like he was swatting away a bad smell. 'No need to worry about the investigation, old fruit. We've got that covered. Consider yourselves in the clear.'

'Great,' Bald deadpanned. 'When do we crack open the bubbly?'

'I'm afraid you'll have to put your celebrations on ice for the time being. We've got another job for you.'

'What's the craic?' Porter asked.

Hawkridge gestured to the two empty chairs facing the desk. 'Why don't you both take a seat, gentlemen.'

Porter and Bald planted their arses on the chairs and waited for Hawkridge to continue. Porter found himself scanning the room, looking to see if there was any booze lying around the place. He wondered how much longer he could go without a drink before the shakes kicked in again. These days he could hardly last more than a few hours without a drop of the strong stuff.

Hawkridge tipped his head at the woman. 'Before we continue I'd like to introduce you to Angela March. She'll be sitting in with us. Angela is with the Foreign Office, and she'll be helping to coordinate the operation.'

'Gentlemen. A pleasure,' March said. She had a husky smoker's voice and a cool, professional manner. Porter nodded a greeting at her. But in the back of his head he asked himself, *Why the hell would some civil servant from the Foreign Office take an interest in an MI5 op?*

March tapped the manila folders. 'I've read both your files. Excellent work taking down Radoslav Brozovic's gang, by the way. You two are practically minor celebrities inside Whitehall, you know. It's a shame you'll never be able to take public credit for what you did.'

'We didn't do it for the glory,' Bald said. 'We did it because Brozovic killed our mates.'

'So I gather.' March went on, 'Actually, it's one of the reasons we've taken an interest in you. I understand you're both experienced operators, capable of surviving alone in hostile environments for extended periods of time. Your fighting skills are second to none. And you're both extremely loyal towards your fellow SAS men. That's important on this particular operation.'

Porter frowned. 'How do you mean?'

Hawkridge sat down and brushed back his thinning hair. 'I trust you're both familiar with a chap called Ronald Soames?'

The name got their attention. Porter sat bolt upright and tensed.

'Soames?' he said, almost spitting out the name. 'Aye, we've heard of him.'

March took a folder from near the bottom of the pile. She opened it up and glanced down at the first page, then lifted her eyes to Porter. 'I understand Ronald was Commanding Officer of 22 SAS during your time in the unit.'

'For a short while. He transferred a few months after I passed Selection, as I remember it.'

March read from the page in front of her. 'Ronald Soames, born in Esher, Surrey in 1947. Born into a prestigious military family. Father Onslow served in the Corps of Guides in the Indian Army, later elected as Conservative MP for Henley-on-Thames. Ronald received his commission from Sandhurst in 1969 and joined the Household Cavalry Division. Promoted to the rank of Captain and passed SAS Selection in 1977. Later promoted to the rank of Lieutenant-Colonel. Commanding Officer of 22 SAS from 1987 to 89. Became Director Special Forces in 1994 before retiring in 1997. After he retired from the MoD Ronald set up his own private military contractor, Janus International. They operate security contracts, mostly in Africa.'

She stopped reading. Unclipped a photograph from the front of the file and slid it across the desk. Porter and Bald leaned over for a closer look. It was a snap of Ronald Soames, a recent one by the look of it. Post-Whitehall. He looked good for his age. He was dressed in an expensive-looking linen suit, light blue shirt underneath with the collar button popped. Everything about him oozed money. The suit, the watch, the neatly stubbled jaw. In the photograph Soames was gazing off somewhere to the left of the camera. His eyes were cold and black, like wet stones. His thin lips curled up at the edges to form an arrogant smile. Soames somehow looked both charming and cold-blooded. The kind of guy who acted as if he owned the world and everything in it, and ruthlessly dealt with anyone who thought otherwise.

Porter looked up at March and shrugged. 'Looks like Soames had done well for himself.'

March said nothing. She closed the folder and dug out a pack of Camels from her Marc Jacobs handbag. Then she plucked out a tab, lit it and took a long drag.

'Ronald isn't just another retired general. He's one of the most decorated soldiers in the British army.' She read from his CV again. 'He was awarded the Military Cross for his actions during an IRA ambush outside Belfast. In addition he's a recipient of the Distinguished Service Order and received the honour of Knight Commander of the Order of the British Empire.'

'That doesn't mean a thing.' Porter laughed. 'They're bullshit medals.'

March gave him a stern look. 'I think that's just jealousy speaking, don't you?'

Porter felt a spark of anger flare up inside his chest. He shook his head and said, 'Do me a favour. It's the worst-kept secret in Hereford that Soames didn't earn that MC. That cunt was sitting behind a desk at barracks while the other lads were out on the top. He wrote up his own citation afterwards.'

'Whatever you may think, the plain truth is that Ronald is a highly valuable asset,' March replied curtly.

'How do you mean?' asked Bald.

March paused while she took another drag on her cigarette. 'Ronald does us favours, from time to time.'

Bald grinned. 'So do the girls at Spearmint Rhino, love.'

March glared at him before she replied. 'Ronald has a particular set of skills. He's good at working in the grey areas, the shadows. He also happens to be very well connected. He knows everyone worth knowing. More importantly, he knows everything about them.' She tapped ash in the ashtray and smiled thinly. 'Let's just say he knows how to get things done.'

'That's one way of putting it,' said Porter. 'Here's another. The bloke's dodgier than a late-night kebab. He stitched up plenty of lads in the Regiment. He's a professional back-stabber.'

'Perhaps,' March conceded. 'But Ronald is useful in those places where it's politically inappropriate for us to be involved. Places where we need influence, but we can't be seen to be using it. The world is changing. Transparency is everything now. The days of direct intervention are over. Men like Soames buy us power without putting boots on the ground.'

'Must pay well and all,' said Bald. 'I never served under Soames in the Regiment, but I've heard that the guy is rich as fuck.'

'Ronald doesn't do this for the money,' Hawkridge countered. 'He's a patriot. He has plenty of friends inside Whitehall. People who are grateful for the work he's done on our behalf. And right now he's in trouble.'

'What kind of trouble?'

Hawkridge drummed his fingers on the table, shifting his small dark eyes from Bald to Porter. 'Tell me,' he said. 'How much do either of you chaps know about the situation in Sierra Leone?'

'It's a shithole full of chogies and AIDS,' Bald quipped.

Hawkridge coughed politely. 'That's a rather succinct way of putting it, I suppose. Although the reality is somewhat more complicated. As you're probably aware, Sierra Leone is in the grip of a decade-long civil war. Nine years ago the armed forces of the Revolutionary United Front, backed by soldiers from Liberia, attempted to overthrow the Sierra Leone government under President Joseph Momoh. The RUF, led by Foday Sankoh, quickly took control of large swathes of the country and forced Momoh into exile in a military coup. Ever since, the RUF and the civilian government have been at war. We're talking an endless cycle of coups, revolts and mass killings.'

'Like every other African hellhole, then,' said Bald.

'Not quite. You see, Sierra Leone has huge diamond deposits. Vastly more than any other country in the region, and located close to the surface. Which means that one doesn't need expensive machinery to mine the land for diamonds. Which means the RUF has had a ready-made source of funds for its military operations.'

'Blood diamonds,' said Porter.

Hawkridge nodded. 'Exactly. In the past the RUF has relied heavily on the blood diamond trade to pay for their rebellion. Their soldiers smuggle the deposits south of the border to Liberia, where they are processed and cleaned by Lebanese fences, then sold onto Western markets. We're talking about a trade worth hundreds of millions of dollars per year. Money which goes directly into the RUF's war chest.'

March said, 'Four years ago, HMG decided to intervene. A resolution was passed and UN peacekeepers were put on the ground. The country voted for its first democratically elected president, David Ibrahim Fofana.'

March took a last drag on her Camel. Blew out smoke and stubbed the butt out in the ashtray. Then she brushed her hair back and went on.

'The electoral process wasn't smooth. And it wasn't exactly clean. But it was clean enough for HMG and our cousins in Washington to throw our support behind the new man. However, Fofana's position is weak. Large parts of the country remain under rebel control. Outside Freetown, the country is a war zone. If Fofana was going to stay in power, we had to secure the diamond mines and stop the rebels from seizing the deposits. Which is where Ronald came in.'

'How so?' Bald asked.

'Janus International was awarded a contract to protect the mining fields in Kono, in the rural east of the country,' March said. 'Kono is the biggest diamond mining region in Sierra Leone. Which makes it potentially the biggest in West Africa. Which makes it potentially one of the biggest in the world.'

'The Kono mining fields are critical to President Fofana's hopes of staying in power and defeating the RUF,' Hawkridge cut in. 'If the rebels managed to seize Kono, they'd be able to bankroll their operations for years to come. Any hopes of ending the conflict would be dead in the water.'

He turned to March. She said, 'Soames was operating in Sierra Leone with our implicit consent. You might say we have a vested interest in Soames running security on the diamond mine.'

'Or rather we did,' Hawkridge said. 'Until twenty-four hours ago.'

Porter said, 'What happened twenty-four hours ago?'

Hawkridge paused and glanced at March.

'The situation changed,' he said.

'How?' Bald asked.

'The rebels launched a new offensive. No one was expecting it. They took everybody by surprise, swept through the government checkpoints and reached as far as Port Loko, less than fifty miles from Freetown. President Fofana and his advisors fled across the border to Conakry, Guinea.'

March cleared her throat. 'Without Fofana, the civilian government has effectively collapsed. The rebels have taken great encouragement from the president's departure. We believe that they are preparing for a full-blown assault on the capital. There's widespread panic on the streets. Everyone remembers what happened the last time the RUF rolled into town. Their soldiers engaged in an orgy of violence. Looting, rape, murder. Thousands were killed, many more displaced.'

Porter scratched his jaw. 'Where's Soames in all this?'

'Somewhere inside Freetown,' Hawkridge said. 'Overseeing the Kono contract. It's imperative that we get him out of the city immediately. Before the security situation deteriorates any further.'

Bald gave a casual shrug of his shoulders. 'So stick the guy on a plane. You don't need to send us halfway across the world just so we can hold his fucking hand.'

'It's not as simple as that.'

Bald stared at the guy. 'There's a fucking surprise. When is it ever, with you lot?'

Hawkridge stiffened his jaw and said, 'Yesterday morning GCHQ picked up chatter in Moscow. Their intelligence people at the FSB. It appears they're dispatching a team to Sierra Leone.'

Porter did a double-take. 'The Russians? What's their involvement in all this?'

'We're not entirely sure. But we think it might be to do with the diamond mines.'

'Here's what we know,' March said. 'The Russians have cut a deal with the military leader of the RUF rebels. A charming man who calls himself General Mosquito. The deal is, weapons in exchange for concessions on the diamond mines, in the event the rebels take over the country.'

Porter nodded. 'That's why the rebels have suddenly got their shit together. They've got brand-new kit from the Russians.'

'Exactly,' said Hawkridge. 'We think the Russians have sent in a team to expedite matters. Take advantage of the chaos on the ground and knock Soames on the head. Once he's out of the way they can seize control of the Kono mines. That would simultaneously cut short any attempt by Fofana to regain power and hand the keys to the country to the RUF.'

'And Russia's new president gets an early win,' March added.

'So Soames is a target,' Porter said.

March gave a cautious nod. 'At this moment Downing Street is discussing options for a military response to drive back the rebels and help Fofana regain the initiative. But our first priority has to be to get Ronald out of the country. He's under threat and he needs our help.'

Porter listened in silence. His head throbbed with pain. As if someone was stabbing the backs of his eyeballs with an ice pick.

'What's the plan?' Bald asked.

'Ronald has gotten us out of some tight spots in the past,' March said. 'Now we're going to return the favour. We need you to fly to Freetown and find Soames. Then get him the hell out of the country. Before the Russians get to him first.'

FOUR

Nobody said anything for a while. Porter felt the temperature inside the soundproofed room plummet. Silence filled the air. March sparked up another tab and watched the operators carefully. Like she was trying to gauge their reactions. Finally Porter broke the silence.

'If you're so worried about Soames, why don't you just tell him to hop on a plane?'

'Two reasons.' March took a puff of her cigarette, then propped it on the side of the ashtray. Smoke drifted lazily towards the foam-covered ceiling. 'One, the situation on the ground is increasingly unstable. We have unconfirmed reports of armed groups sympathetic to the rebels already inside Freetown. That makes any Westerner a potential target. We're advising all British nationals inside the city to stay indoors unless absolutely necessary. If Soames tries to check out of the country alone, he might run into trouble. Especially since he's a close friend of President Fofana. Which makes him a sworn enemy of the RUF.'

Bald said, 'What about a military evacuation? All them other expats will need rescuing if the country goes to shit. Get them to bail the old bastard out.'

'It's on the agenda.' Hawkridge took off his horn-rimmed glasses and rubbed his tired eyes. 'But it's a question of time. We have no ships in the area and the nearest troops are over in Senegal.' He set the glasses back on the ridge of his long nose. 'It will be a couple of days before we can mobilise a force to evacuate British nationals. At least. By then it might be too late.'

Porter said, 'What's the second reason?'

'We've tried contacting Ronald several times since we learned of the threat,' March replied. 'But there's no answer at his company offices.'

'What about his gaff?' Bald asked.

'Same thing. No answer.'

'It's possible that the comms are down,' Hawkridge added. 'They're unreliable at the best of times. Or Soames might be trapped somewhere else in the city.'

'Wherever he is,' March cut in, 'we have no way of reaching out to warn him of the Russian threat.'

'Isn't there anyone else on the ground locally?' Porter said. 'Someone who can make a run across town and knock on his door?'

Hawkridge said, 'Unfortunately not. The only local resources we have are the staff at the British High Commission. It's a skeletal staff. As you can imagine, they're swamped dealing with expats trying to get out of the country. Even if we could spare somebody to warn Ronald, it doesn't solve the problem of getting him on a plane without running into a team of armed Russians. Locating Soames is only half the problem. Once you find him, you're going to have to watch his back closely.' He shrugged. 'For all we know, the Russians are already inside Freetown.'

'Besides,' said March. 'It's not just a question of protecting Soames. It's about safeguarding the national interest.'

Bald furrowed his brow. 'How's that?'

March said, 'Ronald is practically a Whitehall institution. He spent twenty years at the forefront of the MoD and is well versed in matters of national security. If the Russians get to him, there's a serious risk that they might interrogate him and find out what he knows.'

Porter said, 'You're afraid he'd spill his guts?'

'It's a concern.' March paused and smoked some more. 'Even if he didn't talk, his capture or death would be highly embarrassing. Soames is a man with plenty of friends. He's on first-name terms with members of the royal family, not to mention several politicians and high-ranking public officials. If anything happened to him, it would reflect badly on his associates. Needless to say, those people are keen to make sure that he is returned safely to London.' March paused and levelled her gaze at Porter. '*Very* keen.'

Porter listened and nodded. He could picture the headlines splashed all over the front pages of the red tops. A top international fixer with links to the Windsor set, on a questionable mission in Sierra Leone, being executed by a bunch of savage guerrillas. The media would have a field day.

'Fair enough,' he said. 'So the old boys' network is shitting bricks and they want us to rescue one of their own. But how are we supposed to find Soames?'

'Try the office first,' Hawkridge replied stiffly. 'It's a more secure location than his apartment, and there's a guest room on the ground floor. It's quite possible Soames might be there, waiting this whole thing out.'

'And if he isn't?'

'There's a houseboy based at the office. Young fellow called Vandi. If Soames has gone off somewhere, he might be able to point you in the right direction. In the meantime, we'll keep trying to reach him from our end.'

'You'll have to move fast,' March said. 'The situation in Sierra Leone is getting worse by the hour. The latest intelligence reports indicate that we have forty-eight hours until the rebels mount an attack on Freetown. Maybe less. You'll need to land, locate Soames and extract him before the city falls.'

'What if Soames has already bugged out of Freetown?' Bald said. 'He might have seen the way things are going and decided to leg it.'

'Unlikely,' Hawkridge replied with a sharp wave of his hand. 'Most of the territory outside Freetown is held by the rebels. They've got checkpoints all over the place. Even if Soames did manage to avoid the rebels, there's still the risk of running into the West Side Boys.'

'I've heard of them,' said Bald. 'Bunch of chogie crackheads who dress like pooftas.'

45

Hawkridge grimaced. 'That's certainly one way of putting it. The West Side Boys aren't aligned with any of the rebel factions. Their leader is a fellow by the name of Brigadier Foday Kallay. He's a big fan of rape, looting and murder. Most of their soldiers were abducted as children and forced to torture or kill as part of their initiation. They dress in women's wigs and flip-flops to intimidate the enemy, and they're permanently drugged up on marijuana and heroin.'

'Sounds like a Friday night in Brixton,' said Porter.

'Don't be fooled. The West Side Boys are volatile, and danger-ous. Two months ago Kallay's men entered a village south of Freetown and rounded up anyone suspected of collaborating with the government. Twenty-three men, women and children in total. They took them down to a pit and executed them, one by one. Trust me, Soames won't have left the city. Not with the West Side Boys running amok in the countryside.'

Porter listened in silence. His hands had started to shake. He was half-tuned in to the briefing, half-tuned in to the voice in the back of his head. The one that told him he badly needed a drink. Just a little while longer, Porter told himself. He grabbed his right hand in his left and stilled it.

Hawkridge clasped his hands together. 'Questions, gentlemen?'

'What about weapons?' Porter said.

Hawkridge made a sucking sound with his teeth. 'I can't help you there, old fruit. We can't get you clearance to take guns aboard a commercial flight. Not without going through the official chan-nels. And we'd prefer to have as few people as possible know about this operation, for obvious reasons.'

Porter glanced at his mucker. Bald looked incensed. His brow creased into a deep frown. The muscles on his neck strained like tensed rope.

'What are we supposed to do if we bump into the Russians?' he growled.

'Forage and supply yourself locally. You'll just have to be resourceful.' Hawkridge smiled. 'Isn't that what you Hereford chaps are supposed to be good at? Fending for yourselves?'

Bald made no attempt to mask his anger. 'Fucking great. So we've got to rescue some old Rupert in the middle of a coup, and now we're going in half-cocked as well. This op just keeps getting better.'

The briefing room descended into another bout of silence. Hawkridge stared down the barrel of his nose at the two Regiment men.

'If you have misgivings about the mission, now is the time to say so. You can walk away from the mission, if you prefer. I'll see to it that you spend the next two years on secondment as PSIs instead. Your call.'

Porter tensed and felt a wave of anger surge up inside him. Permanent Staff Instructors were the guys in charge of the TA units. There could be no greater shame for a Regiment man than having to bark orders at a bunch of weekend warriors for the next two years. Porter looked across at his mucker. Could tell he was thinking the same thing. *Lifting some ex-Rupert out of an African hellhole might be a crap mission, but it's still better than being posted as a PSI.*

'Fine,' he said to Hawkridge. 'We'll do it.'

Hawkridge relaxed his face into a slight smile.

'You'll fly out today,' he went on. 'This afternoon, in fact. We've booked you in on the next available flight from Heathrow to Freetown. Once you land you'll be greeted by a local handler. Fellow by the name of Mike Shoemaker. He'll be waiting for you at the airport. He's got your descriptions. Which reminds me.'

The agent slid out of his chair, paced over to the AmSec safe at the back of the room and punched in a six-digit code on the backlit keypad. The safe made a bunch of whirring and clunking noises. Then Hawkridge cranked the heavy door open and retrieved a set of documents from the top shelf, plus a dark green Motorola satellite phone the size of a brick with a long black aerial as thick as a tube of Smarties. He dumped the items on the desk in front of Bald and Porter.

'For your travels,' he said. 'I think you'll find that everything is in order.'

Porter reached for the set of documents. There were two business-class tickets for a British Airways flight from London to Lungi International Airport at 1355 hours, with a stopover in Morocco. The return portions of the tickets were open-ended. There was a third ticket in the name of Ronald Soames. Also in business class. Along with the tickets there were four bands of cash. Two thick ones in Leones, the local currency, and two smaller wads of US dollars. Porter picked up a couple and thumbed them. He counted five hundred in twenty-dollar bills in the US bundle, and two hundred and fifty thousand in the Leone one. A total of a thousand dollars in Yank currency, and roughly the same again in the local coinage. Probably not a lot to a guy like Soames, Porter thought. Probably less than the bloke earned in a day.

'Walking-around money,' Hawkridge explained. 'You'll need it. You can't get anything done out there without greasing a few palms. Bribery is the second biggest industry in Sierra Leone, after diamonds. But try not to blow the lot. This isn't some government jolly we're sending you on.'

'Sure,' Porter said, grinning. 'We'll just ask the rebels for receipts.'

Hawkridge made a face. Then he pointed to the sat phone. 'Iridium Motorola 9500. There's a UK number stored on the SIM card. Call it and you'll be put through to a secure line over at Vauxhall. As this is an overseas affair Angela and I will be liaising with Six on this operation. Contact us once you've located Soames. The battery only lasts for sixteen hours on standby, although I doubt you'll be on the ground for much longer than that. Understood?'

Both men nodded. Then Hawkridge stood up and glanced at his watch.

'It's quarter to eight, chaps. We're already on the clock. A driver will pick you up at ten o'clock sharp and drop you at the airport.' He buttoned up his jacket. 'Now, unless you have any further questions ...?'

Bald and Porter looked at one another. Porter turned back to Hawkridge and shook his head.

'Good. Then I suggest you both get leave and pack your bags.'

The two operators stood up simultaneously and turned to leave. Then Hawkridge cleared his throat. Bald and Porter both looked inquiringly at their handler.

'A word of warning,' Hawkridge said. 'A lot of people are desperate to make sure that Ronald stays out of trouble. People higher up the food chain than us. There's more at stake here than the diamond mines inside Sierra Leone. Ronald is a high-value asset. If the Russians get to him first, our past operations involving him will be at risk of being exposed. Operations we prefer to remain secret. Do whatever it takes to get him out of Freetown. Am I clear?'

'Yeah,' Porter replied tersely. 'Crystal.'

'Good.' There was a hard look in Hawkridge's eyes. But there was something else there too, thought Porter. Something unexpected. A cold blue glimmer of fear. 'If you fuck up, heads are going to roll inside Whitehall. And I'll make damn sure that yours will be the first ones on the block.'

FIVE

The car pulled up opposite the safehouse at exactly ten o'clock. A plain grey Ford Mondeo. The kind of anonymous car the Firm specialised in. Bald and Porter were waiting a few doors down from the safehouse, outside a grubby B&B called the Grosvenor Park Hotel. As soon as the briefing had finished the two Blades returned to their Firm-owned flats across town and grabbed their overnight bags and passports. Both guys also changed into civvies better suited to the tropical Sierra Leone climate. They wore 5.11 Tactical khakis and olive-green t-shirts under short-sleeved Valiant Softshell jackets, and XPRT urban boots. With their plane tickets and their travel bags, Bald and Porter looked like just another couple of out-of-towners waiting for a lift to the airport.

They dumped their bags in the boot and climbed into the back of the Mondeo. They didn't ask the driver for his name and he didn't offer it. The Firm had plenty of drivers on the Thames House payroll, ferrying agents and contacts around the country, and they all kind of looked the same. The guy gunned the engine and set off for Heathrow, arrowing slowly through the choked London streets. Porter gazed out of the tinted window and sipped from a bottle of Evian water he'd brought along for the flight. He'd emptied the bottle back at his flat and topped it up with Asda own-brand vodka. A neat little trick he'd learned from his old man. You take a sip whenever you need it, and it doesn't even look like you're on the piss.

Now I'm thinking like a true alcoholic, just like my father, Porter thought to himself. *Well, fuck it.* He took another swig and felt the warm soothing glow spread through his chest as the booze juiced his bloodstream. Bald stared at him with obvious contempt.

Fuck him too, thought Porter. *Twelve hours from now I'm going to be in the middle of the worst fucking city in the world. Might as well have a drop of the good stuff while I still can.*

The drive to the airport took forty-six minutes. They trundled west past Lancaster Gate and Queensway, skirting around the edge of Kensington Gardens, hung a left at Notting Hill Gate and rolled down High Street Kensington, past the overpriced designer shops and organic food halls and the imposing redbrick apartment blocks worth more than Porter would earn in his lifetime. Then past Hammersmith onto the M4. The road finally opened up. From there it was a straight drive west for ten miles to Heathrow. Porter took regular sips from his bottle. Twenty minutes later the Mondeo eased to a halt outside the entrance to Terminal 3. A little over three hours until their flight.

Bald and Porter unfolded themselves from the back seats and grabbed their bags. Then they swept into the departure hall and made for the BA desk. They got the business–class treatment, which meant they skipped the long lines at check-in and breezed through security. By the time they arrived at the duty-free shops Porter was practically gasping for another swig of his voddie. They found a bar on the first floor with Guinness on tap, garish lighting and a big-screen TV in the corner tuned to Sky News. There was a report on the TV about the deteriorating situation inside Sierra Leone. A solemn-looking brunette reporter stood at the side of a road outside Freetown. Behind her, a long line of scrawny locals were passing by, dragging carts piled high with their worldly possessions.

Everyone else is leaving the city, thought Porter Except us. *We're the only fuckers heading in.*

Bald pulled up a pew and browsed the food menu while Porter knocked back a long slug of vodka. The alcohol burned the back of his throat, slicked down into his guts. After a few seconds his hand stopped shaking. The sharp stabbing pain behind his eyes faded to a dull, rhythmic ache.

Ah, better.

'Fucking sad, that,' Bald said.

Porter wiped his mouth and frowned. 'What are you talking about?'

'You, mate.' Bald nodded at the Evian bottle. 'I wasn't born yesterday. I know what you've got in that bottle. It's not fucking water in there, is it?'

Porter looked away at the TV. 'I don't know what you're talking about.'

'Piss off,' Bald snapped. 'You might have them pen-pushers over at the Firm fooled, but I'm not buying it. You're on the drink again. I can smell your fucking breath from here.'

'It's a nightcap, that's all,' Porter replied defensively. 'A little something to help me sleep on the flight.'

Bald screwed up his face. 'Call that a bloody nightcap? There's enough booze in there to knock an elephant out.'

'Chill the fuck out.' Porter gripped the bottle tightly. 'I've got it under control. I know how to handle myself. It's not like you don't like a drink yourself, Jock.'

'True, but I'm Scottish. I can handle it. You bloody can't. I mean, just look at you. You look like a ten-pound shit stuffed into a one-pound sack. I've taken dumps that look better than you, mate.'

Porter set his teeth on edge. Anger coursed through his veins, mixing with the booze. Part of him knew Bald was right. The other part of him just wanted another drink.

'I'm fine.'

Bald snorted. 'Yeah, right. Just like you were fine back at the townhouse with them Albanians. You almost took my fucking head off.'

Porter clamped his jaws shut. 'I told you, that gun was dodgy. It won't happen again.'

'Bollocks.' Bald shook his head angrily. 'You used to be a good operator. Some of the younger fellas at Hereford looked up to you, hard as that is to believe. Now fucking look at you.'

Porter balled his hand into a fist but said nothing. *Maybe Bald is right*, he thought. *Maybe I am a disgrace to the Regiment. But I've got my reasons.* No alcoholic drank because they wanted to feel good about themselves. That wasn't the point. You drank to forget. To try and numb the pain. *And I need to feel as numb as fucking possible.* All Porter had left in this world was his daughter. Now they were taking Sandy away from him as well. She would grow up calling some other bloke 'Daddy'. I'll just become some sad, distant memory, he thought. A few years from now, she probably won't even recognise me in the street.

I've got nothing left in this world. So I might as well have another bloody drink.

'I've still got what it takes,' Porter muttered under his breath.

Bald laughed cynically. 'Just keep telling yourself that, pal. All I know is, where we're going, we're gonna have to be on top of our fucking game. Especially with those chogie nutters running all over the place.'

'I'll be fine.'

'Bullshit.' Bald stared levelly at his mucker. 'Look, I couldn't give a good fuck what you do on your own time. But as long as we're on this op, you're off the drink. Or you and me have got a problem. Got it?'

For a moment Porter was tempted to hit back at Bald, but then he bit his tongue. The two of them had their differences in the past and hadn't always seen eye-to-eye. They had barely socialised during their time together in the Regiment. They weren't friends, but they had developed a grudging respect for one another over the past year while working for the Firm. Deep down, Porter knew Bald was right. *I've got a problem.* He'd hit the bottle hard eleven years ago after a hostage-rescue mission in Beirut had gone tits-up, leaving three Blades dead. Porter had taken the blame. The other lads at Hereford had lost their respect for him, and he became a Regiment outcast. Eventually, he turned to the drink. The booze had nearly cost him his career in the Regiment, as well as his family. *Unless you sort yourself out, the drink is going to kill you.*

I've just got to get through this mission first, thought Porter. *Just this one last op, then I'm good.* He cast a forlorn look at the half-empty plastic bottle in front of him. Then he looked up at Bald. Nodded.

'Fine,' he said. 'I'll stay off the booze. For now.'

Bald studied his mate for a moment, then looked away. Over on the TV the camera cut away to the next news item, a live interview with an overweight Tory MP wearing small wire-framed glasses and a crumpled suit with a garish yellow shirt and purple tie. Porter vaguely recognised the MP from his smug grin and shiny bald pate. One of the new breed of career politicians. They all looked the same, sounded the same made the same empty promises. Porter hated them.

'You think we'll get to Soames before the rebels attack?' Bald said.

Porter mulled it over as he rubbed his jaw. 'Even if we do get there first, we've still got to bug out of the city without bumping into the Russians.'

Bald grunted. 'If we manage to get that ex-Rupert on a plane before the country goes tits up, it'll be a fucking mirade.'

1340 hours.

Two-and-a-half hours later, Porter and Bald boarded the Boeing 767. Their business-class tickets got them each a luxury reclining seat the approximate size of a single bed, a free copy of the *Financial Times* and a warm smile from a chatty blonde stewardess called Tiffany. It was a long way from the all-inclusives Porter had gone on with Diana and Sandy, in the days before he'd started draining their joint bank account to pay for his drinking binges. He eased back in his chair, resting his head against a plump white pillow. I could get used to this, he thought. The travel, the service. The five-star lifestyle. But he'd been working for the Firm long enough to know how they operated. They only picked up the tab for as long as they needed you.

Once you've extracted Soames, they'll soon send you back to your dingy flat and the crap surveillance missions.

The captain went through the usual litany of pre-take-off announcements. Then the engines droned into life, and the plane taxied across the runway. Outside it had started to rain. Big drops tumbled down from the lead-grey clouds, spattering the asphalt, pebble-dashing the plane windows. As the Boeing lifted into the sky Porter felt a tingle of excitement running up his spine. Ever since he and Bald had transferred to MI5, they had been itching to get back into the frontline.

Back to where the action was.

I don't give a crap about some shady ex-Rupert. But this is still better than gunning down crackheads in Hackney.

The plane banked as it climbed through the clouds. Porter gazed out of the window and watched London disappear behind a dense bank of grey. Then the seatbelt lights switched off, and the stewardess called Tiffany pulled the curtain across the divider between business and economy. A short while later she did the rounds with the drinks trolley. Porter greedily eyed the selection. They had miniatures of Johnnie Walker, Woodford Reserve and Glenlivet 18-year single malt, plus a large selection of beers and vodkas. Bloody hell, he thought. They've got everything here. It's all complimentary too. He was sorely tempted to get a few rounds in. But he could see Bald turning in his seat, giving him the evil eye.

'Just give us a Diet Coke, love,' he said sourly.

The stewardess smiled and handed Porter a miniature-sized can, plus a plastic cup half-filled with ice. Then she moved on.

'Fuck me, mate,' Bald said under his breath, turning in his seat and gazing admiringly at the stewardess as she bent over to serve another customer. 'That bird's giving me a hard-on a cat couldn't scratch.'

He unbuckled his belt and stood up from his seat. 'Where are you going?' Porter asked.

'Need a piss,' Bald said, his eyes planted firmly on the stewardess. 'Then I'm gonna try some of the old John Bald magic on that lass. See if I can persuade her to join the Mile High club.'

He shuffled past Porter then marched down the aisle towards the toilets at the rear of the plane. Porter reached inside his jacket pocket and fished out the Evian bottle. He'd lied to Bald back at the airport, telling him he'd emptied the vodka in one of the public restrooms. Now Porter was glad he'd saved it. There was still a decent amount sloshing around in the bottle. He discreetly emptied a generous measure into his cup. Took a sip and smiled. That's more fucking like it, he thought. Sod what Jock says. He doesn't have the right to tell me what to do.

Bald returned to his seat several minutes later. Porter sipped at his vodka mixer. Within a few minutes the booze had started to work its magic. Bald gave him a suspicious look but said nothing. That's the difference between me and Jock, Porter thought. He actually enjoys a drink. The bastard can put it away with the best of them, but he always stays functional. He doesn't need to drink himself into oblivion. He doesn't understand why I need it. Because it's the only way of blocking out all the shit in my head.

The only way I can put a lid on the pain.

'What's the deal with you and Soames?' Bald said. 'I saw the look on your face when that FO lass mentioned his name. You looked ready to snap.'

'Nothing.' Porter shrugged. 'You know what all them Ruperts are like, mate. Soames was no different. The guy's a tosser. That's all there is to it.'

'Except he's got the Firm in his pocket.'

'It's not important,' Porter said.

'Yeah,' Bald said. 'It fucking is. Soames is our objective. We need him on our side if we're gonna pull him out of Freetown. If there's bad blood between you and him, I've got a right to know about it.'

Porter looked away. 'Soames was the CO when I joined the Regiment. He was calling the shots when that clusterfuck in Beirut went down. He blamed me for what happened.'

'Them three lads who died?'

Porter nodded. 'After the debrief, Soames did his best to shaft my career. He made my life fucking hell.'

He fell silent and looked out of the window. The bad memories came rushing back at him. All the guys in the SAS were divided into two streams, A and B. The guys in A stream were the

56

ones who were really going places. They were fast-tracked onto all the courses, given the best postings, and nailed-on for one of the RSM spots down the line. The guys in B stream were the ones who got left behind. Back then Porter had a promising future in the SAS, a young wife and a child on the way. He had his plans all laid out. First Troop Sergeant, then Squadron Sergeant Major, then RSM.

'I was in the A stream before the Beirut job,' he continued. 'But after the op, Soames bumped me down to the B stream. The bastard sent me on shitty postings and gave us a crap write-up in my confidential. He even got me cross-promoted to one of the crap squadrons and replaced us with a load of yes-men. That prick stitched me up good and proper.'

Porter went quiet again. He remembered how some of the officers tried to persuade him to chuck in the towel, no doubt encouraged by Soames. The other lads kept their distance from him, after that. They could smell the failure coming off him. His career in the Regiment left in tatters. All because of Soames.

Bald eyed his mucker carefully. 'You sure it was Soames who shafted your career?'

'The fuck's that supposed to mean?'

'I heard that's when you started hitting the bottle. Right after the Lebanon op.' Bald shrugged. 'Just saying.'

Porter clenched his jaws. 'It wasn't the fucking booze, Jock. Soames hung me out to dry so he could cover his own arse. He's a slippery bastard. That bloke's got his fingers in more pies than a leper on a cookery course.'

'So what? Every bloke who's ever made their fortune has to get their hands dirty sometimes.'

'Not like Soames they haven't. This guy is on another level.'

'Maybe,' Bald responded. 'But all I know is, Soames has done well for himself and we're being paid a crap salary to fly out and rescue him. So who are the real mugs here?'

Porter didn't answer. He shook his head and returned his gaze to the window. Bald doesn't know what Soames is really like, he thought. Most of the Ruperts in the SAS followed the same career path. They came into the Regiment straight out of staff college and started throwing their weight around, acting like they were Lawrence of Arabia. Then they pissed off after a few years and ended up with a corner office in Whitehall and a pension pot the size of a Premier League footballer's salary. Most of them were tossers. But Soames was worse. Far worse. The guy had been a ruthless bastard, willing to do over anyone who dared to cross him.

Porter remembered how he used to hang around the base, being chummy and acting as if he was just another one of the lads. Soames would put on a front and stroll through the junior ranks' cookhouse, buying pints for the sergeants down the local pubs. But Porter had seen through the act. He'd noticed the wicked gleam in Soames's eyes, the way he looked down on the other Blades. And then there were the rumours that had floated around Hereford during his time in charge. The stories about Soames's dodgy dealings, fiddling the books and stealing money from diplomatic bags. Anyone who asked questions quickly found themselves in trouble. Soames blackballed some of the lads on the Circuit. He sabotaged the contracts of rival PMCs. He fucked with the careers of his enemies. Just like he fucked with me, Porter thought.

Too many bad memories, Porter thought. *Time to forget about them*. He took a long sip of his vodka mixer, sat back in his chair and tried not to think about the past.

SIX

0204 hours.

The rest of the journey passed in an alcoholic blur. Bald and Porter landed at Mohammed V International Airport in Casablanca at 1825 local time. Four hours later they boarded an ageing Boeing 737 for the last leg of their trip. The plane was more than half-empty. The only other passengers on the flight were a few locals and a handful of nervous-looking Arab businessmen who stank of cheap cigarettes and cologne. No one was flying to Freetown if they could possibly avoid it.

The fight from Morocco took a little over three hours. Porter passed the time sipping from his vodka mixers whenever Bald had his back turned. By the time the pilot announced that they were making their final approach to Lungi airport he was feeling thoroughly well-oiled, and better about himself. As the creaking old Boeing dipped through the clouds Porter knocked back the dregs of his vodka and glanced out of the window at the landscape below. Sierra Leone wasn't much to look at. Not by night, at least. Most of the surrounding jungle was buried under a dense blackness. Like soil heaped on top of a coffin. Further along the coast a cluster of lights glowed sporadically in the distance. Freetown, Porter realised.

Twenty-two minutes later they had landed.

0235 hours.

They stepped off the plane into a suffocating wall of tropical heat. The air was so thick and hot, Porter could hardly breathe at first. It was like wearing a scuba-diving suit into a steam room. He and

Bald shouldered their bags and climbed down the flight stairs, then boarded the airline bus. It was a million degrees inside the bus. Porter could feel the sweat slicking down his back as they rumbled across the runway and approached the main terminal building. Sixty seconds later they drew to a halt. The doors hissed open, and the passengers disembarked at the front of the terminal. The building façade was riddled with bullet holes. A battered sign above the main doors said: COCA-COLA WELCOMES YOU TO FREETOWN INTERNATIONAL AIRPORT. Next to it there was another smaller sign: DON'T RAPE WOMEN. YOU MAY GET AIDS.

Welcome to Africa, thought Porter.

It was chaos outside the terminal. Armed guards stood anxiously in front of the glass doors, clutching their AK-47 assault rifles and barking orders at the passengers stepping off the bus. Across the asphalt a team of airport workers were busy unloading crates from the back of an old Russian Antonov An-225 cargo plane. Several locals were hanging around the front of the terminal, bartering with the passengers. A skinny porter hobbled over to Bald and Porter and tried to grab their bags, offering to escort them into the city. Bald shoved him aside. Then he looked up and spotted their handler beyond the heaving throng.

He was easy to identify. Partly because he was the only other white guy in sight. But mostly because he was doing his best not to look like a handler. He stood to one side of the terminal building, clutching a clipboard in his right hand and chewing on a wad of tobacco. He had a pair of Ray-Ban Aviators strapped across his face, under a baseball cap with the words EVERGREEN CARGO stencilled across the front in big gold lettering. The guy was medium-height, medium-build. Medium-everything. He looked about as anonymous as a white man could be in a place like Sierra Leone. The handler caught sight of Bald and Porter and quickly approached them, threading his way past the crowd.

'You're John Bald, right?' the guy said, thrusting out a hand. He had a gruff Midwestern accent, Porter noted. He didn't take off his shades.

'Aye,' Bald replied, pumping the guy's hand. 'That's me.'

'Mike Shoemaker. Logistics manager here at Evergreen Cargo. I was told to expect you guys.' Shoemaker looked towards Porter and gave a barely perceptible nod. 'That makes you John Porter, I guess.'

Porter grinned. 'You're Catholics in Action?'

Shoemaker scratched his beard. 'Excuse me, sir?'

'CIA,' said Porter, pointing to the guy's baseball cap. 'That's you, right?'

Shoemaker stared at him from behind his shades. His expression was neutral.

'Sir, with all due respect I have absolutely no idea what you're talking about. I'm just the logistics manager.' He adjusted the brim of his cap and said, 'Now, if you gentlemen both follow me . . .'

He turned and marched purposefully towards the terminal. Bald and Porter followed him a short distance behind. Bald glanced at his mucker. 'What was all that about?' he asked in a low voice, so that Shoemaker wouldn't overhear.

'He's from the CIA,' Porter whispered in reply, pointing to the back of the guy's cap. 'I recognised the name of the company he's working for.'

'Evergreen Cargo?'

Porter nodded. 'It's a front business the CIA uses for operations in Africa. Their mob were working for the same firm down in Zaire, back when Mobutu threw his toys out of the pram.'

'You sure, mate?'

There was a note of scepticism in Bald's voice. Porter said, 'I might be an alcoholic, but that doesn't mean I'm losing my marbles. This guy is definitely working for the Company, Jock.'

They caught up with Shoemaker and followed him into a low-ceilinged hall with a loose line of immigration cops, a customs counter and a Hertz desk with nobody manning it. There was a tense mood in the air. Some of the armed guards stood huddled around an old radio set, listening intently to the broadcast and pulling on their cancer sticks. Shoemaker led Bald and Porter past the queues and made for a side door. He paid twenty bucks to an immigration official and slipped another Andrew Jackson to the customs guy to stop him rooting through their bags. Shoemaker seemed to be on first-name terms with everyone at the airport. He was that kind of guy. In a few minutes they were breezing out of the terminal building. *I don't care what this guy says*, Porter told himself. *He's with the CIA. I'd stake my life on it.*

Which made him wonder: Why would the CIA give a toss about helping to extract some British ex-Rupert? What's in it for the Yanks? I don't know, he thought. *But I get the feeling someone's not telling us something.*

Outside the airport Porter noticed a long line of people stand-ing around outside the departures hall. There must have been four hundred people in the line, he guessed. They were mostly Westerners, along with a few locals. They looked like the richer ones. The ones who could afford a two-hundred-dollar plane ticket, in a country where the average wage was less than a dollar a day. Some of the travellers sat on the ground, surrounded by their hastily gathered belongings. Men argued with the armed guards, offering them cash bribes. Their voices were laced with desperation, and fear.

'What the fuck's going on?' Bald asked as they paced towards a line of vehicles parked across the road from the main airport building.

Shoemaker took off his cap and wiped sweat from his brow. 'Right. I forgot you guys have been off the grid for a while. Things just got real bad here. RUF forces have entered Freetown.'

Bald frowned heavily. 'When?'

'Yesterday evening. General Mosquito's men broke through the army checkpoints at Port Loko and entered Freetown at around 1930 hours.'

Porter stopped in his tracks. 'The city's fallen?'

'Sure looks that way,' Shoemaker replied. 'Details are a little sketchy right now. But we've got reports of the rebels going nuts. Looting World Food Programme warehouses, stealing Red Cross vehicles, stripping luxury homes. Last night they reached the Pademba Road Prison and released all the convicts. Co-opted the fuckers into their army. We've also heard reports that some of their guys launched mortar attacks on the American embassy a few hours ago.' He waved a hand at the line of people stretching outside the airport building. 'Everyone's trying to get out while they still can. The smart ones, anyhow. The rest are locked up inside their homes, praying the rebels don't come for them.'

'Our timing's fucking impeccable,' Bald muttered. 'As per bloody usual.'

Porter felt unease dripping like acid into his guts. He turned back to Shoemaker. 'How the fuck are we supposed to get into the city if the rebels have taken control?'

'That's going to be the least of your problems. Most of the rebels will be too busy lining their pockets and settling scores to pay you much notice. As long as you stick to the back streets and try not to draw any attention to yourselves, you should be okay. If it gets too hot, you should make your way to Lumley Beach, to the west of Freetown. Where all the expensive hotels are. The rebels won't dare approach that area. Not yet.'

'Why's that?'

'One word,' Shoemaker said. 'ECOMOG.'

'The fuck is that?' said Bald. 'Some new sort of fancy new version of AIDS?'

'It's the local peacekeeping force here in Sierra Leone. Soldiers drafted in from Nigeria and Guinea to help keep the peace after the last rebel coup. There are about three hundred Nigerian troops based in Freetown, under the command of Major-General Godwin Bassey.'

Porter rustled up a smile. 'You know a lot about Sierra Leone for a logistics manager.'

Shoemaker looked at him but his expression gave away nothing. 'As long as Bassey and his guys are stationed in the city, the rebels will be wary about attacking the hotels. They're mad motherfuckers, but they're not crazy enough to want to get into a pissing contest with the Nigerians.'

'That's assuming the Nigerians stick around,' Bald countered. 'What happens if they pull out?'

Shoemaker just shrugged. 'Then, brother, you do the smart thing and get the fuck out of Dodge City.'

He stopped in front of an eggshell-white Range Rover. Dug a set of keys out of his cargo pocket.

'Here,' he said, chucking the keys at Porter. 'She's got a full tank in her, plus four extra jerry cans in the back if you run out of gas. It's an hour and a half from the airport to the city. How you get there is real simple. You follow the road south all the way until you hit the crossing at Tagrin. You can't miss it. Buy yourselves a couple of VIP tickets, and the ferry will land you at Kissy, on the other side of the Sierra Leone river.'

Bald said, 'Isn't there a quicker way into the city?'

Shoemaker took out his pouch of chewing tobacco. Took a pinch and thumbed it into the back of his mouth. 'Usually, yeah. Couple of Russian pilots own an Mi-17. They run a helicopter service that can get you into the city in twenty minutes or so, but the chopper's out today. They're going where the money is. And right now, that's flying expats from Freetown to Conakry. You guys are going to have to slum it on the ferry instead.' He shrugged. 'It's not your lucky day today.'

'Tell us something we don't know, mate.'

Shoemaker half-laughed and pointed south down the road. 'There's a government checkpoint half a mile outside the airport. The soldiers are on edge, what with the shit that's going down across the river. Also, they'll be suspicious about why a couple of white guys want to head into Freetown in the middle of a coup. You just smile, stay calm and hand out a few bucks to each of the soldiers. Keep the denominations low. A dollar or two apiece ought to do it. Hand over too much and they'll think you're hiding more cash and will likely rob you. The trick is to make them think you're broke, and handing over all the dollars you have left in the world. Got it?'

'Don't worry about us,' said Porter. 'We're big boys. We can take care of ourselves.'

'I don't doubt it.' Shoemaker took out a business card from his wallet and handed it to Porter. It was plain, no-nonsense, with the Evergreen Cargo logo and a local number at the bottom. 'You guys run into trouble at the checkpoint, or if you need anything, you give me a call. No promises, but I'll see what I can do.'

'Sure,' said Porter, pocketing the card. He started to turn away.

'A word of advice,' Shoemaker continued.

Porter stopped. Half-turned back towards Shoemaker. 'What's that?'

'I don't know what your business is inside Freetown. Frankly, I don't want to know. But whatever it is, make it quick. Word on the grapevine is that the rebels are gearing up for an attack on the airport. If that happens, don't expect the government troops here to put up a fight. Trust me, they'll run at the first sight of the RUF.'

'What about the Nigerians?' Bald asked.

'They're strictly based in the city. Their orders are to guard key government buildings and protect the expatriate community. Their jurisdiction doesn't extend to the airport. If the rebels attack here, the ECOMOG troops won't be in a position to help.'

'And if the airport falls,' Porter said, 'we'll be trapped.'

Shoemaker nodded. 'All I'm saying is, do what you gotta do, but don't stick around for a second longer than you have to.'

They shook hands. Then Shoemaker turned and hurried back in the direction of the terminal building, shouting at one of the airport officials. Bald and Porter climbed inside the Range Rover. Porter took the wheel. He shoved the keys in the ignition and fired up the wagon. Then he steered out of the airport and bulleted south on the main airport–ferry Road. Headlamps burning in the near-dark, tyres throwing up fists of purplish dust into the pre-dawn sky. Porter felt his hangover giving way to a raw sense of unease. They were heading into a city in the grip of a violent coup, crawling with murderous rebels and escaped convicts looking for easy targets. And to make matters worse, they were both unarmed.

The more he thought about it, the more Porter started to realise that this op was a really bad fucking idea.

SEVEN

The drive south to the ferry took a little under thirty minutes. After half a mile they hit the government checkpoint. Just like Shoemaker had said. Twenty or so scruffily dressed soldiers stood in a line blocking the road, next to a pair of beaten-up pickup trucks. Some of the guys were brandishing AK-47 assault rifles. Others were armed with RPG-7 rocket launchers or pistols. The soldiers looked tense and edgy, and itching for a scrap. Porter kept his cool, played the ignorant Westerner and dished out the dollar bills. The sight of hard cash instantly changed the mood. The soldiers grinned as they waved the Range Rover through. Porter hit the gas and carried on down the airport–ferry road.

They passed an unending line of locals trudging along the side of the road in the opposite direction. It seemed to Porter as if half of Sierra Leone was trying to flee the city. Men walking barefoot and dressed in filthy t-shirts shuffled alongside women in dirty patterned skirts. The locals stared indifferently at the Range Rover as it rolled past, their bulbous eyes glowing in the faint pre-dawn light. Some of the locals were missing arms or legs. Many of their faces were horribly scarred, a legacy of the last time the RUF rebels had rolled into town. It never changes, thought Porter. He had been on previous missions to Africa and he never ceased to be amazed by the level of shit that people put up with in this part of the world. The grinding poverty, the desperation, the constant threat of violence. It doesn't matter who they put in the president's office, he thought. These people had fuck-all before, and they'll go on having fuck-all long after the dust has settled too.

At Tagrin they pulled up in front of the shabby ticket office and paid 10,000 Leones for two seats on the next available ferry, plus another 5,000 for a space on the ferry for the Range Rover. Roughly three dollars in US currency. A few bedraggled souls hung around by the jetty, staring out at the dirty grey waters separating Tagrin from the capital. Porter steered the Range Rover up the metal ramp and onto the back of the ferry moored at the side of the jetty. The vessel looked like an old fishing trawler with a couple of extra decks stacked onto the front end of it. The railings were scabbed with rust and the glass was missing from most of the upper deck windows. A smell of vomit and diesel fumes hung in the air, mixing with the rancid stench of the river waters. Porter and Bald climbed out and stretched their legs, staying close to the railings so they could keep a close eye on the Range Rover.

As Porter gazed out across the jetty he saw a trio of smaller wooden boats with outboards arriving, filled to the brim with people who had managed to escape the bloodshed across the river. Hundreds of panicked civvies clambered off the boats before beginning the journey north towards Lungi airport. Porter couldn't help but notice that there were only a handful of passengers on the ferry heading in the opposite direction.

Bald shook his head.

'We must need our fucking heads examined.'

'How's that, Jock?' Porter asked.

'Heading into the city.' Bald tipped his head at the river 'This old Rupert better be grateful when we get our hands on him. Maybe he'll give us a cushty job with his PMC once this is over.'

Porter laughed cynically. 'Don't get your hopes up. Soames won't be doing us any favours. That bastard only cares about himself.'

'Sounds like good career advice to me.' Bald shrugged. 'Anyway, I'd rather work for him than that twat Hawkridge any day of the week.'

'No.' Porter shook his head bitterly. 'Trust me, you wouldn't.'

Bald stared at his mucker. 'You must really hate his guts.'

Porter didn't reply. He hardened his gaze at the few glowing lights in the distance, on the far side of the dark mouth of the river. Then he said, 'Let's just focus on finding Soames. All I give a shit about right now is getting him out before the rebels take over the rest of the city.'

'We won't have much time, then. You know what them chogie squaddies are like. Piss themselves at the first sign of trouble. If the shit hits the fan, them Nigerians will quit the place faster than a Scouse at a job interview.'

At five o'clock in the morning the ferry sounded its horn as it slid away from the jetty and began its journey south-west towards Kissy. The first streaks of sunlight were visible on the horizon, creeping out of the guts of the earth. As they left behind Tagrin and the crowds of wailing locals, Porter felt a knot of cold fear inside his bowels. This was it, he told himself. There was no going back now. They had to hope they could locate Soames and lift him out of the city in time. Before the Russians got to him first. Before the rebels swept into the airport and cut off their exit route.

The ferry chugged deeper into the glum, inky abyss.

Towards Freetown.

Towards Ronald Soames.

0547 hours.

They reached Kissy forty-six minutes later. The ferry shuddered to a halt at the shabby terminal, the ramp came down, and Porter and Bald hopped back inside the Range Rover. Then Porter reversed the wagon back down the ramp onto the road leading out of the terminal. Two minutes later they were breaking free of the loose crowd hanging around the litter-strewn jetty, and rolling south past the dockyards on the ferry road.

The streets were choked with traffic. People on foot, weighed down by their belongings or dragging carts piled high with food and clothing. Knackered old motors with mattresses and furniture lashed to their rooftops. Everyone seemed to be in a mad hurry to catch the next available ferry to Tagrin. Most of the civvies were dressed in filthy torn rags or faded trousers with patches missing. Porter nosed the Range Rover through the traffic at about five miles per. They passed more mounds of festering rubbish and rivers of shit running into the drains. They passed decaying buildings with weeds growing out of the cracks, and murals splashed down the side.

One mural caught Porter's attention. It had been painted in bright colours on the side of a bullet-riddled apartment block, and it depicted several African women marching through the streets, holding up placards bearing the faces of young boys and girls. Below the painting was a slogan in bold red lettering: 'Mothers of the Lost Children'.

'What's that all about, do you think?' said Porter.

'No fucking clue,' Bald replied. 'Let's just get to the office and get out of here.'

After half a mile Porter made a left onto Kissy Road, leading into the west of the city.

The streets in this part of the city were deserted. Everywhere they looked there were signs of the recent RUF attack. Shop windows had been smashed open, the ground littered with glass and rubbish. Several burnt-out cars lay at the sides of the road, the toxic smell of burnt rubber stinging the early-morning air. There were piles of rubble all over the place, and Porter glimpsed several dead bodies lying slumped at the side of the road, the blood pooling under their bullet-riddled torsos. Bald frowned.

'I thought the rebels had the run of this side of the city?'

'That's what Shoemaker said.'

'Then where the fuck is everyone?'

Porter thought for a moment. 'Probably still asleep, working off their hangovers from last night's looting session. These guys aren't trained soldiers. They're not gonna be up at the crack of dawn unless there's something in it for them.'

Bald screwed up his face in soldierly disgust.

'Fucking useless.'

'At least we've got a couple of hours until they wake up. Let's hope we find Soames before then.'

A hundred metres further down the road Porter caught his first sight of the rebels. Half a dozen of them were robbing an electronics store, three of them lugging TVs and radios out and dumping them on the back of a stolen UN vehicle. They were too busy looting the place to spot Bald and Porter ahead of them in the Range Rover. Three other rebels were leaning against the side of the UN vehicle. They were wearing designer shades and red t-shirts and passing around a bottle of poyo, the local home-made brew.

As Porter drove past two more rebels emerged from the store, dragging out a skinny girl dressed in a bloodstained skirt and dirty white blouse. She looked to be no older than thirteen or fourteen. The rebels dragged the girl over to the UN vehicle and tried to bundle her inside. She resisted, kicking out and screaming at the top of her voice, begging for help. One of the rebels grabbed his AK-47 and gave her a sharp dig in the ribs with the rifle stock. The girl dropped to the dusty red ground. Then the guy pinned her down, ripped off her skirt and knickers and pulled down his shorts. The other six rebels started whooping and hollering, firing automatic rifle bursts into the air as their mucker forced himself onto the girl. She screamed at the top of her voice, to the amusement of the rebels crowding around her. Bald twisted in his seat and looked back at the crowd.

'Stop the wagon,' he said.

Porter shook his head. 'We can't get involved.'

Bald turned around and glared at his mucker. 'You're just gonna let those fucking animals rape that girl?'

'There's nothing we can do. There's seven of them, and they're packing rifles. We don't even have a bloody pea-shooter. If we try and intervene, they'll turn their weapons on us.'

Bald stared at his mucker for a long moment. Then he looked away, clenching his fists. 'This is fucked.'

Porter tightened his grip on the wheel and drove on. The girl's screams sounded above the steady growl of the engine.

After another hundred metres he turned off the main road and made for the back streets leading through the shanty areas. He'd studied the maps of Freetown during the flight out of Heathrow, and he broadly knew his way around. The roads in the slums were practically deserted. Which made sense. There was less action here for the rebels. Less valuable staff for then to loot. There were hardly any locals outside. Thin, drawn faces peered out of half-opened doors or through grime-coated windows at the Range Rover trundling past. As Shoemaker had predicted, many of the residents were bottled up in their homes, waiting until the killing frenzy was over. A few locals sat down in the streets, portable radios glued to their ears. Porter drove on, the still of the dawn air broken by the distant crack of gunfire and the heavy bass of rap music blaring out from the rebels' trucks. In the distance he could see columns of smoke drifting into the air from several burning buildings. Black, swirling smudges against the dirty copper sky. Dawn was breaking. It seemed to Porter as if the entire city was on fire.

The route to Soames's office was long and winding and fraught. It took Porter forty-five minutes to arrow the Range Rover through the back streets before they hit Spur Road. Practically twice the time it took to cover the same distance in London. The deeper they ventured into Freetown, the more signs of devastation they encountered along the way. Dozens of bodies hacked to bits by machetes lay face-down in the streets. The bigger houses and businesses had been stripped bare, right down to the fittings. Twice Bald and Porter nearly ran into gangs of rebel fighters tearing through the streets, hanging out of the back of battered old Jeeps as they cheered and laughed. On both occasions Porter weaved in and out of the side streets, narrowly avoiding them. Once they hit Spur Road they hooked left at the British High Commission and made their way down a heavily-potholed street lined with gated houses and abandoned hotels. After two hundred metres, they pulled up outside a grand old colonial block with a wrought-iron gate and a brass plaque next to it that said INDIA HOUSE.

'Looks like the old boy has done well for himself,' said Bald as he cast an approving eye over the driveway. 'I can definitely see myself working for him in the future.'

Porter shot a look at his mucker. 'You're talking about the bastard who wrecked my career.'

'Maybe you should bury the hatchet with him. He might give you a job and all. You never know.' He grinned.

Porter had stopped listening. He was frowning at the driveway. 'What's wrong with this picture?'

Bald scratched his jaw. Then he saw it too. 'The gate. It's wide open.'

'In the middle of a rebel coup? When they're looting every property in sight?'

'Maybe Soames isn't here,' Bald suggested. 'Maybe he checked out as soon as the rebels moved into the city.'

Maybe, Porter thought to himself. *Or maybe the Russians got here first.*

He pointed the Range Rover through the gates and rolled down the entranceway. There was a large garden at the front of the house fronted with palm trees and bushes leading towards a wide two-storey mansion twenty-five metres away, with a whitewashed portico at the entrance. It looked less like the HQ of a PMC, and more like the house of a slave plantation owner.

There were no other cars outside the mansion. Which was the second thing that struck Porter as odd. *If Soames is still here, then where the fuck is his vehicle?* He pulled up outside the front door, cut the engine, and climbed out of the Range Rover. Then he glanced down and noticed the third thing.

'Jock. Look. Over here.'

Bald chased his line of sight. 'Shit.'

Spent brass was lying around the portico, glinting in the bleary morning light. Porter counted at least a dozen jackets around his feet. Some of them were close to the front door. The rest had been discharged further down the driveway, amid a scatter of broken glass. Porter noticed a pair of bullet holes pockmarking the wall next to the main gate. He glanced around the mansion, a noose tightening around his guts.

We think the Russians have sent in a team to take advantage of the chaos on the ground, March had said at the mission briefing.

Bald stooped down to inspect some of the spent brass. 'Looks like you were right. Someone paid Soames a visit. Not a friendly one.'

'The Russians,' Porter said. 'We might be too late.'

'Only one way to find out.'

They approached the front door. Porter tested the handle. Unlocked. He shoved open the door and Bald followed him into the shadowed cool of the hallway. Porter slowed his pace and pricked his ears as he glanced around, listening for any signs of life inside the mansion. But there was nothing except a cold, still silence and the sound of their footsteps echoing on the tiled floor. Porter led the way past several unfurnished rooms and headed for the stairs. He knew from the mission briefing that Soames kept his office on the first floor as an extra security precaution. If the guy was hiding out in his mansion, that's where he would be.

He moved quietly up the stairs, hit the first floor landing, and made for the office door to the left. Brass lettering etched across the glass told him this was the office of Ronald M. Soames, Director of Janus International Ltd. The door was ajar. But the wood panelling was splintered down the middle and when Porter reached for the doorknob it rattled loosely in his grip. As if someone had kicked the door open. *Someone who had been targeting Soames.* He inched forward and gently pushed the door back on its hinges. Then he stepped through the opening and entered Soames's office ahead of Bald.

· The office looked as if the occupants had left in a hurry. Everything was still switched on. A Psion laptop noisily hummed away on a desk in the middle of the room. There was an ancient-looking HF radio set on a side table, along with a fax machine and a stack of printed pages. There was no sign of Soames inside. Porter took another step into the room and heard something crunch underfoot. He looked down. Shards of glass were scattered across the tiles. There was a dark stain on the carpet next to a shattered glass bottle with a Grey Goose label.

Then Porter lifted his eyes and stopped cold.

Sprawled on the floor next to the desk was the bloated, purpled form of a dead man.

EIGHT

Porter didn't move for a beat. Neither did Bald. The two Blades just stood in the middle of the office, staring in silence at the dead guy on the floor. Porter dropped down beside the body for a closer look. The dead man wasn't Soames. That much was obvious from his appearance. This guy was younger than the ex-Regiment CO. Much younger. His face had puffed up in death, distorting his features. His hands looked like a couple of rubber gloves that had been filled with water, and there was a dark patch on his trousers from where the guy had shat and pissed himself in the last seconds of his life. A strip of plastic cable-tie was fastened tight around the guy's throat, Porter noticed. There were bloody claw marks around the flesh on his neck. Presumably from where the victim had tried to prise the cable-tie free. A tattoo was visible on his neck above the cable, depicting the head of a wolf with its jaws open in a snarl.

'The body's stiff,' Porter said. 'He must've been dead for a while. Long enough for rigor mortis to set in. Maybe a day or two.'

'Who is he?'

Porter padded the guy down. Found a brown leather wallet in his breast pocket and flipped it open. There was two hundred dollars in US bills, a few bills in the local currency, and a plastic warrant card the size of a credit card with a passport-style photograph of the dead guy and a bunch of words in a foreign language Porter couldn't read. Some kind of Cyrillic script. He showed the card to Bald.

'Looks Eastern European,' he said. 'Russian, maybe.'

Porter thought back to what March had told him at the briefing. About the Russians looking to get rid of Soames. 'We think the Russians have sent in a team to expedite matters,' she had said.

Maybe the Russians have already lifted Soames, Porter thought.

Or maybe Soames knew they were coming for him.

The pounding in his head came back. The effects of the booze starting to wear off. He spied a drinks cabinet in one corner, stocked with enough spirits to keep an off-licence in business. It was mostly posh gins and brandy, but Porter wasn't fussy. He just needed something to take the edge off the pain he was feeling. *Right now I'd drink a pint of battery fluid if someone offered it to me.* He made a mental note to help himself to a bottle or two before they checked out of the office.

'We need to call it in,' said Bald.

Porter nodded absently and reached for the sat phone stashed inside his bag. Just then he heard a noise. A soft, muffled whimpering, coming from somewhere close by. He scanned the office again. His eyes were drawn to the balcony doors at the far end of the office. The doors were closed, with the frayed dark curtains pulled across the length of the frame, blocking out the sunlight. Porter nodded at Bald. Both operators thinking the same thing. *Someone else is inside this room.*

Porter set down the sat phone and slowly manoeuvred around the stinking corpse towards the balcony door. The sniffing sound grew louder now. There's definitely someone on the other side of that door, thought Porter. Maybe it's Soames. *Maybe the old bastard has been hiding here the whole time.*

He reached for the brass handle and yanked the balcony door open. The figure on the other side gave a tiny childlike yelp. Porter thrust out onto the balcony and found a scrawny black kid crouched against the railings. The kid was no more than eleven or twelve. He was dressed in a pair of stained shorts and an Arsenal shirt that was at least two sizes two big and hung like a tent from his skeletal frame. The kid looked panicked. His arms were raised high above his head in a pose of surrender. His hands were trembling. He looked up at Porter, his eyes wide with terror.

'Please, mister,' the kid said. 'I want no trouble. Don't hurt me. Please.'

'Who the fuck are you?' Bald demanded. He had moved over to the balcony next to Porter, his icy blue gaze fixed on the kid.

'My name is Vandi.' The kid swallowed as he looked from Bald to Porter and back again. Tears streamed down his face. 'Please. Vandi not bad person. Vandi don't make trouble. Vandi just work for Mister Ronald.'

'You're the houseboy?' Porter said.

The kid nodded.

Every rich household in Africa had a houseboy, Porter knew. Usually a poor kid from the slums who did all the chores around the place, mowing the lawn, buying supplies from the shops and sweeping the floors, in return for board and food. It stood to reason that Soames would have hired one to help him with the day-to-day maintenance of the mansion. Then another thought tickled at the back of his throat. *Maybe this kid knows where to find Soames.*

And can tell us why there's a dead Russian in the office.

'Get up,' he growled.

The kid rose unsteadily to his feet and dropped his arms by his side. Bald grabbed him by the collar of his Arsenal shirt and shoved him through the doors and into the musty gloom of the office. The kid stumbled inside, weeping and shaking. Bald ordered him to sit down on the leather chair in front of the desk. The kid did as he was told, looking up at Bald and Porter with a mixture of fear and helplessness.

'Don't kill me, mister. Please, I beg you,' he said, frantically shaking his head from side to side. Like he was trying to shake something out of his ears. 'It wasn't me. I swear. Vandi is not bad.'

'Shut the fuck up,' said Bald.

The kid started wailing again, rocking back and forth on the chair, tears welling up in his eyes. Porter could see they were getting nowhere with the heavy-handed approach. Someone had put the frighteners on the houseboy. He dropped to a knee beside

Vandi, placed a hand on his shoulder and addressed him in a soft tone of voice.

'Listen to me, kid. We're not here to hurt you, all right? We're friends of Ronald.'

The kid stopped snivelling. He wiped the tears from his eyes and looked up at Porter. His face relaxed slightly, the fear replaced by something closer to curiosity.

'Friends? You know Mister Ronald?'

Porter grinned. 'That's right. Ronald is an old mate of ours. We're worried that something might have happened to him. So if you know anything that might help us find him, you need to tell us now.'

Vandi sniffed. 'Okay.'

Porter pointed to the dead guy and said, 'Did you see who did this?'

The kid bowed his head. 'Mister Ronald,' he said in a barely audible voice. 'Mister Ronald killed him.'

Porter did a double-take. Dread squirmed inside his guts, chilling the blood in his veins. He suddenly forgot about the booze in the drinks cabinet. Now he understood why Soames had disappeared off the grid. Why Hawkridge and March had been unable to locate him in the hours before the op briefing.

Because Soames is on the run. He murdered someone and then bolted.

He looked back to the kid. 'What happened?'

'Mister Ronald, he had a meeting with this man. Day before yesterday.' He glanced across at the dead guy. The stench of faecal matter inside the room was becoming unbearable, mixing with the heat and the sweat and the dust. Porter felt a wave of nausea surge up inside his chest.

'Who is he?' he asked.

'Mister Ronald did not say. But it was a very important meeting.'

'What was the meeting about?'

'I don't know. I am just the houseboy. I show the man into Mister Ronald's office. Then I leave.' Vandi paused. 'But I overheard them. The doors here, they are not so thick. I could hear them arguing. The other man threatened Mister Ronald. He said he was going to rob him.'

Porter swapped a look with Bald. He turned back to Vandi. 'Go on.'

The kid rubbed his knuckles and lowered his head. 'Then the bad men arrived. I saw them. So I went back to warn Mister Ronald. That's when I saw the dead man.'

Porter stared intently at the houseboy. 'Hold on. What bad men?'

'The men with guns.'

'Rebels?' Porter asked.

'No. White men.' Vandi pointed with his wide eyes at the dead man. 'Like him.'

'How many?'

'Four of them,' the kid said. 'They had guns.'

'The Russians,' Bald said. 'Has to be.'

Porter nodded. That could only mean one thing. *We're too late. The Russians got to Soames first.*

'What happened to Ronald?' Porter asked. 'When the bad men arrived.'

'Mister Ronald, he ran away,' Vandi replied. 'The bad men tried to shoot him. I heard their guns go bang bang.' The kid mimed a pistol action with his forefinger and thumb. 'Then Mister Ronald drive off in his car. The bad men left and followed him.'

Bald nodded at the houseboy. 'Where were you in all of this?'

'I was hiding in there.' Vandi pointed out a wardrobe in the far corner of the room, next to the balcony doors. A big old thing with dark wooden panels and worn brass handles. 'I waited until all the bad men leave.'

Porter said, 'Where is Soames now?'

Vandi shrugged his bony shoulders. 'This I do not know. I don't go outside now. Not safe. Too many rebels. I stay here. Wait for Mister Ronald.' He made a pained face. 'But he not come back.'

'That's why you hid in the balcony just now,' said Bald.

The houseboy nodded. 'I heard a car outside. For a moment, I think maybe Mister Ronald is coming home. That he has not abandoned me after all.' He sighed. 'Then I see your faces. I think maybe you are with the bad men. Maybe they come back to kill me.'

'Any idea where Soames might have gone?' said Bald. 'Any clue at all?'

Vandi eyed the two men suspiciously. 'You swear you are friends of Mister Ronald?'

'Aye,' said Porter. 'We're best mates, us. We go way back.'

The kid considered them both for a moment. Then he said, 'There is a friend of Mister Ronald. They were talking on the phone before the bad men arrived.'

'Who?' Bald asked.

'I don't know his name. I have seen him a few times. He has visited this house before. He and Mister Ronald are close. Like this.'

Vandi crossed his index and middle fingers to illustrate the point.

'Did you hear what they were talking about?' Porter said.

'Not really. I only heard them talking for a few minutes. But Mister Ronald, he was worried about Kono.'

'The diamond mine?'

Vandi nodded. 'Yes. He sounded very worried. He said the Russians knew about Kono and were planning to steal everything from him. I've never seen him look so worried.'

Porter digested the int then dug the Iridium Motorola 9500 out of his back pocket. He had switched off the sat phone before their flight in order to preserve battery life. Now Porter twisted up the bulky antenna and hit the red button to power up the unit. A basic graphic played out on the small digital screen while the sat phone began searching for a signal. He told Bald to keep an eye on the houseboy, then stepped out onto the balcony, pointing the antenna at the sky until he got three bars flashing on the monochrome display. Once he had a signal Porter tapped the Menu button, bringing up the Contacts list. He scrolled down to the single pre-installed number, hit Dial. There was a pause of static while the call patched through to London. Then the phone rang. After four rings, a voice on the other end of the line answered.

'John? Is that you?'

He recognised the nasal voice at once. Hawkridge. The guy sounded breathless, thought Porter. Harassed. Angry.

'It's me,' he said. 'Listen, we're at the office. Soames isn't here. Looks like the guy's done a runner.' He looked over his shoulder at the body slumped on the floor. 'And he's left a present behind for us.'

'Eh?' Hawkridge snorted down the line. 'What the hell are you talking about, man?'

'There's a dead guy in Soames's office. We found some ID on him. We're not sure, but we think he might be Russian.'

There was a long pause. Then Hawkridge said, 'We know.'

Porter jolted. 'What the fuck do you mean?'

'We're one step ahead of you, old bean.' There was a pause, followed by the sound of rustling papers. 'The dead man's name is Viktor Sergeyevich Agron. He's a senior agent with the Russian Federal Security Services. Height six-three, dark hair, tattoo on his neck of a wolf, the mark of members of a Moscow biker gang. The new Russian president is a big fan of the Night Wolves, apparently. They're proven themselves very useful at roughing up the political opposition, kidnapping journalists, that sort of thing. He's placed several of them in the FSB. According to our intelligence Agron arrived in Freetown three days ago on a diplomatic passport.'

A pulse of hot rage swept through Porter's veins. He gripped the sat phone so hard it threatened to crack open.

'How long have you known?' he said.

'About the murder? A few hours. GCHQ picked up incoming messages to the FSB from one of their field agents, openly discussing Agron's murder. They're convinced Soames is responsible.'

'You should have told us.'

'We've been trying to reach you, but your sat phone was switched off.'

'We're trying to save the battery.'

'Going against orders, you mean.' Hawkridge's voice took on an edge. 'From now on, you will do as I damn well tell you and keep the phone switched on at all times. Understood?'

'Fine,' said Porter.

'Did you find anything else?'

'There's a houseboy.' Porter glanced at the kid. 'We found him hiding in the back of the office. He reckons Soames killed the Russian, then legged it when the guy's mates rocked up.'

A pregnant pause. 'The boy is certain of this?'

'Positive.'

'And you believe him?'

'He's got no reason to lie.'

Hawkridge muttered something inaudible. 'Did he say anything else?'

'The kid overheard Soames and the Russian having an argument. Sounds like the Russian made some kind of a threat against Soames. He lost his rag and strangled the guy to death.'

'That does make a certain amount of sense. It ties in with a theory we've been working on, ever since we learned about Agron's death. We think Viktor Agron made an offer to Soames, on behalf of the FSB.'

'What sort of offer?'

'Hand over control of the diamond mines, or die. Soames naturally refused. He could never agree to such a deal.'

'But he still went ahead with the meeting.'

'He had to. Otherwise Agron would have gone public with the rumours.'

Porter tensed. 'What rumours?'

Hawkridge took a few moments before he answered. 'There are reports that Soames may have been smuggling diamonds out of the mines illegally, using his inside knowledge as the security contractor to bypass the guards. Then he'd sell the diamonds onto the black market for a tidy profit.' He added hastily, 'Nothing has been proven, of course.'

'Why didn't you share this with us before? Or do you lot over at Thames House just have a fucking allergy to telling the truth?'

'We didn't consider it vital to the operation. You don't need to know everything, John. You're just the collection team.'

Porter shook his head in anger. 'So Soames planned to kill Viktor Agron all along? The meeting was just a convenient way of getting the Russian alone?'

'It appears that way. Unfortunately, Soames didn't count on the Russian having backup. Which explains why he's gone to ground.'

'What do you want us to do?'

'As far as we're concerned, this development changes nothing,' Hawkridge said flatly. 'Your mission remains the same as before. Find Soames, and get him on a plane back to London.'

'What about the dead Russian?'

'I'm sure Soames had his reasons. The fact remains, Soames is a vital British asset and it's imperative you find him before his enemies do. Especially now the Russians know he's killed one of their own.'

'How are we supposed to locate the guy?' Porter snapped. 'In case you hadn't noticed, there are rebels all over the fucking place.'

'Already taken care of, old fruit,' Hawkridge replied airily. 'We now have a fix on Soames's location. The Ambassadors Hotel, on the western side of Freetown next to Lumley Beach.'

'What's he doing in the hotel?'

'Hiding out. Along with every other expat inside the city. Since the events of yesterday most Westerners have fled for the hotel. Aid workers, consulate staff, journalists. As of this moment, it's the last safe place in Freetown. Hundreds of people are cooped up inside. Including Soames.'

Porter remembered what Shoemaker had told him back at Lungi airport. *If it gets too hot, you can always retreat to Lumley Beach*, the guy had said. *The rebels won't dare approach that area.*

Not yet.

'How do you know he's there?'

'Because we have someone watching him.'

'One of our own?'

'A friend, more like,' Hawkridge said. 'Angela March has a contact inside the British High Commission. Dominique Tannon. She's the deputy commissioner. A colleague from Angela's days in the Foreign Office. Tannon is ex-army intelligence. She's been helping to keep tabs on Soames during his stay in Freetown.'

'Making sure he stays on the straight and narrow?'

'Something like that. One of Tannon's contacts reached out to her earlier this morning and said someone checked into the Ambassadors Hotel under Soames's name. Tannon called it in straightaway.'

'When was this?'

'An hour ago.' A note of urgency tinged Hawkridge's voice as he went on, 'We don't know how much longer Soames is going to remain at the hotel. You must hurry, John. Get there immediately. Before he disappears again.'

Porter consulted his G-Shock Mudman. It said 0728 hours. According to the map of Freetown he'd studied earlier, the western tip of Lumley Beach was roughly four miles from their present location. A fifteen-minute journey by car. Maybe thirty minutes if they stuck to the back streets and steered clear of the RUF. Which meant he and Bald could be at the hotel by 0800 hours.

Hawkridge said, 'Deputy Commissioner Tannon will be waiting there for you. She'll lead you directly to Soames.'

'We're leaving now,' said Porter. He went to hang up.

'One more thing,' Hawkridge added hastily.

'What's that?'

'The dead Russian. He's a problem. We don't want anyone stumbling on the corpse and putting a warrant out for Soames. Can you get rid of him?'

Porter glanced down below at the rear garden. Amid the weeds and spent shell casings he spied a square manhole cover covering a low brick rise in one corner of the garden. From the shape of the manhole cover he figured he was looking at a septic tank built under the rear of the property. A thought took shape in his head.

'Well?' Hawkridge asked.

'I think I know a place,' Porter replied.

'Get it done. Then get the hell out of there and find Soames. Hurry, man. There's no time to lose.'

NINE

Bald and Porter bugged out of the mansion nineteen minutes later. They spent sixteen minutes disposing of the dead Russian. They dragged his distended corpse out of the office, down the stairs and into the rear garden, the two of them buckling under the heavy mass of his dead weight. They dumped him beside the manhole while Porter jimmied open the cover using the pair of lifting keys that Vandi had retrieved from the garden shed. A rancid stench wafted up from the tank as Porter removed the cover, his eyes stinging from the potent fumes. The opening was roughly the size of a storm drain. And Viktor Agron was a big guy. It took both of them to force him into the half-empty tank head-first. The body landed with a wet splat in the festering pool of excrement. The dark brown slime quickly closed around his body. Then he was gone.

'What about me?' Vandi said, looking up hopefully at the operators as they prepared to leave.

Porter said, 'Have you got somewhere else you can go?'

'My aunt,' the kid replied. 'She lives in the old town. But it is long way from here. Many bad men on the streets.'

Porter sighed, took the sheaf of bills from the dead Russian's wallet and handed them over to Vandi. A little over two hundred dollars in US currency. Practically a year's salary in Sierra Leone. The kid's eyes threatened to pop out of their sockets.

'Here,' Porter said. 'This should be enough to get you past any checkpoints. Take this, find your aunt and get on the next ferry out of here.'

Vandi nodded quickly. 'Yes, boss. Next ferry.'

He pocketed the bills and ducked out of the garden, heading for the front door. Bald stared wide-eyed at his mucker as Vandi left the house. 'That's all the Russian had in his wallet? A couple of hundred dollars?'

Porter nodded.

'Fuck me,' said Bald. 'I knew the Russians were hard up, but that's taking the piss. They'll be sending out their field agents with luncheon vouchers soon enough.'

As they were leaving Porter cast a mournful look at Soames's drinks cabinet. An idea occurred to him, and he considered sneaking out a bottle. But there was no time. Bald had spotted a group of rebels looting one of the colonial-style hotels located a hundred metres further north on the main road. One or two of the looters had started to take an interest in Soames's office, pointing out to their mates the Range Rover parked in the driveway. Porter knew they couldn't afford to stick around the office for a moment longer than necessary. We've got to get out of here and get to the Ambassadors Hotel, he thought.

Before Soames gives us all the slip.

Once they'd replaced the manhole cover on the tank they hurried out of the front door and climbed inside the Range Rover. Thirty seconds later, they were rolling south on Spur Road and heading towards Lumley Beach.

The sun was fully up now. There were far more rebels out on the streets than there had been earlier that morning, Porter noticed. They were out in force now, looting everything in sight. Scores of them were darting in and out of the hotel to the south of Soames's office. Some were running out brandishing ornaments or paintings. Others emerged with radios and DVD players. They whooped in excitement, raising their stolen goods above their heads as if they had just won the World Cup. A few rebels were fighting over the loot, arguing about who had stolen what. Among them Porter spied half a dozen guys wearing army and police uniforms.

Fucking hell, Porter told himself. Even the local authorities are abandoning their duties to join in the fun. *The situation must be getting desperate now.*

A hundred metres further on he saw smoke billowing up from a local police station on the side of the road. The bodies of three cops lay face-down on the ground next to the burning structure, while a couple of rebels gleefully handed out the dozens of AK-47 rifles, shotguns and pistols they had nicked from inside. Six rebels stood in a semi-circle over the bodies of the dead cops, passing round bottles of poyo and ganja joints. Some of the rebels were dressed in layer upon layer of clothes. They were wearing athletic shorts over brightly patterned trousers and several t-shirts underneath their jackets, and mismatched Nike and Reebok trainers.

Porter steered off the main road and guided the Range Rover through the cramped back streets. Everywhere he looked he could see wrecked motors and smashed shop windows and trashed homes. He counted at least a dozen bodies lying slumped along the roadside, some burnt or hacked to bits. Others were riddled with bullets. Bald turned on the radio and worked the tuner. Every station was playing the same message in broken English. A spokesman for the RUF was on the air, announcing that the rebels had seized the state media and the treasury and now effectively controlled the country. The spokesman threw in the usual bullshit about a brave new era for Sierra Leone, and urged the civilian populace to carry on as usual. Bald laughed.

'No fucking chance,' he said. 'Not with these chogie bastards running riot.' He nodded at another group of rebels lurking by the side of the road, beating a guy in civvies with canes while a woman and her child looked on, screaming hysterically. 'It's always the locals who suffer the worst.'

Porter glanced warily at the rebels. 'I wonder why they haven't turned on us yet.'

'They won't, mate,' Bald said as he shook his head firmly. 'Not as long as they've got easier targets to rob. It's when this lot run out of stuff to loot that we need to start worrying.'

Porter took a deep breath. *The quicker we get to the hotel, the sooner we can grab Soames and get out of this shithole.*

They drove on. After a mile of crawling through the cluttered back streets Porter took a sharp right turn onto Lumley Beach Road. The landscape abruptly shifted as they motored north. Slab of shimmering white sand and palm trees to their left, abandoned villas and apartment blocks to their right. Further on they swept past a derelict golf course, the course green pockmarked with mortar round craters and littered with shrapnel. It looked like a honeymoon resort that had been dumped in the middle of a war zone. Gunfire cracked and whipped in the distance. Smoke darkened the horizon in the east. Like someone had taken a blow torch to the sky.

They passed through two checkpoints. The rebel troops at both checkpoints looked tense and restless and moody. Probably disappointed that they were having to man the roads while their mates indulged in a frenzy of raping and looting. Bald dished out the packs of fags and bundles of Leone currency to the troops, defusing the uneasy atmosphere. On both occasions the troops eagerly seized the goods and waved Porter and Bald through.

After three miles the road opened out and they hit the northwestern tip of the city. The secluded beaches were replaced by a sprawl of luxury whitewashed apartment blocks, beachfront bars and trendy restaurants, all of them closed down. Half a mile to the north of the peninsula Porter could see a jetty facing out across the bay, the waves glittering like shards of broken glass beneath the sun. He hooked a right at the next roundabout and motored east for two hundred metres down the Cape Road. Three minutes later, they reached the Ambassadors Hotel.

The place looked like a Seventies tower block that had been cut in half and given a fresh lick of paint. The seven-storey building was set fifty metres back from the street, at the end of a narrow access road lined with palm trees and grass so green it looked like it had been painted on. There was a helipad a hundred metres to the west of the hotel, and a mile to the east Porter could see the faint outline of the Aberdeen Road Bridge stretching over a narrow creek, connecting the coastal peninsula to the rest of Freetown.

Thirty Nigerian soldiers were standing guard at the front of the access road, forming a line two-deep in front of a restless crowd of civvies. Another twenty troops were stationed behind two separate piles of sandbags either side of the access road, keeping a wary eye on a crowd that had gathered opposite. The soldiers were all decked out in green army uniforms and helmets covered with camouflage netting and twigs. The ECOMOG troops, Porter realised.

'Looks like it's all kicking off here,' Bald said, gesturing at the crowd.

Porter ran his eyes over the heaving throng. They were mostly locals, and there had to be at least a hundred of them. Some had radios glued to their ears, listening to updates from the state-run news station about the coup attempt. Others were arguing with the Nigerian troops, begging to be let through to the relative safety of the hotel. The Nigerians shouted at the crowd to stay back, lashing out at anyone who came too close with their night sticks. Porter cast a professional eye over the troops and noted that they were armed with self-loading rifles. A couple of them were shouldering RPG-7 anti-tank launchers. One guy brandished an FN MAG 7.62mm belt-fed general-purpose machine gun. At least they looked the part, he thought.

Porter slowed down and eased the Range Rover to a halt at the side of the Cape Road. Then he and Bald clambered out of the wagon and paced towards the crowd standing in front of the ECOMOG troops. There was a tense atmosphere outside the hotel. Porter could sense it in the air as he threaded through the dense press of bodies and made for the line of Nigerians guarding the access road. As far as he could tell, there seemed to be some kind of standoff between the locals and the Nigerians. A few Westerners and Lebanese waved their passports at a burly-looking sergeant. His subordinate cross-checked each of their names against a list on a clipboard before the sergeant waved them through. Every time one of the Westerners slipped through the cordon, the crowd shouted of vitriolic abuse at the soldiers. Some of the locals pleaded with the Nigerians to let them through but they stood firm, keeping the crowd at bay.

Porter elbowed his way past a couple of civvies and approached the sergeant. The man stepped forward from the ranks and flashed a sweaty palm at the two Blades, ordering them to halt.

'Passports!' The Nigerian had a deep, booming voice that was dripping with hostility.

Bald and Porter handed over their documents. The sergeant thrust them at his subordinate, who referenced their names against a long list on his clipboard. The man shook his head then passed the documents back to the sergeant.

'Turn around,' the sergeant ordered. 'You are not on the list. Only guests are allowed to enter the hotel.'

Bald glared at the Nigerian. 'We've got business inside.'

The sergeant stood his ground. 'That isn't my problem. You can't come in unless you're a guest, or registered with the charities. Major-General Bassey's orders.'

Bald took a step closer to the soldier. Made a face like he was chewing on a bag of dicks. 'I couldn't give a crap what your boss said. We've got orders to RV with our contact, and she's inside that hotel. For fuck's sake, let us through.'

'No. I cannot allow it.'

Porter could see that his mucker was about to snap. He stepped forward and pressed twenty dollars into the Nigerian's palm. 'Look, mate. We're friends of the deputy commissioner. Dominique Tannon. She's inside that hotel, and we need to talk to her right now. If you don't let us through, the commissioner's going to go through the fucking roof. It won't be us getting it in the neck then. It'll be you.'

The sergeant closed his fist around the twenty bucks and stared warily at Porter. Then he stepped aside and nodded in the direction of the hotel entrance. 'Okay. You may go. But make sure you have something for me when you leave, okay?'

Porter and Bald headed back to the Range Rover while the Nigerians started clearing a path through the crowd. As Porter opened the driver's side door a panicked shout went up from the crowd. He looked east down the Cape Road and caught sight of a Toyota Hilux racing towards them. Four RUF fighters were standing on the back platform, their AK-47s pointed at the sky. The Hilux slowed as it passed the crowd, the rebels on the back shaking their fists and making throat-slitting gestures at the Nigerians in front of the access road. The Nigerians stood their ground but looked around at one another uncertainly.

One of the rebels loosed off a three-round burst at the sky, causing panic. People ducked low, grabbing hold of their children and screaming. Then the Hilux driver gunned the engine and the truck took off down the road, the rebels roaring with laughter, jeering as they fired more volleys into the sky. Porter watched them speeding off west in the direction of Lumley Beach.

'Is that supposed to scare us?' he said, grinning.

But Bald didn't share the joke. He simply stared at the shrinking Hilux and tensed his jaw. 'That show wasn't for us, mate.'

'What do you mean?'

Bald cocked his chin in the direction of the Nigerians. 'The rebels are testing their nerves. Trying to unsettle them. Psych them out.' He pursed his lips. 'Looks like it's working and all.'

Gritting his teeth, Porter glanced back at the Nigerians. Bald was right, he realised. The soldiers' faces were stitched with fear. With a restless crowd breathing down their neck and the rebels threatening them, Porter figured it was only a matter of time before the ECOMOG troops bricked it and abandoned their post. If they did, the guests inside the Ambassadors Hotel would be left at the mercy of the rebels. They'd be fatally trapped inside.

And we'd be trapped in there with them.

TEN

0812 hours.

Porter gunned the Range Rover engine, steered past the security cordon and barrelled down the access road leading towards the hotel entrance. Fifteen metres from the entrance, the access road split into two, separated down the middle by a grassy verge. The left side of the road led directly to the glass doors at the front of the hotel. The right side sloped down into an underground car park. There were no free spaces outside the front of the hotel, so Porter pointed the Range Rover down into the car park, a subterranean space bathed in apricot light. He found a spot close to the service doors, parked and cut the ignition. Then the two Blades debussed and quick-walked towards the nearest stairwell. They pushed through the service door and climbed the concrete steps leading to the reception.

A tidal wave of humanity confronted the operators as they swept into the lobby. It seemed like every foreigner in Freetown had crammed inside the hotel. Porter heard more languages than a Hong Kong whorehouse. French, German, Scandinavian, plus a smattering of American accents. A group of twelve Lebanese businessmen in bright-coloured suits crowded around the reception desk, shouting demands at the harassed-looking receptionist. People clustered in tight knots in every inch of free space, with groups sleeping on the floor or resting against the walls. Luggage was strewn everywhere. In one corner of the lobby several aid agencies had set up emergency stalls using tables and chairs. They were struggling to process the huge crowd of people inside the hotel, shouting to make themselves heard above the sounds of angry businessmen and anxious expats.

Bald said, 'Fuck me. There's hundreds of people here.'

'Five hundred,' Porter guessed. 'Maybe more.'

'If the Nigerians scatter, the rebels will have a field day cutting this lot up.'

Porter said nothing as he scoped out the lobby, looking for their contact. A few moments later a professional-looking woman pushed through the crowd in front of one of the aid agency desks and beat a quick path over to Bald and Porter. She looked to be in her mid-thirties, with mousy-brown hair that ran down to her shoulders and slender lips and big round eyes that glowed like a pair of polished coins. She wore a plain white blouse under a black jacket, with a dark knee-length skirt. She looked corporate, athletic – and out of her depth. It was there in the uncertain way she carried herself, the forced smile, and the nervous look in her eyes. Like a mid-level manager who had suddenly been promoted to company CEO, Porter thought.

'Dominique Tannon. Deputy at the High Commission here in Freetown,' she said, offering her hand. She had a Home Counties accent, and she spoke a little too quickly, he thought. 'I'm assuming you're the two gentlemen Angela told me about.'

'That's us, love.' Porter shook her hand and the two Blades introduced themselves. Tannon struck him as very businesslike and corporate. Part of the new breed. The Firm was chock-full of them these days. The ones who drank herbal tea and snacked on gluten-free bars and got up at five a.m. for their morning run. They were sober, dependable, clean. *The opposite of guys like me and Bald.*

'I'm afraid you've joined us at a difficult time.' Tannon smiled apologetically and swept her hand across the lobby. 'As you can see.'

'What's going on?' said Porter.

'It's mayhem,' she explained. 'We're still managing to hold the fort over at the High Commission, but virtually every other institution has been forced to abandon their offices and flee here.'

'Along with half the fucking city, by the looks of it,' said Bald.

Tannon shrugged. 'There's nowhere else for people to go. All the international radio stations are carrying the same broadcast. If you're an expat and you're still inside Freetown, head to the Ambassadors Hotel. Right now, the city is a ghost town.'

'We know, lass,' Bald replied. 'We just drove through the bastard.'

'Why aren't these people heading for the airport?' Porter said, casting his eye around the lobby.

'Not that easy,' said Tannon. 'The rebels have seized the area south of the ferry terminal at Kissy. They're also in control of most of the roads in and out of the city. It's too dangerous to risk a run to the airport.'

Bald said, 'How the hell are we supposed to get Soames out of the country, then?'

'We'll have to take our chances.' Porter turned back to Tannon. 'What about this lot? What are they going to do?'

'There's going to be an official evacuation. My boss is over at the High Commission right now, trying to thrash out an agreement with Downing Street. The Americans and French are doing the same with their respective governments. But nothing will happen until tomorrow at the earliest. This isn't Bosnia. Sierra Leone is way down on their list of priorities.'

'What are you supposed to do until then?'

'Wait here. We don't have a choice.'

Tannon attempted a smile, but it was trembling at the edges. She's worried, Porter thought. With bloody good reason. There's an army of nutters out there, itching to carve up every civvy in this hotel.

'Where's Soames?' he said.

'In his room.' Tannon pointed to the staircase at the far end of the lobby. 'He took off as soon as the lobby started filling up. Him and his friend.'

Porter glanced at his mucker before looking back to the deputy commissioner. 'Soames is staying here with a mate?'

Tannon nodded. 'A friend, or maybe a business partner? I didn't recognise him. But they seemed close. They were hanging out in the lobby for a while this morning, checking the situation outside. Then they headed upstairs.'

'What room is he staying in?'

'Room 201. He checked in under his own name. The hotel manager's a friend of mine.'

Porter gave her a look. 'Are you friendly with all the managers in Freetown?'

'Only the ones who are nice to me.' She flashed Porter a smile. It wasn't as nervous as her first attempt. 'I thought Soames might come here. Especially considering there aren't many safe places for a white man in Freetown right now. So I asked my friend to keep a lookout. As soon as Soames arrived he found him a room, then called me.'

Porter arched an eyebrow at Tannon. This bird might be anxious, he thought. But she's smart. He wondered what someone with her talents was doing in a backwater like Freetown.

'What are we waiting for?' Bald cut in. 'Let's get Soames. The sooner we grab him, the sooner we can get the fuck out of here.'

The three of them moved quickly across the lobby and made for the stairs at the far end, picking their way past the baggage scattered across the marble floor. The air was muggy and dry and Porter was sweating profusely beneath his t-shirt. Both he and Bald had ditched their short-sleeve jackets in the back of the Range Rover immediately after leaving the mansion.

Suddenly at their six o'clock they heard a burst of distant gunfire coming from the front of the hotel. They turned and caught sight of the rebels making another broad sweep past the security cordon in their pickup truck, emptying rounds into the air. Porter felt a cold fear slither down his spine. He wondered how long the rebels would wait until they decided to try their luck against the Nigerians.

He turned and vaulted up the stairs after Bald and Tannon, and almost bumped into a party of five white guys descending at the same time. They were burly-looking and sunburnt, and dressed like a bunch of dentists on a safari jolly. They wore long-sleeved bush shirts, dun-coloured knee-length shorts, hiking boots and wide-brimmed leather hats. They were chatting amongst themselves in a language Porter thought sounded a bit like French, or maybe Dutch. They all had the same broad-shouldered, calloused look of manual labourers. Porter had spent enough time on ops in Africa to know the type. Construction workers, maybe. Or engineers flown in to repair the machinery used in some of the bigger mines. Some kind of job that involved specialist knowledge, a lot of outdoor work and heavy lifting.

As Porter brushed past one of these guys he abruptly stopped and spun around, muttering under his breath. Porter turned to face the safari guy and his mates. Like he was assessing a threat. The guy he'd bumped into had thick nostrils, a small black goatee, and a curious scar that ran from his upper lip to his left nostril. Like the scar following corrective surgery on a cleft lip. For a moment the guy just stood there, glowering at Porter. As if he was debating whether to throw a punch. Porter stood his ground. The foreigner worked his lips into a slight smile, revealing a set of stained teeth. Then he turned and muttered something else to his mates. They laughed as they carried on down the stairs. Porter watched them leave.

'The fuck was his problem?' said Bald.

'Fuck knows. Come on. Let's go.'

He hurried up the stairs alongside Bald and Tannon. They turned right at the second-floor landing and the two operators followed Tannon down a drab and sparsely furnished corridor with soft ceiling lights and cream-coloured walls. Everything was understated and beige. It looked like any other corridor in any other five-star hotel in the world, thought Porter.

Except there's an army of madmen outside desperate to hack us to pieces.

At the end of the corridor they hung a left and continued on for twenty-five metres until they drew to a halt outside the door to room 201. Porter felt a twinge of nervous excitement in his guts. This is it, he told himself. My old CO is behind that door.

We've finally tracked the bastard down.

Tannon slid between Bald and Porter and produced a shiny black key card from her jacket pocket with the name of the hotel printed on it. 'Spare key to the room.' She grinned. 'Courtesy of the manager.'

Bald looked impressed, and a little jealous. 'This bloke must be a good mate of yours.'

'Not really. But he's a man. Which means he'll do anything for a glimpse of my tits.'

Bald grinned at her. 'Do you need anything doing?'

She ignored him and inserted the card into the slot below the door handle. The tiny light next to the card reader flashed green. Then Tannon tried the handle. The door wouldn't open. She tried again. Same thing.

'It's locked,' she said.

'Here.' Bald stepped forward. 'Let me try.'

'Because you're a man, and you know best?'

Bald shook his head. 'Because I pick locks for a living.'

Tannon handed him the key card. Bald approached the door and repeated the process. Card into the reader, out again, green light, handle. The door still refused to budge.

'No good,' he said, turning to Porter. 'Bastard must have jammed it shut.'

Soames is bricking it, Porter thought. *The guy's expecting trouble.*

He stepped between Bald and Tannon and banged his fist on the door three times. 'Open up!' he boomed. 'Ronald, this is John Porter speaking. I'm here with John Bald. We're two friendlies. We know you're in there. Now open the fucking door!'

A beat passed. Nothing. Then Porter heard a bunch of muffled noises coming from the other side of the door. Voices arguing. More than one. Soames must be in there with his mate, Porter realised. *They seemed close*, Tannon had said. He wondered again about this mystery friend of Soames's.

Then the handle lowered and the door cracked open. Porter looked up. A tall, lean figure stood in the hallway, dressed in a sand-coloured shirt and a pair of combat trousers, wearing a surprised look on his face.

Porter froze.

The man in the hallway wasn't Ronald Soames.

It was a face he hadn't seen for six years.

ELEVEN

0823 hours.

Nobody moved for what felt like a while. Porter stood rooted to the spot, staring at the guy in front of him. The guy in the doorway had black, dull eyes like a couple of drill holes, thinning brown hair, and a long broken nose. His expression hovered somewhere between blank and cold. He looked like the kind of guy who could butcher a family, then sit down afterwards to enjoy a glass of fine Merlot.

Porter recognised him instantly. Bob Tully, the bastard of the Regiment.

He thought, Tully must be the friend Tannon was talking about. The one she saw hanging out with Soames in the lobby.

Then he thought, What business has Tully got with Soames?

'Bob,' Bald said. 'What the fuck are you doing here?'

Tully smiled. His thin lips curved dangerously at the corners. 'I was about to ask you two fellas the same question.' He spoke in a thick, grating Brummie accent.

Tannon glanced from Tully to Porter and back again. 'You know each other?'

'Aye,' said Tully. 'That's right, sweetheart. We served together at Hereford. Isn't that right, fellas?'

Porter said nothing. Their time in the SAS had overlapped for four years in the early Nineties. But he knew enough about Bob Tully to be wary. He had a reputation as the most dangerous man ever to set foot inside Hereford. The guy was so loose he was practically unhinged. He was also a professional bridge-burner. Six years ago he'd left the SAS in disgrace, jumping before he was pushed.

Since then, Porter had heard the rumours on the Hereford grapevine. The ones that said Tully was into some dark stuff. The last Porter had heard, Tully had been working for several dodgy PMCs in South Africa, spending the months between jobs indulging in his two favourite hobbies. Drinking and shagging hookers.

'A long time ago now,' Porter replied eventually.

'Six years,' Tully said. 'Not that long ago. Tell you what, though — best decision I ever made, leaving the Regiment. I'm making a killing these days on the Circuit.' He grinned, then gave Porter the once-over. 'Fuck me sideways. You've aged a bit, mate. You look like shit.'

Porter felt a rising tension in his chest. He forced himself to bite back on his anger. 'We're looking for Ronald Soames. He's registered as checking into this room. Have you seen him?'

Tully frowned. 'Our old CO? What do you want with him?'

'We're with the Firm,' Bald explained. 'We've got orders to escort Soames back to London immediately.'

'Sorry fellas.' Tully shook his head. 'Can't help you. He's not here.'

Porter studied the guy's expression. Looking for the slightest telltale hint that Tully was hiding something. But his face gave nothing away. Either Tully really didn't know, or he was the world's greatest liar.

He saw the sceptical look on Porter's face and said, 'Come in and have a look for yourselves if you don't believe me.'

He ushered Bald and Porter inside. They followed Tully down the dimly lit hallway and into the main living space. The furnishings were stylish but dated. Like a Hilton that hadn't been refurbished since the seventies. A dark-skinned woman in a tube-top and latex mini-skirt sat on the edge of the king-sized bed, glancing warily at the three figures standing next to Tully. On the far wall a glass door led out to a balcony overlooking the front of the hotel. There was a bathroom to the left and another door to the right, with a lock on it that Porter figured led through to an adjoining room. In the distance he could hear the cracks of weapon discharges, the faint screams of terrified civvies and the jeers of rebels. But there was no sign of Soames.

He looked back to Tully. 'What are you doing in his room, Bob?'

'Soames is my boss,' Tully replied.

'You're working for Soames?' Bald said in surprise.

Tully nodded. 'For the past six months, aye. Got myself a job guarding the diamond mine over in Kono. It's good hours, and the pay is top whack. And there are loads of perks too,' he added, winking at the woman by the bed. 'You can do anything you want in these parts. Anything at all.'

Porter said, 'If you're being paid to look after the mine, what are you doing here?'

'Boss's orders. The work force at the mine's thinned out, what with them rebels stirring things up. We've been called back to Freetown until things settle down. Thought I'd take the opportunity to let off a bit of steam with Claudette. We were stuck in here when the rebels moved into the city.'

Tully beckoned over the black woman. She hesitated at first, then stood up from the bed and nervously approached. As she drew closer Porter noticed she had a cut to her upper lip. Her jaws were swollen and she had painful-looking bruises on her neck. She shivered as Tully wrapped an arm around her waist.

'You should check out the local hookers,' he said to Bald, grinning. 'The women here are cheap as fuck. You can get a blowjob around these parts for the price of a Big Mac. They even let you slap them around for a few extra quid. You'd love it.'

He laughed and gave the prostitute a peck on her swollen cheek. Bald stared back at him, the expression on his face hovering somewhere between jealousy and disgust.

'What's the deal with Soames?' Tully asked. 'Is he in some sort of trouble?'

'We can't say,' Porter said. 'You know how it is. All we can tell you is, we've got to locate him and get him on a plane as soon as possible. If you know where to find him, you need to tell us.'

'Like I said, fellas: I don't know.'

Just then Porter heard the clack of a latch unlocking. The door to the right swung open and a figure stepped in from the adjoining room. Tully looked towards the man. So did everyone else in the room. The man smiled menacingly at Porter.

'Hello, John,' Ronald Soames said.

Porter stared at his old CO for a long beat. Soames had hardly aged since the last time Porter had seen him. His hair was a little greyer and thinner. His jowls looked a little softer. But the guy still had the same broad-shouldered physique. The same cold look in his eyes. He looked like a public school rugby coach, Porter thought. Or a City banker in early retirement. He was dressed in a dark short-sleeved shirt, a pair of beige trousers and spit-polished Timberland boots. The Blancpain watch clamped around his wrist was probably worth more than Porter and Bald earned in a year.

'This is something of a surprise, I must admit,' Soames said, in voice so smooth you could have played snooker on it. 'You were the last person I expected to run into here.'

Soames forced a smile and tried to relax into himself. But his eyes betrayed him. They were darting left and right, as if searching for another escape route from the room. He looked nervous, thought Porter. Edgy. As if he was wearing a shirt that was too tight around the collar.

Tully took a step forward, putting himself between Porter and Soames. Like a bodyguard protecting his client from an angry mob. Soames waved a hand at him. 'It's all right, Bob. I can handle this.'

Tully gave a grudging nod and kept his eyes locked on Porter and Bald, ready to leap into action if either of them tried to make a move. Soames turned to Porter and straightened his back, dropping the smile.

'Five sent you here, did they?' Soames chuckled. 'I'm surprised they've given you a job, given your track record. They must be getting desperate over at Whitehall these days.'

Porter clenched his jaws. 'We're here to protect you. We've got orders to escort you out of the country immediately.'

Soames smiled again and shook his head. 'That's very thoughtful of my friends at Thames House. But you can tell them I don't need protecting. I'm safe enough here.'

'We're not asking you nicely,' Porter said between gritted teeth. 'You're coming with us, no ifs or buts.'

Soames ignored him and turned his attention to Bald. His eyes narrowed to pinpricks. 'Jock Bald, isn't it? Not had the pleasure of meeting you before. I've heard lots about you, of course. You're the one who caused that diplomatic incident in Belfast a few years back, aren't you?'

'Aye,' said Bald. 'That's me.'

Soames nodded his head sagely. Everyone at Hereford knew the story of how Bald had crossed the Irish border, tracked down a kidnapped MI5 agent and killed several high-ranking members of the IRA's notorious Nutting Squad. His bravery had almost caused a major incident between the British and Irish governments, but earned him the instant respect of the other lads in the Regiment. Even Porter had been impressed when he'd first heard about it.

'That took balls, that,' Soames said. 'Big balls. Now it appears you've been relegated to nursemaiding duties. Such a waste of talent.'

Bald said nothing. Porter glared at Soames. 'Why were you hiding in that other room?'

'I thought you might be someone else.'

'The Russians?'

Soames tilted his head at Porter. 'So you know about that.'

'We know about Viktor Agron too. We found his body at your gaff. Had to clean up your fucking mess.'

'Yes,' Soames replied, wringing his hands. 'A pity I had to kill him. Viktor's friends arrived just as I was preparing to leave. Then the rebels entered the city and I had to find somewhere to lie low while I waited for the rebellion to burn itself out. So I found Tully at his, ah, lady friend's place, and came here.'

'But the hotel computer had you listed as staying in this room,' Porter countered. 'Not the one next door.'

Soames nodded. 'I thought it better if Tully stayed in the room under my name and I stayed in the adjoining room under the name of a local businessman, an acquaintance of mine. I didn't want to take any chances.'

The sly bastard, Porter thought. *The guy persuaded Bob Tully to take his room so that he'd get the heads-up if anyone came looking for him.*

'So that's why you're really here?' Soames eyed the two operators carefully. 'To arrest me?'

'You can't do that,' Tully protested. 'Not without a fucking warrant.'

'It's not like that,' Bald said. 'No one's pushing an agenda. You're in a difficult situation and we've been sent to get you out of it. There's nothing else going on here.'

Bald's tone struck Porter as surprisingly calm and even. Like he had a certain degree of respect for Soames. Like he didn't want to piss the guy off.

'You're wasting your breath,' Soames responded curtly. 'I'm not going anywhere.'

Porter took a step closer to his old CO. Tully moved forward too. Like pieces being moved on a chessboard.

'We're not giving you a choice,' Porter said. 'You're coming with us. Now pack your fucking bags. We don't have much time.'

'You don't understand. I can't leave. Not now. My business interests are in Sierra Leone. I'm one of President Fofana's closest advisers, not to mention one of his main backers. He'll need me once he returns from exile. It's vital that I remain here.'

Porter gestured to the balcony. Gunfire popped and cracked in the distance. 'You can't stay put. In case you hadn't noticed, the entire country's about to go to shit. We've got to get out here while we still have a chance.'

Soames flashed a patronising smile. 'You thick bastard, Porter. I've been here long enough to know how this works. This isn't the first time the rebels have tried to overthrow the government, and if I'm being perfectly frank it won't be the last. But they never succeed. In a few days our boys and the Yanks will kick the rebels out and Fofana will fly back from Guinea. The truth is there's simply too much at stake for HMG to allow President Fofana's regime to fail.'

'You mean the diamond mine at Kono?'

Soames shifted on his feet and nodded. 'Our fortunes here are intimately tied in with those of President Fofana. If his regime is toppled, then our interests will be under threat. I'm far better off staying put and waiting for this whole thing to blow over.'

He folded his arms across his broad chest and stared defiantly at the two Blades. After a moment Porter said, 'You've got five minutes to pack your bags. Then we're leaving. We'll be getting the next flight out of Lungi airport. We've got your ticket ready, it's all sorted.'

Soames looked at Porter as if he was mad. 'You want to drive to the airport? With hundreds of armed rebels roaming the streets? You can't be serious. It's a suicide mission.'

'Our hands are tied,' Bald said. 'We're just the messengers. If you've got a beef, it's with that mob over at Thames House, not us.'

Porter raised an eyebrow, taken aback by Bald's friendly tone. I know what's going on here, he thought. Bald is trying to stay on good terms with Soames, in case the guy offers him a contract down the line. Not for the first time since they had worked together, Porter wondered whether he could really trust Bald. He looked back at Soames.

'Get a move on. We're wasting time.' He nodded at Tully. 'You might want to think about getting the fuck out of here too, Bob.'

'Nonsense!' Soames growled. 'Listen. I've been in this country long enough. I know how things work here. And I'm telling you, this hotel is the safest place for us all.' He waved a hand at the window. 'There are fifty ECOMOG troops guarding this hotel. Another hundred Nigerians are stationed at the Aberdeen Road Bridge leading in and out of the city centre. They'll keep us safe until our American friends have sent the rebels packing.'

Tully nodded in agreement. 'Ronald's right. It's madness out there. Last we heard, some of the soldiers have started to join in with the looting. Them rebels will have us surrounded the moment we set foot outside the hotel. We're better off staying put.'

Bald threw his arms up in the air in frustration. 'How long do you think those chogies will hold out once it starts getting noisy? They'll raise the white flag as soon as the rebels train their sights on this place.'

'Our decision is final,' Soames said. 'We're staying in Freetown.'

Something snapped inside Porter. He rounded on the ex-CO, his teeth clenched in anger. 'I'm not going to ask you again. You're coming with us and getting on that plane, or you and me have got a fucking problem.'

Soames stared icily at him. 'Don't forget who you're talking to, Porter.'

He stood firm and refused to budge. For a few moments no one moved. Porter felt an irresistible urge to slog his old CO in the guts. His veins pounded with rage as all the bad memories came rushing back at him. How Soames had shafted his career in the Regiment after the Beirut op. He recalled how the other lads had looked at him differently after the debrief, steering clear of him in the pubs and looking the other way in the guard room at Hereford. They all knew the score. Everyone knew that Porter was damaged goods. Once Soames had blackballed him, no one wanted anything more to do with him. Anyone who associated with him risked getting dumped in the B stream.

This bastard ruined my life. I didn't travel three thousand miles to take shit from him.

A sharp trilling sound cut through the tense silence. Porter dug out the sat phone from his pocket and saw the screen glowing. Incoming call. A UK number. He flipped up the long tubular antenna. Hit the green key and pressed the phone to his ear.

Hawkridge's voice came down the line, buzzing in his ear.

'You've kept the satellite phone switched on, I see.' His voice was barely audible above a roar of interference. Like he was in a tunnel. 'Thank God. Listen, where are you now?'

Porter gave his back to Soames and moved towards the balcony for a better signal. 'The Ambassadors Hotel. We've located Soames. He's staying with one of the lads attached to his PMC outfit.'

'Who?'

'Bob Tully. We know him. He's ex-Regiment. Bob was shacked up in the hotel room with some night fighter when Soames reached out to him. The guy's been hiding out here for the past couple of days.'

'Well done.' There was a long bout of silence. Then Hawkridge cleared his throat and said, 'Unfortunately, we have a problem.'

'Let me guess. You're out of Viagra.'

'This is serious. There have been some developments in the past hour.'

'What developments?'

'The bad kind. The rebels have taken control of the airport at Lungi. All friendlies have been ordered to evacuate the area. All flights suspended until further notice.'

Shit.

'So there's no way out?' Porter said.

'Not until we retake the airport, no.'

'How long will that take?'

'A couple of days. Elements of 1 Para are mobilising as we speak. But they're currently on exercise in Dakar. Best-case scenario, they'll mount an operation in the next forty-eight hours.'

Anger coursed through Porter as he listened. Beyond the hotel, the sounds of distant gun battles raged across the city. Directly below the balcony he could see the crowd outside the hotel becoming more agitated, heckling the Nigerians and showering them with abuse. More and more rebels were cruising up and down the main road in stolen UN vehicles. One or two of the peacekeepers shook their fists at the rebels in a show of defiance, but most of them looked as nervous as the crowd. Porter pressed his finger to his left ear and tried to shut out the noise.

'If the airport's down, how the fuck are we supposed to get out of the country?'

'You can't,' Hawkridge responded sharply. 'The only other route is to drive north to the border and cross into Guinea. But it's a long, dangerous drive and the route is teeming with rebel checkpoints. We can't risk it. Not unless it's absolutely necessary.'

'What the fuck is the plan'

'Stay where you are. We're mobilising friendlies for an emergency evacuation plan with our American cousins. One of their aircraft carriers happened to be returning from a patrol off the coast of Gabon when the rebels launched their coup. The USS *Lauderdale*. The plan is to land a squadron of Sea Stallion helicopters at the hotel and lift people out to the *Lauderdale* as soon as possible.'

'How long until they get here?'

'Tomorrow, at the earliest,' said Hawkridge. 'We're still awaiting confirmation. I'm sure you can appreciate that the situation on the ground is extremely fluid.'

Porter shook his head. 'I don't give a fuck what the situation is. You're not hearing me. The rebels are already scoping this place out. I'm telling you, they're gearing up to have a crack at us. If that happens, we're shafted.'

There was a pause down the other end of the line, and for a moment Porter thought he'd lost the signal. Then Hawkridge's voice came back.

'I understand your concerns. Rest assured, we'll continue to monitor the situation at our end. If there's a problem with the evacuation, then you'll have to extract Soames via land. But that is strictly a last resort. Your orders are to protect Soames at all costs. Do you understand?'

'Fine,' Porter replied.

I'll keep Soames safe, he thought. I'll follow my orders. *But if the worst happens, I'm not taking a bullet for that prick.*

Hawkridge said, 'I'll be in touch as soon as we have more details about the evacuation. In the meantime, stay put and don't let Soames out of your sight. If he comes to harm, both our necks are on the line. Make sure it doesn't come to that.'

TWELVE

0849 hours.

Porter stood listening to the dead air, feeling the hot wind blasting against his face. He shaded the sat-phone screen against the sun and checked the battery icon. Three bars. Which meant the phone had maybe eight hours of battery life left. *Stuck in a hotel in the worst city in the world, surrounded by psychotic rebels, with no weapons and a half-dead sat phone for company.* He stashed the phone in his pocket then stepped back through the balcony door into the hotel room. Soames stood up and looked across at him.

'Well? What's going on?'

Porter gave them the bad news. Once he had finished explaining the situation, Soames folded his arms across his chest, smiling triumphantly.

'What did I say? I told you it was too dangerous to leave. Even your bosses agree with me. Perhaps next time I offer my advice, you should try listening to it.'

Porter tensed his neck muscles and glared at the ex-Rupert. Another twenty-four hours cooped up in the hotel with this smug bastard, he thought to himself. *Another twenty-four hours putting up with this shit.*

Tannon said, 'What's the plan?'

'First things first, we need to secure the hotel,' Porter said. A plan was already taking shape inside his head. He nodded at Tannon. 'You reckon you're friendly with the hotel manager?'

'That's right,' she said.

'Let's go and have a chat with him.'

'Right now?'

Porter nodded.

'I'll go with you,' Tully cut in, glancing quickly at Soames. 'It's getting hot out there. You're going to need all the help you can get.'

Porter considered it, then nodded. 'Fine.'

The hooker pulled a sour face at Tully. 'What about me?'

Tully grinned at her. 'You stay here, sweetheart.' He stroked her swollen jaw. 'Now, remember. You'd better be here when I get back. Otherwise I'll be pissed off. And you don't want to piss me off, do you?'

The hooker bowed her head obediently.

'No,' she whimpered.

'No, what?'

'No, master.'

'That's more like it.' Tully ran his fingers over one of the bruises on her neck, causing the hooker to wince in pain. He gave his back to her and nodded at Porter and Bald. 'Right, fellas. Let's go.'

'What am I supposed to do?' Soames said.

Porter turned to him. 'You can stay here and keep Tully's night fighter company. Keep the door locked, and for fuck's sake stay away from the window.'

He turned away before Soames could reply and marched out of the room. Tannon, Bald and Tully hurried after him. All four headed swiftly down the stairs to the ground floor. The lobby seemed even busier than it had been earlier, if that was possible. There had to be at least seven hundred people crammed inside the lobby now, Porter reckoned. With the guests bottled up in their rooms, the total number of civilians inside the hotel was probably close to a thousand. A steady stream of bewildered and terrified expats filtered through the front doors, seeking refuge in the hotel. Many of them carried little or no luggage. Exhausted men and women slumped against the walls, drenched in sweat, some of them looking on the verge of passing out in the stifling heat. Charity workers rushed over to those worst affected, handing out bottles of water.

Porter could feel his heart thumping fast as Tannon led them past the crowd towards a door at the side of the reception desk.

The situation inside the hotel was becoming critical, he realised grimly. He glanced over at the front of the hotel at the Nigerians manning their defensive cordon at the end of the access road. They were looking agitated, reacting nervously every time the rebels roared past in their pickup trucks. It was only a matter of time before the soldiers abandoned their posts and legged it inside, Porter knew.

Tannon pushed through the door to the manager's office and ducked into a cluttered office. There was a cheap metal desk next to the window and a bunch of certificates hanging from the walls. A portable fan in one corner whirred noisily. An overweight guy in a short-sleeved white shirt sat behind the desk, cradling a Cisco phone receiver under his chin. He hung up and stood up to greet Tannon, acknowledging the three guys standing next to her with a terse nod of his head. The guy was in his mid-fifties, Porter guessed. He had thinning grey hair, deep frown lines and sweat patches under his armpits the size of China.

'Jim, I'd like you to meet some friends of mine,' Tannon said. She motioned towards the three Hereford men standing next to her and briefly introduced them. 'Jim Crowder is the manager here at the Ambassadors Hotel,' she added.

'So you guys know Dominique,' Crowder said. He spoke in a slow hillbilly twang that stretched every word out into a long and lazy note. American, thought Porter. But not from either of the coasts. Somewhere to the South or Midwest, he figured. 'What can I do for you? I'm afraid we don't have any free rooms left, if that's what you're after. Things are kind of hectic round here.'

'We're not after a room,' said Porter. 'We're here to help defend the hotel.'

Crowder leaned back in his chair. He studied Bald and Porter carefully. 'That's a kindly offer. Truly. But we've got all the help we need.'

Porter tried again. 'Listen, mate. We've all served in the British Army. Take it from us, that lot outside are going to have a crack at us sooner or later. We need to put the hotel on lockdown before it's too late.'

'We've already taken precautions. Those Nigerians outside will have our backs.'

'No,' said Bald. 'They won't.'

Crowder wrinkled his features into a deep frown. 'What makes you think that?'

'There are fifty soldiers guarding this hotel. There are ten times that many chogies running about in the streets. At least. Once they've cleaned out the rest of the city, they'll be making a play for the loot in here. The Nigerians won't be able to stop them then.'

'So you say. But the Nigerians are telling me different. I've just got off the phone with their colonel. He's given me his word that his men will protect us in the event of an attack.'

The manager was digging his heels in. Porter could see they were getting nowhere. The man's professional pride was at stake. He had a hotel crammed with guests, and three strangers telling him he was making a serious mistake.

'Even if that's true,' Porter said, 'don't you think we should be planning for the worst?'

Crowder looked unconvinced. He steepled his fat fingers on the desk. 'You really think we're in danger?'

Bald nodded. 'We've been in situations like this before. This is what we do. And we're telling you, we have to act now if we're going to stand a chance of stopping the rebels. It's that, or we sit back and wait to get chopped up.'

'We should really listen to these guys, Jim,' Tannon interjected. 'They know what they're talking about.'

Crowder looked at her. 'You trust these guys?'

'I do.'

Crowder paused as he chewed on a thought like it was a pound of beef. Then he held up his sweaty hands.

'Okay,' he said. 'I'm listening. What do you propose we should do?'

Porter had been working through the plan in his head and he addressed the manager in a calm, authoritative tone. 'Our first priority is to clear out the ground floor. The front entrance is the most obvious target. If the rebels break through those doors, anyone in the lobby is going to be a target. Same goes for the first floor.'

'Where the hell are all these people supposed to go?' Crowder asked, his frown deepening.

'The upper floors. That's the safest place in case of an assault.'

'That's not going to be easy. We've got almost a thousand people in the hotel, with more folk coming through those doors all the time. Some of these people have been hiding out in their basements for days. They're scared shitless. I can't turn them away.'

'How many rooms are there in the hotel?' Porter asked.

'A hundred and eighty. Plus a dozen suites on the top floor, junior and Presidential.'

'That works out to roughly five people to a room. Six if we leave out the rooms on the lower floor. Which means everyone's going to have to quadruple up. Families take priority. They'll room together. Couples too. Everyone else will have to share with strangers. They're to stay in their rooms at all times and draw up rosters for keeping the bathrooms and showers clean. It won't be comfortable, but it's our best chance of keeping everyone safe if things get noisy.'

Crowder made a pained face and squirmed in his chair. Like he had piles. 'Some of the guests won't be happy about that. There are guys on the top floor who come here for a little R&R, if you know what I mean. Businessmen. Europeans, mostly. They won't appreciate the interruption.'

'Tough,' said Bald. 'The situation takes priority. We need to get everyone to safety as quick as possible. If the rebels start popping rounds at the hotel, anyone on those lower floors is going to be vulnerable.'

'I'll see what I can do.'

Porter nodded. 'Just make sure that everyone knows to stay away from the windows at all times. Get them to take the mattresses off the beds and shove them against the windows. We need to turn the hotel into a fort.'

'Where will everyone sleep?' Tannon said.

'On the floor. Safest place for them.'

Crowder nodded. 'I'll brief my staff. Get them to spread the word.'

'Good,' Porter replied. Then another thought occurred to him. 'How many people can you squeeze into the restaurant?'

The manager stroked his chin. 'Two hundred. Two-fifty at a push. Why?'

'We'll have to draw up a roster for meal times. One hour for each group. Once they've finished their meals they're to head straight back to their rooms. Make sure everybody knows the drill.'

Crowder clicked his tongue. 'Feeding everyone is going to be tricky. We're running low on supplies. The rebels have cut off the route to the warehouse across town. There's no chance of us bringing in more provisions.'

'Then we'll start rationing water and all the non-perishable food. From what we've heard, it could be a day or two until help arrives.'

Tannon said, 'There's another problem. We need to keep people updated. There are a lot of anxious faces out there. If we keep them in the dark, it's only going to make them more worried.'

Porter thought for a moment, then nodded. 'We'll hold daily briefings, twice a day. Once after breakfast, and then again after the evening meal. That way we can update everyone on the evacuations, and they can ask questions and air any grievances. The most important thing is to reassure everyone that help is on the way, and under no circumstances is anyone to leave the hotel. If they do that, they're gonna get themselves carved up by the rebels.'

Crowder said, 'Anything else?'

'We'll need to barricade every entry and exit point around the hotel. Any entrance that the rebels might use to sneak inside will need to be sealed or boarded up.'

A brief look of alarm registered on Crowder's face. 'Is that really necessary?'

Bald nodded firmly. 'The Nigerians have got the front door covered. For the moment, anyway. But that still leaves the rest of the building unguarded.'

'You think the rebels might creep around the back?'

'Probably not. But we should block up all the exits just in case.'

'We'll need volunteers as well,' Porter added. 'Six to a floor. They'll be responsible for organising the rooms and getting everyone's luggage sorted.'

'Shouldn't be a problem,' Tannon said. 'There's a ton of aid workers out there wanting to help.'

'What are we going to do about Soames?' said Bald. 'We can't just leave him in his room.'

'Why not?' Tannon said.

Porter said, 'Jock's right. He might try and escape. He's not exactly enthusiastic about leaving Sierra Leone. We need to put him somewhere secure, where he can't escape. Somewhere we can keep an eye on him.'

Crowder said, 'There's a janitor's storeroom on the second floor. No windows, reinforced concrete walls, sturdy lock on the door. Your buddy can stay in there.'

Porter nodded. 'We'll get him moved.'

'How much notice will we have?' Tannon asked. Something like concern flashed behind her pale green eyes. 'When the rebels attack.'

Porter considered. 'Not much. If there's gonna be a surge, it'll be just before first light. That's what I'd do, if I was in their boots. Build up my forces first, then assault at dawn while everyone's still fast asleep. Right now they're just strengthening. They won't have a pop until they're confident they've got enough men for the job.'

The concern in Tannon's eyes grew larger. 'How long until that happens?'

'I don't know,' said Porter.

Tannon bit her tongue, took a deep breath, nodded. The anxiety spreading from her eyes to the rest of her face.

'What's to stop them attacking us at night?' Crowder said.

'They won't. They'll be too busy getting pissed.'

'So you say.'

'We're not dealing with Delta Force here,' Bald said. 'We've seen these guys out on the streets. They're piss-poor shots and badly trained. Trust me, when they hit us, it won't be anything sophisticated. They'll come at us from the north and hit us with everything they've got.'

'What'll we do then?' Tannon asked, her voice wavering.

Porter looked at her. 'Got a sat phone?'

She nodded. 'All the senior staff are given one.'

'Get on it,' he said. 'Put in a call to everyone who owes you a favour and get them to apply pressure behind the scenes. Tell every other embassy official in the hotel to start doing the same thing. We have to make everyone understand that evacuating this hotel is a priority. Because if we're still inside when the rebels break through, we're royally fucked.'

THIRTEEN

0928 hours.

The meeting broke up. Porter emerged into the lobby with Bald and Tully and Tannon. While Crowder headed off to round up his staff, the others started working the crowd in the lobby to round up volunteers. The growing threat from the rebels outside had concentrated everyone's minds, and within a few minutes they had thirty people offering to help.

As they moved through the crowd Porter spotted the five guys he'd bumped into earlier. They were dressed like they were going on a safari jaunt, milling around in the far corner and doing their best to look casual, their hands stuffed in their pockets as they scanned the sea of faces in the lobby. As if they were looking for a friend. The guy with the dumb goatee who'd bumped into Porter stood to one side of his mates. He had a chunky mobile phone pressed to his ear. From his animated body language the guy appeared to be having an argument with the person on the other end of the line.

Tannon kept glancing anxiously over at the hotel entrance while Bald and Tully assembled the army of volunteers. Porter noticed her right foot tapping on the marbled floor.

'You okay, love?'

She nodded. Quickly. 'I'll be fine. Just, you know ... I hope you're wrong.'

'About the Nigerians?'

Tannon nodded again.

'Me too,' said Porter.

Several moments later Crowder returned with a dozen hotel work- ers in tow. He directed them into the restaurant on the south side of the ground floor, overlooking the grounds to the rear of the hotel. Porter, Tully and Tannon followed along with the group of volunteers. Two of the workers cleared away the dining tables to make space for everyone. Then Crowder gave Porter the floor. He tried to sound as diplomatic as possible as he explained the situation.

'Help is on the way. There's an evacuation plan in place. But in the event of an attack we need to make sure the guests are safe and the hotel's as secure as possible. From now on, no one enters or leaves the building.'

One or two of the staff muttered amongst themselves. One of the volunteers raised her hand. A middle-aged woman with a heavy French accent A Médecins Sans Frontières accreditation danged from her neck.

'What about the people outside who are injured?' she said. 'We can't just leave them in the streets. Some of them need medical attention. They'll die.'

'We can't help them,' Porter replied. 'Our priority is to care for the people inside the hotel. That means fortifying the hotel against a possible enemy assault.'

Another volunteer raised his head. A Red Cross worker. 'If we're in danger, why don't we start evacuating the hotel now, before the rebels attack us?'

Some of the other volunteers murmured in agreement. Bald stepped forward and said, 'It's too dangerous. The streets are crawling with hostiles. We'd run into an enemy checkpoint before we could get everyone to safety. There's only one route out of the city, and it would take us in the direction of the rebels.'

'Then what do you expect us to do?' the Frenchwoman asked, throwing up her arms. She looked despairing. 'Sit here and hope for the best?'

'We bunker down in the hotel until help arrives,' Porter replied forcefully, making sure everyone in the room understood the gravity of the situation. 'This is where we'll make our stand. You'll need to make that clear to everybody inside the hotel. Anyone who loses their nerve and bolts will fall into the hands of the rebels and end up dead. Got it?'

117

There was a general bobbing of heads around the room. Porter nodded in satisfaction. His words had helped to focus the volunteers' minds on the task ahead, and they listened in silence for the rest of the briefing as he went over the plan in detail. He divided the volunteers into fifteen pairs, with each group given responsibility for a specific area. Two pairs would help clear the luggage from the lobby and stow everything in an unused conference room on the first floor. Another eight volunteers would help clear the corridors and stairways on the upper floors, so that the staff could easily relocate guests to the rooms. The remaining twenty volunteers were tasked with fortifying the upper floors by putting all the internal furniture up against the windows, as well as transferring the non-perishable foodstuffs upstairs.

At the same time the hotel workers would knuckle down to the task of organising the guests into the rooms on the top four floors, while the kitchen staff were tasked with rationing supplies and drawing up a meal roster for everyone. Guests would be told to report to the main restaurant at 0900 hours and 1700 hours each day for a daily briefing led by Deputy Commissioner Tannon. When he had finished, Porter went through the plan again so that everyone understood their jobs. Then Crowder called an end to the meeting and they went to work.

There was a bustle of activity in the lobby as the hotel porters began ushering the guests towards the stairs. Volunteers scurried around the lobby, grabbing suitcases and holdalls and backpacks and anything else cluttering the space, lugging everything up to the conference room on the first floor. Kitchen staff hurried in and out of the restaurant, bringing in extra tables and chairs for the evening meal. As the crowd started to filter out of the lobby Crowder made a beeline for Porter and Bald. A squat old white guy in overalls and a utility belt marched alongside him.

'This is Fischer,' Crowder said. 'He's our handyman. He'll show you the exit and entry points.'

'You know your way around?' Porter asked him.

Fischer nodded. 'Been working here since they opened the place,' he said in a thick Afrikaans accent. 'Nobody knows this building better than me, bru. Not even the guys who built it.'

Porter nodded then looked to Tully. 'You go with Fischer. Any exit points other than the fire doors should be nailed shut. Staff entrances, delivery bays. Board them up with whatever you can find.'

'What about the front doors?' Fischer asked.

'Leave them open for now. We've got the Nigerians covering the front. They're our barricade. But everything else needs to be sealed or blocked off.'

'We'll sort it,' said Tully. 'Where are you fellas going?'

'Upstairs. Me and Jock will do a recce of the upper floors. Set up fire points on each floor. Some of those rebels we saw on the drive over are packing RPGs. If one of them fuckers lets off a round and hits the hotel, the whole place could go up in flames.' He turned to Crowder. 'We'll need fire extinguishers at each fire point. We'll give you a list once we've done the rounds. Have your people fill up the bathtubs and sinks in the upper-floor rooms. If the water supply gets cut off, we're going to need drinking water for everyone inside the hotel.'

'Sure,' said Crowder. 'I'll get on it now.'

He turned and wandered back towards the reception desk. Tully followed the handyman across the lobby. As Porter turned to head for the stairs he heard a scuffle coming from the direction of the entrance. He looked across and saw one of the volunteers arguing with a trio of dark-haired guys in garish suits. From their accents and clothes Porter guessed they were Lebanese. Wherever there were diamonds in Africa, you could find a community of Lebanese running the merchant side of the business, fencing diamonds to the big companies in the West. He and Bald paced over to the Lebanese men as they continued to shout at the volunteer. At the sound of their approaching footsteps one of them turned towards the Blades. A hairy, morbidly obese guy with a pencil moustache and chunky gold rings on every finger. The man reeked of rich cologne.

'What's the problem here?' Porter asked, directing his question at the volunteer.

'This woman says we aren't allowed to leave the hotel,' the Lebanese scowled, waving a fat hand at the volunteer blocking the entrance doors.

Porter nodded. 'That's right. Everyone is to say inside from now on. It's for your own safety.'

The Lebanese shook his fat head. 'This is unacceptable! We have businesses to run. How are we supposed to protect them from the rebels if we're stuck inside here?'

'The hotel is on lockdown,' Bald cut in. 'Now shut the fuck up and deal with it.'

The Lebanese glowered, his sweaty features bristling with rage. 'You have no authority here. You're not in charge.' His eyes shifted to Porter. 'Either of you. We're leaving.'

He reached for the door. Porter stepped forward and planted his palm flat on the door, slamming it shut then stepping between the Lebanese and the entrance. He glared at the businessman.

'Step away from the door.'

'You can't tell me what to do.'

'If you step outside, you're a dead man. The rebels will get to you before you get anywhere near your precious shops. They'll take you alive and torture you in ways you can't even imagine. By the time those animals are done with you, you'll be begging them to put a bullet between your eyes.'

The Lebanese hesitated for a beat. His eyes narrowed to tiny dots and twitched at the corners. As if he was trying to decide whether to turn away or barge past Porter, and which one was more profitable for him. Then one of the other Lebanese cleared his throat and placed a hand on the fat guy's shoulder. A younger man dressed in a bright blue suit, with a thick beard and bushy eyebrows.

'Perhaps this man is right, uncle,' the younger Lebanese said. 'Maybe it is safer if we stay.'

Pride demanded that the Lebanese hold his ground for a few more seconds. Then he snorted at Bald and Porter and spun away, cursing under his breath. Bald watched them disappear up the stairs with the rest of the guests.

'Let's hope no one else tries to leave,' he muttered. 'We've got enough problems on our plate without the guests kicking up a fuss.'

Once the lobby had emptied, Bald and Porter got to work. They moved steadily up each floor of the hotel, checking that the fire doors were properly sealed and unobstructed, inspecting the emergency stairwells to make sure the volunteers could easily move from one floor to the next. As they went around Bald made notes with a pen and a pad of blank paper he'd taken from one of the staff at the reception, identifying where the fire points on each floor should go. By midday they had cleared most of the floors and as they climbed the stairs to the top floor Porter breathed a slight sigh of relief. They had restored a semblance of order to a chaotic situation, and given the people inside the hotel a fighting chance of survival.

I don't give a toss about protecting Soames, thought Porter. But there are a thousand people in here depending on me to keep them alive. I'm not going to let them down. No fucking way.

As they reached the sixth floor a high-pitched scream split the air. Porter and Bald both stopped cold as they hit the landing, and glanced down the corridor to their left. They saw a guest standing ten metres away, in front of the door to one of the luxury suites. He was arguing with one of the hotel porters. He wore the hotel uniform of short-sleeved white shirt, dark trousers and polished black shoes.

He was maybe the biggest guy Porter had ever seen. His shoulders were like a pair of basketballs stuffed into sacks. His neck was as wide as a lampshade. He towered over the guest. The latter looked to be in his sixties. He wore a pair of chinos and a wrinkled linen shirt. He had a liver-spotted left hand clasped around the wrist of a rakishly thin black woman standing next to him. The woman wore the same kind of clothes as Tully's night fighter. She had the same deadened look in her eyes too. She could have been the hooker's twin sister, thought Porter. The woman screamed again as the old man yanked her towards him.

'Sir, please,' the porter said. 'You need to let her go.'

'Shut the fuck up,' the guest spat.

The porter tried again. 'Sir, as I have already explained, all the guests must share their rooms. The boss has ordered it.'

'Tell your manager to fuck off.' The old man spoke in a harsh, guttural accent. German. 'I'm not sharing with anyone. I paid for this room, just like I paid for this whore. She stays with me.'

'Please . . .' the woman whimpered as she struggled to break free from the man's grip. 'Let me go. You're hurting me.'

'Shut up, whore!' the German snapped at her. 'Get back inside the room. I won't ask you again.'

The woman shrieked as he shoved her inside the room. The man-mountain looked on, his hands clenched into fists the size of bowling balls. The veins on his neck bulged like water in a couple of twisted hosepipes.

'Sir, I cannot let you do this.'

The German spun back to face the porter. Scowled at him. 'I don't give a shit what you think. You have a problem, take it up with your boss. I'm sure he'll be interested to hear about how you've treated one of his most important guests. Now get out of my face.'

The porter didn't move. He just stared at the old man. The guest stared back at him and smiled arrogantly. Then there was a flash of movement as he reached a hand around to the back of his chinos and whipped out a pistol from under his shirt. A stubby black Russian-manufactured PSM pistol with a steel barrel and a long curved trigger guard. The old man swung up his right arm and brought the PSM level with the porter, training the muzzle on a spot between his eyes.

The porter threw up his arms. His eyes were glued to the black hole of the PSM's muzzle six inches from his face. Beads of sweat trickled down his head. His hands trembled.

'Sir, please,' he said. 'I beg you. Don't do—'

'Don't tell me what to fucking do!'

The old man tensed his finger on the PSM trigger. All his energies were concentrated on the gun in his hand and the vast spread of a target standing in front of him. Which meant he didn't see

Bald charging at him from behind. At the last second the German heard the pounding of footsteps on the soft carpet and spun away from the man-mountain to face the new threat. Bald sprang forward before the old man could react, swinging his right arm in a rapid chopping motion and aiming for the guy's neck. The German gasped as the outer ridge of Bald's hand slammed against his windpipe, driving the air out of his throat. He folded at the waist in shock, his right arm falling away as the semi-automatic tumbled from his grip and thudded against the carpet.

The guy tried to retreat from Bald. He didn't get very far. Bald grabbed the German by the hair and brought up his right leg in a sharp upward jerk. There was a sickening crack as the bony edge of Bald's knee slammed into the bridge of the man's face, shattering the bones in his nose and breaking several of his teeth. Bald released his grip and the old man stumbled backwards, groaning nasally as he pawed at his broken nose. Then Bald stepped forward, throwing a sharp uppercut at the German that caught him square on the underside of his chin and sent his jaw crashing into the roof of his skull.

The old man grunted and fell backwards, landing on the floor next to the man-mountain. He rolled over and reached for the semi-automatic glinting on the carpet. Bald stepped forward again, kicking the weapon out of range. He slammed his boot down on the man's balls for good measure. The German gasped for breath, cupping one hand to his groin while the other staunched the flow of blood from his broken nose.

Bald quickly scooped up the PSM, racked the chamber and slid out the mag. He counted eight rounds of 5.45x18mm brass in the clip. A full magazine. He inserted the clip back into the heel of the grip and stashed the pistol in the waistband of his combats. The man-mountain stared at him in open-mouthed astonishment.

'You saved my life, sir,' he said softly. 'Thank you.'

'Forget it, mate. That wanker had it coming.' Bald rolled the German onto his front and pinned his arms behind his back, pressing down on his spine with his right knee.

'Bastard!' the old man rasped. 'Get off me!'

'Give us a hand here,' Bald called out. 'Help me restrain this cunt.'

Porter ducked inside the suite, looking around for something to tie the old man's hands together with. The hooker was lying on the king-sized bed, rubbing her sore wrists and staring in horror at the scene outside. Porter paced over to the window, grabbed the thick cord tied around the curtains and yanked it free. Then he approached the bed and offered his hand to the prostitute. She stared at him for a beat before accepting it. Porter helped her to her feet, escorted her out of the room and handed the curtain cord to Bald. The old man groaned as Bald bound the cord tight around his wrists, until he'd almost cut off the blood supply. When he'd finished, Bald hauled the German to his feet and shoved him towards the man-mountain.

'Dump this prick in one of the rooms on the first floor. He can sweat it out down there.'

'This man . . . he was going to kill me.' The porter bowed his head at Bald. 'Sir, I am in your debt. If there's anything I can do to repay you—'

Bald waved him away. 'Buy me a drink when this is over.'

'Please, sir. Call me Solomon.'

'You'll regret this,' the German snarled at Bald. 'You and your nigger friend. I've got friends in the police. I'll make sure they hear about this. They'll make you pay. Both of you.'

Before Bald could reply a staccato burst of cracks sounded outside, rumbling across the city like distant strokes of thunder. Porter glanced at his mucker. Both men recognised the noises instantly. The unmistakeable sound of gunfire.

A look of alarm flashed across Solomon's face. 'What was that?'

'Nothing,' Bald lied. 'Probably just an engine backfiring.' He pointed to the German. 'Take him away, and make space in one of the rooms for the hooker. Go!'

Solomon turned and manhandled the old man down the corridor towards the stairs. The hooker grabbed her handbag and hurried after them. Then Porter and Bald turned back into the junior suite and rushed over to the window.

Three hundred metres to the east of the hotel Porter could see a worn athletics track with a ramshackle pavilion at one end. Three hundred metres further east of the track there was a massive roundabout with a large baobab tree in the middle of it, the tree's copper-coloured trunk topped with the strange distinctive branches that resembled a bunch of upturned roots. Beyond the roundabout Porter spotted a loose cluster of injured ECOMOG troops hurrying up the road from the direction of the Aberdeen Road Bridge. At least a dozen of them. Some of the Nigerians were limping or had makeshift bandages wrapped around their heads or limbs. More gunfire erupted in the distance. The Nigerian troops picked up the pace as they scrambled past the roundabout, away from the sound of the firefight and towards the fifty other ECOMOG troops stationed at the front of the access road. Porter felt his guts turn to ice.

'Looks like the rebels are attacking the bridge,' he said.

'Bastards are getting closer,' Bald growled.

'How much longer do you think the Nigerians on the bridge will hold out?'

'Fuck knows. But whatever evacuation plan Hawkridge and his mates are cooking up, they'd better hurry up. We won't be able to hold out for long once things start going noisy here.'

'No.'

'At least we've got this,' Bald said, digging out the PSM pistol he'd nicked from the German.

Porter raised an eyebrow. 'What good is that gonna do us against hundreds of bloody rebels?'

Bald shook his head. 'This isn't for the chogies.'

Porter stared at his mucker in horror.

Bald said, 'There's no way I'm letting those fuckers outside take me alive, pal.'

Porter turned away from the window and made for the corridor.

'Where are you going?' said Bald.

'To move Soames,' Porter said. 'Before that lot outside come crashing through the doors.'

FOURTEEN

1322 hours.

The gunfire continued to crack and boom in the distance as Bald and Porter bolted down the stairs. They hit the second-floor landing and paced down the corridor leading towards Soames's hotel room. There was no sign of Tully. Porter guessed he was still busy with Fischer sealing off the exits on the ground floor. He passed a loose line of forty or so distraught-looking guests being escorted out of their rooms by the volunteers. They were led down the corridor, towards the landing and the safety of the upper floors. Most of the guests left their rooms without complaint. A few kicked up a fuss with the volunteers, but they quickly shut up once they heard the sounds of the firefight raging in the distance. The air inside the hotel was stale and hot and Porter could feel the sweat pasting his shirt to his skin. I could murder a cold beer right now, he thought. Christ, I can almost taste it on my lips. But the moment passed and he focused his thoughts on the mission.

Protect Soames. Protect the wanker who torpedoed my career.

All we've got to do is keep him away from the Russians for a few more hours, Porter told himself. As soon as the evacuation is sorted we'll get him on the first chopper out of the city and fly him home. Then it's job done and I can get back on the voddie.

Unless the rebels kill us all first.

He swiped open the door to room 201 with the key card Tannon had given him earlier. The door clicked open and Porter swept inside, with Bald a step behind him. Tully's hooker sat on the edge of the bed, staring sullenly at her feet. Soames was pacing up and down in front of the balcony, wearing a trench line into the faded carpet. He stopped and looked up as the two operators entered.

'What the devil's going on out there?' he said.

'The rebels are assaulting the bridge,' Porter answered. 'Some of the Nigerians have fallen back to the cordon in front of the hotel. We don't know how long the others will hold out.'

Soames looked startled. 'Shit. The rebels have never managed to get this close before.'

'We don't have a lot of time,' Porter said. 'Get moving.'

'Where are you taking me?'

'To a more secure room.'

The ex-CO narrowed his eyes at Porter. 'Somewhere you can keep an eye on me?' he sneered.

'It's for your own safety.'

'I'm fine where I am. Anyway, I doubt we're in any serious trouble. The Nigerians won't abandon their positions. People like myself are too important to be left to the mercy of the rebels. President Fofana knows that. So do the Nigerians, I'm sure.'

He stood his ground, smiling. Porter stared at him, his anger rising in his throat. *This tosser might be a close mate of the Whitehall set, but he's not my fucking CO any more. He's not pulling the strings now.*

'It's not up for debate,' he said. 'You're moving rooms and that's the fucking end of it. Now go. Jock will show you to your room.'

Soames stood still for a moment longer. Then he picked up his jacket and headed for the door, muttering under his breath. Bald followed him out of the room. Porter gestured to the hooker.

'You too, love. Hurry up.'

The hooker watched the door for a few moments, waiting until she was certain Soames and Bald were out of earshot. Then she manoeuvred around the bed and approached Porter. For a fleeting moment he thought she was going to make a pass at him. She must be desperate for business, he thought. Then he looked into her eyes, and saw the fear in them.

'Please,' she said. 'I must get away. I can't stay here.'

Porter shook his head. 'No one's allowed in or out of the hotel. Not until the rebels have cleared off.'

The hooker took a step closer to Porter. Her lower lip was purpled and trembling, he realised. 'You must help me,' she said. 'You have to keep me away from him.'

'From who?'

'Mister Tully.' She paused and flashed an anxious glance at the door. 'He hurts me.'

Porter hardened his expression. 'I can't help you.'

She reached out and placed her hand on his. 'You don't understand. He used to slap some of the girls about. Everyone knows Mister Tully likes it rough. But now it's worse. He chokes me. Sometimes he kicks me in the stomach and punches me in the face.'

'Why haven't you left him?'

'I tried. He caught me before I could escape. Then he said he was going to teach me a lesson I wouldn't forget. He raped me twice. Then he told me he knew where my family lived, and if I tried to leave him again he would find my brothers and sisters and kill them.'

Tears rolled down the hooker's face. She looked away in shame. Porter listened in stunned silence. He remembered what Tully had told him earlier that day. *You can do anything you want in these parts. Anything at all.* Bob Tully had always been unbalanced, even back in the Regiment. But now the guy was running wild. Raping prostitutes and threatening to murder their families. Bob's losing the plot, Porter thought.

What else is he capable of?

He shrugged off the disturbing thought as the hooker stepped closer to him. Close enough that he could smell her perfume, feel the warmth of her breath on his face. She looked at him with pleading eyes.

'You have to save me from Mister Tully,' she said, reaching a hand down to Porter's groin. 'I can give you good time. Better than any other woman. I make you happy.'

Porter grabbed her hand by the wrist and pushed it away. 'Maybe another time, love. Let's go.'

'You keep me from Mister Tully?'

'I'll see what I can do.'

That seemed to calm the hooker down. Porter led her out of the room, turned left and hurried down the corridor. Ahead of them dozens of guests were being ushered towards the upper floors. Among the faces Porter caught sight of Bald and Soames. They were pacing towards the stairwell leading down to the first floor. Porter quickened his stride and caught up with his mucker. He shoved the hooker towards Bald.

'Here,' he said. 'Take her and put her in one of the other rooms. Wherever there's space. I'll take Soames down to the storeroom.'

Bald frowned at the prostitute. A question formed in his eyes but then he simply shrugged, took the hooker by the wrist and ushered her in the direction of the guests being led up towards the upper floors. Porter grabbed Soames by the shoulder and thrust him down the stairs leading down to the first floor.

'You don't have to do this,' Soames said. 'You can still do the right thing and let me go.'

'Why would I do that?'

'I can give you and Bald both a job.'

Porter laughed.

'I'm serious,' Soames continued. 'You two did well to track me down, after all. It can't have been an easy mission, especially with the situation outside. I'm always on the lookout for good men. Once this business with the RUF blows over, I'll need extra security for the mine. You could do well for yourselves. Very well indeed.'

'If you think I'm taking orders from you again, you're fucking deluded.'

'Don't be a fool all your life, man. Things are different on the Circuit. Talk to your friend Tully if you don't believe me. Life here is dirt cheap. You get all the women and drink you want, whenever you want it. And the salary is competitive. Extremely competitive. You'd be making a lot more money than you do working for some line manager over at Thames House.'

They hit the first-floor landing. Porter gritted his teeth, listening to Soames argue his case as they paced along the corridor.

'Think about what I'm offering you! What happens if you take me back to London, eh? You'll just go back to being a grunt again, working for the Firm for a pittance. That's no kind of existence for a good Hereford man. Let me go, and you and Jock Bald will live like kings. You have my word.'

Porter still said nothing. Soames kept arguing with him as they marched towards a door at the far end of the corridor. Giving him the hard sell. *Maybe Soames is right,* the voice inside Porter's head said. *Maybe you should walk away from the Firm. What have they ever done for you?* For an instant he was tempted to take up Soames on his offer. But then he remembered who he was dealing with. *You can't trust this guy,* a second voice told him. *You know what Soames is like. He's more slippery than a butcher's prick. He'll say anything to get what he wants. Five minutes ago Soames was slagging me off. Now he's offering me the job of a lifetime.* Which made Porter wonder: *Why is my old CO so desperate to stay in Sierra Leone?*

They arrived in front of the storeroom. An unmarked brown door situated midway down the corridor. Porter dug out the set of keys Crowder had given him. He tried a bunch of them until he found the one that unlocked the storeroom door. He pushed Soames into the room and flicked the light switch on. A single fluorescent bulb sputtered into life, casting weak light over the room and revealing a cramped space with bare breeze-block walls and shelves at the back piled high with cardboard boxes. There was a desk to the right of the storeroom and a dirty sink to the left with a toaster and a kettle. Several large bottles of industrial cleaning agents were stacked in a cabinet above the sink. Every surface was coated in about an inch of dust. Soames glanced around. Wrinkled his face in disgust.

'You're not going to leave me in here, surely.'

'I'll have someone bring you food and drink when the evening meal's ready,' said Porter. 'As soon as the evacuation is underway, we'll come and fetch you. Until then you'll stay here.'

Soames's expression hardened. 'You can't do this to me, Porter. Think about who you're dealing with. I've got friends, you know. They won't be pleased when they find out how you're treating me.'

Porter shook his head. 'I don't give a crap what your mates think. Right now, all I care about is keeping us alive.'

'What if I need to go to the bathroom?'

'Piss in the sink.'

Porter pulled the door shut then twisted the key, locking Soames inside. The guy shouted obscenities through the door as Porter made his way back down the corridor towards the main landing. Ahead of him Bald trotted down the stairs from the upper floors. He marched over to Porter, nodded at his mucker.

'That's the night fighter sorted. What now?'

'Now, we sit tight and wait,' said Porter.

And pray that the evacuation team gets here in time.

The afternoon passed in a frenzied blur. Bald and Porter regrouped with Tully in the lobby and the three men did a quick recce of the exit and entry points on the ground floor, checking that each one had been securely boarded up. They took a brief detour into the underground car park to check that the metal shutters had been lowered over the exit and all the service doors were blocked. Once they were satisfied the hotel had been sealed off, they beat a path to the manager's office and made photocopies of the map Bald had drawn up indicating the fire points on each floor. Crowder handed the copies to his staff and ordered them to be distributed to the volunteers, so that everyone would know where to go in the event of a fire breaking out.

Out in the lobby, the hotel staff and volunteers were like an army of termites, boosting furniture from the lounge and carrying it across to the back of the ground-floor restaurant, blocking the windows and doors overlooking the grounds to the rear of the hotel. Rendering the weak points in the structure impassable. Others carried fire extinguishers upstairs or lugged up boxes of non-perishable goods in case the enemy breached the lower floors and the guests found themselves cut off from the food supplies stored in the kitchen. Porter, Bald and Tully supervised the operation. Tannon had set up shop in the back office, putting in regular calls to her superiors, demanding updates on the evacuation. Only the twelve Lebanese refused to help. They hung around in a corner of the lobby, smoking foul-smelling cigarettes and nervously watching the Nigerian troops.

For the rest of the afternoon Bald and Porter alternated between keeping an eye on the situation outside through the lower-floor windows, and checking in with Tannon for any new information. Porter also periodically checked in on the sat phone to see if Hawkridge had tried to reach out to them. But he heard nothing. At least battery life wasn't an issue: Tannon had managed to source a spare satellite-phone charger from a staffer at the Dutch embassy, allowing Porter to keep the unit plugged in on a side desk in the back office.

Sporadic bursts of gunfire continued to ripple across the peninsula as the day wore on. Bald, Porter and Tully did a quick recce of the rooftop to try and get a better view of the situation to the east. By now several plumes of jet-black smoke were drifting lazily up into the sky from the direction of the Aberdeen Road Bridge as the gun battle there continued to rage. A steady trickle of wounded Nigerians staggered back towards the hotel from the bridge, and Porter privately feared that the remaining troops would abandon their position before long. Once the main body of enemy soldiers had broken through there would be nothing to stop them attacking the hotel, he knew.

The gunfire ceased some time around dusk. The distant crack of rifle reports faded as the dying embers of sunlight burnt themselves out on the horizon. Like a cigarette being stubbed out in a giant ashtray. Then the sky went dark, and the streets of Freetown were soon filled with wild cheers and the booming thud-thud of gangsta rap as the rebels celebrated another day's looting. After the final roster of guests had taken their evening meal and returned to their rooms, Porter divided the staff into groups of six and detailed them to take turns on the night watch. They would work in three-hour shifts throughout the night, making sure the landings were empty and looking for any signs of a potential breach by the enemy. Then Porter left to have a drink.

He crossed the litter-strewn lobby, glancing outside as he made for the bar adjacent to the hotel restaurant. Through the double-doors at the front of the hotel he could see the Nigerian troops on stag at the end of the drive. They were sitting around in small groups and smoking cigarettes, their belt kits off and their guns resting on their laps. They didn't exactly look like a determined force to Porter. There's not a good fighter amongst them, he thought.

The bar doors were closed but unlocked. Someone had turned the lights off, but Porter could see several bottles of spirits on a rack behind the bar. He breezed past the tables and chairs and made a beeline for the counter. Most of the good stuff had already been cleared out by thirsty punters but there was a bottle of Absolut vodka hidden behind a couple of flagons of empty Cockburn's Special Reserve port. Porter grabbed the vodka bottle and slumped down in a chair at the nearest table. Then he unscrewed the cap and took a long pull straight from the bottle. His first sip in almost twenty-four hours. The liquid slicked down his throat and flowed into his veins, dulling his nerve endings. A warm glow washed over him. Sweet Jesus, but that felt good.

He felt a sudden wave of tiredness wash over him. Porter glanced at his watch and realised it had been well over two days since he'd had a decent night's kip. For the past several hours he'd been running on fumes, and now the stress and exhaustion came rushing back at him with a vengeance. His eyelids felt heavy, as if someone had sewn hockey pucks into them. A kind of dull fog settled behind his eyeballs. He closed his eyes for a moment and sighed.

'Mind if I join you?'

Porter looked up and saw Tannon standing a few feet away. She had removed her jacket and rolled up the sleeves on her crinkled white blouse. Strands of her brown hair clung to the slender lines of her face. The deputy commissioner looked stressed, Porter thought. *I know the feeling.*

He nodded at the bar. 'Help yourself.'

'Freebar,' she said. 'The best kind.'

She sauntered over to the bar, grabbed a glass from the rack under the counter and slid down into the chair opposite Porter. Poured herself a double measure of the Absolut and tipped it down her throat in one gulp. Either she's a heavy drinker, thought Porter, or she's even more worried about the situation than she's letting on.

'How long do you think we've got?' she asked, setting her glass down.

Porter shrugged then took another hit from the bottle. 'Not long. My guess is the rebels will have another crack at the bridge first thing tomorrow. Strike while morale is low with the Nigerians. It won't take them long to smash through. We've got twenty-four hours at the most. Probably less.'

Tannon poured herself another slug of vodka. 'Let's hope you're wrong. I just got off the phone with the commissioner. Seems like Downing Street finally understands how serious the situation is. The evacuation's been set for tomorrow afternoon. We're still waiting for an exact time. It'll be a joint US–British operation. Details are scant but we'll brief the guests in the morning.'

She looked up her from drink. Smiled nervously. Her eyes were half filled with hope, and half with fear.

'You think we'll make it?'

'It'll be close,' Porter said. 'But I've survived worse.'

Tannon sipped at her drink. 'I guess you'll be leaving on the first chopper?'

Porter nodded. 'We've got our orders. What about you?'

'I'll be flying to Conakry with the commissioner to meet with President Fofana. We'll return here as soon as it's safe. Downing Street wants us to take the lead in negotiating a truce with the rebels.'

'Won't work. Never does when you're dealing with scum like this lot. Trust me, love. The only language they understand is bullets.'

'It's different this time.'

'How do you mean?'

'The rebels have the people on their side now. In the past, they didn't have much in the way of public support. It was mostly a bunch of self-interested army officers looking to make a name for themselves. This time the rebels have the sympathy of a large number of people in the south of the country. If the president comes down hard on them, he'll lose the next election.'

'I thought the locals were terrified of the rebels,' Porter said.

'They are. But they're also angry with the president. Because of the missing children.'

Porter frowned. 'What missing kids?'

'Haven't you heard?' Tannon saw the puzzled look on his face and went on. 'Hundreds of children have gone missing in Sierra Leone in the past year. Mostly from the poorer villages and farms to the south. At first, everyone assumed they'd been abducted by the West Side Boys.'

'Makes sense. They're the ones recruiting all the child soldiers.'

'Right. Except for two things. One, the kids going missing are too young, even for the West Side Boys. We're talking about six- and seven-year-olds. Kids that age aren't old enough to hold a rifle properly, let alone use it.'

'What's the second thing?'

'Not long after the disappearances, Fofana's men captured one of the West Side Boys' commanders. He confessed to a bunch of stuff, but he swore blind his men hadn't abducted these kids.'

'So who took them?'

'We don't know. But whoever's responsible, it's got the locals pretty worked up. They think Fofana isn't doing enough to find the missing children. Some of them even formed a pressure group here in Freetown to petition the president. Mothers of the Lost Children.'

Porter nodded. 'I've seen the posters.'

'The mothers have caused quite a stir. The rebels took advantage of the public anger and advanced on the city. The president is on the brink and they smell blood. The only way Fofana will survive is if he can form a truce with the rebels and put an end to the bloodshed. But it's going to be tough. The rebel chiefs won't agree to a ceasefire until the president cuts his ties with Soames.'

'Will he?'

Tannon laughed and shook her head. 'He can't. Fofana needs Soames for his political comeback.'

'Because Soames protects the mines?'

'Correct. Without control of the diamond fields, Fofana is a lame duck. Besides, Soames has the political connections in Westminster to make things happen. Securing foreign investment, that sort of thing. Without Soames, the money dries up.'

'Is that why Angela March has had you keeping tabs on Soames?'

Tannon nodded. 'Whitehall is worried about blowback.'

'Against the president?'

Tannon nodded. 'Some people at the FO are concerned that Soames isn't exactly clean. Angela included.'

'The diamond smuggling. Hawkridge and your friend Angela told us during the briefing.'

'The rumours have been floating around for a while. Angela was concerned that if Soames got caught with his hand in the till, it would reflect badly on the president and strengthen the rebels' hand. We can't afford any scandals. Not if we want to keep Fofana in power, obviously. So I looked into it.'

'Did you find anything?'

'I tried. But I couldn't get close to the diamond mines. Soames has got a tight security presence there. Which struck me as odd.'

'We're talking about a diamond mine in the middle of the most dangerous country in Africa. Security in these places is tighter than a nun's snatch.'

'This is different. The mine makes Fort Knox look like a branch of Abbey National. I'm telling you, Soames has got something hidden there. Something big.' She paused. 'And then there's unannounced visits.'

Porter said, 'What visits?'

'In the past several months, a number of prominent military personnel and politicians have made unscheduled trips to the mine. We're not sure, but we think they might be checking on something.'

'Such as?'

'We don't know.'

Porter said nothing. He thought back to the conversation with Hawkridge after they had found the murdered Russian in Soames's office. Remembered the MI5 agent telling him the rumours about Soames stealing diamonds from the mine and selling them on to dodgy fences for a profit.

Nothing has been proven, Hawkridge had said.

But I know Soames, Porter thought. I know how the bastard's mind works. He doesn't care about money. He's already minted. All he gives a toss about is climbing the greasy pole, getting a knighthood, and the lifestyle that goes with it. The parties with the super-rich on their yachts in Monte Carlo. The weekend invites to Chequers. Chummying up to media tycoons and future prime ministers.

But if he's not smuggling diamonds, then what the fuck is he up to?

He forgot about all this as Tannon knocked back the rest of her drink. She brushed a strand of hair behind her ear and smiled at Porter. Shyly at first. The hint of a smile, rather than the full thing. It carried the promise of something more than a smile, somewhere down the line. Then she leaned across the table and pecked Porter on the cheek. He caught the scent of her skin as she leaned over, and felt something hot stir in his blood. He wondered if Tannon was coming on to him. *Bloody hell. I might actually be in here.*

'Thank you,' Tannon said as she straightened up. She smiled more fully at him now. The booze breaking down her anxieties. 'For everything that you've done for us today.'

Porter took another swig of vodka, then waved a hand at her. 'Don't thank me yet. We've still got to get through tomorrow first.'

Tannon poured herself another shot and downed it, giving herself more confidence. Then she broke out the full smile. It was less like a smile, and more like an invitation. She wet her lips and ran her finger around the rim of the shot glass.

'I might not see you after tomorrow,' she said. 'I wish there was some way I could thank you.'

Porter sat dumbfounded. He could hardly believe what he was hearing. It had been a long while since he'd had a woman. His last shag had been a drunken fumble in the dark with an Irish waitress with a face like a bag of ferrets. Porter had simply assumed his days as a bedroom warrior were behind him. Nowadays most women ignored him. Or worse, took pity on him. They could smell the moss on his dick from a mile away. *Here we are in the middle of a war zone, and this bird is gagging for it.*

Tannon leaned in closer to Porter. Lowered her voice to a whisper.

'You know, I've got a room to myself on the fourth floor. Crowder insisted. There's a fully stocked mini-bar in there too. How about you and I take this party upstairs?'

He didn't need a second invitation. He set down the vodka bottle and shot to his feet. Tannon slid out of her chair, turned on her heels and sauntered out of the bar, her wide hips swaying hypnotically from side to side. Porter stared at her cracking arse, grinning widely as he followed her out into the lobby. He could hardly believe his luck. *Five minutes ago I was going to spend the night with the bottle, drinking myself into oblivion. Now I'm in with a chance of shagging the deputy commissioner, someone with direct access to a minister in the Foreign Office.* He smiled to himself as he imagined the look on Jock Bald's face when he found out he'd spent the night with Tannon.

He felt his heart pounding with anticipation as he followed the deputy commissioner into her room. Porter glanced around the room while Tannon kicked off her shoes and retrieved a couple of miniatures from the mini-bar. The double mattress had been propped against the window and the rest of the furniture shoved against the wall. A makeshift bundle of pillows and duvet covers lay on the floor next to the bedside table. There were several bottles of prescription pills arranged on the table, Porter noticed.

He read the labels. Zoloft, Xanax, and a generic brand of sleeping tablets.

'For my anxiety,' Tannon said as she wandered back over to Porter, clutching a pair of Jim Beam miniatures. 'I get panic attacks sometimes.'

Porter tipped his head at the miniatures. 'Should you be mixing that stuff with all them pills?'

'It's no big deal. I'm used to it by now. Besides, you're hardly one to talk. The amount you drink, you should be dead by now.'

'Who told you that?'

'Don't look so surprised. Angela sent me your file. It was all in there.'

She handed one of the miniatures to Porter and unscrewed the cap on the other. Then they sat on the bedframe side by side, her long legs touching against his thighs as they sipped at their drinks.

'What happened to your hand?' Tannon asked, pointing to the two stumps where his index and middle fingers had once been.

'We were on an op in Beirut. Me and some other lads were sent in to rescue a British businessman being held hostage there. Things got noisy. I took a round from one of the guards.'

Tannon reached down and touched the stumps. 'I'm sorry,' she said softly.

Porter shrugged. 'I got off lightly. Three Regiment lads died that day.'

'What happened?'

'There was a kid. He was one of the guards.' Porter knocked back half the miniature before continuing. 'I remember his face even now. He must have been thirteen or so. I knocked him out cold during the mission. A blow from a bloke my size, the kid should have stayed down. But he didn't. He got back to his feet as we were bugging out and dropped three of the lads. If I'd slotted the kid, those three lads would still be alive.'

'How long ago was this?'

'Eleven years. Back in '89. Not long after I passed Selection.' Porter fell silent and stared down at his drink. 'There's not a day goes by that I don't think about those three lads.'

Tannon took her hand and placed it on top of Porter's. 'You can't blame yourself for what happened.'

Porter looked her in the eye. 'I did what I did. There are no easy decisions in a battle. If I'd shot the kid, I would have broken the Geneva Convention and I'd probably be rotting in a prison cell right now. I made my choice and paid the price for it. A heavy price. But I can't forgive Soames.'

'Why? What did he do?'

'He was the CO of the Regiment at the time. He blamed me for the Beirut op. What happened to me could have happened to any of the lads at Hereford, but Soames didn't see it that way. As far as he was concerned, I'd flunked the op and made him look bad. He needed a scapegoat. So he hung me out to dry. I went from being on the fast track to being thrown on the scrapheap.'

'He ruined your career?' Tannon said. 'That's why you hate him?'

Porter nodded. 'I wasn't the best operator in the Regiment. Far from it. But I was a decent soldier and I had a good future ahead of me. I've got blood on my hands, and that's on me. But Soames wrecked my career over it. He should have had my back. Instead he blackballed me just to cover his own arse. That bastard was more concerned with looking good in front of the top brass than losing three of his men. Now everyone thinks he's a bloody hero.'

Tannon traced her fingers up the tight knotted muscles of his arm. 'It can't be easy. Having to protect Soames, after all that's gone on between you in the past.'

'I didn't have a choice. The Firm sent us out here. And your mate Angela over at the Foreign Office. Seems Soames has got half of Whitehall under his thumb.'

Tannon frowned. 'How comes you're working for Angela, anyway? I didn't know the SAS was in the habit of working with the Foreign Office.'

'We're not.' Porter shook his head. 'We're on secondment to the Firm. We did a job for them a year ago, and they decided to keep us on. Been working for them ever since. They're the ones who brought Angela on board.' He looked up at Tannon. 'What about you? How did you end up here?'

Tannon teased a wry smile out of the corner of her mouth. 'Sometimes I ask myself that very question. I come from a military family. Dad was an officer in the Coldstream Guards, my grandad fought in Sicily with 1 Para. I followed the family tradition and joined the First Military Intelligence Battalion. Did four years, then left to join the Foreign Office and got posted here. Needless to say, Daddy wasn't very happy about it. He always thought I'd marry some rich bloke in the City, settle down and pop out a couple of kids. But that was never what I wanted.'

'What did you want?' Porter asked.

'Adventure. A chance to see the world.' She lowered her eyes. 'I guess at some level I wanted to prove my father wrong. Show him I was capable of being more than a stay-at-home mum.' She looked up and shrugged. 'Guess I have unresolved Daddy issues.'

'I'm sure he'd be proud,' Porter said. Because he felt he had to say something.

The awkward silence was punctured by another distant burst of gunfire. Tannon glanced at the window as the sounds of the rebels' cheering and whooping carried across the night sky.

'Do you think we'll make it through tomorrow?' she asked, looking back to Porter.

'I don't know. But I can promise you two things. If the rebels have a crack at us, me and Jock will give them the fight of their lives. The fuckers won't know what's hit them.'

'What's the second thing?'

Porter smiled weakly. 'Once this is over, Soames will probably get a bloody medal. That wanker's like Tefal. Nothing sticks to him. He always come out smelling of roses.'

Tannon went quiet for a beat. Then she looked deep into his eyes and said, 'I don't care about Soames and his medals. I know who the real hero is.'

She leaned over and kissed him, hard. It was the kind of long, feverish kiss that left them both breathless and trembling as they sought out each other's tongues. Then they were tearing each other's clothes off. Porter ripped open her blouse and unlatched her bra with his big clumsy fingers. Her small, pert breasts popped out. Porter cupped a hand to one, drawing a moan of pleasure from Tannon. Then she drew back, making noisy inhalations as she stood up from the bedframe and took Porter by the hand and moved over to the bed. She peeled off his shirt, paused when she caught sight of the scars on his chest then pulled him close, socketing her groin to his. Porter felt the warmth of her breasts flattened against his bare chest as he kissed her pale neck.

'Fuck me,' she gasped. 'Fuck me hard.'

Tannon slid her hand down to his crotch and unbuttoned his khakis. Then she reached around to the back of her pencil skirt and pulled down the slip, letting the material slide down the length of her smooth legs. For a moment Porter just stood there, his head spinning as he admired her stunning figure. She wasn't just pretty. She was transformed. A totally different woman from the awkward, shy creature he'd first met in the hotel lobby. Tannon had the kind of body that looked better naked than clothed. She had wide curved hips and powerful thighs and a flat, smooth belly. She was lean, but not skinny. Slender, but not bony. The kind of woman who took care of herself, but knew how to have fun as well. Porter grinned.

Just wait until Jock Bald hears about this, he thought again as he watched Tannon slink out of her black lace knickers. She smiled at him with moist lips and a sweet, playful look in her eyes.

'Well?' she said. 'What are you waiting for?'

Porter grinned. He forgot about his mucker. He forgot about the booze and the mission, and Soames and the rest of it. *This time tomorrow we might all be dead. So I may as well enjoy tonight.* He pulled Tannon tight and clamped his hands around her firm buttocks, and kissed her like it might be the last kiss he ever had.

FIFTEEN

Harsh sunlight spilled into the room the following morning. Porter woke early, glowing with satisfaction and listening to the light sound of Tannon's breathing as she rested her head against his chest. A pungent aroma of sex and perfume lingered in the cool air of the room. He was hungry, and content. *Waking up in bed with a beautiful woman by my side, and without a massive hangover splitting my skull in half. So this is what it feels like to be sober,* Porter thought. *Bloody hell. I could get used to this.*

The silence was broken by a sudden rasping whoosh followed by a loud crash. RPG, Porter realised. It sounded close to the hotel. Dangerously close. He leapt out of the makeshift bed, grabbed his clothes, and quickly dressed. Then he rushed over to the window and peered out through a gap next to the mattress.

The window faced north, giving Porter a partial view of the security cordon at the far end of the access road, fifty metres away. Down below, the fifty Nigerians who had been guarding the access road began retreating towards the hotel entrance, under sporadic bursts of gunfire. They were accompanied by the twenty or so other Nigerians who had withdrawn from the bridge the previous afternoon. Further north Porter saw the crowd of locals on the main road rapidly disperse, people running for cover in every direction, screaming in terror. More gunshots ripped through the air, with several rounds slapping into the ground around the access road. Two ECOMOG soldiers were slumped on the ground next to the sandbags, blood pooling around their corpses.

Behind him Tannon stirred in the bed and immediately sat upright.

'What is it?' she asked anxiously. 'What's going on?'

Porter said nothing. He turned away from the window and made for the door as another RPG round whooshed towards the hotel. There was a deafening boom and shudder as it struck the palm trees lining the main road.

Shit, he thought.

It's started.

'John?' Tannon said.

Porter stopped and turned back to her. He tried to keep his voice calm. 'I'm going to have a look downstairs. Wait here.'

'But—'

Porter didn't catch her reply. He yanked the door open and stepped outside, then marched quickly down the hallway as the urgent sounds of gunfire continued to ring out from the front of the hotel. He quickened his stride as he hurried on towards the landing, the dread tightening around his throat. Ahead of him he saw Bald and Tully waiting by the stairs, ordering everyone back into their rooms. They turned to face Porter as he rushed over.

'What the fuck's going on?' he said between snatches of breath.

Tully jerked a thumb in the direction of the lobby. 'The bridge has fallen. The rebels are headed this way. Hundreds of the fuckers. It's all kicking off.'

'Where's Soames?'

'Still locked in the storeroom,' Bald said. He frowned. 'Where have you been all night?'

Before Porter could reply several shouts echoed from down in the lobby. The voices sounded desperate, and scared. The three men glanced at one another. Then they turned and sprinted down the stairs, clearing the treads two or three at a time. A furious volley of cracks and thumps sounded in the distance as they made their way down to the lobby. The sounds were getting closer.

This is it, Porter thought as he raced after Bald and Tully. *We're under attack.*

Forty or so guests stood huddled by the lobby stairs. Early risers who'd ventured downstairs to see what was going on. Crowder and a few of the staff stood close by. Porter, Bald and Tully battled their way through the crowd and looked towards the entrance twelve metres away. More than forty Nigerian troops had backpedalled from the access road, fleeing through the double doors that had been left unblocked the previous day. Porter marched over to the front entrance and gazed outside. He saw the remaining thirty troops further north along the drive. The Nigerians had lost all sense of discipline and were retreating towards the entrance, firing wild rounds at the Cape Road to cover their retreat.

As soon as the Nigerians hit the lobby they began shedding their kit. SLR rifles, secondary pistols, RPG-7s, belts of 7.62mm link. The Nigerians dumped the lot. Even the guy with the GPMG discarded his guns. Once the soldiers had ditched their guns they started taking off the rest of their kit. Helmets, camo jackets, utility belts and boots.

'What are they doing?' Bald snarled.

'Ditching anything that might identify them to the rebels,' Tully said.

Bald's expression tightened with impotent rage. 'We've got to put a stop this. Get them back to their positions.'

But Porter could tell just by looking at the Nigerians that it was pointless arguing with them. They were gripped by a combination of crap training, indiscipline and sheer terror. *There's nothing we can do.*

Amid the melee Porter spotted the heavyset sergeant they had ran into the previous day outside the hotel. Bald immediately made a beeline for the sergeant, his face twisted into a disgusted scowl. Tully and Porter hurried after him. The Nigerian looked up at Bald as the latter stepped into his face.

'The fuck you think you're doing?' Bald said.

The sergeant gave him a long, hard stare. 'Protecting my men. There are too many rebels out there.' He gestured outside, to the sandbags at the far end of the access road. By now the last of the soldiers had pulled back from the cordon and retreated inside the hotel. 'We can't hold them off any longer. If the enemy captures us they'll kill us all. The only way to keep my men alive is to make the rebels think we're guests here.'

Bald jabbed a finger at the Nigerian's chest. 'What about everyone else in here? You can't just abandon these people.'

The sergeant shook his head. 'There's nothing more we can do for them. My men will wait here and hope the rebels spare us. If you want to leave, that's up to you.'

'We can't. The whole place is fucking surrounded.'

The Nigerian stared at Bald with a cold indifference. 'This isn't our problem. We can't help you. Now get out of my way.'

He brushed past Bald and headed for the stairs with the rest of his men, yelling at them to grab whatever clothes they could find to disguise their appearance. Bald shaded white with rage as the Nigerians barged past the guests and scurried up the stairs. The guy was grinding his teeth so hard, Porter could hear the scrape of enamel.

'Fucking useless,' Bald muttered.

'What do we do now?' Tully said.

As he spoke a flurry of three-round bursts erupted along the Cape Road and a pair of stray bullets thwacked into the concrete walls either side of the glass doors. The rest of the Nigerians picked up the pace and vaulted up the stairs after their mates. Some of the guests turned and followed them, unnerved by how close to the lobby the rounds had struck. Porter narrowed his eyes at the Cape Road and searched for movement. There was no sign of the enemy, but he knew they had to be close. Most of the rebels he'd seen on the streets were kitted out with AK-47s. Probably Chinese or Eastern European knock-offs. The AK-47 had a maximum effective range of four hundred metres, and a stray round might carry on for another two or three hundred metres beyond that. Which put the rebels at anywhere between seven hundred and four hundred metres away from the hotel grounds. Close, thought Porter. But not too close.

146

There's still time.

He gave his back to the entrance and looked the two others in the eye. 'We still have a chance to stop them. We can use the weapons the Nigerians have dumped. Set up firing points on the rooftop and start putting rounds down on these bastards before they hit the entrance. It's our only chance.'

Tully pulled a face. 'Just the three of us? I'm all for knocking the bastards down. But there's no way we'll be able to hold them off until help arrives.'

'We've seen them chogies in action,' Bald replied. 'They're shit shots.'

Tully looked uncertain.

Porter said, 'It's our only option. Either we start hitting the enemy right now, or we're gonna get our heads chopped off.'

'What about Soames?' Tully asked. 'We can give him a weapon too. That'd make four of us.'

'We can't risk it. If he gets clobbered, we're the ones who'll end up taking the blame. He stays in the storeroom.'

Tully pressed his lips shut. Then he shrugged and said, 'Fuck it, then. Let's go.'

The three men rushed over to the stack of weapons the Nigerians had discarded. Bald grabbed the GPMG, plus several belts of 7.62mm brass lying amid the pile of helmets and jackets. Porter grabbed one of the SLRs and chucked it to Tully. Took another rifle for himself. The weapon felt good in his grip. Reassuringly familiar. Like all Hereford men Porter had broken his balls with the SLR. Over the years he'd fired thousands of rounds with that rifle on the ranges in the Brecons. It was a sturdy, dependable weapon. In a straight gunfight the SLR would be more than a match for the shoddy AK-47s that Porter had seen most of the rebels packing in the streets of the capital.

A quick glance at the fire selector told him the rifle was one of the L1A1 variants, with only two settings instead of the usual three. Semi-automatic, and safety. Porter thumbed the mag release located on the side of the receiver and gently slid out the clip. A full clip of 7.62 rifle cartridges gleamed dully in the box mag.

Twenty rounds in total. He scooped up four additional clips, plus two more from another pair of SLRs. Six extra clips, as well as the twenty in the mag. A hundred and forty rounds in total. As much ammo as he could carry.

As he stuffed the clips into his pockets one of the guests stepped forward from the crowd and cleared his throat. Porter recognised the man with a start. The guy with the scar above his lip. One of the five guys dressed for safari he'd seen hanging around the hotel. A few paces behind the guy stood his four mates, to the right of the small crowd of guests. They were still wearing their African hunting gear, watching the scene at the entrance with a keen interest. The guy with the scar above his lip glanced at Tully and Bald before turning to address Porter.

'Forgive me,' he said. 'But I couldn't help overhearing your conversation. I think me and my friends might be able to help.'

'You can help us out by getting the fuck back to your rooms,' Bald said as he hefted up the GPMG, belts of ammo draped across his shoulder. 'It's not safe down here.'

The man smiled weakly. 'You need more men to keep the rebels at bay, no?'

'Yeah,' said Porter as he stood up. 'So what?'

The guy with the scar above his lip reached into his shorts pocket and dug out a shiny leather wallet. He plucked a business card out and handed it to Porter. The card gave the guy's name as Vincent Nilis, Senior Engineer for Worldwide Exploration for a company called Perutz Mining Corp. There was a telephone number below the company logo and a postal address in Antwerp.

'We arrived a few days ago to carry out inspections on our company's mining equipment. We've been trapped here since the rebels entered the city.' Nilis gestured to his mates. 'But my friends and I did our national service in Belgium. We all know how to handle a rifle. Let us help.'

Porter handed the business card back to Nilis. Ran his eyes over the four other Belgians standing a few metres away. They all looked to be in their late thirties or early forties, and Porter guessed it had probably been a long time since any of them had fired a shot in anger. Then another burst of gunfire crackled outside from the direction of the main road. It sounded louder than the previous reports and sent the last remaining guests darting up the stairs after the Nigerians. The rebels are getting closer, Porter thought.

We have to act now, or we're all dead.

'Well?' Nilis asked.

Bald leaned in close to Porter. 'Maybe we should clear this with Hawkridge. If this lot fuck up, we'll be the ones carrying the can.'

Porter shook his head. 'There's no time.' Then he looked back to Nilis and said, 'How long ago did you do your national service?'

'For me, eighteen years. The others are about the same.'

'Ever used an SLR before?'

'No. But we trained with the FN FAL battle rifle many times.'

Porter nodded. The British SLR was an inch-pattern variant of the FN FAL. Built to British imperial measurements, rather than metric. But the rifles were practically identical. Like twins separated at birth. Both weapons were chambered for the same 7.62x51mm NATO round. Both had some interchangeable parts. They had the same sighting posts and similar effective ranges. Which meant the Belgians should be able to get to grips with the SLR easily enough. *As long as they remember their basic training*, Porter told himself.

'Fine,' he said to Nilis. 'You're with us. Tell your muckers to grab themselves an SLR each. Take as much ammo as you can carry and follow us up to the rooftop. Hurry. We don't have much time.'

The Belgian called over his mates and told them the plan. While they grabbed weapons and clips from the stash by the doors, Porter marched over to Crowder and pointed to the front doors.

'Get that last entry point sealed,' he said. 'Now. Before the rebels, start attacking us.'

Crowder jolted into action. He barked at the four staff in the lobby. They rushed forward and shoved a wooden piano across the lobby, blocking the glass doors. It wasn't an imperetrable barricade, Porter knew. But it was better than nothing and would buy them valuable seconds to respond if the enemy managed to breach the hotel. Satisfied, he turned away from the staff and joined Bald, Tully and the Belgians by the foot of the staircase. Then they launched themselves up the stairs.

They moved as fast as they could, equipment clattering and clinking, struggling under the weight of the rifles and the extra rounds they were carrying. Bald gripped the gimpy by its carry handle, belts of ammo slung across his shoulders. Porter raced up the treads alongside him, adrenaline pounding inside his veins. He suddenly forgot about the tiredness. The dryness in his mouth, the dull ache in his bones. His mind was entirely focused on doing whatever it took to stop the rebels. The lives of a thousand civvies, depended on him now. Even if the rebels did spare the majority of the guests, he doubted they would show any mercy to a couple of SAS operators.

The rebels won't take the hotel. Not today. Not if I can bloody help it.

He ran into Tannon on the fourth-floor landing. The deputy commissioner had dressed in a hurry and she had a flustered look on her face. She glanced at the five Belgians as they raced up the stairs.

'What's going on?' she asked Porter.

'The rebels have broken across the bridge. They're coming right for us.'

'What about the Nigerians?'

Porter shook his head. 'Abandoned their posts. They're trying to pass themselves off as guests.'

Tannon composed herself, took a deep breath. 'What can I do?'

'Get on the blower your boss,' said Porter. 'Tell him it's fucking urgent. The Yanks need to get a move on and bring the choppers in to evacuate everyone before this mob overruns us.'

'How long do we have?'

'We'll hold them off for as long as we can. But I can't make any promises?'

Tannon nodded quickly. Then she turned and paced down the corridor leading back to her room. Porter, Bald, Tully and the Belgians continued upstairs. The landings on the upper floors were eerily silent except for the occasional wail of a child from inside one of the rooms. Two more explosions echoed in the distance as the rebels fired more RPG rounds at the hotel. It seemed to take forever to reach the rooftop and by the time Porter climbed the last set of stairs he could feel his thighs burning, his calves swelling with exertion. He reached the exit a couple of paces ahead of Bald. Slammed his palm down on the crash-bar and charged through the open door. Ready to face down the enemy.

SIXTEEN

0710 hours.

A thick wall of heat hit Porter as he stepped out onto the rooftop. He blinked sweat out of his eyes and glanced around to establish his bearings. The rooftop was forty metres long and twenty-five metres wide. Roughly half the length of a football pitch, and half as wide. There was a water tower in the middle of the rooftop with a set of concrete stairs leading up to it and an iron ladder nailed to one side. An air-conditioning duct snaked across the dusty ground, with several smaller feeds and pipes branching off in every direction. A metre-high parapet ran the perimeter of the rooftop with square drainage holes built into the wall, spaced at one-metre intervals. Each one was big enough to fit a gun barrel through. Porter clambered over the air-con duct and sprinted over to a section of the parapet overlooking the north of the hotel. He worked his way along the roof, scoping out the ground below.

Sixty metres to the north of the hotel stood the access road. Porter could see the abandoned security cordon and the two dead Nigerian soldiers. Directly beyond the sandbags on an east–west axis was the Cape Road, a horizontal grey bar amid patches of brown and green. An abandoned garage with a blue-painted roof was situated on the other side of the Cape Road at Porter's one o'clock, two hundred metres from the hotel. Eight clapped-out motors were parked in front of the garage, rotting under the sun like metal carcasses. A hundred metres further to the east, at his two o'clock, Porter spotted a row of half-finished buildings with piles of festering rubbish heaped in the narrow alleys. Urban tumbleweed. The derelict structures backed onto a banana tree plantation, four hundred metres away. East of the plantation stood the main roundabout with the big baobab tree in the middle, six hundred metres from the hotel. Further east, at his three o'clock, Porter could just about see the faint outline of the Aberdeen Road Bridge, a mile in the distance.

As he looked on four rapid bursts of gunfire split the air. Porter flicked his gaze back to the banana plantation to the north-east. He saw a group of rebels moving down the road parallel to the treeline, four hundred metres from the hotel. Twenty of them, Porter counted. They were wearing brightly coloured shirts and moving in an asymmetrical pattern as they fired wildly, discharging bursts from their AK-47s at a cluster of a dozen or so civilians running for their lives across the Cape Road. Three of the civilians were cut down by the raking bursts of gunfire. The rest ran in the direction of the hotel, desperate to escape the killing frenzy. There was no pattern to the rebels' approach, as far as Porter could tell. No tactics of any kind. They were tearing through the streets and murdering anyone in their wake in an uncoordinated charge, fuelled by drugs and bloodlust. Heading straight for the Ambassadors Hotel.

'Over there,' Bald said, appearing at Porter's shoulder. 'Another twenty X-rays. East of us.'

Porter looked in the direction his mucker was pointing, shading his eyes against the rising sun. Six hundred metres east a second group of rebels was streaming towards the hotel from the direction of the roundabout. The black shapes of several slaughtered civilians dotted the ground either side of the Cape Road. Half of the second group of rebels hurried along the Cape Road, racing after the first group of rebels to the east. The other half broke south and charged across the open ground towards the eastern side of the hotel.

'More coming this way,' one of the Belgians to the south cried.

Porter looked towards the Belgian. He had a shock of blond hair in a widow's peak, muscles like granite, and skin so bronze it looked spray-on. The guy looked like Dolph Lundgren's long-lost twin.

'How many?' Porter asked.

Spray-Tan strained his eyes. 'I count at least fifteen.'

Porter hurried over for a better look. He spotted a tight cluster of rebels manoeuvring in a loose formation through the barren field three hundred metres south of the hotel. They were heading for the low wall backing onto the swimming pool and tennis courts at the rear of the hotel grounds.

Porter thought, *Twenty rebels to the north. Twenty more to the east. Fifteen to the south. At least fifty-five rebels in total.* With more on the way, judging from the shooting and voices in the distance.

And there's only eight of us.

He tensed his neck muscles and turned to the other guys.

'This is what we're gonna do. We'll work in pairs.' He pointed at Nilis. 'You'll go with Bob Tully and take the east. Take two of the Belgians with you. The other two can cover the south. Jock, you're with me,' Porter added, turning to Bald. 'We'll take the north. That way we'll have all the approaches covered.'

Bald smiled grimly. 'About time we gave these pricks a good kicking.'

Porter turned back to the Belgians. 'Kill anything with two legs and a weapon. We've got the advantage of surprise, since the rebels won't have spotted us yet. Make those early rounds count.'

'No problem,' said Nilis, giving a thumbs-up and smiling. Bald rolled his eyes at the guy.

'One more thing,' Porter said, looking at each of the other Belgians in turn. 'Keep an eye out for any fuckers packing RPGs.' He tipped his head at Nilis. 'Your mates know what an RPG looks like?'

'Yes. We used them in training before. Don't worry, we know what to look for.'

'Good. You see an X-ray carrying one, you make sure you put them down. They're the main threat. The AKs only fire 7.62mm short. At this range they won't be able to do much damage. But if they get one of them RPGs on target, anyone inside the hotel room won't stand a fucking chance.'

There was no need for Nilis to translate. His four mates all spoke decent English and understood Porter's instructions. They swiftly divided into two pairs and spread out across the rooftop, lugging their SLRs and spare clips. Tully and Nilis raced over to the section of the parapet overlooking the north-east corner of the hotel, facing out towards the roundabout, with one pair of Belgians setting up shop at the south-east corner. Spray-Tan and the fourth Belgian took up their positions on the south side of the rooftop. Porter and Bald turned back to the north-facing wall and peered down at the Cape Road. The first wave of rebels were three hundred and fifty metres from the hotel now. All twenty of them were rushing across the main road, showing no caution, gesturing at the access road with their machetes and assault rifles. Any half-decent soldiers would have been making their approach behind cover, thought Porter. But these guys weren't trained operators, he reminded himself. They were rapists and thieves and murderers. They weren't technically minded. All they wanted to do was kill the civvies trapped inside the hotel.

Not today.

As he watched, half a dozen of the rebels surged ahead of their mates. Four of them were clutching AK-47 rifles. The fifth guy wore a replica Liverpool shirt with HESKEY on the back, and shouldered an RPG launcher. A sixth rebel wearing a pink skirt ran close behind the guy with the RPG. He was carrying a bag of spare rockets for the launcher. The lead group of rebels were three hundred metres from the front of the hotel now. Porter pointed them out to Bald.

'I'm gonna drop the one with the RPG,' he said calmly. 'Get him wriggling. I'll slot his mate too. Then you light the rest of the fuckers up.'

'Roger that, mate.'

Bald looked on whilst Porter hefted up the SLR and tugged on the bolt handle located on the right-hand side of the receiver. The SLR ker-chacked as the first round of 7.62 milli shunted into the chamber. Porter tucked the stock tight to his right shoulder, with his legs shoulder-width apart and his left arm directly under the rifle supporting its weight. Resting his cheek on the receiver, he peered down the rear iron sighting post and lined up the rebel in the Heskey shirt. The one with the RPG. He was the most immediate threat, because a badly-aimed rocket could do a lot more damage than a badly aimed burst of ammo. Heskey was racing to catch up with his mates several metres further ahead of him, with the rebel in the pink skirt running close behind. Porter relaxed his right shoulder, slid his index finger onto the trigger. Rested the sights on Heskey's groin. Porter didn't want to kill the rebel. A head-shot would merely send the other five rebels running for cover. Which was not ideal, because moving targets were always trickier to hit than static ones. But if he wounded the rebel, one of the other guys would automatically rush over to help. Simple guerrilla warfare tactics, perfected by the Viet Cong against US troops.

He took a deep breath.

Exhaled.

Fired.

The SLR made a satisfying crack as the first round spat out of the snout. The spent jacket flung out of the ejector and landed a few feet away to Porter's right. Down on the main road, Heskey folded at the waist as the round smacked into his balls.

'Target down,' Porter reported, keeping his voice flat and steady. Like a surgeon giving instructions during an operation. All of his mental and physical energies concentrated on making sure he achieved the maximum kill rate.

Heskey released his grip on the RPG and fell to the tarmac in the middle of the Cape Road, squirming in agony and screaming to the others for help. The bait was set. *Now I just need someone to take it.*

The four rebels ahead of the wounded rebel stopped dead in their tracks and glanced around the hotel, looking for the direction the shot had come from. Several metres behind them, the guy in the pink skirt dropped the bag of rockets and bolted forward. His instincts were kicking in. He wouldn't have a clue where the shot had come from, Porter knew. The guy probably wasn't even aware a shot had been fired. But he would have seen his mucker tumble to the ground, and his first instinct would be to go over and help his mate. His second instinct would be to pick up the RPG launcher and get off a shot in revenge. It was basic human psychology.

Porter hovered the SLR sights over the injured rebel and waited for the guy in the pink skirt to rush over. He was unnaturally calm and focused. He was in control of the situation. Setting the stage for the next shot, directing the action.

Waiting for the target to make himself static.

Porter counted to two. He watched the second rebel move directly into his sights.

The guy stopped. Reached down for the RPG launcher.

Then Porter pulled the trigger again.

The SLR kicked up. There was a puff of bright red behind the rebel's head. Or what was left of it. The guy jerked and did the dead man's dance. He dropped like a marionette with the strings cut, landing next to the wounded rebel.

The four rebels ahead saw their friend's head explode and simultaneously turned towards the rooftop, hefted up their rifles and returned fire. They didn't bother to aim properly. They just emptied bursts in the general direction the shooting was coming from. The rounds struck harmlessly wide and low of Porter and Bald's positions.

'Nail those fuckers, Jock,' Porter said.

'About fucking time,' Bald said.

He stepped into view at Porter's right, squeezed the bipod legs together and folded them into the clip on the underside of the barrel. Bald propped the gun on the top of the breeze-block parapet, and adjusted the dial for the sights. Then he pressed the safety button above the pistol grip, switching it from SAFE to FIRE. Down on the Cape Road, the four rebels who had been returning fire ran for cover at the slum dwellings north of the road. Bald depressed the trigger. The gimpy made a deep thunderous roar, blasting Porter's eardrums. Like a chainsaw cutting through a car engine. The GPMG muzzle flashed. The first couple of two-round bursts fell short of the targets by nine or ten metres. The fifth round was the tracer. The marking round. Guiding the shooter towards the targets. It scorched through the air like a bright red arrow pointing to treasure on a map, leaving a puff of smoke on the ground.

The four rebels in the lead group ran on, straining every sinew to reach cover. Like sprinters leaning forward at the finishing line. They were fast. But not fast enough. Bald followed the line of the tracer. Adjusted his elevation. Aimed.

The rebels were ten metres from the slums when he let rip again.

Bald unloaded a dozen rounds at the rebels in two quick bursts. At eight hundred metres a burst from the GPMG was capable of smashing through solid brick walls. At less than half that distance, the rebels didn't stand a chance. The bullets literally chopped one guy in half, severing his torso at the waist in a spray of blood and viscera. The brass punched holes the size of Coke cans in another target, the velocity of the rounds sucking his guts out through his exit wounds. Bald kept firing. The other two rebels disappeared in a cloud of dust and blood and bone fragments.

Porter turned his attention to the other rebels in the first wave, fifty metres further east. Some of them saw their mates getting slotted and ran for cover at the banana plantation north of the Cape Road. One rebel with a bright-yellow beanie hat dropped to a knee beside the road then aimed his RPG launcher at the rooftop. Bald raked him down with a four-round burst before he could fire. The impact knocked the guy off his feet, his right arm jerked up and his finger automatically depressed the trigger. The RPG hissed out of the launcher and burred across the road, thumping into a vehicle parked at the side of the street. The back-blast from the RPG engulfed the rebel immediately behind the target, tearing at his flesh and ripping off his left leg at the knee. One of his mates heard his screams, rushed over and started to drag the wounded rebel away from the kill zone. Porter put a round through the guy's groin and watched him keel over, writhing in agony on the ground. He kept the sights trained on the wounded rebel. Looking to see if any of his mates came to the rescue. But none of the rebels emerged from cover. They had learned their lesson. They had seen what happened to the last guy who tried to help his injured mate, and wisely decided to stay out of sight behind the banana trees. They were getting plenty of on-the-job training today.

Nine targets down, Porter thought.

Forty-five left.

He glanced over his shoulder to see how the other guys were getting on. Over on the eastern side of the parapet, Tully and Nilis were putting down a steady burst of rounds on the rebels advancing from the direction of the roundabout. The pair of Belgians stationed at the south-east corner were dropping the targets trying to make their approach from the direction of the athletics track. Spray-Tan and the fourth Belgian knocked down the rebels advancing from the direction of the barren field to the south of the hotel. The Belgians were communicating with one another in their own language, operating like a separate entity from the other guys. Their shots were striking the enemy with impressive regularity, Porter noticed. None of the Belgians showed any sign of fear or nerves at the situation they were facing. Like pros, he thought.

Nilis took another shot and pumped a fist in delight at scoring a kill. He looked over at Porter and gave him the thumbs-up, grinning with delight.

'Prick,' Bald muttered under his breath.

'He can Fucking shoot, though.'

'So can his mates.'

'I thought they were supposed to be rusty,' Porter said.

Bald shrugged. 'Maybe they're not labourers.'

'What do you mean?'

'Maybe they're with the Belgian military. Maybe they're special forces. Either way, I couldn't give a toss. As long as they know how to fire a weapon.'

Porter looked back to the north and trained his sights on the banana plantation. He caught sight of four enemies scuttling forward from the treeline, running low while their mates at the trees put down covering fire. The rebels were making for the slum dwellings to the west, Porter realised. The reckless bursts from their muckers at the plantation landed well short, hitting the front of the hotel several floors below the rooftop. *These guys might have the upper hand in numbers and firepower*, he thought. *But they can't shoot for shit.*

'Movement,' he said to Bald. 'One o'clock. Four X-rays, heading for the slums.'

'I see the bastards.'

Bald zeroed in on the targets and put down a rapid series of two- and three-round bursts with the gimpy. The bullets thudded into the ground, throwing up geysers of smoke and dirt, forcing the rebels to turn around and head back for the trees in an attempt to escape the blistering gunfire. Porter dropped one guy wearing a Chicago Bulls jersey, nailing him in the leg. The man fell forward, pawing at his rag-order ankle as he screamed at his mates for help. He was still crying when Porter put a single round in the back of his head. His skull exploded in a shower of gristle and brain matter. Porter cut down a second, lanky guy wearing shades before he could scramble for cover, firing twice and nailing him in the upper back. He fell away, the shades tumbling from his face. Bald arced the gimpy across and pulverised the other two retreating rebels, their bodies thrashing wildly as the rounds smashed into them, severing another of the targets at the waist in a glistening bright red shower of entrails.

'More X-rays incoming!' Tully shouted. 'Three o'clock. Thirty of 'em, six hundred metres away.'

'Great,' Bald muttered. 'Just what we fucking need.'

Just then a muzzle flashed at Porter's twelve o'clock. In the next instant a volley of bullets struck much closer to the rooftop, six of them striking the air-conditioning duct two metres to Porter's left, glancing off the metal sheeting and making a din like a thousand hammers banging against a lead pipe. Porter arced his sights across the road and glimpsed another flash coming from the side of the garage west of the treeline. As he watched, three more rebels crept out from behind the banana trees snaked around to the back of the garage before he could line up a shot.

They're changing their tactics, Porter realised. They know they're getting walloped whenever they set foot on the main road. Now they're trying to sneak around us instead. He pointed the garage out to Bald.

'X-rays on the move. Three hundred metres to the front. The building with the blue roof. Get some rounds down on the fuckers.'

'With fucking pleasure, mate.'

Bald trained the GPMG sights on the dwelling. Two shooters fired rounds at the rooftop before ducking out of sight. The rebels figured they were safe behind the side wall of the garage. They were wrong. Bald emptied ten three-round bursts at the wall, aiming for a point midway up, roughly level with the enemies' torsos. The bullets chewed through the concrete as if it was made out of papier-mâché, punching a hole in the wall a foot in diameter and knocking down the rebels hidden behind like they were bowling pins in an alley. The targets collapsed in a tangle of limbs and clothes.

Five more rebels scurried forward from the plantation to the garage. Two of them stopped to fire their rockets at the rooftop before they ducked behind cover. The rockets corkscrewed way off target and burred high over Bald and Porter's heads before whistling into the distance. Bald dropped both of the rebels with the gimpy. Bullets tore through the concrete wall, riddling the targets with hot lead.

'How many more of these fuckers are there?' he said.

Porter had no answer to that. He faced forward and searched for his next target. The rebels were definitely acting more cautiously now, he thought. They were shrinking behind cover as much as possible, loosing off bursts at the rooftop. But they were still crap shots. They were still operating in small, uncoordinated gangs rather than attacking the hotel in an organised military pattern. *As long as they keep this up, thought Porter, we've got a chance of holding them at bay.*

But if someone with proper military experience takes command of this lot, we're in fucking trouble.

A three-round burst walloped into the parapet six inches to his left, flinging hot dust into his face. Porter looked for the tell-tale flash of the muzzle to identify the shooter. Caught a glimpse of the guy in the periphery of his vision, crouching by the wall of one of the derelict structures at his one o'clock. The guy stepped back behind cover before Porter could get a shot off. Porter didn't panic. He just kept his hands steady, trained the SLR's iron sight at the spot where he'd last seen the rebel. Racked the handle just enough to cock the hammer, and waited.

He didn't have to wait long. Two seconds later, the guy popped his head out from the side of the dwelling. He was still hefting up his AK-47 when Porter squeezed the trigger in a smooth, controlled movement, keying into thousands of hours he'd spent on the field firing ranges in Brecon. A hot tongue of flame licked out of the SLR snout. There was a spray of red mist behind the target as the bullet bored through the man's skull before exiting out of the back of his head. Like someone shaking a bottle of Veuve Clicquot then uncorking it.

Now Porter glimpsed two more rebels scuttling around the back of the banana trees. They were heading towards the eastern-most dwelling, taking the place of their slotted mate. He swept the SLR across, lined up the first guy in the metal sights, and nailed him in the chest. The target was still falling away as Porter emptied two rounds in the back of the second rebel moments before he reached cover. The guy tumbled forward, blood spraying out of his exit wounds in bright red torrents.

Thirteen rounds down, Porter reminded himself.

Seven left in the clip.

'Second wave approaching!' Tully shouted from the eastern side of the rooftop. 'Four hundred metres.'

Porter said, 'How many guys will this lot sacrifice until they piss off home?'

'They won't.' Tully wiped sweat from his brow. 'They're like rats, fella. They'll keep coming until they find a way through. They won't stop until they're all dead.'

Porter gritted his teeth and turned back to the rooftop. He looked towards the second wave of enemies approaching the hotel from the direction of the roundabout. He counted thirty of them, moving forward in a fast, loose formation. Bald raked the approaching targets with a few bursts from the gimpy, killing three in quick succession and scattering the rest. Porter traced his sights back to the north, concentrating his fire on the patch of open ground between the banana trees and the slum buildings, dropping any rebels who tried to make a run for cover. Bald peppered the plantation with furious bursts from the gimpy, forcing the rebels massing there to displace. The two operators were working like a well-oiled machine, anticipating each other's moves and providing covering fire the moment either one of them needed to reload. The ground around their feet became littered with spent brass. The air was filled with the continuous crack and whip of gunshots and the hysterical cries of the wounded and dying.

'What's happening with the evacuation?' Bald asked, glancing over his shoulder at the crash door as he spoke. As if he expected to see Tannon come rushing out at any moment with news.

'No fucking idea. Let's deal with these bastarcts first.'

'What happens if we run out of ammo before the rebels run out of bodies to throw at us?'

'We won't,' Porter said. 'It's just a matter of time till help gets here.'

But in truth, he had been thinking the same thing as Bald. If the rebels keep attacking us, eventually we're gonna have to start conserving ammo, he thought. Even these idiots soon figure out that we're running low on rounds. When that happens, we're gonna be in the shit.

Big time.

By now the sun had fully risen above the bay, bleaching the sky an acid blue. Porter glanced at his G-Shock and was amazed to see it was a few minutes past eight o'clock. Which meant they'd been putting rounds down on the enemy for over an hour. But the rebels showed no signs of giving up their assault. Ten or so rebels from the second wave had managed to advance across the gap from the banana trees to the slum dwellings, while the other fifteen rebels bunkered down at the plantation to provide covering fire, unleashing erratic volleys of 7.62mm short at the rooftop. They were emptying entire clips with no regard for conserving their ammo.

They're being careless with their rounds, Porter noted. Which could only mean one thing.

They must have a lot more ammo than us.

By nine o'clock in the morning, the rebels' gunfire had become increasingly accurate. At least twenty enemies had migrated from the slum dwellings to the garage directly north of the hotel, taking up firing points that brought them closer into range of the rooftop. A four-round burst landed dangerously close, slapping into the wall several inches to the right of Porter. The rebels were also shrinking back behind cover before Porter could put the drop on them.

'Twelve o'clock,' he said to Bald. 'The garage. The old cars outside.'

Bald dropped to his front and folded out the legs on the GPMG bipod. Then he pointed the muzzle through the drainage hole located midway up the parapet and rattled off shots at a group of three rebels crouched behind one of the abandoned motors in front of the building. Still the rebels kept pouring forward. Tight clusters of six or ten arrived to reinforce their mates at the plantation, allowing the other rebels to scurry forward under suppressive fire. By mid-morning the enemy had managed to advance to within three hundred metres of the hotel. Half a dozen had reached cover inside the garage itself. Bald and Porter kept applying the pressure with frequent well-aimed bursts. More than twenty bodies now lay sprawled across the ground north of the hotel. Porter dropped another rebel, emptied his clip and grabbed a fresh mag from his trouser pocket. He was on his fourth clip now. Which meant he had expended more than sixty rounds. *Eight rounds left before I run out of ammo.* He glanced over at Bald and saw that his mucker had used up two belts of ammo. Between them they had fired almost five hundred rounds.

Every time one attack stalled under the oppressive weight of gunfire, the rebels switched their efforts to one of the other approaches to the hotel. Twice Bald and Porter had to migrate across the rooftop to reinforce Spray-Tan and the fourth Belgian. The operators couldn't clamber over the air-con duct since that risked making them visible above the parapet to the targets below, so they had to crawl around the vents on all fours to reach the other sides of the roof. Wave after wave of rebels attacked the hotel from the east and south in groups of six or eight. Rounds chipped away at the concrete and ricocheted off the water tower.

They're getting closer, Porter thought. He felt a pang of anxiety in his guts. *Whatever help is on the way, it had better get here soon.*

'Need some help over here!' Spray-Tan called out from the south-facing parapet.

Bald and Porter dashed across the rooftop. Nilis joined them, leaving Tully and the two other Belgians to put down fire on the rebels advancing from the north-east at the roundabout. Porter hit the southern-facing wall and peered out through one of the drainage holes. Two dozen fighters were closing in on the rear of the hotel. They had cleared the barren field to the south and reached the low wall a hundred and fifty metres away, a short distance beyond the swimming pool. Bald cut down a loose cluster of rebels climbing over the wall with a savage hail of gunfire, the gimpy barrel glowing red as the bullets tore into the enemies, ripping apart their limbs and decapitating some. A couple of the smarter rebels hunkered down behind the far side of the wall. Porter picked them off as soon as they poked their heads out of cover.

As Porter searched for his next target he saw with horror that two of the rebels had managed to clear the wall to the rear of the hotel grounds. They were making for a row of storage sheds a hundred metres from the back doors leading into the restaurant.

These two rebels looked to be much younger than the others, Porter noticed. They were no older than eleven or twelve years of age. They were seventy metres from the storage sheds now. Porter tracked the nearest child through his iron sights. A bony kid dressed in a blood-red tank top, with a green bandana tied around his shaven head. He looked less like a killer, and more like a kid in fancy dress playing Rambo.

Porter saw Bald line up the kid.

'Do we have to put them down too, Jock? They're just kids, for fuck's sake.'

Bald hesitated. Before he could respond Porter heard the crack of a rifle discharge at his nine o'clock as Nilis fired a single shot from his SLR. The bullet smashed into Rambo's gut and sent him tumbling to the ground fifty metres from the sheds. The second kid made the mistake of looking over his shoulder at his mate, stopping momentarily in his tracks. Long enough for Nilis to reset his aim and pop the kid through his left shoulder. The second kid dropped to the ground a few paces from Rambo. The two of them clutching their wounds, their hysterical screams piercing the burnt air.

'Got them!' Nilis said, grinning. He gave Bald the thumbs-up again. 'Now that's what I call shooting, my friend.'

The two wounded kids continued wailing. Bald lined up the two screaming children with the gimpy, ready to put them out of their misery. Nilis thrust out a hand and rested it on top of the machine gun. Looked Bald hard in the eye.

'No,' he said. 'Let them suffer.'

He stared at Bald a moment longer. Then he grinned again and went back to his firing position on the parapet, putting down rounds on the dozen or so rebels still picking their way across the hotel grounds. Porter stared at Nilis in disbelief, stunned at the casual way the Belgian had dropped the two kids. Like it was nothing at all, he thought. Like this wasn't the first time he'd killed somebody. Maybe Bald's right, Porter told himself. Maybe these guys really are Belgian SF. *But if that's true, what are they doing here in the first place?*

A shout from Tully drew his attention to the north.

'Technical!' he yelled. 'Three o'clock. Coming your way, fellas!'

Bald and Porter scrambled back across the rooftop, rounds striking the parapet and the air-con duct. Porter slid off the duct half a second before three bullets struck the metal sheeting. He ducked low at the northern wall and looked in the direction of the roundabout to the east. Saw a dust trail drifting up into the sky. A battered white Hilux was rolling down the Cape Road, doing twenty miles per. Four rebels were jogging alongside the pickup, using it to cover their approach to the hotel. A fifth guy stood on the platform on the back of the Hilux. He was manning a heavy machine gun mounted on a tripod, ammo belt swaying in the breeze. Even at a distance of four hundred metres, Porter readily identified the weapon as a Russian-manufactured Dushka. An anti-aircraft gun chambered for the 12.7x108mm round, the Soviet equivalent of the NATO .50 calibre bullet. The kind of weapon that could put down a herd of elephants from a mile away. At a range of four hundred metres, it was lethal.

'Where the fuck did they get that thing from?' Bald said.

'Probably from one of the army units that defected,' Porter said. 'Or maybe they grabbed it from one of the armouries the bastards looted.'

Either way, if the rebels get that thing on target, we're shafted.

Bald and Porter instantly switched their focus to the approaching Hilux. They both swivelled their weapons away from the foot soldiers, training their sights on the immediate threat. Bald unloaded a quick burst at the pickup, aiming for the guy manning the Dushka. Not an easy shot, Porter knew. A fast-moving target at a range of three hundred and fifty metres, with a weapon like the GPMG, presented a formidable challenge even for a seasoned SAS man like Bald. The gimpy thundered. The six rounds missed their target, striking the tarmac two metres to the left of the pickup.

'Bastard,' Bald cursed.

'Three hundred metres,' Porter said. 'Hurry.'

The Hilux driver suddenly hit the gas. The pickup lurched forward, tyres screeching as it bulleted west along the road, leaving the four gunmen trailing in its wake. In the same beat the guy manning the Dushka swung the heavy machine gun up and across, and there was a white-hot flash at the muzzle as he discharged six rounds at the rooftop. Gases snorted out of the sides of the barrel. A series of deep low thumps echoed across the sky as the rounds spat out. Porter saw the Hilux jolting with the weapon recoil. Rounds the size of beer bottles pinged out of the side of the ejector. Two of the bullets chopped into a palm tree directly in front of the hotel, felling it. Three rounds struck higher, slamming into the concrete below the parapet, each one landing higher than the last. Like notes in a musical crescendo. The sixth bullet blew a hole in the section of the wall six inches to the left of Porter, smothering his face with bits of concrete and a cloud of hot dust.

'Drop him!' he yelled. 'NOW, JOCK!'

Bald zeroed his aim and fired again. The first two bullets zipped over the top of the Toyota. The next three rounds were the bullseye shots. They smacked into the rebel on the machine gun in a close grouping, ripping open his bowels. His arms fell away from the handles of the heavy machine gun as Bald trained his sights on the front cab and unleashed another five-round burst. The rounds struck the driver's side door and bored through the metal like a ticket punch through a paper card, nailing the bloke behind the wheel. Blood splashed across the front windscreen. The Hilux veered sharply off to the right, crashing into one of the knackered motors parked in front of the garage. There was the shrieking of twisted metal and the shattering of glass. The car horn sounding its urgent blaring note, like a mechanical scream.

'Still fucking got it,' Bald said, flashing a grin.

Porter switched his attention east, to the four gunmen in the middle of the road. They suddenly began racing towards the knackered pickup. Porter instinctively grasped what was happening.

'Four X-rays going for the Dushka,' he said. 'Knock that fucker out!'

'On it, mate.'

One of the gunmen climbed onto the back platform of the Hilux and reached for the Dushka. Bald unloaded a burst at him as he grabbed the handles. The rounds hit him with such force that they knocked him off the back of the pickup. Bald adjusted his aim slightly and directed a continuous stream of rounds on the fuel tank located at the rear of the Hilux. The first six rounds punched through the tank. The next six caused the tank to burst into flames. The three other gunmen who had been running towards the pickup stopped short as the fire consumed the vehicle, the heat and fumes making it impossible to operate the Dushka. They turned away from the burning pickup and scurried towards the rear of the garage twelve metres away. Porter and Bald put down a series of raking bursts on the rebels, dropping all of them.

Another ten rebels advanced from the derelict buildings, reinforcing the dozen or so camped out at the garage. Porter was down to his last two clips. Forty rounds left, he thought. There were more clips downstairs but if the waves of rebels kept coming, he knew that eventually they would have to start rationing ammo.

He looked out across the Cape Road. Saw a larger group of rebels emerging from behind the slum dwellings, racing towards the access road. Fourteen of them. Half of the enemy were equipped with RPGs. They were less than two hundred metres from the hotel now. Dangerously close.

'Shit,' Bald said.

'Some more firepower over here!' Porter called out.

Tully and Nilis hustled over from the eastern flank to help deal with the threat, leaving the two Belgians to put down rounds on the rebels at the pavilion. Spray-Tan and the fourth Belgian continued to brass up the enemies along the southern flank of the hotel. Porter went to fire but then Tully shouted out at him and Porter ducked low as a rocket fired over his head, missing him by less than a foot. Then his training kicked in. Porter immediately, raised his SLR, following the evaporating trail of smoke. He trained the iron sights on a rebel crouching beside one of the slums. Porter dropped the guy as he finished loading another round into the RPG. He jack-knifed and fell forward, firing the RPG into the ground. The rocket detonated and sent a violent hissing surge of soil and debris and body parts high into the air. Another target knelt down to fire his launcher. Porter gave him the good news as well.

'Down there, mate!' Bald roared. 'Twelve o'clock!'

As Bald spoke another RPG thudded into the vacant lower floors of the hotel. Glass shattered. Acrid black smoke swept up and across the roof, burning the operators' lungs and obscuring their view of the targets along the Cape Road. The smoke cleared. Then Porter saw them. Seven rebels, directly below his position on the rooftop. They had reached the turn in the access road leading down to the front of the hotel. In his determination to slot the guys with the RPGs, Porter had missed them. They had already raced past the sandbags and were now zigzagging their way down the left-hand side of the road towards the entrance to the hotel. They were thirty metres away, Porter figured. Way ahead of their muckers.

Closing fast.

He raised his gun arm and arced his sights down at the onrushing targets. From a height of forty metres the angle was tight and Porter had to lean over the side of the parapet to get a fix on the enemy. Any moment now they were going to slip out of sight, he knew. He had one chance to nail them. He stilled his breath, depressed the trigger twice. The first round missed. The second hit the rearmost rebel in the groin and sent him dropping to the ground like a hot brick. But the six other rebels disappeared from view before Porter could adjust his aim. They rushed past the shuttered entrance to the underground car park and made directly for the main entrance.

Porter spun away from the wall. Looked to Tully. Said, 'Stay here and keep this lot back. Keep firing until no one's left standing. Got it?'

Tully nodded. 'Where are you going?'

'To stop those lunatics from getting inside the hotel.'

Nilis overheard them and said, 'I'll come with you. There's six of them. Two of us stand a better chance of stopping them than one.' He grinned. 'Besides, it's a chance to kill more of these savages.'

The Belgian looked relaxed. Confident. Like he wasn't afraid. Porter wondered again about that. But there wasn't time to worry about Nilis and his mates. He thought about the flimsy barricade at the entrance to the hotel, and knew it wouldn't take long for the rebels to break through it. *Unless we hit these fuckers hard and fast, everyone inside this hotel is done for.* He nodded quickly at Nilis.

'Follow me.'

Then he turned and hurried across the rooftop towards the stairwell.

SEVENTEEN

1058 hours.

Porter launched down the stairs. Blood rushing in his ears, muscles aching with the strain of combat. The sounds of the firefight rattling through the upper floors of the hotel. Nilis lagged a couple of steps behind, breathing hard. A crashing boom sounded from one of the lower floors. The walls shook as another RPG struck the front of the hotel. Porter could hear the broken glass hailstoning, the flames seething. He ran on. He didn't think about dying. He didn't think about what might happen in the next few hours, or whether the enemy might win the battle. He thought no further ahead than the next ten seconds. *Get down to the ground floor. Kill the rebels. Stop them from massacring the civilians.*

As they raced down the main stairwell Porter and Nilis passed several small groups of Nigerian soldiers hunkering down on the landings. Others were slumped against the walls of the corridors branching off to the left and right of the stairwells. A few had crammed inside whatever empty rooms they could find. They stared back at Porter with their wide round eyes as he swept past. There was no shame or embarrassment on their faces at avoiding the firefight. Just evident relief that they weren't having to take the battle to the enemy. Porter gritted his teeth in anger at their cowardice as he pushed on.

A thick cloud of black smoke greeted the two men as they reached the second floor. Porter glanced to his left. Saw the reflected orange glow of a fire raging inside a room at the far end of the main corridor, twenty metres away. Crowder and a trio of volunteers stood inside the doorway of the north-facing room, dousing down the flames with fire extinguishers and buckets of water. Other teams of volunteers rushed up and down the corridors, struggling to deal with the fires that had broken out when the RPG rounds had struck the hotel. Porter swept past them and made for the staircase leading down to the first floor. He ran into a heavily bearded guy in a bright blue suit scrabbling up the stairs. One of the Lebanese businessmen he'd seen trying to leave the hotel the previous day. The guy waved his arms at Porter, calling out between ragged gasps for breath.

'Help!' the man cried, panting heavily. 'Please. They're killing them!'

Porter halted and said, 'Who?'

'My uncles,' the man replied, pointing down the stairs. 'They went down to the lobby, to see if they could leave. Then the rebels came in and attacked. You have to help them!'

'Wait here,' Porter ordered.

He stepped past the terrified Lebanese and moved more slowly down the next flight of stairs, with Nilis falling in a metre behind. Weapon stocks tucked against their shoulders, eyes scanning the floor below. Ready to bring up their SLRs and shoot at the first sign of movement. Porter stopped at the first floor and checked both sides of the main corridor. Once he was sure the landing was clear he inched around to the left and paused at the top of the stairs, checking the area immediately below. There was an intermediate landing halfway down before the stairs changed direction by 180 degrees and led straight to the ground floor. Porter couldn't see any sign of the rebels on the lower landing but he heard several shouts echoing from down in the lobby. He knew then that the rebels had broken through the front barricade.

An unsettling thought prodded at him. *Why aren't the rebels charging up the stairs?* That's what I'd be doing, he thought. Heading straight for the upper floors to ambush the shooters camped on the rooftop. But these guys are still on the ground floor.

Why?

He shoved aside the thought and signalled to Nilis, motioning for the Belgian to follow him. They crept down the treads and hit the lower landing. Then Porter stopped at the blind corner. The shouts were louder now. They sounded almost delirious. Like a bunch of football fans cheering a penalty decision for their team. Porter moved over to the edge of the banister, motioned to Nilis and moved down the first tread. Then the second, and a third. He crept down until he was halfway down the stairs. Then he turned to his left and looked beyond the banister at the front of the lobby.

Six rebels stood around in a semi-circle in the middle of the lobby, fifteen metres away from Porter, either side of a pair of lavish marble pillars. Behind them, Porter could see the upturned piano and a sea of shattered glass from where the rebels had forced their way through the makeshift barricade blocking the entrance. He glanced through the open doors at the hotel grounds. Empty. No sign of any other advancing enemy forces. Which made sense, Porter knew. The rebels were operating independently of one another, attacking in uncoordinated waves. Somehow these guys had slipped through the net, but the rest of the enemy fighters were still struggling to advance under the weight of fire raining down on them from the rooftop. There was no immediate danger of reinforcements arriving, Porter decided.

He turned his attention back to the six rebels. In front of them lay a pair of bloodied Lebanese. One of the victims was slumped against one of the pillars. Dark blood pumped out of a puckered wound to his throat. He was already dead. The other Lebanese was on the floor next to him, kicking and screaming on the floor as one of the rebels hacked away at him with his machete. The victim gasped in pain as the rebel slashed open his guts in a single clean blow. Then the guy with the machete grabbed a handful of the man's intestines and ripped them out of his stomach and held them aloft. Like they were some kind of trophy. The other rebels had their backs to the stairs as they hooted and cheered with excitement, fuelled by drugs, alcohol and bloodlust. Porter took one look at the rebels and understood why they hadn't charged up the stairs. *These guys aren't thinking tactically.*

They just want to kill.

Porter brought up his SLR as he edged further down the stairs alongside Nilis. The Belgian had his weapon raised too. Index finger tense on the trigger.

The rebels didn't see them coming.

Porter looked down the length of the barrel at the rebel holding up the intestines. There was no time to aim properly. The target was too close. At a range of fifteen metres, it all came down to instinct. A combination of reflexes, muscle memory and thousands of hours of weapon-handling. Porter double-tapped the guy. The rounds struck just below the neck and passed through him, thumping into the rebel standing to his rear and nailing him in the broad trunk of his chest.

Two targets down.

Everything happened in a blur. The three other rebels spun away from their slotted mates and turned towards the stairs. One guy in a bright orange shirt and Ray-Bans snapped up his weapon and fired at Porter, spraying bullets from the hip. The classic Hollywood pose. The rounds thwacked into the stairs half a metre in front of Porter and chewed up the bannister to his left, spitting wood into his face. Porter moved swiftly down the stairs and dropped the guy before he could fire again, emptying two rounds into his groin. The rebel grunted as he fell back, cupping a hand to his shredded balls. Then Porter put a third round between his eyes.

In the same breath a fourth rebel trained his AK-47 at the stairs. Porter saw the new threat too late. The guy had time to aim his rifle while Porter had been knocking down the three other rebels. He had half a second to react before the guy fired, Porter realised. Not enough time to pivot, adjust his aim and squeeze off a round. Not even close. For a cold instant Porter thought he was going to die. Then there was a brilliant flash of orange at his three o'clock as Nilis surged forward, rattling off a three-round burst at the target. He fired and moved with precision, displaying the kind of shooting skills that wouldn't have looked out of place in the Regiment. The rebel's head snapped back as the bullets tore into his skull. His gun arm tilted upwards, reflexively pumping out a burst at the ceiling before he stacked it, the bullets punching out lights on the tacky chandelier.

The fifth rebel stood to the immediate right of the guy Nilis had dropped. He was dressed in a patterned skirt and sandals, and he was the slowest of the bunch. Nilis unloaded a three-round burst at the rebel before he could loose off a shot. The rounds struck the guy in the upper chest, tunnelled through his vitals and exited through his back, spiderwebbing the glass doors behind him. He stumbled backwards and crashed into the stack of weapons and kit left by the Nigerians. He didn't get back up.

One rebel left to kill. Porter hit the lowest tread, his weapon still raised. The sixth rebel swung his weapon towards Porter in a blur of motion. A muscular guy in knee-length basketball shorts and pecs the size of hubcaps. He had a black leather grenade belt slung diagonally across his bare chest with half a dozen hand grenades secured in the elastic loops. Hubcap shaped to open fire at Porter. His three-round burst struck high, zipping over Porter's head and thudding into the treads at his nine o'clock. The guy reset his aim. He wasn't a great shooter. But at a range of fifteen metres, he didn't need to be, Porter told himself. *He just needs to get lucky.*

Make the next shot count.

Porter stayed calm. He lined up the barrel with Hubcap's centre mass. Aiming for the biggest target, to give himself the best chance of a hit. He squeezed the trigger a fraction of a second before Hubcap fired. The round struck ten inches high. The upper half of Hubcap's face exploded. Blood squirted out of the lower half, spraying the pillar with brain matter and bits of skull. The guy dropped, landing on top of the gutted Lebanese.

Porter scrambled forward, sidestepping the slotted rebels. He hit the entrance and through the doorway sighted two more rebels. They were picking their way down the access road forty metres away. One guy had the greyhound build of a long-distance runner. He was sprinting ahead of his mate, chopping his stride. He was thirty-five metres away from the front of the hotel now. He never made it to thirty-four. Porter swiftly dropped to a crouching firing stance, lined up the target and squeezed the trigger twice. Nailing Greyhound in the throat and upper chest. The second guy kept on running. He wore a blonde wig and a floral dress and waved a machete above his head, screaming madly. Porter emptied three rounds into Blondie's torso, knocking him down.

'Secure the breach!' he yelled to Nilis.

The two men hurried over to the lounge area to the right of the entrance. A trio of worn mid-century sofas arranged around a long, dark-wood coffee table, enclosed by a bunch of exotic plants. Porter slung his SLR over his shoulder and pointed to the coffee table. He grabbed one end of it while Nilis heaved up the other. They lugged the table over to the entrance and tipped it onto its side so that the smooth top surface was pressed up against the door, with the table legs pointing out at the lobby. Like the pins on a plug.

They were still dragging over one of the sofas to reinforce the barricade when Porter heard the crisp, urgent shattering of glass at his six o'clock. He stopped what he was doing and looked south of the lobby. Nilis looked in the same direction. Down the corridor, past the manager's office and the staff room. Towards the tall glass windows fifteen metres away at the far end of the corridor, overlooking the terrace at the rear of the hotel. The windows had been sealed off the previous day, Porter recalled.

Then he saw the rebels.

Two of them had climbed through one of the barricaded windows, smashing apart the glass pane and knocking aside the stack of interlocking chairs that had been placed in front of the window. Furniture and broken glass lay scattered across the lobby floor. Porter looked on in horror as a third guy clambered through the opening and dropped down from the window, clutching his AK-47 and joining his two mates. In another couple of seconds, they'll have sighted us, Porter realised. We've got nowhere to take cover. They'll slaughter us.

Nilis sprang into action. He rushed over to Hubcap, knelt down beside his corpse and grabbed one of the F1 grenades from his leather belt. Then he yanked out the pin and launched the grenade in an overarm throw at the three rebels. It hit the floor, bounced up and then the ground shuddered and there was a dull boom as the grenade detonated. Porter heard a scream as the rebels disappeared in a cloud of smoke and splintering steel. The explosion ripped through the targets and blasted the pictures hanging from the walls either side of the corridor, scarring the corridor. The rebels were strewn across the floor in front of the window, their skin shredded and blackened. Blood everywhere. Chunks of masonry collapsed from the ceiling, falling on their lifeless bodies like burnt snowflakes.

More voices sounded from the other side of the window. Nilis snatched another grenade from Hubcap's belt, sprinted forward and lobbed it through the window opening. There was another dull, damp crack of thunder from the terrace as the second grenade detonated. Porter heard the hideous screams of those rebels trapped in the fragmentation area. He trained his SLR on the window in case any more rebels attempted to climb through the breach. But no one came.

Nilis stepped back from the window and flashed a chummy smile at Porter. 'That showed those sons of bitches, no?'

Porter stared at the Belgian. This guy is a complete nutter, he thought. Once this is over, I'm going to find out who this bloke and his mates really are.

He heard footsteps to the left. Coming from the restaurant. Porter instinctively swung to face the restaurant, his index finger curling around the SLR trigger. Three shadowed figures approached the lobby. For a cold second Porter feared more rebels had broken into the hotel. But then the figures stepped out of the shadows and he saw that the guys were dressed in the same cheap suits as the two dead Lebanese. They had the same dark features and thick moustaches. The same tacky gold watches strapped to their wrists. They were identical to the dead guys. Except they hadn't been carved up with a machete.

One of the Lebanese stepped warily towards Porter, his chubby hands raised above his head. Then he saw his dead friends, and his expression crumbled. His face trembled with unspeakable grief.

Porter had no time to comfort the guy. 'Anyone else back there?' he said, pointing at the restaurant.

The fat guy regained his composure and shook his head. 'No. Just us. We hid in the kitchen as soon as we saw the rebels coming.' His eyes wandered back to the dead Lebanese. 'We heard them. We heard our friends screaming for help and we did nothing.'

'Make yourselves useful,' Porter said, pointing to the window. 'Get that fucking breach barricaded properly. Stack it with furniture and anything else you can get your hands on. Anything to stop them fuckers getting in. Unless you want to end up looking like your mates.'

The Lebanese stared at his dead friends and nodded vaguely. Porter looked towards the two other Lebanese.

'You. Search the rebels for weapons and ammo.'

One of the guys stared in trepidation at the slotted rebels.

'Search . . . these men?' he asked anxiously.

'Aye,' Porter replied. 'We're going to need every round we can get our hands on. Whatever you find, bring it up to the roof. Get a move on.'

The Lebanese nodded at his mate. They both took a deep breath and tentatively approached the corpses. Porter gave his back to them and looked towards Nilis.

'Back to the roof. Let's go.'

They hurried past the slotted rebels, boots brushing aside the spent jackets as they pounded back up the stairs. The non-stop whip-cracks of gunfire had faded to the occasional dull boom now, and Porter figured the rebels outside must be in retreat.

We might win this battle after all.

Keep going.

Don't stop now.

They hit the second floor and moved down the corridor. Crowder and his team of volunteers were still tackling the blaze. They had extinguished most of the bigger fires and were now dousing down the few remaining pockets. Now, suddenly, above the crackle and hiss of the flames, Porter could hear dozens of cries and shouts from the rooms on the floor directly above. Nilis stopped and tilted his head at Porter.

'You think they've managed to breach the upper floors?'

Porter listened then shook his head. 'They've been screaming for a while. If they were being hacked up, they would have fallen silent by now.'

But the screams did tell Porter something. The civilians must be absolutely terrified, he thought. They reminded him of the awesome responsibility that lay on his shoulders. There's a thousand people in this building, relying on us to keep them safe. We can't let them down.

We can't let the rebels win.

As he moved towards the stairwell he heard Soames beating his fists on the storeroom door. The guy's muffled voice shouting from the other side of the door, demanding to be let out. Porter breezed past a pair of Nigerian soldiers sitting on their arses by the stairwell, and made for the storeroom. Dug out the set of janitor's keys from his trouser pocket. Twisted the key in the lock. Shoved the door open.

In the doorway, wearing a face like an Arab at a Gay Pride parade, stood Soames.

'Porter. Christ!' he said in a hoarse tone. 'Took you long enough. What the bloody hell is going on out there?'

'The rebels are throwing everything they've got at us,' Porter replied firmly. 'RPG rounds, heavy machine-gun fire, the lot. There's a hundred of them out there and more arriving every minute.'

'What happened to the Nigerians?'

'They fucked off at the first sign of trouble.'

Soames looked stunned. 'Then who's protecting us?'

'We are,' said Porter. 'Me and Jock and Bob Tully. And a few of the guests,' he added, gesturing to Nilis.

Soames clapped eyes on the Belgian. A brief look of suspicion crossed his face. Then Soames swung his gaze back to Porter. 'I see. Perhaps you and I might have a word in private.'

Porter nodded at Nilis. 'Go on. I'll catch up with you.'

The Belgian stared curiously at Soames for a beat. Then he nodded. 'Sure. Whatever you say, chief.'

He turned away from the storeroom and bounded up the stairs. Soames watched him, waiting until the guy had disappeared from view before he spoke again.

'Who's that fellow?'

'An engineer,' Porter responded. 'Him and his four mates work for a mining company. They're helping us out on the roof.'

That look of suspicion resurfaced on Soames's face. His left eyebrow arched up a couple of inches. 'They can handle a weapon?'

'They did national service in Belgium. If it wasn't for them, we'd be fucked by now. As it stands, we're just about holding the fort.'

Soames nodded gravely. 'Listen to me. We need to leave right now. There's a jetty to the north. I know it well enough. There are usually a few fishing boats moored there, and I'm sure we can bribe the fishermen to lend us one of their boats. It won't be enough to get everyone out, of course, but we can escape up the coast.'

Porter thought for a beat, then shook his head. 'I can't. If we leave, everyone inside this hotel is dead.'

'They're dead anyway. Face it. You don't stand a chance. A handful of defenders against an army? It's no contest. You and I both know the people in here are done for. But we still have a chance to get out.'

'We?'

'You, me, Jock and Bob. Who else do you think is going to come? Those boats don't hold many. It's our only option.'

181

'We'd never make it to the jetty,' Porter said. 'The rebels have got this place surrounded. The minute we set foot outside, they'd cut the lot of us down. We're better off waiting for help to arrive.'

'Don't be a damned fool! You won't be able to hold the rebels off for long. Can't you see? This whole place is going to be over-run. They'll massacre the bloody lot of us.'

His booming voice carried down the corridor, reaching the ears of the volunteers dealing with the fires. Porter stepped towards Soames and stared levelly at him.

'Keep your fucking voice down. Unless you want everyone inside this hotel to start panicking.'

Soames snorted in derision and folded his arms across his chest. 'I don't take orders from you, Porter. You have no authority here.'

'Maybe not.' Porter shrugged. 'But this is my world now, not yours. I'm the one calling the shots. Now get back in that room and keep your mouth shut, or you and me have got a fucking problem.'

Soames glowered at him but said nothing. *He's not even offered to give us a hand on the rooftop*, thought Porter. This arsehole doesn't give a toss about anyone but himself. *Even when our necks are on the line.*

'Think about what you're doing,' Soames said.

'I have,' Porter said. 'And I'm not leaving. That's final.'

'At least give me a gun, then. I need to be able to defend myself if the worst happens.'

Porter shook his head. 'Ammo's in short supply. We need every spare round for the rooftop.'

'What am I supposed to do, for God's sake?' Soames protested, throwing up his arms. 'Just sit here and wait to die?'

'Write yourself a fucking citation. You're good at that.'

He yanked the door shut and locked it before Soames could reply. Then he turned and raced up the stairs, as the sounds of the battle continued to rage outside.

EIGHTEEN

The gunfire had almost petered out as Porter hurried towards the roof. He passed a couple of Nigerian soldiers who'd sought cover in the concrete stairwell leading to the top side of the hotel, swept through the crash door, and stepped out into a blinding white heat. Porter shaded his eyes against the sun as he glanced around. Bald had manoeuvred across to the east-facing side of the rooftop with Tully, Nilis and two of the four Belgians, picking off the rebels with occasional bursts from the GPMG. Spray-Tan and the fourth Belgian were still manning the south side of the roof over-looking the rear of the hotel. Porter dropped to his front and crawled around the air-conditioning duct, careful not to present himself as a target to the enemy. Bullets pinged against the side of the water tower as he edged over to the eastern section of the parapet. Porter rejoined the fight alongside Bald, resting his SLR on top of the wall. He peered through the sights as he searched for his next target.

Most of the rebels had begun beating a hasty retreat from the fight. Around forty of them were withdrawing east along the Cape Road. Several rebels stopped to fire at the rooftop, wild bursts that fell hopelessly wide and short. The rest of the enemy had already turned their backs on the defenders and fled towards the main roundabout in the east. A pocket of six rebels stubbornly held their ground at the plantation, but Bald hosed them down with blasts of 7.62mm brass every time they tried to advance and they soon began falling back after their mates. Porter sighted one rebel dragging away a wounded mate with a bloodied patch on his right leg. He lined up the injured rebel in the SLR's sights and finished the job, shooting him twice in the upper chest. The second rebel let go of his dead mucker, turned and ran on towards the roundabout. He disappeared behind the baobab tree before Porter could put the drop on him.

Bald emptied another burst at a pair of fleeing rebels. A tracer round flashed across the bullet-scarred tarmac and smacked into one of the rebels at the hip, severing his leg. The guy toppled over, blood squirting out of his ragged stump. Bald pumped another burst into him, stitching his guts with lead. The shooting stopped as the last rebels withdrew out of the line of fire. Then a heavy silence settled over the rooftop. Porter eased his finger off the SLR trigger. A palpable sense of relief washed over him. No one said anything for a while. Bald grinned at Porter.

'That's the last of them chogie bastards. Looks like we've taught them a lesson they won't forget in a hurry.'

'Don't count on it, fellas. They'll be back soon enough,' Tully said. 'The rebels won't give up that easily. They're stubborn fuckers. Once they've licked their wounds, they'll have another crack at us.'

'How long until they hit us again?' Porter said.

Tully shrugged. 'Depends.'

'On what?'

'On whether any of those chogies has got green-army experience. If someone shows up with a military background, they'll take their time to assess the situation before attacking us. Otherwise, they'll attack once they've smoked a few joints and given themselves some confidence. Either way, we're gonna get hit again soon. This afternoon, probably.'

'How long are they gonna keep this up?' said Bald.

'As long as it takes,' Tully responded. 'Until they run out of bodies.'

Or until we run out of ammo, Porter thought.

Nilis kept his rifle sights trained on the road to the east. 'X-rays still active at the roundabout,' he reported. 'Twenty of them. Seven hundred metres away.'

184

'Keep eyes on,' said Porter. 'Check the other approaches too. We need 360 coverage. The minute those bastards are on the move again we need to know about it.'

Just then Porter heard a grating groan. He glanced over his shoulder and saw Tannon emerging from the crash door at the top of the concrete stairwell. She stopped by the door and gazed around the rooftop in a kind of daze. Gunpowder and lead particles and smoke hung in the air like a thin, dirty film. A couple of rounds thundered in the middle distance as the rebels grouped by the roundabout continued to take pot-shots at the defenders on the roof. They couldn't hit a barn door from this distance but Porter didn't want to take any chances. 'Stay low!' he shouted at Tannon. 'Don't make yourself a target.'

She snapped out of her daze and dropped low. Then she inched forward, tentatively working her way around the air-con duct to join Porter and the others at the parapet. Tannon cautiously surveyed the bullet-chipped wall and the brass and debris scattered across the ground. Then she stared at Porter with a horrified look. A quick glance at the others explained her reaction. Porter and his fellow defenders cut a terrifying sight. Their hands and faces were blackened with smoke. Their clothes caked in dust, blood and sweat.

'Is it over?' she asked.

'Not by a long shot,' Porter said. 'What's going on with the evacuation?'

Tannon shook her head. 'I can't get through. My sat phone is dead, and all the telephone lines in the hotel are down. The radios too. The only station still on the air is the state-run radio, and that's just repeating the same message from the RUF spokesperson. Nothing's working.'

'The rebels must have taken over the main telephone exchange,' Porter said.

Bald nodded. 'Oldest trick in the book. Spread your propaganda message over the airwaves and get everyone to turn against the government.'

'What are we going to do?' Tannon said.

Her voice was shaking. Like someone plucking a length of tautened string. Her eyes kept returning to the bullet-riddled parapet, as if she expected the rebels to attack again any moment. She's trying to act as if it's business as usual, he thought. *Trying to put a lid on the anxiety she's feeling. But she's not fooling anyone.*

Porter dug the sat phone out of his back pocket. The handset was coated in a layer of dust and there was a massive crack running down the screen. But it was still in working order. The battery icon on the display was showing two bars. Roughly three hours of battery life, Porter thought. He passed the phone to Tannon.

'Use ours. Keep trying until you get through to your boss. This thing only works in open ground. As long as you're on the rooftop you should be able to get a signal.'

Tannon frowned. 'You expect me to stay up here? With all this going on?'

'We don't have a choice,' Porter replied in a firm but calm tone. 'Your boss needs to understand that the situation is urgent. If help doesn't arrive in the next hour or so, we won't be able to stop the rebels from storming the hotel. Then we're fucked.' He saw the hesitant look on the deputy commissioner's face and said, 'If you don't believe me, go downstairs and have a look in the lobby. There's a couple of Lebanese down there with their guts hanging out.'

'I can't be here,' Tannon said. 'I just can't.'

Porter pointed to a metal rooftop ventilator mounted on top of a concrete post, roughly a metre high. 'You can stay behind that. The ventilator will cover you from any rounds coming in. Keep calling until you get an answer. And for fuck's sake don't stand up and make yourself a target.'

Tannon pursed her lips. 'You really think the rebels are going to attack us again?'

'It's a question of when.'

She nodded then turned and crawled over to the ventilator. Slid down behind it and started operating the sat phone. Porter watched her for a moment then turned to Bald.

'Find Crowder. Tell him we need water and medical supplies. Plus any ammo. We'll need every spare round going.'

'What about the Nigerians? Some of them might still have a few clips,' Bald said. 'It's not as if they've got any fucking use for them, is it?'

Porter nodded. 'Grab what you can.'

Bald hurried across the rooftop towards the stairwell. Porter moved back from the wall and slumped down. Exhaustion washed over him. Adrenaline had kept him going during the skirmish, along with a grim determination not to let the enemy win. But now Porter felt the tiredness deep in his bones. Like a comedown from a drug. He was sweating hard from the stress of the firefight and the heat emanating from the rifle barrels and the sun beating down on their heads. He was filthy and thirsty and knackered. He wanted nothing more than to close his eyes for a moment and sleep.

You can't rest now, the voice inside his head told Porter. *Push through it. If you fail, a thousand people will die.*

The minutes ticked by. Tannon tried to get through to the commissioner without success. The two Lebanese in their cheap grey suits arrived on the rooftop, carrying the spare rounds they had retrieved from the dead rebels in the lobby. Porter took turns with Tully to keep a mark-one eyeball on the rebel position beyond the roundabout to the east. But the enemy remained hidden behind the vegetation around the baobab tree and showed no signs of movement. Maybe they've had enough, Porter thought. *Or maybe they're just biding their time and waiting for their mates to arrive.* He periodically crawled across the rooftop to the north, his sights switching between the empty garage and the banana plantation. There was no sign of any enemy activity. Just the awful stillness of the downtime, the glinting of spent jackets under the sun and the twisted corpses lying in the road.

After twenty minutes Bald returned with Crowder and the giant, Solomon, in tow. Crowder was carrying a multi-pack of one-litre bottles of mineral water. Some expensive-looking French brand that Porter had never heard of. He also carried a medical supply kit in a green satchel bag slung over his shoulder. Bald lugged a bucket filled with clips for the SLRs while Solomon carried a couple of metal boxes of ammo. Each box was the size of a toolbox, painted green with yellow text stamped down the side: 200 RDS. 7.62mm BALL. L2A2. UN 0012. They looked tiny in Solomon's huge grip. Like a couple of kids' lunch boxes.

Solomon carted the ammo boxes over to Porter and Tully and dumped them beside the GPMG. At the same time Crowder started distributing water bottles among the shooters. Porter grabbed one, tore off the cap and took a long, refreshing gulp. Twenty-four hours ago I was necking vodka out of a water bottle, he thought. Now I'm grateful just for the plain stuff.

Bald emptied the clips onto the ground, then ducked back inside the stairwell with Solomon and Crowder to fetch the rest of the supplies. After the second trip Crowder looked like he might have a heart attack. Sweat rolled down his face and his cheeks were reddened with the effort of bounding up and down seven flights of stairs. Along with the extra mags for the SLRs they retrieved two RPG launchers, plus a pair of binoculars and three old Makarov semi-automatic pistols chambered for the Russian-manufactured 9x18mm round. They dumped everything in the middle of the rooftop and handed out the spare clips among the defenders. Porter counted up the spare ammo. Four hundred rounds for the gimpy, plus ten mags for the SLRs. Which worked out to two extra mags each. Forty more rounds per man. Two hundred rounds in total for the rifles. Not much, Porter thought.

If they come at us with everything they've got, we're fucked.

While the rest of the guys loaded up on supplies, Bald decided to instruct Solomon in how to piece together belts of ammo for the gimpy. He knelt down beside the machine gun and scooped up a handful of the discarded link that had ejected from the feed tray and collected at the foot of the parapet. Then he called over Solomon. The man-mountain watched as Bald spread out the small black metal clips in front of him. Some of the links were a little rusty but they were all in a reusable condition. Bald took the first round from the first box of 7.62mm brass, gathered up two pieces of link, and pushed them together to line up the two sets of loops. Then he pushed the bullet through the loops to make the first round in the link. He pieced together a few more rounds before leaving it to Solomon. The guy fumbled awkwardly with the clips at first. But he soon got the hang of it and began assembling the belts, his face a picture of concentration.

'Don't suppose any of the Nigerians stuck their hand up and offered to help out?' Porter said, looking from Bald to Crowder.

The hotel manager wiped his brow and made a wry smile. 'You're kidding, right? They couldn't wait to hand over their ammunition. As far as they're concerned, this isn't their fight any more.'

Crowder made his excuses and left the rooftop to check on the guests cooped up on the upper floors. Porter smiled weakly at Bald. 'Looks like it's just us, then. At least the Belgians are making themselves useful.'

'First time their country's been good for anything,' Bald said. 'Fucking liberals.'

The two operators shared a half-hearted laugh. Then a shout went up from across the rooftop.

'Movement, lads!' Tully cried. 'East, six hundred metres away. Multiple X-rays, plus technicals.'

Bald and Porter glanced at each other. Then they darted across the rooftop and hit the section of the parapet next to Tully. Porter strained his eyes at the main roundabout, with Bald looking in the same direction through the pair of binoculars he'd lifted from the Nigerians. Around sixty rebels were creeping forward from the roundabout and heading for a two-storey building at the side of the road, a hundred metres due west of the baobab tree. The building was partially obscured by a clump of trees and a sign above the entrance said ABERDEEN POLICE STATION. With the trees restricting their view it was impossible for Bald and Porter to get off a clean shot at the rebels. Besides, at a distance of six hundred metres the rebels were at the maximum range with iron sights, and Porter knew their chances of hitting a moving target were extremely low. They couldn't afford to waste ammo on long shots. So they looked on helplessly as the enemy disappeared around the back of the building.

In the next beat a couple of pickup trucks came hurtling towards the roundabout at a fast clip. They swung past the round-about and steered into the patch of muddy ground to the side of the old police station, concealed behind the trees.

'Supply trucks,' Bald reported as he peered between the trees using the binoculars. 'RPG rockets, plus a couple of mortars. Soviet 82 millis, as far as I can tell. Looks like they're setting up a forming-up point.'

Porter said, 'They know they'll get clobbered if they go just steaming in at us again.'

'Maybe this lot aren't as useless as they look.'

'Maybe,' Porter said. 'Or maybe they've got someone in charge who knows what the fuck they're doing for a change.'

He looked on with a rising sense of dread as another wave of forty or so rebels flooded west across to the old police station from the roundabout. Like a crowd flocking towards the turnstiles for the FA Cup Final. Among the rebels he noticed several guys decked out in soldiers' uniforms and he realised these must be some of the government troops who had defected to the rebel side after the coup. Fighting against a bunch of machete-wielding nutters is one thing, Porter thought to himself. But now we're dealing with trained soldiers too.

This next assault is going to be a whole lot noisier than the first one.

Bald said, 'How long do you reckon we have?'

Porter squinted at the road and considered. 'The rebels will wait for the rest of their forces to arrive from the bridge. Whoever's calling the shots down there, they won't want to hit us again until they've got all their ducks in a row. I reckon we've got an hour, at best. If that.'

'Fuck.' Bald shook his head. 'We need to get some top cover over here. A couple of Black Hawks would go down nicely. They'd soon wipe out these bastards.'

They lapsed into an uneasy silence, both men privately absorbing the seriousness of their situation. Porter observed the enemy for a few moments longer then turned to Bald.

'Wait here.'

He spun away from the parapet and hastened over to the ventilator. Found Tannon hunkering down behind the concrete post. The sat phone pressed to her right ear, a deep frown lining her brow.

'Any luck?' he asked.

'Not yet.' Tannon's fingers were shaking as she hit the red button to end the call. 'No one's picking up the phone at the High Commission. I've tried the Embassy in Conakry too. I'm getting nowhere.'

Porter thrust out his hand. 'I'll try our handler. See if he can help.'

Tannon passed him the sat phone. He scrolled through the menu. Selected the number for Hawkridge that had been saved to the contact book, and hit Dial. Then he waited. After a pause the call patched through. Hawkridge picked up on the sixth ring.

'John? Is that you?' He sounded tired, and out of breath.

'Aye,' said Porter. 'It's me.'

'You're alive. Thank God.' Three thousand miles away, Hawkridge sighed in relief. 'Where are you?'

'On the roof of the Ambassadors Hotel. We've been up here since first thing this morning. The rebels have been making repeated assaults on our position, trying to break through the lines to the hotel. Everything's going tits up.'

'I'm well aware of what's happening,' Hawkridge said irritably. 'I've just been briefed on the developments, as a matter of fact. We've had numerous reports of fighting in your area. What's your current situation?'

'We've held the bastards off for the time being. But they've got reinforcements coming in. We've got eyes on them right now.'

'What about Soames?'

'He's safe,' Porter said. 'Look, we don't have much time. We've got a hundred-plus enemies converging on our position, plus technicals. With more arriving every minute. They're gearing up to have another crack at us, and the next time they attack it's gonna be serious. We need some help down here.'

'The Sea Stallions will be en route to you shortly,' said Hawkridge. 'We're hopeful they can reach you within the next two hours. Then we can begin the evacuation and get you chaps out of there. You'll be on the first chopper. We're just sorting out the details with the Americans now.'

Porter felt his neck muscles tense. 'We don't need transport helis. We need bloocly hardware. Someone who can come in and knock these fuckers on the head and send them packing.'

Hawkridge made a sound like a guy sucking juice out of a lemon. 'That's going to be difficult. We don't have the local resources to provide air support ourselves. One Para will be in your area to retake the airport but they won't be able to deploy until late this evening, I understand.'

'That's too late. What about the Yanks?'

'I've already asked the question. Believe me. But the Americans aren't especially keen to get involved in what they view as a domestic squabble. Neither is Downing Street, quite frankly. They don't want it to look like we're undermining President Fofana's authority.'

Porter felt the blood boiling in his veins with anger. Here we are surrounded by rebel fighters, and no one wants to lift a finger to help out. *The world is changing*, Angela March had told him back at the mission briefing. *The days of direct intervention are over. Men like Soames buy us power without putting boots on the ground.*

'You're not hearing us,' he said. 'There are a thousand people trapped in here, and I'm telling you, the next time these fuckers attack it's going to go bad. We've already slotted a fair few of them. When they break through they'll be gagging for revenge. They'll carve up everyone inside the hotel. Including Soames.'

'You've managed to hold them off so far, haven't you?' Hawkridge said.

'This is different. They're not attacking us in small groups this time. They're building up their forces for a major assault. We're short on ammo and they've got the upper hand in terms of numbers and weapons. The next time the rebels attack us they'll break through. You've got to get on the phone with the Yanks. Tell them the situation here is critical and we need air support.'

There was a long pause before Hawkridge answered.

'I'll see what I can do. But I can't promise anything. This is a complicated situation, John. There are a lot of parties involved. A lot of parameters to consider. It isn't simply a matter of making a call.'

'I don't give a toss,' said Porter. 'Do whatever it takes. If you don't get some hardware down on our position in the next hour, you're talking to a dead man. Along with everyone else in this hotel.'

NINETEEN

1226 hours.

Porter killed the call. He flipped down the antenna and handed the sat phone back to Tannon. As she reached for it a bottle of pills fell out of her jacket pocket and rolled across the ground, stopping next to Porter's boot. One of the bottles he'd seen up in her hotel room. Tannon hurriedly scooped up the amber plastic bottle and shoved it back inside her jacket, ignoring Porter's quizzical stare.

'If you're going to lecture me about the evils of prescription medicine, now really isn't the best time,' she said.

A shout went up from the other side of the parapet as Bald called out from his observation point overlooking the roundabout. Porter left Tannon with the sat phone and worked his way back across the rooftop, dropping down at the northern parapet. Bald was peering out through the binoculars at the Cape Road to the east.

'What is it, mucker?' Porter said. He could see a couple of dust trails in the distance, nothing more.

'Take a look.' Bald slid back from the wall and offered his binos to Porter. 'More supply trucks, seven hundred metres away. North of the petrol station.'

Porter took the binos and concentrated his gaze at the point Bald had indicated. A hundred metres east of the roundabout he sighted a disused petrol station at the side of the road, its bare forecourt covered with weeds and broken glass. Porter shifted his line of sight to the road. Then he saw the pickups. There were four of them, bowling west down the road at a decent speed towards the roundabout, with a gap of four metres between one truck and the next. Each truck was loaded with stacks of ammo crates, Porter observed. At seven hundred metres the trucks were too far away for a clean shot with the SLRs. The palm trees on both sides of the road partially obscured the targets, stopping Bald from giving them a blast from the GPMG.

The four pickups hit the roundabout, swung north and disappeared around the back of the police station, six hundred metres north-east of the hotel. The supply vehicles were swiftly followed by a pair of old Toyota minibuses. Both were crammed full of rebels. Like Tube carriages at rush hour. There had to be at least thirty fighters in each bus, Porter figured. They followed the same route as the wagons, tooling north past the roundabout then turning left off the road. It pulled up out of sight, somewhere behind the police station.

Tully took in a sharp intake of breath. 'Jesus. There must be a hundred of the fuckers down there now.'

'They're gearing up for something big,' Porter said.

'Looks like you were right, mate,' said Bald. 'The chogies have got someone in charge down there who knows what they're doing.' He spat on the ground. 'Those Yanks better hurry the fuck up. Otherwise we're shafted.'

The mood on the rooftop changed. There was a quiet tension in the air now. Which was understandable. When the first wave of rebels had poured forward, Porter had been reasonably confident in their ability to keep the enemy at bay. But now the odds had shifted.

He shoved aside the unease brewing in his guts, turned towards Tully, and pointed to the spot where the rebels were massing.

'We need eyes on the main street. Two of you watch that fucking spot. Get the other Belgian lads to cover all sides of the hotel, in case the bastards try to flank us. If there's movement to the left or right of the gathering point, we need to know about it.'

'Roger that,' Tully said. Then he moved off with Nilis to brief the other Belgians and set them up at each side of the rooftop.

Porter drew back from the parapet and passed the binoculars to Bald. 'Keep eyes on the rebels. Watch for approaching vehicles. We need to know how many more of those bastards are forming up over there.'

Bald nodded. 'Where are you going?'

'To see if we can get someone to pull a few strings with the Americans.'

He pushed away from the parapet, moving past Nilis and the four other Belgians. He stopped briefly beside Solomon. The man-mountain had finished linking together the rounds of 7.62mm brass through the two ammo belts. Porter nodded his approval at Solomon's efforts and sent him back downstairs. Then he made his way over to Tannon. She was crouching beside the ventilator, craning her neck at the parapet. Her eyes quickly snapped to Porter as he approached. He could see the nervous strain written across her face.

'What's happening down there?' she asked.

'The rebels are forming up over at the police station. More than a hundred of them. Looks like they're getting ready to have another pop at us.'

The colour drained from Tannon's face. 'How long can you hold them off?'

'I don't know,' he replied honestly. 'We're talking about a large force with heavy ordnance, and we're down to the bare bones.'

Tannon took a deep breath and nodded. 'What do you need me to do?'

'You're mates with Angela, right?'

'Sure. We go way back. Angela and I joined the Foreign Office at the same time.'

'Get on the phone to her. Tell her we need whatever hardware the Yanks have got, and we need it right this fucking instant. Gunships, fast air. Anything that can buy us some time until the evacuation team arrives.'

'You're asking me to bypass my boss.'

'We've got no choice. We've tried our handler but he's messing us about. We need someone who can cut through the noise. Make the Yanks understand there are lives at stake here.'

Tannon looked uncertain. 'I'll see what I can do. Angela knows some people over at Langley. She might be able to put a word in and get something done.'

Porter said, 'Whatever strings you can pull with Angela, get them pulled. Tell her if we don't get some gunships on our position very soon, there won't be any guests left to evacuate.'

A brief flicker of alarm flashed in Tannon's eyes. 'What'll happen if the rebels break through?'

Porter grabbed one of the Makarovs that Crowder and Bald had brought up to the roof. He pressed down on the heel release on the underside of the grip, slid out the mag and inspected the cut-out. There was a single round in the clip. He gently reinserted the clip, racked the slide back to chamber the round, then thumbed up the safety to the 'on' position and offered the weapon to Tannon grip-first. She stared at it like it was a live grenade.

'What's that for?' Her voice had gone cold and flat and quiet.

'There's one round in the chamber,' Porter said, tapping the side of the Makarov. 'If the worst happens and the rebels take the hotel, you point the barrel at the roof of your mouth and pull the trigger.'

Tannon recoiled in shock. 'You're serious?'

Porter stared at her. 'Deadly.'

She shook her head frantically. 'There must be some other way out.'

'There isn't. This is your best bet. The rebels aren't going to go easy on the guests. If they overrun us, you're better off with a quick bullet to the head than letting those lunatics taking you alive.'

'Why? What would they do to me?'

'You don't want to know.'

For the next forty minutes a continual flow of rebels streamed forward from the roundabout and amassed at the police station. By one o'clock in the afternoon another fifty rebels had reached the forming-up point. Every so often another supply truck skidded to a halt round the side of the station building to distribute more rockets and ammo to the assembled rebels. Bald and Porter took turns to OP the enemy through the binoculars, while Tully and the five Belgians prowled the other three sides of the rooftop, watching for any sign of enemy movement on the flanks. But the rebels were pooling all their efforts into reinforcing their position at the old police station. It was obvious to Porter they were planning to hit the defenders soon with a major frontal assault.

Whoever's calling the shots down there has changed tactics, he thought. They're not going to attack us in small groups like before. They're playing a different game now. Putting their resources together for a coordinated attack.

The next time they hit us, we won't stand a chance.

Bald said, 'Any word on those gunships?'

Porter looked over at Tannon. Shrugged a question at her. She looked up from the sat phone, met his gaze and shook her head in frustration.

'Nothing yet,' Porter said, turning back to face the parapet.

'Fuck's sake.' Bald shook his head bitterly. 'What's taking them so long? If the Yanks don't come up with the goods soon, we won't stand a chance against these scum.'

Porter said nothing. He checked his G-Shock again 1309. Forty-three minutes since he had put in the call to Hawkridge. Down at the police station, the number of rebels arriving at the gathering point had slowed to a trickle. Porter figured at least a hundred and fifty X-rays were now encamped behind the station building. A dead, hot stillness hung in the air. He could feel the nape of his neck burning under the sun's intense rays. Everything was hot to touch. The concrete wall, the plastic water bottles, the trigger guard on the SLR. It had been more than six hours since the first assault on the hotel, and the action had started to take its toll on Porter. He felt physically shattered, and mentally drained. His muscles were aching and weary, the rifle felt twice as heavy in his grip now. He knew the guys on the roof wouldn't be able to keep up the defence of the hotel for long once the enemy attacked.

Every so often he called out to Tannon, asking her for updates. But she had still heard nothing from her bosses or Angela. A bleak thought slowly began to pick away at the base of Porter's skull.

The cavalry's not going to get here in time.

The minutes ticked by. Another nine rebels scurried forward to the forming-up point. A battered old Nissan pulled up, carrying five more fighters. Then everything went quiet. No more enemies advanced from the direction of the roundabout. No more supply trucks arrived. Porter could hear nothing except the palm tree fronds shivering in the breeze, the thump of his heart beating erratically in his chest.

Bald's voice broke the silence.

'They're on the move! Fifty X-rays. Heading west towards the plantation.'

Porter forced his tired body into action once more. He grabbed his rifle and crawled over to the north side of the parapet, centring the SLR sights on the banana trees four hundred metres away at his two o'clock. Dozens of shapes were sneaking forward from around the back of the police station now. They were approaching the banana plantation a hundred metres to the west of the forming-up point. At least twenty of the rebels were lugging RPGs, Porter observed. The remainder were equipped with assault rifles and he spotted a few mortars in there as well. *It's starting again*, he thought as he watched the enemy advance.

They're going to attack. And this time they're going to hit us with everything they've got.

'Get into position!' he roared at the other defenders, waving them over. 'Fucking move yourselves!'

Tully and four of the Belgians scrabbled over, taking up firing positions either side of Porter along the north-facing wall. Nilis formed up to his left, with Bald, Tully and two of the Belgians at his right. The other two shooters were left guarding the eastern side of the rooftop, watching for any enemies who might try to break off from the main group and outflank them. Bald set down the binos and inserted the last remaining belt of 7.62mm brass into the left-hand side of the feed tray on the GPMG. He ratcheted the cocking handle. Stared down the sights as another dozen rebels poured west from the back of the station building, joining their mates behind the treeline.

'Here they come, guys,' Nilis said. 'Let's fucking do this.'

He gave Bald the thumbs-up then went back to peering down the sights of his rifle. The Belgian didn't look too worried, thought Porter. *He sounds almost cheerful.*

Porter cupped a hand to his mouth and shouted over at Tannon. 'Anything?'

'I'm on hold. Someone's trying to find Angela.'

'Whoever it is, tell them to fucking hurry up and pull their finger out. We're about to get hit here.'

He flicked the safety on the side of his weapon to semi-automatic, tensing his muscles as he trained his weapon on the banana plantation. Ready to fire as soon as the first target popped into view. The rebels had clearly absorbed the lessons of the earlier attacks and stayed behind cover. Porter could see a few brightly-coloured shapes flitting into view between the palm trees, their clothes visible amid the dense shade. He held fire, painfully aware of how little ammo they had. Then he saw a glimmer of movement at the left of his fire picture. He swung his sights across just in time to see a rocket fizzing out from the edge of the treeline.

Then another.

'Incoming!' he yelled.

The rockets struck the front of the hotel in a furious torrent. The first RPG round hit low, slamming into one of the upper floors with a juddering boom, pulverising glass and concrete. Two more rockets whizzed over the top of the parapet, missing the defenders by less than a metre. Everyone involuntarily ducked as three more RPGs burred overhead in a fury of noise and heat. One of the rockets slammed into the concrete base below the water tower in the middle of the rooftop, spewing out bright orange flames, the shock of the impact blowing off the tower's corrugated steel roof. Acrid black smoke gushed across the rooftop, blocking out the sunlight and showering Porter with debris. He rubbed the dust out of his eyes, ignored the burning in his lungs and swung the SLR's iron sights across to the left of the plantation, following the smoke trail.

Four X-rays with RPG-7s were visible in the hollow ground next to the banana trees. They were taking turns to fire rockets at the hotel, darting back into cover behind the trees to reload. Porter centred his sights on one guy in a kneeling firing stance, shouldering his RPG as he shaped to fire. He calmly centred the foresight on the man's chest and fired twice. Both rounds hit their target, knocking the rebel off his feet. Like he'd been hit by a two-ton truck. Bald raked down two of the other guys with a burst from the gimpy. But a seemingly endless stream of rebels kept pouring forward from the trees to fire their rockets.

Porter arced his sights across the treeline and fired again, clobbering another rebel dressed in a Hawaiian shirt and flip flops. His mate disappeared behind the trees before Porter could cut him down. Around him the other defenders on the roof were all concentrating their fire on the plantation, but the rebels still managed to unleash a few rockets. As Porter searched for his next target he saw another rebel creep into view at the edge of his vision. A guy in an army uniform. One of the soldiers who had defected to the rebels. He carried an RPG launcher, and he moved like he knew how to handle the weapon properly. The rebel soldier took up a position in the hollow ground next to the plantation. He pointed his launcher at the rooftop, and fired before Porter could take aim at him.

The RPG whirred towards the parapet. Directly towards the spot Bald was occupying. Bald had moved up into a kneeling position to drop a trio of rebels with a couple of bursts from his gimpy, and his attention was drawn away from the soldier with the rocket launcher. He didn't see the round heading towards him.

But Tully did. The guy was four metres to the right of Bald when he sighted the soldier lining up his RPG-7. There was no time to shout a warning. Tully shot to his feet and threw himself at Bald a split-second before the rocket struck the parapet. The two men barrel-rolled across the ground as the RPG slammed into the lower section of the wall where Bald had been kneeling a moment earlier. The explosion shook the rooftop, blasting away chunks of the concrete and exposing the steel rebar. Smoke gushed over the rooftop. Bald and Tully landed on the ground next to Porter, bits of incinerated rubble raining down on them. Nilis staggered back from the parapet, hacking and coughing. Porter tasted grit in his mouth, felt the debris nicking at his hands and face. The smoke fizzled out. Bald scraped himself off the ground, his clothes coated in dust. He glanced in shock at the huge hole in the wall where the rocket had struck.

'Fuck, that was close.' He nodded at Tully. 'Thanks.'

'Thank me later, fella. We've got to survive this clusterfuck first.'

Porter looked over at the two Belgians who had been to the right of Tully. One of the guys had been knocked back by the blast. He lay in a dazed heap next to the air-conditioning duct, his face covered in cuts and his clothing torn in several places. The other Belgian was slumped on the ground next to the wall. Half his face had been blown off. There was a soup of bone and gristle and sinew where his eyes and mouth and nose used to be. The other half of his face was blistered and blackened. Like overcooked meat left on a barbecue.

The other Belgian stared at his dead mate uncomprehendingly.

'Get up!' Porter roared at the man. 'Get back on that fucking wall!'

The Belgian snapped out of his trance. He scooped up his SLR and moved back over to the parapet, stepping around the guy with half his face missing. The RPG rounds were coming in thick and fast now as the rebels swarmed closer to the hotel, breaking across the open ground and rushing towards the garage. Somewhere behind the plantation the enemy had set up a mortar. Porter heard the shrill whistling sound of grenades arcing through the sky, like someone letting off a ton of fireworks simultaneously. The mortar rounds landed well short of the rooftop, slamming into the access road immediately to the north of the hotel, belching smoke and flames several metres into the air. More grenades launched through the air and landed to the rear of the hotel, some thirty metres behind the men on the rooftop. The temperature on the rooftop went from boiling hot to furnace.

'There's too many of them!' Bald shouted above the crack of rifle rounds being discharged and the whoosh of rockets fizzing out from between the trees.

'Keep them on the move,' Porter said. 'Don't give the fuckers a chance to settle.'

The two Blades fired well-placed bursts at a group of rebels swarming towards the garage and the derelict buildings to the west. But it wasn't enough. For every one X-ray they cut down, two more targets made it to cover at the slums. The rebels were now two hundred metres from the hotel, edging closer with every passing minute. Those rebels based at the plantation kept up their vicious rate of gunfire, mortar rounds and RPGs. We can't hold them off for much longer, thought Porter. Fifty minutes had passed since he'd put in the call to Hawkridge. There was still no sign of any top cover coming in.

He shifted his focus back to the plantation. Two figures were kneeling beside a mortar unit. They were visible in the shaded ground between a couple of trees. One guy was securing the base plate while his mate fetched another round from a wooden crate to slide into the tube. Porter depressed the trigger and gave the guy with the mortar grenade the good news. His mate had just enough time to look up and see the other guy's brains spurting out the back of his skull. Then Porter lined up the second target with the sighting post and sent him over to the dark side with a two-round burst.

Another mortar team rushed forward to set up shop at the plantation. Porter was about to line them up when he heard a deep low rumble in the distance.

'Technicals!' Tully screamed. 'Incoming, two of them!'

Porter swivelled his gaze to the roundabout. A pair of Toyota pickups were bombing down the Cape Road at a decent clip, tearing towards the hotel. Both trucks were carrying heavy machine guns mounted on tripods on the back platforms. One of the weapons was a 12.7mm, identical to the one Bald had neutralised during the earlier assault on the hotel. The second machinegun was even bigger. Porter identified it as a 14.5mm ZPU Russian anti-aircraft gun. The double-barrelled variant. A serious piece of hardware. The 12.7mm looked almost puny by comparison.

If the rebels get that ZPU on target, we're done for.

He shouted at the others to get down. In the next instant the 14.5mm let rip. Porter threw himself to the ground as a series of deep, loud booms echoed across the road. Four massive rounds sliced through the thinner upper section of the parapet, half a metre to the left of Porter. The top of the wall disintegrated. It was there one moment, and then suddenly it wasn't.

'This fucker's mine,' Bald said.

He shuffled over to the nearest drainage hole as another furious volley of 14.5mm rounds pounded against the air-conditioning duct. The technical had dropped its speed dramatically to allow the rebel manning the 14.5mm to properly aim the weapon at the rooftop. Bald rolled onto his stomach, shoved the gimpy muzzle through the opening and aimed at the moving target. The 14.5mm sparked up again, punching fist-sized holes in the concrete and keeping the men on the rooftop pinned down behind the thicker, lower section of the parapet. Through another drainage hole Porter could see scores of rebels taking advantage of the savage bursts from the ZPU, darting out of cover from behind the plantation treeline and dashing over to the garage, two hundred metres from the hotel.

Bald pulled the trigger before the technical could fire again. Porter watched through the drain hole as his mucker pasted the rebel operating the ZPU with a long rattling burst from the GPMG. Bullets shredded the pickup, nailing the two rebels in the front cab. Bald smoothly lined up the pickup equipped with the 12.7mm and peppered that vehicle with rounds too. The second vehicle rolled to a halt in the middle of the road. Two guys tried to climb on the back of the truck and mount the 12.7mm. Both were swiftly cut down by a couple of bursts from the gimpy.

The relief was temporary. Porter and Bald switched their attention back to the plantation, brassing up rebels with short bursts as soon as they popped out of cover. To his left, Tully and Nilis were concentrating their efforts on the rebels at the abandoned garage. Some of the enemy had set up a firing point on the first floor of the garage and a steady flow of RPGs whooshed towards the hotel, striking the lower floors a few metres below the rooftop. Several more X-rays had taken up positions at the adjacent windows, spraying the parapet with continuous bursts from their AK-47s. Despite the best efforts of the men on the roof, the rebels continued their relentless advance, gradually closing the distance to the hotel. Around thirty X-rays had taken up firing positions at the garage. With forty based at the plantation. And more pushing forward all the time.

We can't hold out much longer.

A group of four rebels broke across the open ground to the garage. Porter clipped one of them in the back with the last round in the magazine. He ejected the empty mag, dug a fresh clip out of his back pocket and reloaded. Down to my last twenty rounds, he realised grimly. He looked over to his right and saw Bald had worked his way through more than half the belt of 7.62mm. The guy had fewer than ninety bullets left on the belt.

'Shit,' one of the Belgians on the eastern parapet called out in a frantic tone of voice. 'They're flanking us!'

Porter and Bald broke into a crouching run and hurried over to the Belgians. They were ducking low beside the wall as rounds buzzed overhead in vicious little bursts, sounding like a hive of yellow jackets right after someone had trashed their nest. Porter looked through the nearest drainage hole. He could see scores of rebels jumping down from half a dozen pickup trucks that had pulled up next to the athletics track three hundred metres to the east. Forty of them. A 12.7mm machine gun mounted on the back of a Nissan pickup spat round after round at the parapet, providing covering fire for the rebels as they debussed. Porter and Bald started putting rounds down through the openings, picking off the closest targets. The pickup responded with a hailstorm of gunfire from the 12.7mm, forcing the two Blades to bunker down. Bullets pinged off the duct behind Porter, ricocheting off the water tower. Others smashed apart the upper wall. Porter tried to return fire through the drain hole. But there were too many rounds coming in and as he looked down he noticed a cluster of rebels had broken forward. Fifteen of them. They were racing south towards the low wall that enclosed the rear of the hotel. Closing in.

'I'm almost out, lads!' Tully called out from the northern wall.

Tully shrank back from the parapet as another RPG round whizzed low and struck the top floor immediately below the rooftop, throwing up a cloud of smoke and shattered glass.

'Fuck,' Porter said. 'There's too many of them.'

'If we had bayonets,' Bald said, 'we'd be fixing them right about now.'

The two operators shared a look. Porter half-smiled at his mucker. They both knew what the other was thinking. It's curtains for us now. There's no way out. *Not this time.*

Anyone else in our position, would be bricking it, thought Porter. But that's not who we are. I'm not scared of the rebels. I'm not afraid of bloody dying. I'm not even angry at dying for nothing, in a shithole country I don't give a flying fuck about, protecting some twat of an ex-Rupert. *I just wish I'd had the chance to see Sandy's face one more time. To say goodbye to my daughter. Tell her that her old man's sorry for fucking everything up.*

There was a lull in the rounds chipping away at the wall. Porter crawled back over to the drain hole and hefted up his SLR, ready to put down the enemy with his last twelve rounds. He was about to pull the trigger when he heard Tannon's voice calling out to him above the rumble of gunfire and the hideous pained screams of the dying. He shrank back from the drain hole and hurried over to the ventilator. Tannon handed him the sat phone.

'It's Angela,' she said breathlessly. 'I've got her on the line. She said she wants to speak with you.'

For a moment Porter couldn't believe what he was hearing. He snatched the phone and pressed it to his ear, plugging his other ear with his thumb to block out the noise.

'Angela?'

The voice on the other end of the line said, 'Dominique tells me you're in a bit of a tight spot.'

Porter almost laughed. 'That's putting it fucking mildly. The rebels have got the hotel surrounded. We're about to be overrun here. We need some help.'

March said, 'That's why I'm calling. Look, I've been discussing your situation with the American Secretary of State. It wasn't easy, but she's agreed to intervene personally. We've got air support coming in as we speak. Two gunships.'

'About fucking time. What's their ETA?'

Rounds buzzed over the wall and pinged against the side of the water tower, pinballing across the rooftop. March said, 'I don't have the details. The USS *Lauderdale* will be calling you any minute now to confirm. Keep this line clear, okay?'

She hung up before Porter could get another word in. He didn't feel any immediate sense of relief. The situation on the ground was still critical, he knew. The rebels are closing in on all sides, and we've got fuck-all ammo. *We're not out of the woods yet.*

Thirty seconds later, the sat phone beeped again. Porter answered, heard nothing but static. 'Hello? Anyone there?'

There was a long pause. Then the static faded. A stern, humour-less voice came over the line.

'Sir, this is Colonel Joshua Hendricks,' the voice said in a strong Texan accent. The kind that made every word sound like the twang of a guitar string. 'I'm the commander of the 11th Marine Expeditionary Unit here on the operations bridge of the USS *Lauderdale*. Am I speaking with John Porter?'

Yanks, Porter thought. *Never say one word when ten will do.*

'That's me.'

'Sir, I'm authorised to report that we have two Black Hawks inbound to your position. ETA is nine minutes. I repeat, two

Black Hawks inbound, ETA nine minutes. What is your present situation?'

Porter said, 'Not fucking good. We've got about a hundred and fifty X-rays here, plus two technicals with 12.7mm machine guns approximately a hundred and fifty metres from our position. We've had at least forty RPGs fired on us and the enemy has got a mortar set up somewhere too.'

'Sounds like y'all are in more trouble than you can shake a stick at.'

'Put it this way, mate. Now I know how General Custer felt.'

The Texan didn't laugh. Officers in the Yank military didn't have a sense of humour, in Porter's experience. Must be something in the water over there. 'Well, sir, our boys are fixing to level things up some. Think you can hold them off till our guys get there?'

'We've halted their advance for the moment. Should be able to keep them off for a few more minutes.'

'Good to hear it, sir. We'll check in once our guys have a visual on your position.'

'Roger that.'

The call ended. Nine minutes, Porter thought. It's going to be close. But at least we've got a fighting chance now. He looked across at the rooftop. Then up at the cloudless sky. Then over at the smoke billowing up from the exploded mortar shells north and south of the hotel. A thought occurred to him just then. He waved Tully over, leaving Nilis and Spray-Tan to deal with the rebels on the northern side of the hotel. Tully got down on his hands and knees and inched his way over, hugging the ground as bullets cut through the air above, ripping into the wall and showering him with fragmented concrete.

'I need you and Jock to run downstairs,' Porter said once Tully had reached him. 'Get to the underground car park, grab a car tyre and one of the jerry cans from the back of the Range Rover. Take a knife from the kitchen, too. Bring everything up to the roof. Make it quick.'

'What the fuck for?'

Porter pointed to the sky. 'We've got top cover coming in, nine minutes from now. We need to mark our position to the pilots so they know we're friendlies. We don't want to find ourselves on the end of a fucking blue-on-blue.'

Tully nodded, sensing the urgency of the situation. He turned and broke into a crouching run with Bald at his side. The two men edged around the air-conditioning duct, moving as fast as they could under the intense weight of fire bearing down on the rooftop.

Once they had departed Porter moved over to Tannon. He nodded at her. Pointed to the stairwell.

'You need to get off the rooftop. We've got Black Hawks coming in less than ten minutes from now. They're going to be blasting everything that moves. You'll be safer downstairs.'

'What about you?'

'We've got to stay up here to direct the fire. Get down to the upper floors and find somewhere to keep your head down. It's gonna get noisy as fuck up here.'

Tannon got up and left. Porter watched her disappear into the stairwell, then returned to his position at the drain hole to operate the gimpy, putting down a three-round burst on the pavilion. Another ten rebels sprinted out from behind the structure and darted south, hooking around to the wall perimetering the rear of the hotel. They were gone before Porter could cut them down. He crawled over to the south-facing parapet, his knees scraping over the chunks of concrete and spent rounds littering the ground. Then he poked the gimpy muzzle through an opening and sprayed a short burst at six rebels scaling over the low wall. He killed three of them. The survivors sought cover behind the sheds at the far end of the grounds, a hundred metres back from the hotel.

Fifty rounds left in the belt.

For the next five minutes Porter madly scrambled from one side of the rooftop to the other, desperately trying to keep the rebels at bay with short, controlled bursts from the GPMG. But the enemy was growing bolder all the time. He kept glancing at the horizon, straining his ears as he listened for the telltale sound of the rotor blades that would signal the arrival of the Black Hawks. He checked his watch. Six minutes since he'd got off the sat phone with Colonel Hendricks.

Three minutes till the choppers arrived.

If everything went according to plan.

Sixty seconds later Bald and Tully charged out of the stairwell, carting a black rubber tyre with worn treads and a dented alloy rim. They dumped the tyre beside the bullet-riddled water tower. Then Bald ducked back inside the stairwell. He returned a few beats later clutching a jerry can in his left hand and a huge kitchen knife in his right. Bald took the knife and slashed open the tyre as if he was gutting a fish. Air hissed violently out of the gash in the rubber. Then he took the jerry can, unscrewed the cap and poured the fuel inside the tyre, filling it up. He emptied the dregs of the can over the top of the tyre, chucked it aside and dug a box of matches out of his back pocket. Struck one against the side of the box. Tossed it onto the tyre. Stood well back.

The tyre burst into flames. The fire quickly consumed the wheel, filling the air with the pungent stench of burning rubber and channelling coal-black smoke into the sky. Porter could feel the heat from the fumes scolding his back as he moved over to the eastern parapet. The temperature on the rooftop was unbearable now. Suffocating. Like wearing a wetsuit inside a sauna. Every time Porter breathed it felt as if someone was taking a blowtorch to his lungs.

After eight minutes he heard an incessant thump-thump noise at his nine o'clock. Coming from the north of the hotel. The noise grew louder by the second, until the whole building seemed to reverberate with the beat. Porter looked beyond the north parapet, shading his eyes against the savage sun. Three quarters of a mile out a helicopter swung into view above the bay and surged towards the hotel. Even at this range Porter easily recognised it as a Black Hawk, with its long, waspish design and bulbous cockpit, rotor blades slicing and dicing the air like a couple of giant blenders. A pair of General Electric M134 miniguns were mounted on fixed metal brackets, protruding from the doors on either side of the main fuselage behind the cockpit. Six-barrelled monsters capable of firing up to 6,000 rounds per minute. Porter felt his spirits soar as he watched the Black Hawk sweeping inland.

Finally. We're in business.

The sat phone sparked into life.

Porter grabbed it. Hit Answer. 'Hendricks?'

'Our boys are one minute out,' Colonel Hendricks drawled. 'Can you confirm your coordinates?'

Porter replied in a slow, clear voice so there was no misunderstanding. 'Our position is the black smoke on the rooftop of the Ambassadors Hotel. Repeat, we are directly under the black smoke rising from the hotel rooftop.'

'One moment,' Hendricks said. There was a pause while the ops officers checked in with the pilots. Then the colonel came back on the line. 'Confirmed. We have a visual on the black smoke. Repeat, our guys have a visual on your location.'

Porter said, 'The area surrounding the hotel is not deemed friendly. Neutralise anything 360 of this building. I say again, anything surrounding the black smoke is hostile territory.'

There was another pause. Then Hendricks said, 'Understood. Sir, we're going to patch you through to the pilots now. Communicate directly with them from now on. We'll be listening in from the bridge.'

Hendricks's voice disappeared. Porter heard a series of whirrs and clicks. He chucked the binoculars at Bald and gestured for him to begin identifying targets east of the parapet. The throb of the Black Hawk's blades was deafening now as it came in fast towards the hotel. On eight-and-a-half minutes the connection went through. A voice cut through the static.

'Ambassador 1, this is Helo Z-1. We are inbound to your position and ready to engage. Helo Z-2 is two minutes out.'

Porter said, 'Helo Z-1, this is Ambassador 1. We have enemy forces in technical, three hundred metres east of our location. Engage, engage.'

Porter craned his neck up and tracked the Black Hawk as it banked heavily to the left and circled the hotel in a wide arc. Then the heli swung around and came tearing down towards the athletics track on the east side of the rooftop. The humming noise of the blades drowning out every other sound on the rooftop, sunlight reflecting off the cockpit. The Black Hawk swooped down on its target. At this distance Porter could see the loadies manning the M134s behind the cockpit. They were tied to lanyards to stop them from falling out. He looked away and shouted at the other guys on the rooftop, cupping a hand to his mouth.

'Incoming friendly fire! Everyone get the fuck down. NOW!'

Tully, Nilis and the other Belgians hit the deck. The Black Hawk bore down on the technical stationed next to the pavilion. Most of the rebels blindly stood their ground, continuing to fire at the rooftop. Others pointed their AK-47s at the Black Hawk and emptied pointless bursts at the heli. They were either really bold, or really fucking stupid.

On nine minutes, the Black Hawk opened fire.

One of the miniguns screamed. It sounded like the world's biggest chainsaw carving through the world's biggest tree. Porter thought his eardrums might explode from the noise. He saw the minigun barrel light up. Saw the rounds smashing into the technical in a red-hot stream. The burst lasted five seconds. Which equalled approximately five hundred rounds of hot lead, concentrated in an area the size of a bathtub. A deadly cocktail of heat, pressure and brass. Nothing could survive that. The technical was vapourised in front of Porter's eyes. There was a patch of blackened land and smoke and flames where the vehicle had been. And not much else. The rebels camped around the pavilion instantly turned and ran for the roundabout. The minigun chainsawed again. The fleeing targets weren't cut down. They were simply turned to dust. The gun stopped whirring. The Black Hawk flew back out towards the bay.

The pilot came back over the sat phone and said, 'Ambassador 1, this is Helo Z-1. On target. Repeat, on target. Helo Z-2 incoming.'

'Roger that,' Porter said.

A second thumping sound boomeranged across the sky. Porter looked up, squinted, saw the second Black Hawk slingshotting in from the bay. The second heli flew past its twin and closed in on the hotel. Everything was happening very quickly now. Like a game of chess being played at a hundred miles an hour. Bald had already scuttled across to the south side of the rooftop, scoping out the next targets.

Porter noticed something in the corner of his eye. Smoke spooling into the sky from the wreckage of the technical to the east. Black smoke. Close to the plumes rising up from the car tyre. Close enough for the two plumes to be mistaken for one another.

Porter spoke into the sat phone. The second Black Hawk was already banking towards the hotel, circling it in the same broad arc as the first heli.

'Helo Z-2, this is Ambassador 1. Be aware, vehicle is on fire. We have smoke coming off vehicle to the east, three hundred metres. Be advised, we are still on the rooftop. Repeat, the black smoke to the east is not our position.'

The line squawked with interference. Then the pilot said, 'Read you loud and clear, buddy. Smoke to the east is not you guys. Helo Z-2 ready to engage next targets when you are.'

Bald said, 'Ten X-rays south of us, mate. A hundred metres away, at the sheds.'

Porter got back on the blower. 'Go south, go south. One hundred metres south of black smoke. Ten enemies with weapons. Engage, engage.'

The second Black Hawk banked steeply off to its left. Porter watched it perform a low fly-over south of the hotel. The mini-gun roared. The rebels seeking cover at the sheds were turned to mincemeat. Spent rounds poured out of the tubes attached to the side of the minigun and rained down on the swimming pool behind the hotel. Like coins out of a fruit machine hitting the jackpot. Half a dozen rebels legged it back towards the low wall in a desperate bid to escape the fire. The Black Hawk tore them to pieces and took out most of the wall too. The targets had literally been scrubbed out of existence.

Over at the bay the first heli had completed its turn and now swooped inland again for a second fly-over. Tully called out from the north side of the rooftop, where he'd returned to his firing position alongside Nilis. Rounds were spattering the top of the parapet in long, continuous bursts.

'Need to get some fucking fire over here, fellas. They're getting close!' Tully shouted, his voice barely audible above the rounds lashing past his head.

Bald and Porter crawled over to the north side, moving as quickly as they could without raising their heads above the parapet. Porter's combats were frayed at the knees from constantly scraping against the debris strewn across the roof. His elbows were bleeding, he had more nicks and cuts on his body than a Chinese torture victim. He stopped by the north wall next to Tully and immediately lay flat on the scorched concrete. More bullets tore into the rooftop in a deafening racket. One of the other Belgians had curled up in a foetal position in sheer terror at the storm of unrelenting gunfire.

In the distance Porter could hear the buzzing of the first helicopter as it neared their position. The mechanical whine of its engines getting loader.

The pilot's voice came over the sat phone. 'Ambassador 1, this is Helo Z-1. Ready to engage next targets.'

We've got to deal with the rebels at the garage, Porter told himself. *Before they brass us all up.*

He grabbed the binos from Bald, swapping them for the sat phone. Then Porter scrambled to his feet before his mucker could say anything, shifted over to the north wall and gazed out through the glasses at the Cape Road, trying to pinpoint the enemy. Round after hot round whipped past him. Porter tried to remain calm in spite of the terrifying rate of fire bearing down on him. A burst rattled the top of the parapet six inches to his right, scattering chunks of concrete across the rooftop. Porter knew he was taking a massive risk by exposing himself to enemy fire. But he also knew he didn't have a choice. The Black Hawks had missed the rebels camped out in the garage on the previous fly-overs. Unless Porter could point out their coordinates, the rebels were going to keep on peppering the rooftop with accurate gunfire. He glimpsed one of the rebels firing from the window on the first floor of the garage. Then he turned to Bald.

'Twenty-five X-rays north of us!' Porter shouted. 'At the garage with the blue roof. Two hundred metres. Get some fire down on those cunts.'

Bald got on the sat phone and relayed the int to the pilot. He had to shout to make himself heard above the bursts of gunfire and the howl of RPG rockets. Porter saw the Black Hawk banking sharply to the left, her rotors straining under the pressure of the turn. Then the M134 on the left-hand side buzzed. A river of fire spurted out of the minigun, blasting the garage. Porter couldn't see much of the strike area. There was a lot of dust and debris, and occasional flashes of bright red light as tracer rounds sliced through the walls. Pulverising any targets camped out inside the building.

Five or six rebels had managed to escape the garage before the minigun struck. Porter heard the *pa-pap-pa-pap-pa-pap* of the M134 on the right-hand side as it fired again. The fleeing rebels disappeared in cloud of blood and smoke. Like a killer magic trick. Further to the east some of the enemy emerged from behind cover at the banana trees and tried to bring down the heli with their small-arms fire. The Black Hawk blitzed them with a long squirt from the minigun, chopping up the plantation and everyone in it. By the time the heli flew back out to the bay, the entire road had been decimated.

Porter stepped back from the parapet. Bald stared at him with a look of grudging respect.

'Fuck me, mate. Maybe I was wrong.'

'What d'you mean?'

Bald grinned. 'Maybe you've got a pair of balls on you after all.'

'Fuck off, Jock.'

They went back to work, racing from one side of the roof to the other as the Black Hawks took turns to make sweeps of the hotel. The operators worked like a married couple. Porter sighting the next target through the binos, determining the distance and number of enemies. Bald transmitting the int back to the pilots on board each heli. After five or six minutes Porter looked past his shoulder and noticed that the flames on the car tyre had almost burnt themselves out. He dispatched Tully and Nilis down to the car park to fetch more wheels before the fire extinguished. Then he ordered the other three Belgians to spread out across the north, east and south sides of the rooftop, watching in case any more rebels attempted to advance on the hotel. But he figured it was unlikely the enemy would try to attack again. Not with the Black Hawks on the prowl. The few remaining rebels were now camped out behind the old police station. They were taking pot shots at the rooftop, accompanied by the occasional RPG rocket or mortar round.

Porter got a visual on the enemy's location. Bald called it in.

The heli swept inland. The minigun chainsawed.

The bullets shredded the police station.

After eight sweeps the rebel guns began to quieten. Hardly any rounds were coming in at the rooftop now. One rebel stepped into the Cape Road and pointed his RPG skywards as the second Black Hawk swung back in from the bay. Big mistake. The M134 chopped him up into pieces so small they were practically molecular. A few pockets of rebels stood their ground but most of the survivors were driven back under the huge rate of gunfire raining down on them in clinical bursts. Fires had broken out across the Cape Road and towards the roundabout in the east as the Black Hawks laid waste to the technicals and outlying buildings, obliterating anywhere the enemy tried to hide. The sky blackened. The palm trees swayed under the hot blast of the helis' blades. Dust swirled over the mutilated bodies strewn across the tarmac. Everywhere Porter looked he could see smoking piles of rubble and limbs.

After twelve sweeps the guns stopped firing.

The dust settled. Porter gazed out across the Cape Road. The enemy was in full retreat. Twenty or so rebels had managed to escape the killing spree. They had ditched their weapons and were scrabbling back past the roundabout, running away from the helis as fast as their skinny legs could carry them. Overhead the two Black Hawks sequenced into a holding pattern, circling the hotel rooftop and searching for any more opportune targets in the surrounding buildings. But none of the enemy showed their faces or returned fire. They've given up the fight, Porter realised.

It's over.

He slumped back against a ruined section of the wall. Looked down at his watch. 1342. They had been directing the top cover for more than half an hour. It felt more like three hours. It had been the longest thirty minutes of his life. His head was mashed, his clothes glued to his skin, his forearm muscles burning. He reached over and grabbed a half-full bottle of water. The plastic was hot to the touch. The water tasted warm when he pressed it to his lips. Porter didn't care. He took a long gulp, wiped his dry lips with the back of his hand and closed his eyes for a beat.

Bald got off the sat phone with Hendricks. Porter chucked him the water bottle. He took a deep swig, blinked sweat out of his eyes. 'Fucking hell that was close. If them helis had been a minute or two later, we'd have been toast.'

Porter nodded at his mucker. 'You all right?'

'Nothing a pint of Bell's won't sort out.' He shook his head and laughed at the madness of it all. 'That was fucking wacky, mate. When they briefed us on the op, I wasn't expecting us to end up in a remake of *Zulu*.'

'Me neither,' said Porter. 'I thought we were done for back there. Good job you were handy with that gimpy, or we'd have been in serious shit.'

Bald nodded grudgingly. 'You're not such a bad operator yourself. Even if you are a southern cunt.'

'Scottish wanker.'

'Says the poof who can't handle a drink.'

Porter managed a weak smile as the Black Hawks circled above. Neither of them said another word. They didn't need to. Both of them had stared death in the eye, up there on the rooftop.

There was a special bond that existed between operators who had faced certain death and survived to tell the tale. It put everything else into perspective. All the petty bullshit of the world, all the pointless crap that people stressed over. None of it mattered.

Maybe I was wrong, Porter reflected. Bald isn't such a bad guy after all. We might have our differences, but he had my back today on the rooftop. When the shit hit the fan, he stepped up. You can't ask for more than that in a bloke. Bald had a mean streak and a savage tongue, but underneath it all he was loyal. And that was all that mattered, really.

He said, 'When we get back to London, we'll owe that Angela bird a pint.'

'Just the one? For saving our bacon?' Bald pulled a look of horror, then shook his head. 'And everyone says us Jocks are tight bastards.'

They lapsed into a casual, friendly silence for several moments. Then Tully called out from the south side of the rooftop. Porter and Bald picked themselves up, moved stiffly across the roof. They kept their heads low, in case any of the rebels had managed to avoid the pummelling dished out by the Black Hawks. Unlikely, but neither of them wanted to take a chance. They passed the noxious fumes rising up from the burning car tyres and the damaged water tower. Smoke hung like a veil over the rooftop.

The smoke cleared. Porter saw Tully kneeling at the air-conditioning duct beside one of the Belgians. The guy was all kinds of fucked-up. His stomach was slashed open and his guts were hanging out of the wide gash, like the inner tube spilling out of a slashed car tyre. His face and hands were pockmarked with bits of shrapnel. A puddle of glistening blood had formed around his entrails. The guy's breathing was shallow and his eyes were dancing wildly in their sockets. Porter dropped beside the Belgian to examine his injuries. Bald cocked his head at Tully.

'What happened?'

'Poor cunt must have been hit by one of them RPGs.' Tully pointed to a huge hole in a lower section of the southern wall.

Chunks of concrete were scattered all over the place. 'Right when one of the helis was making a pass over us.'

Porter tore a strip off the guy's shirt then covered it over the wound as a temporary dressing. The Belgian moaned in pain, muttering a few incoherent words under his breath. Porter had done enough basic medical training in the Regiment to know his chances of survival were grim unless they medevacked him to a hospital immediately.

He finished applying the dressing, then looked up at Bald. 'What did Hendricks say about the evacuation?'

'Rescue choppers on their way now. Sea Stallions.'

'How long till they get here?'

'Hendricks reckons twenty minutes,' Bald said. 'They're going to land at the helipad west of the hotel with a detachment of marines then start ferrying everyone out to the aircraft carrier. Yanks and Brits first. Then Europeans. Then everyone else.'

Porter nodded. He thought, one thousand civilians. Plus the staff. The Sea Stallions had a maximum capacity of fifty-five passengers. Which meant they would have to make twenty trips in order to get everyone out of the country. He gestured to the wounded Belgian.

'We'll have to take him with us on the first chopper out of here. He's a priority case.' He looked to Tully. 'Get us some water. We need to stop his vitals from drying out.'

Tully headed off in search of a discarded water bottle. Porter stood up and noticed Bald frowning at something over at the southern wall. He looked in the same direction. Saw nothing. Turned back to his mucker.

'What is it?'

'Nilis and the other Belgians,' Bald replied. 'They're not here.'

Porter glanced around the rooftop again, scratching the back of his head. *Bald's right.* He couldn't see the other three Belgians. Just the guy with half his face missing to the north and the guy with his guts hanging out to the south. Porter did a quick recce of the area, noting that the Belgians had taken their SLRs with them. As if they'd simply upped sticks and left as soon as the battle was over.

'Where the fuck did they go?' Porter wondered aloud.

'They must have pissed off downstairs,' Bald suggested. 'Maybe they're helping to put out some of those fires that were breaking out.'

Porter shook his head. 'We don't have time to worry about them. Let's get Soames. We've got to put him on that first heli.'

'Fine by me, mate. I don't know about you, but I've had enough of this shite country to last me a lifetime.'

'What about this fella?' Tully asked, pointing to the Belgian with his guts hanging out. The guy was conscious but totally out of it.

'Watch over him until the helis get here,' Porter ordered. 'Keep pouring water over his vitals. We'll put him on the first chopper with us.'

Porter crossed the rooftop with Bald and ducked into the cool shade of the stairwell, leaving Tully behind to watch over the rag-order Belgian. The blasting noise and fury of the Black Hawks circling overhead faded to a dull hum as the two Blades made their way down the steps. The adrenaline of the firefight had started to wear off. Porter willed on his tired muscles.

Just a little further. *We're almost there now.*

Keep going.

They descended the stairs at a brisk pace. The landings were brimming with smoke from where the RPG rockets had scored direct hits. Dense curtains of it choked the upper floor landings. Some of the guests were poking their heads out of the rooms, but the vast majority were still hiding inside, praying to gods they didn't believe in, waiting for someone to knock on the door and tell them everything was okay. That they could go back to their nice, cosy lives.

Porter ran into Tannon and Crowder on the way down. They were busy coordinating the small army of volunteers, dispatching them to various floors with fire extinguishers and first aid kits, and blankets for anyone suffering trauma. News of the rebels' defeat had quickly spread among the staff and volunteers. Tannon looked visibly relieved, but Crowder appeared dejected. Porter didn't blame the guy. We might have knocked back the rebels, he thought, but this guy's business has been trashed. It would take months before the hotel could open its doors again. If ever.

Porter rapidly outlined the evacuation plan to them both and told Crowder to make sure everyone stayed inside their rooms until the marines were ready to begin transferring people to the choppers. Then he ran on downstairs with Bald.

The smoke thinned out at the second floor landing. Porter hit the bottom stair and almost tripped over a couple of Nigerian soldiers. They were slouched across the landing, their knees pulled tight to their chests. They stared up at the two passing operators with their dull, bovine expressions. Porter breezed past them and pushed down the corridor at a fast pace, Bald hard on his heels. He saw the storeroom door ten metres up ahead. Hurried towards it. Then he froze.

The door wasn't locked.

Porter stepped closer. A splintered crack ran down the middle of the door, and the lock had been busted open. Porter paused in front of the storeroom door and listened carefully. He heard no sound coming from inside. He pushed the door open. It groaned back on its hinges, revealing the dark interior. He saw the light-bulb flickering overhead, the dusty shelves at the far end. Desk to the right, the sink to his left.

Then the realisation hit him, like a knife twisting inside his guts.

Soames wasn't there.

The room was empty.

TWENTY

1356 hours.

Porter stood in the doorway for several beats, staring at the empty space where Soames should have been. Thinking, *Soames has given us the slip.* Bald caught up with him. He glanced inside the store-room. Frowned.

'What the fuck happened? Where's Soames?'

Porter said nothing. He looked back at the door. Something wasn't right with this picture, but he couldn't place it.

'He must have booted his way out while we were on the rooftop,' Bald added.

'No.' Porter waved a hand at the lock. The metal had been twisted out of shape and the surrounding wooden surface was blackened and shredded. 'Soames didn't kick it open. It's been blasted open from the outside. You can see the burn marks. Someone helped him escape.'

Bald's from deepened. 'Who would have done that?'

Porter shrugged. He looked hard at Bald for a moment. The guy had been ambivalent about the op from the beginning, and Porter wondered where his loyalties lay. Above everything else, Bald respected money. Money, and power. And Soames had plenty of both. *Enough to tempt Bald into sabotaging the op?* Porter didn't know. But they'd both been fighting for their lives on the rooftop for the past seven hours. He found it hard to believe Bald would have had time to sneak away and bust Soames free without anyone noticing.

Then he remembered Bald had gone downstairs to fill the tyres. He'd been gone for several minutes. Long enough to make a detour and break Soames free? Perhaps. A question burned in Porter's mind.

Did Bald do a deal with Soames behind my back?

He parked the thought at the back of his mind as he heard the sound of approaching footsteps. Porter turned and saw one of the Nigerian soldiers walking over from the landing. The guy watched Porter with a tight, anxious expression. He had a thin, hollow-cheeked face with a pencil moustache faintly visible above his huge lips. The soldier scratched an elbow and tipped his head at the storeroom door.

'You are looking for the man in that room?'

Porter nodded. 'That's right. Did you see anything?'

'Maybe,' the Nigerian said. 'Then again, maybe I did not.'

He folded his arms across his chest and waited. For Porter to dig his hand into his pocket and fish out a few dollar bills, presumably. Nigerians, thought Porter. Always on the take, even in the middle of a bloody firefight. He stepped closer to the Nigerian and grabbed him by the jacket.

'I'm not fucking around. You'd better tell me what you saw.'

The Nigerian saw the look of rage on Porter's face and relented. 'Three men,' he said. 'I saw three men!'

The soldier held up three fingers as if to emphasise the point. Porter let go of the Nigerian and glared at him. The knife in his guts twisted a little more. 'Who?'

'I didn't get a good look at them,' the Nigerian protested. 'I saw them coming down the stairs, that's all. They smashed open the door and took the man inside with them. There was a lot of shouting, a lot of angry voices. The man didn't sound like he wanted to go with the others.'

'But he left with them anyway?'

'The men had guns. He couldn't refuse.'

'Did you see where they took him?'

'Downstairs. To the car park. That's all I know.'

He spread his hands, palms facing up. Like a poker player revealing a crap hand.

'When was this?' Bald demanded.

'Ten minutes ago, maybe,' the soldier replied.

Bald looked accusingly at the Nigerian. 'And you just stood there and fucking watched?'

The Nigerian folded his arms defensively across his chest. 'It's none of my business what these people do. I didn't want to get involved.'

Bald's face twisted with anger. He snorted in contempt. 'Course you didn't, pal. Just like you and your fucking mates didn't want to get involved with fighting the rebels back there.'

The soldier scratched his elbow again and said nothing. Porter said, 'The blokes who grabbed Soames. Did you notice anything about them?'

'I told you, I didn't get a good look at their faces.'

'What about their clothes? Anything about them? Were they black, white?'

'White men,' the Nigerian said. 'In safari clothes. They look like those families that go on safari in the jungle, you know?'

The knife moved again inside Porter's guts, gouging his vitals and twisting his stomach muscles. Shit, he thought.

'The Belgians.'

That's why they went missing from the rooftop.

They're the ones who took Soames.

Bald said, 'Why the fuck would the Belgians have an interest in kidnapping Soames?'

'No idea, Jock. But there's only one way to find out.'

The wounded Belgian. The guy with his guts hanging out.

We need to find out what he knows.

Porter barged aside the Nigerian and raced back down the corridor towards the landing. Bald sprinted ahead of him. By now several civilians had emerged from their rooms. They crowded the corridors on the upper floors, gossiping amongst themselves.

'Get back in your rooms!' Porter shouted at them.

'What's going on out there?' a podgy French guy in a linen suit demanded. 'Why can't we leave?'

224

'The evacuation hasn't started yet. Everything's under control. Someone will tell you when you're going to be processed. Until then, shut your mouth and stay in your fucking room.'

The Frenchman reluctantly retreated to his room. The other guests swiftly followed. Porter and Bald pushed on up the stairs and accelerated up the bare concrete stairwell leading to the rooftop. Porter could feel his lungs burning, his veins simmering with rage. They hurried over to Tully. He was still kneeling beside the wounded Belgian, splashing water from a one-litre bottle over the man's exposed bowels. He stood up and turned to face the Blades.

'What's going on?' he said.

Porter ignored the question. He dropped down beside the Belgian and grabbed the guy by the throat, clenching his fingers around the man's neck. The Belgian groaned, gasping for breath.

'Where the fuck is Soames?' Porter growled.

The Belgian coughed up blood and groaned again. Porter loosened his grip on the guy's neck so he could talk. The Belgian looked up. His eyes were inked with fear. But there was something else there too thought Porter. Defiance.

'Fuck you,' the guy spat.

His accent had subtly changed. It sounded harsher now. Guttural, and coarse. Definitely Eastern European. Porter tightened his grip around the man's neck again, compressing the cartilage and crushing his windpipe. Tears streamed down the man's cheeks.

'It's only gonna get worse if you don't talk,' Porter said as he released his grip again. 'We know your mates have lifted Soames. Tell us where they took him.'

'Fuck off,' the Belgian rasped, clenching his jaws in pain.

Porter leaned in closer. He tapped his G-Shock and lowered his voice to a sinister whisper.

'That's a nasty wound you've got there. You've got about an hour and a half until you bleed out. There's a heli landing here in twenty minutes. Tell us what the fuck is going on, and we'll put you on the first chopper out of here and get you to a hospital. Or you can keep your mouth shut, and we'll dump you in the basement. It'll be hours before anyone finds you. You'll die in fucking agony. Your choice.'

The Belgian hesitated. His eyes flicked from Porter to Bald to Tully. Then back to Porter. The spark in his eyes faded. The defiance giving way to fear, and uncertainty. Porter ripped off the basic dressing on his stomach wound. The man howled.

'Fucking tell me,' Porter said.

'I swear, I don't know shit.'

'Bollocks! He's lying,' Bald cut in.

Porter bunched his hands into fists. *I didn't survive a battle against hundreds of rebel fighters, only for this guy and his mates to screw the op.* He snatched up one of the jerry cans of petrol lying next to the burnt-out rubber tyres. There was still some petrol left in the container. Enough for his purposes. He moved back over to the Belgian and began pouring the liquid over his exposed entrails. The man screamed as Porter emptied the dregs over his head. Then he tossed the can aside and knelt down next to the Belgian.

'Last chance. Talk, or I'll light your guts up.'

The Belgian broke down in tears. 'I don't know where they've gone,' he sobbed. 'It's the fucking truth, I swear. The plan was to grab Soames and get out of here as soon as the rebels were defeated. We needed him alive. To find out where he was hiding the stuff.'

'What stuff? Diamonds?'

'I don't know. They didn't tell us. We were just following orders.'

'Who sent you?'

The man's eyes dimmed. Like the light fading on a couple of headlamps. Porter grabbed the Belgian by his bloodstained bush shirt and shook him violently. He reeked of petrol fumes.

'I said, who fucking sent you?'

'FSB,' the man replied in a weak voice.

Porter felt the blood draining from his head to his toes.

Shit.

FSB.

Russian Federal Security Services.

'You're Russian?' he growled.

The man nodded weakly.

'Where have your mates gone?' Porter said, shaking the Russian. 'Fucking tell me!'

The man winced. 'I don't know.'

Porter snatched up the kitchen knife lying next to the burnt-out tyres. The knife tip gleamed wickedly. He pressed the tip against the Russian's exposed intestines, drawing an inhuman scream.

'Tell me, or I'll cut your fucking insides out.'

He pressed the knife harder. The tip pierced the man's vitals.

'Shit!' the Russian gasped. 'Fuck, no!'

'Talk.'

The man whimpered and said, 'Our bosses at the FSB, they sent us here to locate Soames. They said he was important to our president. We found out he'd checked in at this hotel, so we came here to look for him. Then the rebels attacked. We had to help you. Stop the enemy.'

'What about the others? Where have they gone?'

The Russian coughed up blood. 'They left with Soames as soon as the attack was over. The plan was to make him talk. Find out where he's hiding everything. Then they were going to rob him.'

He grimaced in pain. Looked up at Porter with pleading eyes.

'That's all I fucking know. You have to believe me.'

The Russian closed his eyes, overwhelmed by the pain. Porter tossed aside the knife. He stood up and turned towards Bald and Tully. Overhead the Black Hawks continued to circle in slow, lazy arcs.

'Fucking great,' Bald said. 'The Russians have lifted Soames and we've got no idea where to look. Now what are we supposed to do?'

Then Tully said, 'I think I know where they've gone.'

Porter said, 'Where?'

Tully stared at the dying Russian as he replied: 'The diamond mine.'

'Kono?' Bald frowned. 'Why the fuck would Soames have taken the Russians there?'

'Soames knew the Russians were on to him,' said Tully. 'He told me a couple of weeks ago over a few beers. He got drunk and told me the Russians were sniffing around, asking questions.'

'What sort of questions?' Porter said.

'About the stuff he's keeping safe at the mine.'

Porter shot a glance at Bald. Swung his gaze back to Tully.

'What stuff, Bob?'

Tully hesitated to reply. His eyes darted back and forth between the two operators. As if he was studying their reactions and debating whether to trust them. Then he took the plunge.

'Soames has got something safe there. Something everyone else has been after. Including these Russians.'

'What the fuck are you talking about?' Porter said.

'Stolen diamonds,' said Tully.

'That's what Soames has got stashed at the mine? A few diamonds he's nicked from under his employers' nose?'

'Not just a few.' Tully shook his head. 'We're talking about a huge stash, fellas. Tens of millions of pounds' worth of diamonds, Soames reckoned. Some of them are the size of fag packets. There's enough in the stash to buy a private island and fill it with high-class escorts.'

Bald puffed out his cheeks and whistled. 'Jesus. I'm in the wrong business.'

Porter said, 'Why would Soames hide diamonds in his own mining field?'

Tully tapped the side of his head. 'Think about it, mate. Safest place in the country. Round-the-clock security, and it's the last place anyone would think to look.'

Bald stroked his jaw. 'Makes sense. Hiding the loot in plain sight. No fucker would think to look there for a stash of stolen bling. It's the perfect hiding place.'

Porter detected a note of admiration in Bald's voice. Not for the first time, he wondered whose side Bald was really on.

'Why would the Russian security services give a toss about some stolen diamonds?' he asked.

Tully shrugged. 'Spoils of war. The Russians have got orders to seize the mine and use it to bankroll their operations in Sierra Leone. Nilis and his mates probably heard about the stash and decided to steal it for themselves.'

'But they didn't know about the stash. Not until they got their hands on Soames.'

Tully rolled his eyes. 'Fella, everyone knows that President Fofana is on the take. There have been rumours doing the rounds for months that Soames has got Fofana in his pocket. The Russians would have heard about the rumours through their mates in the RUF. It wouldn't take a fucking genius to work out that Soames was using the diamonds to bribe the president.'

Porter glowered at Tully. 'Why didn't you tell us about this before?'

'I couldn't, mate. Soames gave me a job on the Circuit when no other bastard was willing to take me on. I've got a good life out here, thanks to him. If he wants to cook up a few dodgy deals in the back office, it's none of my fucking business, is it?'

Porter stayed quiet for a beat. He remembered what Tannon had told him in the hotel bar the previous evening, before the assault. *The diamond mine makes Fort Knox look like a branch of Abbey National.*

The diamond stash, Porter thought. That's what Soames has been hiding there. He stared into the middle distance and thought, *Soames has been nicking diamonds and hiding them at the mine. That's why the Russians were after him. To find out where he had buried the treasure and rob him.* But something was wrong, Porter thought. *I'm missing something here, but I can't figure out what it is.* He nodded at Tully.

'How far is it to Kono from here?'

'Two hundred and fifty miles or so. Six hours, depending on how many rebel checkpoints you've got to pass through. It's mostly dirt roads cutting through the jungle.'

Porter consulted his G-Shock. 1416 hours. According to the Nigerian soldier, the Russians had lifted Soames at approximately

1345 hours. Which meant the Russians had a thirty-minute head start. He shook his head bitterly.

'It's too late. We'll never catch them in time.'

'Not necessarily,' said Tully.

'How'd you mean?'

'I've been here for six months, fella. I've done that trip more times than a hooker to the clap clinic. There's a few shortcuts the Russians won't have a clue about. If we leave now, we can still catch up with them. We can intercept the fuckers before they hit Kono.'

Porter needed about a second to decide. It wasn't a brilliant plan, but it was the only one they had. *We've got to get Soames back. This is our only shot.*

'All right. Let's move. We'll take the Range Rover. Bob, you're coming with us. We'll need you to point out the shortcuts.'

'What about ammo?' Tully said. 'We've got sod-all left.'

'We've still got the two Makarovs.'

Tully shook his head. 'We're gonna need more than that. Way fucking more. The jungle's crawling with child soldiers fighting for the West Side Boys, and they've got some serious firepower. A few pistols won't do us much good if we run into trouble.'

'Then we'll nick whatever we can from the dead rebels outside.'

'What are we gonna do with this cunt?' Bald said.

He pointed to the Russian with his guts hanging out. The guy's lips were dry and cracked, his breathing reduced to a light whimper. He had maybe an hour to live. Maybe less. Porter didn't know for sure. He wasn't a doctor.

The Russian looked up at him with heavily-lidded eyes.

'Please,' he begged. 'Don't leave me here.'

Porter spotted the green satchel bag filled with medical supplies lying nearby. He gave his back to the Russian, reached down for the satchel and unzipped it. Inside was a pair of first-aid scissors, some sterile bandages and gauze swabs, a pack of plasters and a roll of zinc oxide tape. Plus several foil packets of pills with labels on the front. Aspirin, codeine, antihistamines. An impressive variety of sedatives. There were ten pills to each pack. Porter grabbed one of the foil packets and shuffled back over to the Russian. Crouched down next to the guy, and popped all ten pills out of the packet. The noise of the Black Hawks had faded. They were circling a cluster of nearby buildings, scouring for targets.

'Take these,' Porter said, offering the Russian the pills. 'They'll help with the pain.'

The Russian tilted his head forward and opened his mouth. Porter shoved the pills into his gob. Then he took one of the water bottles and pressed it to the guy's lips. He swallowed the pills greedily and croaked a word of thanks.

Porter said, 'We're going to send for help.'

'No,' the Russian gasped. 'Don't go . . . please.'

'We can't move you. You're gonna have to stay put until we can get you lifted to a hospital.'

The guy swallowed painfully. 'But the sun . . . I'll die.'

Porter pointed towards a corrugated steel sheet that had blown off the roof of the water tower. 'We'll put that sheet over you. Keep you shaded. In the meantime, stay quiet. You don't want to make yourself a target for any X-rays that might be hanging around the hotel.'

'You're coming back?'

'I promise.'

Hope flared behind the Russian's eyes. He gave a weak nod of his head. Then Porter stood up and turned his back on the dying man. Bald pulled a face at his mucker as they moved away from the Russian.

'You're going soft. Helping out that bastard.'

Porter laughed and shook his head. 'I didn't give him painkillers. He just popped a load of sleeping pills. He'll die in his sleep before anyone finds him. The pilots won't see him under that sheet.'

Bald looked impressed. 'That's fucking dark, that.'

'Coming from you, Jock, I'll take that as a compliment.'

They shared a warm laugh. Then they hurried across the rooftop. Porter ditched his SLR rifle and retrieved the two remaining Makarov pistols. Porter checked both the clips. Eight rounds in each. Plus the eight rounds in the PSM Bald had lifted from the German the previous day. A total of twenty-four rounds between them. Not enough if they ran into the West Side Boys, Porter knew. But it's all we've bloody got.

He tucked one of the Makarovs in the waistband of his combats and handed the other pistol to Tully. Along with the PSM, Bald carried the GPMG, stuffing his pockets with spare link as he went. Porter figured they could cobble together enough spare rounds from the slotted rebels to piece together a belt for the machine gun. If they were lucky.

As they headed for the stairwell, he heard the dull throb of heli blades beating overhead. He stopped and looked up at the sky just in time to see the first Sea Stallion arrive from the direction of the jetty. The two Black Hawks continued to circle the streets as the Stallion banked to the right, closing in on the helipad a hundred metres west of the hotel. The chopper hovered for a few seconds above the helipad before slowly descending, the downwind whipping up fierce swirls of dust on the ground below. The Stallion touched down, the rotor blades continuing to whir as the ramp lowered and a detachment of twenty-six troops debussed. They were decked out in the Marine Corps uniform of desert cammies, olive-green skivvies and combat helmets. All of them wore wrap-around shades, and they were all equipped with M16 assault rifles.

As Porter looked on, sixteen of the marines formed a protective cordon around the Stallion, facing out across the surrounding territory to watch for any approaching threats. The manoeuvre was smooth, quick and efficient. Typically American. The other ten marines moved at a brisk pace towards the hotel.

'Looks like the evacuation's about to begin,' Bald said.

Porter nodded. He felt a slight sense of relief as he watched the marines enter the hotel. At least the civilians are safe, he thought. Even if the mission is fucked, we did a good thing here today.

'Let's go.'

He closed the door leading to the rooftop. The janitor's key was still inserted in the keyhole. He twisted the key in the lock, then smashed the butt of the Makarov against the bow of the key, bending the metal out of shape and trapping the metal stem in the keyhole. If anyone wandered up to the top of the hotel, they would find the door locked. The wounded Russian would be dead long before anyone managed to gain access to the rooftop.

The three men piled down the stairs at a brisk pace. People were beginning to emerge from their rooms now as word of the imminent evacuation spread. On the third floor, Crowder and a team of half-a-dozen volunteers were moving from room to room, ordering the beleaguered guests down into the lobby so they could begin organising into groups. Tannon was there too, helping to direct the crowd. She was back to her practical, businesslike self. Porter was quietly impressed with the way she had recovered her composure after the hell of the past few hours. She marched over to him.

'The first chopper's just landed,' she said. 'We're sending everyone down to the reception. You should hurry up if you want to make the chopper.'

'We're not going,' Porter said.

'Why?' Tannon glanced at Tully and Bald in turn. Saw the troubled expressions on their faces. Returned her gaze to Porter. 'What's going on?'

'Soames is gone. Some Russians have lifted him.'

He hurriedly explained how the Russians had pulled the wool over their eyes. How they had been watching Soames, waiting for an opportune moment to snatch him and escape. He told her about the diamond mine, and the stash Soames had been keeping there, sharing the spoils with the country's corrupt leaders.

'We're leaving now. We've got to catch up with them. Get Soames back before they reach the mine.'

'I'll come with you.'

Porter shook his head. 'It's too dangerous.'

'I can take care of myself. I'm invested in this thing as much as anyone.'

'Sorry, love. But you need to stay here and sort out the evacuation with the Yanks. Make sure everyone gets on those choppers.

233

The rebels won't come back today, but they'll have another pop tomorrow if there's anyone left behind.'

Tannon gave him a look. For a moment Porter thought she was going to argue the point further. *She looks like the kind of bird who's used to getting her own way.* But then she just nodded and said, 'Okay.'

Porter turned to leave. Bald and Tully were already piling down the stairs ahead of him.

'John,' Tannon said.

He stopped. Looked back at the deputy commissioner.

'Thank you. You saved a lot of lives today.'

She smiled awkwardly at him. Porter nodded back and absently wondered if he'd ever see her again. Then he turned and headed down the stairs after Bald and Tully. I've still got one more life to save, he thought.

The one person I'd rather leave for dead.

My old CO.

TWENTY-ONE

1421 hours.

They hit the lobby fifty seconds later. The first hundred or so guests were already assembling next to the reception. A team of volunteers divided them up by nationality. Yanks and Brits in one group, Europeans in another, and a third group of Chinese, Arabs and a few Indians. The guests stared in mute horror at the mangled bodies strewn across the floor. They had been sheltered in their rooms during the worst of the violence. Now they were seeing it up close, the full scale of the bloodshed was beginning to hit home.

Six marines had spread out across the lobby, keeping a watchful eye on the crowd to make sure the evacuation proceeded in an orderly manner. Another marine and an officer stood beside the entrance, processing each civilian from the first group, checking their documents and patting them down for weapons before they were waved through and directed towards the waiting Sea Stallion. In one corner of the lobby Porter spotted a group of around twenty Nigerians rooting through the kit they had ditched before the initial assault several hours earlier. A few of them had already climbed back into their uniforms. They were trying to get the attention of the Yanks, pointing to their badges and shouting, 'UN! UN! Let us through!'

'Can you believe those wankers?' Tully said.

Bald snorted. 'With that lot, nothing surprises me.'

The Yank officer left the entrance and marched over to Porter. He was a short, wiry guy with a stern, angular face. A stubby cigar stuck out of the corner of his mouth, and he carried a service-issue Beretta M9 pistol in a nylon leg holster. The name tape on the left side of his jacket said HENDRICKS in stark bold lettering. The tape on the right side simply said US MARINES. The officer regarded the three bloodied, sweat-soaked men in front of him, their clothing cut to shreds at the elbows and knees.

'I'm guessing you're the boys who were up on the roof,' Hendricks said in his heavy Texan twang.

Porter nodded. Hendricks relaxed his expression into admiration. He thrust out a hand.

'Colonel Hendricks. We spoke on the phone. I'm guessing you fellas are military?'

'British special forces,' Porter said, shaking his hand.

Hendricks arched an eyebrow in surprise. 'That was some fine work you did up there. I'd be interested to hear the full story. Perhaps you can tell us the whole nine once we're back on the *Lauderdale*.'

'We'd love to, mate. But we've got an alternate mission outside this location, and we don't have much time. Can we hand over to you?'

'No problem,' Hendricks said. 'Ain't much for us to do here anyway, except clear up and get the hell out.' He glanced over at the dead rebels to the side of the entrance. 'Looks like you were really in the shit here.'

'Just doing our job,' said Bald. 'We've been in worse scrapes.'

'I don't doubt it.' Hendricks smiled. 'You fellas need anything where you're headed, just holler.'

Bald tapped the gimpy. 'If you've got any 7.62 milli going spare, we'd be grateful. We're out of ammo.'

'Consider it done.'

Colonel Hendricks barked out an order to one of the marines standing guard. The soldier darted outside and hurried over to the Sea Stallion sitting idly on the helipad. He came back ninety seconds later lugging a box of 7.62mm belt ammo. The marine handed the box over to Tully, saluted, and returned to his post.

'Watch yourselves, wherever you're going,' said Hendricks.

'Cheers,' Porter replied. 'We'll try.'

Then Porter, Bald and Tully made for the doors leading down to the underground car park.

Two minutes later they were racing down the Cape Road.

Porter had the Range Rover wheel. Tully rode shotgun. Bald sat in the back. The GPMG resting across his lap, the box of spare ammo nestled between his feet and the two spare jerry cans next to him. Bald had sniffed the cans to make sure they were filled with diesel before they had set off. With the extra jerry cans they had enough petrol to reach Kono. The clock on the dash read 14:28. Forty minutes since the Russians had bugged out of the hotel with Soames. Porter glanced over at Tully in the front passenger seat.

'How long's it gonna take us to catch up with the Russians?'

Tully narrowed his eyes at the dash clock. 'They've got a good head start. But they'll be taking the Masiaka–Yonibana highway from Freetown all the way to Kono. Which is the newest road in the country. But it's also the longer route. I reckon they'll get there around eight o'clock. We'll follow the highway all the way to Yonibana, then get off the main road and head north. The roads around there are in crap nick, but it'll shave off fifty miles or so from our journey time. If we push it hard, we should catch up with the Russians just before they reach the diamond mine.'

'How do you know they'll stick to the highway?' said Bald.

Tully shrugged. 'It's the most obvious route. The road's brand-new. Less bumpy.'

'What if you're wrong? What if they take the shorter route?'

'Then Soames is fucked.'

And so are we, Porter thought.

They headed west on Cape Road, hung a right and motored south down the coastline along Lumley Beach for half a mile. Then they steered north-east onto the Spur Road and rolled through the city centre, passing the British Consulate and Soames's office. It felt like a lifetime since Bald and Porter had rocked up there the previous morning. Back then, Freetown had been in a state of panic. Now the streets were quiet, and strangely empty. The rebels had long since abandoned their positions, but the evidence of their twisted rampage was all around them. Dead bodies and burnt-out vehicles littered the sides of the road. Small fires blazed amid the gutted remains of looted buildings. Most of the corpses had been stripped of their clothes by scavengers.

Tully directed them south along the Spur Road for five miles, past a low peak with several crumbling mansions built around the base. Then the old colonial buildings and apartment blocks disappeared, replaced by sprawls of ramshackle dwellings and huts built into the surrounding hills. Landslides of human filth and waste. Porter kept the Range Rover ticking along at fifty miles per as the road twisted through the fringes of the Western Area National Park, the vehicle bouncing up and down over the craters in the road. After twelve miles they passed a small village called Waterloo and hit the Masiaka–Yonibana Highway. Or what passed for a highway in Sierra Leone. In reality it was an uneven, single-lane stretch of tarmac that snaked through tracts of vast, sprawling jungle.

Porter kept his foot to the gas as he reached for the sat phone and pulled up the number for Hawkridge. The battery was flashing, indicating it was almost dead. The display showed five missed calls from the same number. Porter hit Dial. Waited.

Hawkridge picked up on the first ring.

'What the devil is going on? Why haven't you been answering?'

'We've got a problem,' Porter said. 'The Russians have taken Soames.'

There was silence on the other end of the line. Then Hawkridge said, 'What Russians? The hell are you talking about? I thought you had Soames safe and sound.'

'We did. The Russians were playing us the whole time. They were posing as engineers from Belgium, helping us out on the rooftop against the rebels. They grabbed Soames as soon as our backs were turned.'

The line kept breaking up. The dense overhead canopy, playing havoc with the signal. Distorting Hawkridge's voice.

'You mean to tell me you can't tell the difference between a Russian accent and a Flemish one? You must be even thicker than I thought.'

'Their cover story was solid. They had business cards and everything.'

'I'm not interested in your excuses. Someone with your training should have seen this coming from the start. This is a fucking disaster. You've really cocked it up this time. Both of you.'

Porter gripped the steering wheel so hard his knuckles shaded white. 'We had our hands full dealing with the rebels. If you'd pulled your thumb out of your arsehole and sorted out top cover for us earlier, we might have noticed the Russians slipping away.'

The line went silent for a beat. Porter thought he'd lost the signal. Then Hawkridge's voice came back. 'Where are you now?'

'On the road to Kono. Bob Tully is with us. He reckons the Russians are taking Soames to the diamond mine. Soames has been stashing a load of stolen diamonds there. That's why the Russians have been after him. They're going to seize the mine and grab the loot for themselves. We're on our way to intercept them.'

'Listen carefully. You absolutely must—'

The line abruptly dropped. Porter glanced down at the sat phone. The display had gone blank. He tried turning it on again. Nothing. Shit, Porter thought. *The battery's dead.* We're on our own now. He chucked the phone on the dash and focused on the road ahead. Questions stacked up inside his head. He felt an intense pressure building between his temples.

'Something doesn't make sense.'

'What's that?' Bald said.

'Why would Soames get involved in the diamond-smuggling business in the first place? He's got the PMC, plus the concessions from the diamond mine. He must be rich beyond all imagining. Why would he jeopardise it all by nicking a few diamonds?'

'That's obvious enough.' Bald rubbed an invisible bank note between his thumb and forefinger. 'Wonga. Soames is a greedy bastard.'

'Maybe,' said Porter.

But he wasn't convinced.

They rumbled on through the pockets of thick tropical jungle, Porter swerving to avoid the deeper potholes as the road became increasingly treacherous. A few locals were walking along the dirt either side of the road, old men and women dressed in threadbare rags with faces like petrified wood. Porter pushed the vehicle as hard as he dared, keeping one eye on the fuel gauge as Tully guided them towards Kono. After an hour Tully directed them off the highway onto a rutted, muddy track with piles of red earth heaped at the sides. They had officially left civilisation behind.

Bald said, 'You sure this is the way, Bob?'

'Course I'm fucking sure,' Tully said.

The track worsened. The jungle closed in. Long creeping vines and palm trees crowded either side of the track beyond the ditch, forming an impenetrable dark mass. Random shafts of sunlight poked through the gloomy canopy, spotlighting the road ahead. Porter slowed the Range Rover down as it struggled along the muddied track snaking through the jungle. They carried on for mile after mile without passing a single pedestrian or village.

Where the fuck is Tully taking us?

Suddenly the road opened up and the jungle retreated. A sign announced that they were entering Masiaka. The last major stop on the road to Kono. Porter knew from studying maps of the area that Masiaka was approximately fifty miles from Freetown. From the hotel to the town was normally a ninety-minute drive. A quick glance at the dash clock told him that they had reached Masiaka in seventy-five minutes. Which meant they had knocked fifteen minutes off their journey time so far. Which meant they were fifteen minutes behind the Russians now. Maybe less.

We're closing the gap.

Porter was forced to slow down as he steered past the crowds and animals lining the road. Masiaka looked less like a town, and more like the last stop on the railroad in the Old West. Most of the structures they passed were crude mud-brick huts with thatched roofs. Scrawny chickens pecked at the dusty red earth.

Naked women and children stood at the sides of the road. The kids stared wide-eyed at the Range Rover, pointing and yelling. As if they'd never seen a car before, or a white person. Hookers jostled for business outside a brothel on the outskirts of the town, pointing into their open mouths suggestively. One of them blew kisses at Tully as they passed by. An overweight woman with chubby thighs and an arse so big it probably had its own longitude and latitude coordinates. Tully grinned at the hooker and waved back.

'Cindy,' he said. 'One of my regulars. That bird's a right goer. Gives a mean tit wank for less than a dollar.'

'Jesus,' said Bald. In the rearview mirror, Porter caught him staring at Tully. 'No wonder you're so familiar with this route. Rather you than me, Bob. AIDS being what it is here.'

'You're missing out, fella. Maybe once this is over I'll show you around. You can sample the locals for yourself.'

'Maybe,' Bald replied non-committally.

Porter focused on the road as he drove on past the hookers. He thought about Tully's night fighter back at the Ambassadors Hotel. Remembered the bruises on her jaw. The look of terror in her eyes. Porter had known one or two guys like that in the Regiment. Guys who had been permanently on the edge. Once they left Hereford, they went off the rails. They got jobs on the Circuit, lived like kings, and did whatever they fucking pleased. But he'd never known anyone as vicious as Tully. Compared to Bob, he thought, Bald is a bloody saint.

They continued east out of Masiaka. After thirty miles Porter checked the time on the digital clock again. 1628 hours. Two hours since they had set off from the Ambassadors Hotel. Three-and-a-half hours until we reach Kono. *If we don't pick up speed, we're not going to catch up with the Russians.* He drove harder, mashing the pedal. All three men kept their eyes peeled for any nearby rebel troops that might delay their journey. But every checkpoint they passed appeared to have been abandoned and Porter figured that most of the rebels had left the area to join in the looting around Freetown.

Keep going, he told himself. We've got to catch the Russians. *If they get to the mine first, Soames is a dead man.*

They passed a series of ransacked villages. Dead bodies in various stages of decay littered both sides of the track. Some had been dumped in shallow graves, mothers heaped on top of their children. Others were left to rot under the sun. A few were no more than piles of bones and rags. Many of the villages had been razed to the ground, Porter saw, leaving nothing behind except patches of scorched earth. They passed another shallow pit piled high with severed hands and arms. Smoke rose from several burning wattle-and-daub huts.

'The fuck happened here?' Bald said.

'The West Side Boys,' Tully replied. 'This is their doing.'

Porter nodded. 'Hawkridge warned us about them.'

He remembered what their handler told them at the briefing. About how the West Side Boys abducted children and forced them to kill their parents. How they dressed up in women's clothing and murdered for fun. *They're volatile and dangerous*, Hawkridge had said.

'They're fucking animals,' Tully said. 'They go round all the villages, rounding up the kids. They get the boys high on smack and teach them how to fire an AK-47. The girls are kidnapped and held as sex slaves for the generals to rape whenever they feel like it. When they get older, they turn a profit as hookers.'

Bald gazed out of the window at the rotting corpses. 'How do you know the West Side Boys did this?'

'This is their neck of the woods.' Tully gestured to the pile of severed hands by the roadside. 'Hacking off hands is their speciality. All the villagers have to swear loyalty to the West Side Boys and hand over their food and savings to their soldiers. Anyone who speaks out against them is taken over to a tree stump and told it's their birthday. Then they're asked if they want a short-sleeve or a long-sleeve. Long-sleeve, they cut off your hand at the wrist. Short-sleeve, they hack off your arm at the elbow.'

'Jesus,' said Bald.

'The West Side Boys are worse than those chogies who attacked us in Freetown,' Tully went on. 'At least the RUF has some kind of political goal. The Boys don't give a flying fuck about overthrowing the government. They're just into rape and murder. That's their bag.'

Porter instinctively tensed behind the wheel. They drove on, tooling along at fifty miles per hour past more abandoned settlements and scorched fields. It was almost five o'clock now. *Three more hours till we hit Kono and catch up with the Russians*, Porter thought. After another four miles they came to a sharp turn in the road. Porter eased off the gas and wrenched the steering wheel hard to the right. The Range Rover growled as it leaned heavily into the corner, passing the apex. The track ahead swung into view.

Half a second later, Porter heard the gunshots.

Four separate cracks, like hammers hitting against a thick sheet of steel. Or a bunch of fireworks popping off at a New Year's Eve celebration. Porter's training kicked in. He slammed the brakes. The Range Rover dipped into a pothole then bounced out and skidded to a halt at an angle in the turn, throwing about the guys inside the wagon. Porter felt his guts lurch into his throat. He looked up.

Then he saw the child soldiers.

There was a gang of twelve of them, eighty metres further along the track from the Range Rover. They were barefoot and dressed in tattered rags. Some of the kids wore olive-green army t-shirts. Two others were decked out in replica football jerseys. One wore Arsenal, the other wore Manchester United. Another kid wore nothing except a grimy pair of bright-yellow shorts. They were standing in a tight cluster in the middle of the track, shooting their AK–47s from the hip or over their heads as they recklessly emptied rounds at the treeline to the left. None of them had spotted the Range Rover. Not yet, anyway.

Porter caught sight of a white Land Cruiser forty metres downstream from the child soldiers. A hundred and twenty metres ahead of the Range Rover. An old Toyota Hilux with a dented bonnet blocked the road directly in front of the Land Cruiser. Half-dozen kids were crowded around the Land Cruiser, putting down more rounds on the same spot at the treeline to the left of the track. The Cruiser was in a shitty state. The tyres had been blown out, and several bullet holes starred the rear window. All four doors were open. Smoke wafted up from the engine. A body lay motionless in the dirt next to the wagon. Both his hands had been chopped off and an axe was embedded in his back. Porter caught sight of the dead man's clothes and felt his stomach muscles clench.

Bush shirt. Dun-coloured shorts. Leather hat.

Safari gear.

Bald said, 'That's one of the Russians. They must have blundered into a snap ambush.'

Shit, Porter thought. *We might already be too late. The West Side Boys might have killed Soames.*

The kids in both the front and rear attack groups continued to put down rounds at the treeline, thirty metres away from their position on the road. They still hadn't noticed the Range Rover. Porter scanned the treeline. He saw a drainage ditch running parallel to the edge of the dirt track, backing onto a dense tangle of lush tropical bushes and palm trees. Amid the gloom of the jungle he spied the outline of two figures in the ditch. They were resting their rifle barrels on the top of the ditch, the muzzles sporadically flashing as they returned fire against the kids. They both wore safari hats, identical to the dead guy.

The other Russians. Nilis and Spray-Tan. They were trying to stem the tide of child soldiers swarming towards them, aiming controlled single rounds at both the front and rear attack groups. One of the children lay slumped on the ground, his belly stitched with bullets. In spite of their piss-poor aim the kids had the Russians pinned down, with no way out. Sooner or later they were going to run out of ammo, Porter realised. Then the child soldiers would be free to move in for the kill. Porter swung around in his seat and pointed out the treeline.

'The other Russians are in that ditch,' he said.

'What about Soames?' Tully whispered, craning his neck at the scene. 'I can't see him.'

'He must be there too. Fucker's probably hiding.'

Bald said, 'Want me to send these kids packing with the chogie popper?'

Porter nodded. 'Do it, Jock.'

All three of them clambered out of the Range Rover. The dozen kids in the rear attack group still had their backs to the Hereford men. They were continuing to pop rounds off at the ditch, their rifle cracks audible above gangsta rap music they now had thumping out of the Hilux stereo. Porter, Bald and Tully still had the advantage. They moved quickly, swinging around to the side of the Range Rover. Using the vehicle as cover. Bald picked up the GPMG, flipped out the machine gun's bipod legs and rested the weapon on the bonnet. At the same time Tully reached into the back seat and broke out the box of 7.62 milli ammo that Solomon had linked together back on the hotel rooftop. He passed one end of the belt across to Bald, who took the first round in the link and inserted it into the gimpy's feed tray. Then he pulled the cocking handle on the side of the machine gun and depressed the safety. Tully crouched to Bald's left, holding the length of the ammo belt. Porter stayed low behind the Rover's front wheel, keeping a mark-one eyeball on the targets. Neither of them reached for their Makarovs. Any pistol was only effective up to a range of fifteen metres. The distance between the operators and the child soldiers was more than six times that. They were going to have to rely on the gimpy to do the heavy lifting this time.

One of the kids in the rear attack group glanced down the road. A scrawny child wearing a filthy LA Lakers jersey that reached down to his knees. The kid looked no older than eleven or twelve. He spotted the Range Rover, spun around and shouted frantically at his mates, pointing to the wagon. The kid in the Lakers jersey was still shouting when Bald depressed the trigger. He fired a short, sharp burst at the child, aiming for the chest region. The kid's upper torso exploded, showering his mate with blood.

The five other kids in the fire group instantly turned to face the new threat. Bald gave them the good news, cutting one of them in half at the waist with a raking burst and dropping another kid who looked young enough to be in primary school. The three remaining children returned fire at the Range Rover. They may as well have been shooting blindfold. The rounds were so far off target that Porter didn't even see where they struck. Bald lined up the GPMG sights with the three kids and emptied four long, controlled bursts. The three child soldiers, fell, screaming.

Porter glanced at his mucker. *He's slotting children and he's not even flinching.*

The child soldiers in the second fire group at the Hilux saw their mates getting dropped and panicked. They spun away from the track, fleeing towards the treeline to the right. They were children first and soldiers a poor second. None of them had ever found themselves on the business end of a machine gun before. Porter drew Bald's attention to the retreating kids. Tully paid out the belt as Bald aimed at the right side of the track and raked the surrounding trees and bushes with six-round bursts. The gimpy rattled as it chugged through the linked rounds. Porter could feel the heat coming off the barrel in waves. A couple of the kids returned fire haphazardly from the edge of the treeline, emptying their clips at the Range Rover. The rounds zipped wide, thwacking into the dirt several metres to the right of Porter.

Bald kept on firing. The last of the kids ditched their weapons and ran for cover, screaming in terror as the incoming rounds ripped into the tree trunks. Bald had almost reached the end of the ammo belt now. Twenty rounds left. Porter glimpsed a stroke of movement at the ditch to the left of the track. He looked across. Saw the two figures springing up from the depression in the ground. They turned briefly towards the Range Rover, presumably wondering who was manning the gimpy. Porter got a clear look at their faces as they looked over. Nilis and Spray-Tan. There was still no sign of soames. He didn't seem to be with the Russians.

So where the hell is he?

The Russians broke north across the track, sprinting towards the Hilux. Porter instantly grasped what they were doing and turned to Bald. *Soames is in the pickup truck. That's where he must been hiding.*

The Russians are going to escape with him.

'They're getting away, Jock!' he shouted.

Bald arced the gimpy an inch across the bonnet. Aiming for the wagon a hundred and twenty metres downrange. Spray-Tan had already climbed inside the front cab and was gunning the diesel engine. Nilis jumped into the wagon as Bald squeezed the trigger. The 7.62mm rounds landed low, thumping into the panelling on the back, shredding metal. One of the bullets struck higher and punched through the rear window. Glass cascaded. Nilis aimed through the shattered window and unloaded a burst from his SLR. Bullets hammered against the Range Rover bonnet, forcing Bald to duck low. Then Spray-Tan hit the gas. Nilis twisted in his seat, grinning as he gave Porter and Bald the thumbs-up. The Hilux truck fishtailed as it picked up speed, churning out clouds of dust in its wake. Bald went to fire again, but the pickup swerved round a tight bend before he could centre his aim.

Then it was gone.

'Bastard,' Bald hissed.

He swivelled the gimpy sights back to the treeline, searching for any more opportune targets. But the kids were long gone. Their screams fading as they fled deeper into the surrounding jungle. The dust settled along the track.

Silence.

Then Porter heard a pained cry.

At first he thought it was one of the wounded child soldiers. But the cry had the gravelly, throated tone of someone much older. Porter and Bald looked at each other. Then they swept out from cover behind the front wheelbase and broke forward, hurrying towards the ditch to the left of the Land Cruiser. Heading towards the cries. Porter picked his way past the slotted kids, avoiding the pools of blood and entrails. He passed the butchered Russian lying in the middle of the track, blood gushing out of the ragged stumps where his hands had once been. The noise was coming from the ditch. He rushed over, stopped by the edge and looked down.

Lying on his back, at the bottom of the ditch, was Soames.

Relief instantly swept through Porter. Thank fuck, he thought. Soames is alive. *The mission isn't a disaster.* His old CO raised his hands above his head, shading his eyes against the stark sunlight as he gazed up at Porter and Bald. His arms and face were streaked with cuts. Bits of loose soil clung to his greying hair, and there was a dark patch on his trousers from where Soames had pissed himself. His hands were shaking, Porter noticed. The guy didn't look like the ex-CO of 22 SAS. Not any more. He looked anxious. Shaken.

Soames squinted at the face peering down at him.

'John,' he croaked. 'Thank God. Help me, man.'

Porter stepped down into the ditch and thrust out an arm. Soames clasped his hand around Porter's wrist and staggered to his feet, groaning as he climbed out of the ditch. He stood upright, breathing hard as he surveyed the carnage along the track. Tully hurried over.

'Are they all dead?' Soames asked.

'Jock dropped half of them,' said Porter. 'The rest scattered. Don't think they'll be coming back any time soon.'

'Good fucking job, too.' Bald nodded at the gimpy resting on the Range Rover bonnet. 'We're out of ammo. That was the last of the link.'

Tully glanced warily over at the treeline. 'We shouldn't stick around. This is the West Side Boys' heartland. Place is crawling with hostiles. They've got training camps all over the fucking shop.'

Soames dusted himself down. 'Bloody savages. They came out of nowhere. I felt sure they were going to kill us all. Thank God you arrived when you did, otherwise it was curtains for us.' He paused. A perplexed look crossed his filthy, blood-encrusted face. 'How did you know where to find me?'

'Bob told us about the stash at Kono,' Porter said. 'Told us the Russians are after the diamonds you've been stealing.'

Soames straightened his back and arched an eyebrow at Tully.

'Diamonds. Yes. Right.' He pursed his lips. 'It's not what you think, Porter. There are interests at stake here, far greater than you can possibly imagine.'

'Bollocks. The only interest you've got is lining your own pockets.'

Soames stared defiantly at him. 'Believe it or not, this has nothing to do with money.'

'That's fucking rich, that. You can dress it up all you want, but when it comes down to it, you've been caught with your hand in the till.'

Soames shot him a stern look. 'We're wasting valuable time. We must leave at once if we're to get to Kono and stop the Russians.'

Porter shook his head vigorously. 'I don't take orders from you. Not any more. If you think we're going to risk our necks to save your stolen loot, you've got another think coming.'

'Don't be a fool, man. This isn't about me. This is about the national interest. If the Russians seize the mine, it will have major repercussions for President Fofana and the future of this country. We're looking at a national security disaster.'

'Over a few poxy diamonds?'

'It's more than that. Much more. We're fighting a proxy war with the Russians for control of this country. If they get their hands on Kono, they'll have the upper hand. The president will be finished. Heads will roll at the Firm. You can add it to the long list of fuck-ups with your name on it.'

Porter stared back at his old CO, but said nothing. He screwed up his right hand so hard his fingernails were digging into his palm. He stood there and thought about slogging Soames in the face. He thought about how good that would make him feel. To wipe that arrogant look off the guy's face.

Porter said, 'How do the Russians know where to find your stash? Tully told us the location of the diamonds was top secret.'

'It was.' Soames shifted. 'It isn't now. The Russians made me disclose the location.'

'You gave it up?'

'I had no choice. They were going to kill me otherwise.'

This bloke really is shameless, Porter thought. *He might be a retired CO, but he's still a fucking coward.*

'The Russians have already alerted their assets across the border,' Soames went on. 'I heard them talking on the sat phone. They're en route from Liberia as we speak. If they reach the mine first, there'll be too many of them for us to deal with. Now, are you going to take me there, or not?'

Porter shook his head. 'Our orders are to get you out of the country. Not go on some wild goose chase into the mountains.'

'For Chrissakes, man,' Soames growled, throwing up his arms in exasperation. 'Use your brain, for once in your miserable little life. Who do you think the Firm is going to blame if the Russians capture the mine? They'll have both your heads on stakes. You'll never work again.' He flashed a smile at Porter like the flick of a knife. 'Ask your chums at MI5 if you don't believe me.'

Porter shook his head bitterly. 'We can't. The phone battery's dead. We've got no way of reaching out to our handler.'

'Soames is right,' Bald said. 'We don't have a choice, mate. We've got to stop the Russians.'

Porter hesitated. I don't trust Soames further than I can piss, he thought. *But whatever he's hiding at Kono, the Russians are desperate to get their hands on it. And we're the only ones who can stop them.*

'Fine,' he replied at last. 'We'll do it. Bob, you're up front with me. Jock, you're riding in the back with this cunt.'

'What about Hawkridge?' Bald asked.

'We'll worry about him later,' Porter said. 'Let's get moving.'

He turned to head back to the Range Rover.

Then he heard the screams.

TWENTY-TWO

1719 hours.

The screams came from Porter's six o'clock. More than one of them. They were high-pitched squeals. Like voices that hadn't broken. He spun around and looked beyond the Land Cruiser. Towards the treeline on the opposite side of the track, eight metres away. Half a dozen child soldiers were charging forward from behind the trees, their puny biceps straining under the weight of the AK-47 assault rifles they were pointing at the four men in front of them. They quickly fanned out across the track, shouting and jeering. The kids were the strangest sight Porter had ever seen. The child opposite him wore a white princess dress and a pair of dirty Nike trainers. His lips were smeared with red lipstick and he'd applied some kind of white paint to his face in long, jagged lines. His index finger twitched nervously on the AK-47 trigger. He looked wired, mad. Ready to kill.

There was no time to displace. No time for Porter and Tully to reach for the Makarovs they were packing. No time to do anything at all. At a distance of eight metres even the worst shooter in the world could hit a human target without much difficulty. Porter stood very still, feeling his guts tighten into a tense knot. Lipstick stood in front of him, scowling.

'Where the fuck did this lot come from?' Bald said.

'No idea, mate,' Porter said. Remembering what Tully had said earlier.

This is the West Side Boys' neck of the woods.

Now we're really in the shit.

A seventh figure emerged from behind the treeline. He was a foot taller than the child soldiers and he sported bumfluff growth

251

on the lower half of his face. Probably in his early twenties, thought Porter. Practically a pensioner, by the standards of Sierra Leone. His dress sense was as weird as the other kids. He wore a threadbare Calvin Klein t-shirt and brightly-coloured trousers with a pair of flip-flops. Glass shards dangled from his hair. He had a necklace knitted out of what looked like pubic hair. The world's largest ganja joint dangled from his lips. Porter guessed that this guy was one of the West Side Boys' senior commanders. Or one of their recruiters. The guy had a hungry look in his eyes. He looked like he'd been living in the jungle for a long time. Months, or maybe even years. In his right hand he gripped an M1911 semi-automatic. A hefty pistol, chambered for the .45 ACP round. A true American classic. Like the Ford Mustang, or morbid obesity. But not well maintained, apparently. The sliding mechanism was covered in rust, Porter noted.

The older guy crossed the track and stomped over to the four men, the child soldiers flanking him on either side. He drew up in front of Porter. Looked him up and down. His breath reeked of booze and weed. The guy thrust his M1911 at Porter and started jabbering at him in the local Krio language. He saw the blank expression on Porter's face and tried again.

'You kill my boys, white man? You tink you kill dem boys and get away wit it?'

The guy had a slow, drugged accent. He sounded like the man from Del Monte, loaded up on amphetamines. Porter said nothing.

'You know who you fucking wit?'

Porter still said nothing. The guy stepped closer. Thumped a fist against his chest.

'Me Captain Big Trouble. Dis my country. Dese my boys,' he snarled, waving an arm at the dead kids littering the track. 'You fuck wit me. Kill my boys. Now me gonna fuck wit you. Me gonna waste all you white crackers.'

'Fuck off,' said Bald.

The captain turned to Bald and flashed a manic grin. Half of his teeth were gold. The rest were missing. Then he shouted an order. One of the kids stepped forward, dropped his shoulder and thrust the butt of his rifle into Bald's midriff. Bald gasped in pain as he folded at the waist, clutching his guts. Porter lunged at the captain but two other kids instantly set upon him, striking out with their rifle butts. A third kid giggled as he clubbed Porter round the side of the head. Porter felt a searing pain explode between his temples, dragging its fingernails down the inside of his skull. He stumbled and fell forward, landing on the baking hot earth. Blood trickled down the side of his face, sticky and warm.

'Enough!' Captain Big Trouble barked.

The child soldiers stopped landing blows. They withdrew a few paces and stood in line next to their mates, keeping their rifles trained on the four men. Porter spat out blood and scraped himself off the ground. Big Trouble was staring at Soames, he noticed. Something like recognition flashed behind his eyes. He took a long toke on his joint. Peered at Soames through the green haze of ganja smoke. Then he took a step forward.

'I know dis face.'

Soames blinked in ignorance. Big Trouble jumped up in excitement and snapped his fingers, like he'd remembered the answer to a quiz show question.

'You de diamond man! I seen your face on de TV. You de friend of dat man call himself de president. Dat's you.'

Soames's expression tightened.

'Let us go,' he said, his voice trembling. 'I can make it worth your while. Just name your price. Whatever you want, it's yours. Diamonds, women. Guns. You have my word. Just let us walk away.'

Big Trouble laughed. There was a wicked gleam in his eyes. 'Me got better idea. We gonna take you back to de village, kill your friends. Den me kill you.'

The colour drained from Soames's face. 'No. Please. I'll give you whatever you want.'

'Shut up!' Big Trouble roared. His eyeballs were inked with hatred. 'Me gonna make you pay, for all the bad tings you did to our people. Me gonna make you hurt.'

He shouted an order at the kids in Krio. Two of the child soldiers marched over to Soames and dragged him away from the others, prodding him along with their weapons. Soames looked towards the captain, shaking his head hysterically.

'Christ, no. Please, don't do this. Please!'

Big Trouble ignored his pleas. He took a final pull on his joint then flicked the butt into the ditch. Then he turned to the four other kids. Pointed his weapon at Bald and Porter and Tully.

'Kill dem,' he said.

The four kids simultaneously raised their rifles. The child aiming at Porter didn't look old enough to shave. His lips quivered with excitement as he curled his finger around the trigger mechanism. Porter stared down the black mouth of the rifle muzzle. His arsehole instinctively clenched with fear. It's over, he thought. We failed. Now we're fucked. The warrior inside him bristled with rage at the indignity of his death. *Slotted in this squalid little corner of the world, by some kid young enough to be my own son.* He closed his eyes. Said a silent farewell to his daughter.

I'm sorry, love. I'm so sorry for fucking everything up.

Then he heard two booming cracks.

Porter opened his eyes after the first crack whipped through the air. Saw Big Trouble's head snapping back, his eyes rolling up into the roof of his skull. The kid's arms slackened. Blood squirted out of a hole in the side of his head, like red paint out of a graffiti spray can. The second bullet struck another one of the kids in the throat, sending him into a tailspin. The kid did a kind of spasmodic pirouette before crashing to the dirt. The AK-47 slipped from his grip, clattering to the dry earth beside him.

Porter looked towards the direction the gunshots were coming from. Towards the Range Rover, eighty metres downstream from their position. A dark-green Land Rover Discovery had pulled up a few metres behind the Range Rover. The front passenger door hung open and a hulking figure stood a few metres ahead of the wagon, his massive head tilted as he aimed down the barrel of an AK-47 at the kids. The weapon looked ridiculously small in the man's giant grip. Like a wrestler brandishing a toy gun. Porter recognised the guy from his huge frame.

The man-mountain.

Solomon.

The five other kids turned to face the new threat from the south. But they were slow to react. They were still processing the trauma of seeing their commander die in front of their eyes. Only one of the kids remembered his training and aimed his weapon at Solomon. The man-mountain fired again. The AK-47 snout flashed. The bullet struck the child in the face, smashing open his jaw and shattering his teeth. Solomon dropped the kid next to him before he could get off a shot, shooting him in the throat and tearing a hole big enough to slide a crowbar through. The child made a hissing noise and fell backwards, landing next to the kid with the missing jaw.

Panic set in amongst the three remaining child soldiers. Two of them turned and bolted down the track, away from Solomon. Tully and Bald lunged after the kids, tackling them to the ground before they could escape. The third child spun away from Porter and raced towards the treeline to the right of the track. Porter dived at the kid and sent him tumbling to the dirt, knocking the AK-47 out of his grip. The kid groaned as he landed on his back, the force of the impact driving the air from his lungs. He struggled wildly as Porter pressed his weight down. Porter gave the kid a few slaps. The fight quickly drained out of him, replaced by an animal-like terror. He screamed hysterically, kicking out and crying for his mother. Porter slapped him again. The kid stopped fighting. Porter slid off and scooped up the rifle, aiming it at a point between the kid's eyes. The kid froze.

Porter turned his attention to Bald and Tully. Bald had disarmed one of the child soldiers and was hauling the kid to his feet. Tully was on top of the third kid, smashing his face in with the kid's AK-47. Each blow landed with a sickening wet crunch as Tully slammed the rifle stock into the bridge of his nose. Porter rushed over to Tully and grabbed him by the shoulders, pulling him away. Tully managed to land another blow before Porter dragged him clear. The guy stood over the battered child, his chest muscles heaving up and down, the rifle's wooden stock glistening with blood and stringy bits of tissue. The child lay on his back, motionless. His face was an unrecognisable mush. Porter looked up at Tully, stunned.

'Jesus, Bob.'

Tully shot Porter a hostile look. Drops of the child's blood glistened on his face.

'Piss off. You don't understand what it's like here. These kids don't watch Power Rangers and play PlayStation. They're stone-cold killers. There's no point trying to reason with them. It's not like their lives are worth fuck-all.'

'They're just kids, mate.'

'No.' Tully shook his head vigorously. 'That's where you're wrong. This lot are scum. Plain and fucking simple. What do you suggest we do with them? Let them go, so they can go back to their camps and butcher a few more villagers? We're doing the locals a favour, killing these animals.'

Porter stared at Tully. It's one thing to take down a child soldier threatening to pull the trigger on you, he thought. But it took a special kind of cold-bloodedness to beat a child to death with your bare hands.

He heard the slam of a car door at his three o'clock. Porter looked over his shoulder and saw Dominique Tannon hurrying over from the Discovery, several paces behind Solomon. The man-mountain breezed past the rest of the group and made a beeline straight for Bald.

'Sir! Are you okay?' he said.

Bald stared at the guy in puzzlement. Solomon just stood there in obedient silence, waiting for a reply. 'Yeah, mate. Never felt better.'

'Never mind him,' Soames barked. 'I'm the one you should be concerned with. I'm the one who got kidnapped by the Russians and almost died in a bloody firefight, for Chrissake.'

Porter ignored him and looked towards Tannon. 'How did you know where to find us?'

'We've been tailing you since you left the hotel,' she explained. 'You told me you were going to Kono, remember?' She shrugged. 'I figured you could use a little extra help.'

'We didn't see you behind us.'

'We left a few minutes after you. It's taken us this long to catch up. Frankly I was beginning to worry that Solomon had us lost.'

The man-mountain smiled. 'Miss Tannon found me after you left. She said you needed someone to follow you into the jungle. I told her I know the secret way. You aren't the only one who knows the shortcut to Kono.'

'You should have stayed at the hotel,' Porter said.

'I'm invested in this thing just as much as you. Besides,' she added, scanning the bullet-riddled Land Cruiser and the corpses, 'it looks like we got here just in time.'

'Bloody good job, too,' Soames piped up. 'At least someone round here knows which side their bread is buttered.' He cleared his throat and flashed a thin smile at Tannon. 'I'll be sure to put in a good word with your bosses once this is over. Pull a few strings. See if we can get you a cosier posting in some more pleasant country.'

Tannon ignored him. She surveyed the ground again and frowned. 'What happened here?'

'What does it look like?' Soames snapped. 'We ran into an ambush. The West Side Boys attacked us. One of the Russians was killed, but the other two got away. Then these three showed up.' He gestured to Porter, Bald and Tully. 'The child soldiers were going to kill them and take me away.'

Porter snorted with contempt. 'Why would the West Side Boys kidnap you?'

'Isn't it obvious? I'm something of a celebrity in this country. Everyone knows my face. That makes me a high-value target. No doubt the West Side Boys thought they could negotiate a large ransom for my return.'

'Good job you brought this brick shithouse along for the ride.' Bald nodded at Solomon. 'If you'd left it any later, we'd have been toast. Those kids had us by the fucking balls.'

'Solomon insisted on coming, actually,' said Tannon.

'Yeah?' said Bald, cocking his brow.

Solomon bowed his head. 'You saved my life at the hotel, sir. That means I am in your debt. When Miss Tannon said she was going to follow you, I was obliged to go along with her.'

Bald glanced over at Captain Big Trouble. Blood pumped steadily out of the hole in the side of the boy's head. 'Consider your debt settled.'

'I cannot. It does not work that way, sir. I must wait for a sign. Until then, I remain in your service.'

Bald stared at the man-mountain, wearing a face as if someone had just given him a turd for Christmas.

Soames cleared his throat. 'This is all well and good, but we must leave now. Every minute we piss about here gives the Russians more of a head start.'

Tannon shot a quizzical look at Porter. 'What's going on?'

'That hardly concerns you, my dear,' Soames replied coldly.

Tannon said, 'We're the ones who risked our lives to follow you into the jungle. We're the ones who saved you from the West Side Boys. I already know about the diamond stash, so you might as well tell me the rest of it.'

Soames clamped his lips shut and fumed for a beat. Then he nodded tersely. 'Very well. The two Russians who escaped are on their way to Kono now. They're planning to seize the mine at Kono and rob me while they wait for reinforcements to show up. If they succeed in capturing the mine, they will control the diamonds. President Fofana's hopes of regaining power will go up in smoke, and any influence we currently have in this part of the world will be lost. It will be nothing short of a disaster.'

'Don't you have anyone guarding the mine?'

Soames shook his head. 'I evacuated my men after the rebels launched their coup. Most of the workforce had left by then anyway. They fled at the first sign of unrest. There's nobody left.'

Tannon said, 'What's the plan?'

Porter said, 'We head to Kono and stop the Russians.'

'But won't they get to the mine first?'

Tully clicked his tongue and nodded down the track. 'The road splits in two about twenty miles to the east. The highway goes south past Yonibana, around the edge of the Kangari Hills. But there's a dirt road that goes north of the Hills. It's not signposted anywhere, but that route will save us some time.'

'How much?' Porter said.

Tully squinted at the road ahead. 'Ten minutes. Maybe fifteen. The Russians will hit the mine before we do, definitely. But until their reinforcements show up, it'll be just the two of them. It'll take a couple of hours for their mates to come up from Liberia. If we take the dirt road, we can still stop them and secure the place before the Russians' mates arrive.'

'That's what we'll do, then.' Porter turned back to Tannon. 'Me, Jock and Bob will ride up front with Soames. You and Solomon follow us. Keep a safe distance behind.'

Tannon said, 'What if we run into another ambush?'

'It's a possibility,' Porter conceded. 'We're going in blind, so we don't know what's out there. But if we get hit again, don't join the fight. You stop the wagon, turn around and floor it back to Freetown. Got it?'

'Can't we call in for help? Warn Hawkridge and Angela that the Russians are en route to the mine? We might be able to divert some local resources to stop them.'

Porter shook his head. 'The sat phone's dead. It's just us.'

'Shit.'

'What about these two?' said Bald.

He gestured to the pair of child soldiers. They stood huddled at the edge of the track, a look of raw fear in their eyes. Deprived of their rifles and captain, the kids suddenly looked a lot younger. They're probably only a few years older than my Sandy, Porter thought. Except she's busy making friends at school, while this lot are chopping up foreigners. It hurt his head to think about it.

He approached one of the kids. Grabbed him by the wrist and dragged him forward. The kid struggled.

259

'Please,' he said. 'No. Please.'

Salty tears traced down the kid's cheeks. His lips trembled. Blood and snot bubbled under his nose. He stopped pleading. So did the second kid. They both had the same look of silent terror. The look of someone preparing to die.

'Please . . .'

'You got family somewhere?' Porter said.

'Aunt,' the kid sniffed. 'In my village.'

'Fuck off back to your village, then. You and your mate.'

The kid blinked at Porter. Then he turned to his mate and said a few words in Krio. The pair of them took off across the track, scrambling past the ditch before they disappeared into the canopied gloom of the jungle. Tully shook his head in disbelief.

'You're actually letting these animals go?'

Porter confronted Tully with an angry stare. 'Just because this is Africa, doesn't mean we get away with anything we want. We start killing unarmed kids, we could end up in jail. Especially if the government turns on us. I don't know about you, but I'm not planning on dying in some hellhole African prison.'

Tully shook his head again. 'This was a mistake. You think those kids will honestly go back to their homes?' He threw up his arms and pointed down the road. 'You saw them villages. Those kids don't have a fucking home to go back to. They'll go running straight to the nearest enemy camp.'

'I'm afraid Bob is right,' Soames said. 'These children are beyond help, sadly. They're like wild dogs. The best thing for all concerned would have been to put them out of their misery. I expected better from you, Porter. For all your many faults, I never figured you were soft. You used to be a real man.'

Porter rounded on Soames. 'Get in the fucking wagon. Now.'

Soames stared defiantly at Porter for a moment. Then he turned and trudged down the track towards the Range Rover, nonchalantly stepping around the bodies of the slotted children. Tannon followed him, beating a path back to the Discovery. Porter and Bald each grabbed an AK-47 from the slotted child soldiers to supplement their pistols. Solomon collected up the spare clips from the dead. With the ammo they had foraged from the West Side Boys they had a total of four thirty-round clips of 7.62x39mm brass apiece. The rifles were in crap nick, and the mags were held together with duct tape. But they were better than fuck-all, thought Porter.

He looked back down the track. Tully was scooping up the M1911 semi-automatic from the beside the dead body of the slaughtered captain. Bald pulled a face.

'You're not taking a rifle, Bob?'

Tully laughed. 'You dopey cunt. This is a collector's item. You don't see many 1911s on the market anymore. It'll fetch me a good price on the black market. Them .45 rounds pack a meaty punch, too.' He grinned broadly. 'Better than those shoddy pieces of crap you and Porter have got your hands on.'

Bald stared enviously at the M1911. Then Tully smiled to himself and beat a path back to the Range Rover. Solomon hurried along behind him, cradling the spare mag clips for the assault rifles. For a moment Porter stood still, waiting until Tully and Solomon were out of earshot. Then he turned to Bald and lowered his voice.

'What do you reckon about that stuff Soames was saying? About the West Side Boys wanting to kidnap him.'

'What about it?' Bald said.

'Do you believe him?'

'I guess. Everyone knows the West Side Boys are in the kidnap-for-ransom business these days. I reckon the president's right-hand man would be near the top of their most wanted list.'

Porter looked away. He thought about the look on Big Trouble's face when he'd confronted Soames. 'Me gonna make you pay,' the captain had said. 'For all the bad tings you did to our people.'

Pay for what?

TWENTY-THREE

1737 hours.

The track narrowed as they motored east out of the ambush site.
After twenty minutes they passed through the derelict town of
Yonibana. Then the road split in two, just like Tully had said.
Porter steered off the highway and took the barely-visible dirt
road north. Soon they had left the jungle behind as the road
climbed into a series of low, broken hills. It was like emerging
from a tunnel. The sky light-blinded Porter. The dense canopy
and foliage shrank into the distance. The air cleared. He steered
the Range Rover along the beaten track, with Tannon behind the
wheel of the Discovery ten metres to the rear. Porter kept the
speedometer needle hovering around the forty mark, the engine
groaning with the strain of the climb. Tully and Bold strained
their eyes at the road ahead, searching for any sign of the Russians
in the Hilux.

Porter guessed that Nilis and Spray-Tan had a fifteen-minute
head start on them. Tully had said the diamond mine was a three-
hour drive east from the ambush site. Which meant the Russians
would arrive at Kono at around 2015 hours. With the short-cuts
Tully knew about, Porter and the others would probably reach
the mine at around the same time. Assuming they didn't run into
any more ambushes. *It's going to be close,* Porter thought.

After an hour they hit the southern fringe of the Loma moun-
tain range. They were in diamond country now. The sun began
sinking behind the hills, burning up in the sky and tingeing the
earth a bloodshot red. Porter kept his eyes focused on the road
ahead, looking for the Russians. In the fading light it was hard to

see very far ahead, but he still couldn't see any sign of the Hilux. The road tightened and narrowed. The diamond hills brooded in the distance, shadowed by the setting sun. Thirty minutes later they reached the outskirts of a place called Koidu Town. They took a left turn and Tully directed them north on a steep track that corkscrewed between rolling green hills dotted with palm trees and bushes. The clock on the dash read 1946 hours.

Just a few more miles to go.

A few more miles until this thing ends once and for all.

They crept along the dirt track for another twenty minutes, rolling over an endless succession of bone-shaking potholes. Thick vegetation overhung both sides of the track, black against the grainy moonlight. Porter slowed down to thirty miles per. He switched off the headlamps and reverted to the sidelights, concealing their approach. According to Tully's directions they were just a mile from the mining field now. He scanned the ground ahead but saw nothing except the track, the moon, the blackness either side. Which could only mean one thing, Porter realised. We're too late. *The Russians must have already reached the mine.*

They continued for another eight hundred metres. Eyes squinting, searching the pitted darkness ahead. Then Porter saw it. A wide compound eight hundred metres ahead of them, faintly illuminated by the ambient light of the moon. There was a chain-link metal fence running the length of the compound, with security lights mounted along the top at regular intervals. Half the lights were dead. An old Toyota Hilux was parked in front of the entrance. Headlamps burning, the doors on both side of the front cab hanging open.

'Shit,' Soames said, panic rising in his voice. 'That's the Russians.'

Porter hit the brakes and steered the Range Rover to the edge of the track, easing to a halt next to the bushes, seven hundred metres from the Hilux. He cut the engine. Tannon pulled up four metres behind them, killing her lights. Porter stuffed the Makarov pistol down the back of his combats and grabbed his AK-47 from the dash, along with the spare thirty-round clip. Bald and Tully snatched up their weapons too. Then everyone debussed. Porter jumped down onto the sun-baked dirt. The temperature outside was close to incinerator level in spite of the late hour. The air was dry and choked with dust. Every time he breathed in, it felt as if someone was shovelling hot coals down his throat.

Tannon and Solomon hurried forward from the Discovery.

'Why have we stopped?' Tannon asked.

Porter gestured in the direction of the compound. 'The Russians are already here. That's their wagon parked outside. We'll have to make our approach on foot.'

Tannon squinted at the Hilux, the bodywork spotlighted under the harsh glare of the security lights. She turned back to Porter and shook her head. 'I can't see them from here.'

'You won't,' Porter replied. 'The Russians might be at the truck, but it's more likely they're inside the compound. But we don't know for sure. That's why we can't risk driving up in the wagons.'

'Won't they have seen us already?'

'Not from here, lass,' Bald cut in. 'It's black as a witch's tit at this end of the track, and those security lights are pointing towards the compound. They'll fuck with anyone's natural night vision. Anyone near that wagon looking out this way won't see anything beyond the light sources.'

'What are we waiting for, then?' Soames said. 'Let's get a bloody move on.'

Porter led the way, moving ahead of the Range Rover with Soames at his side. Bald and Tully followed close behind, with Tannon and Solomon bringing up the rear. They stayed close to the side of the track to make themselves less visible, blending in with the surrounding darkness. As they edged forward Porter strained his eyes at the mine, looking for signs of movement around the pickup truck. He periodically stopped every hundred metres, stilled his breath and listened for any unnatural noise. But he could hear nothing except the chirping of the crickets, the mechanical purr of the Hilux engine.

At two hundred metres he stopped again and scanned the compound. Metal signs had been staked into the ground in front of the chain-link fence, warning that unauthorised visitors would be shot on sight. A small guard hut stood next to the entrance. Just inside the entrance Porter spied a large wattle-and-daub hut with a thatched roof. Where the diggers usually slept, he guessed. Several concrete buildings were situated north of the hut, with a steel-framed Portakabin opposite. In the middle distance he could see a large parcel of land. The diamond field. Porter searched for any sign of the Russians at the Hilux or the compound.

Nothing.

'Place looks fucking deserted,' Bald said.

Porter nodded, remembering what Soames had said about the workers fleeing after the revolt. Nothing here except a bunch of empty buildings and mine pits. *And a couple of Russian killers.*

'Keep moving,' he said.

They crept closer to the entrance, using the dead spots in front of the broken security lights to keep themselves hidden from view. Porter kept his AK-47 trained on the Hilux, ready to brass up anyone who might be hiding inside the pickup. Bald and Tully also had their weapons raised as they searched for activity around the compound. But there was no movement or noise inside. Nothing at all. After a few more paces Porter drew to a halt beside the Hilux. He peered inside the front cab. Turned to Bald and shook his head.

'Wagon's empty,' he said.

'Where the fuck have they gone?' Bald said.

'Over there,' Tully said.

He nodded towards the Portakabin inside the compound, fifty metres downstream from the entrance. Porter looked towards the structure. He noticed a light shining in the cabin window, spilling its fluorescent glow across the ground. Bald narrowed his eyes at the Portakabin and grunted.

'Think the Russians are in there?'

Porter shrugged. 'Where else?'

In the corner of his eye, he noticed Tully frowning at the diamond field. Porter looked towards Tannon and said, 'You and Solomon wait here in case things get noisy. We'll give you a shout once it's clear.'

Tannon glanced warily around the compound and nodded 'Okay'.

Then Porter set off. Bald at his side, Tully and Soames at his six. They crept past the Hilux and swept through the entrance, keeping eyes on the Portakabin, sticking to the dark areas between the functioning security lights. A bank of body scanners had been set up next to the guard hut, to make sure none of the workers tried swallowing a diamond or shoving one up their arse. Tannon had called it wrong, he thought as he picked his way past the scanners. *This mine makes Fort Knox look like a branch of Abbey National.* That's what she told him back at the Ambassadors Hotel. But it didn't look that way from the outside. The guard hut next to the entrance stood empty. There were no gates, no barriers. No kind of security presence at all, apart from the lights and the fence.

They stopped beside the large wattle-and-daub hut. Bald peeked through the opening to check it was unoccupied. Then they moved on. Worn car tyres and broken wooden pallets had been dumped next to the hut. Beyond it stood the cluster of concrete buildings and a standalone shower block. The guards' quarters, Porter figured. The closest thing the mine had to luxury accommodation.

North of the concrete buildings stood the diamond field. It was huge. Bigger than Porter had imagined. In the encroaching darkness it was hard to judge the size of the field, but he figured it had to be around twenty acres. Moonlight reflected off a gentle-flowing river to the west of the field. East of the field there was a worn landing strip, just about long enough to land a light aircraft. Far to the north of the mine, another bank of security lights pricked the darkness.

Porter wondered about those lights.

'The Russians have got to be in there,' Bald said, nodding at the Portakabin.

Soames frowned at him. 'How can you be sure?'

'Every other building looks empty. Where else would they be?'

Soames didn't reply.

Porter turned to Bald and said, 'Take a closer look. We'll cover you from here.'

'Roger that.'

Bald crept forward from the hut and moved crosswise towards the Portakabin at his two o'clock. Porter held back at the workers' hut next to Soames and Tully, his finger on the AK trigger, ready to cover Bald at the first sign of enemy movement. The chances of anyone inside the Portakabin spotting Bald through the window were slim, Porter knew. If the Russians were inside, they would be looking out from a well-lit room into a pitch-black void. The artificial light would screw with their night vision. Which meant they wouldn't be able to see more than a couple of feet on the other side of the window. Bald could be pissing distance from the Portakabin and the Russians still wouldn't see him.

Porter looked on as Bald reached the cabin door. He leaned close and pricked his ears, listening for activity on the other side. Then he looked over his shoulder and waved his mucker over. Porter broke forward from the hut and pushed across the open ground, with Tully covering his approach from beside the workers' hut. Porter hit the front of the Portakabin and drew up opposite Bald to the left of the cabin door, pressing up against the wall. He paused and listened for a few beats. Heard nothing. A sign fixed above the door said MANAGER'S OFFICE. The door was slightly ajar, Porter noticed.

He signalled to Bald, indicating that he would clear the left side of the room. Then he took half a step back from the cabin and raised his AK-47, ready to follow his mucker through the door. Bald moved directly in front of the cabin door, took a deep breath and kicked it open with the heel of his boot. The door crashed back on its hinges. In the next instant Bald rushed inside the Portakabin and pivoted towards his three o'clock, clearing the right side of the room. Porter was hard on his heels, stepping through the open door and in the same motion turning to face the left side of the cabin, searching for opportune targets.

The fluorescent light inside the Portakabin momentarily blinded Porter. He saw a corner desk piled high with papers, an old CRT computer monitor and a portable fan. There was a metal filing cabinet in the other corner with the drawers pulled open and a bunch of folders strewn across the floor. A framed photograph hung from the back wall, showing Soames in his military formals, pressing the flesh with a former prime minister.

He saw no Russians.

'Clear,' said Porter.

'Shit,' said Bald.

Porter swung around. Bald was standing on the other side of the room with his back to Porter, looking down at something in front of him. Porter couldn't see it from where he stood. He lowered his rifle, marched over to Bald and looked down. Then he saw it too. A section of the carpet had been pulled back, revealing the concrete floor underneath. An underfloor safe had been built into the middle of the flooring, Porter noticed. The steel lid on the safe had been flipped open, and the deposit tube inside emptied of its contents. Then Porter noticed the stones. They were scattered across the carpet around his feet. Dozens of them, each one a different shape and colour. Some were white. Others were smoky grey, or yellow, or black. The smaller ones were the size of coffee beans. The biggest was about the size of a golf ball.

Then Porter realised what he was looking at.

Diamonds.

A shit-ton of them. Rough, uncut. Glinting under the fluorescent lights. The golf-ball diamond was the biggest one Porter had ever seen. Bigger even than the one in the Crown Jewels.

'This lot's got to be worth millions,' Bald said, a crafty look in his eyes. 'We could help ourselves to a fortune here, mate. It's not like Hawkridge is ever gonna pay us a decent whack, is it?'

Porter looked steadily at his mucker. 'Don't even think about it. We've got a job to do, for fuck's sake.'

Just then Porter heard the pounding of boots on the dry ground as Soames and Tully rushed forward from the guard hut. They stepped into the Portakabin, glanced around. Soames caught sight

268

of the rough diamonds scattered on the floor. His face went sheet-white.

'No,' he said.

'Why the fuck would the Russians leave diamonds?' said Bald.

Porter thought for a moment. 'They must be after something else.'

Bald unglued his eyes from the rough diamond stash and wrinkled his brow. 'Like what?'

'I don't know.'

Tully stepped forward.

'I think I know where they've gone,' he said.

Porter looked at him. 'Where?'

Tully tipped his head in the direction of the open doorway. 'There's a separate compound at the edge of the mine. That's where they'll have gone. I'm fucking certain of it.'

The security lights, thought Porter. *The ones I saw to the north of the field.*

'What's there?' he said.

Soames paused. 'Military intelligence.'

Porter looked at him.

'The top brass sometimes come here for secret meetings,' Soames continued. 'I'll explain it all later, but right now we don't have time for this. We have to get to the other compound and stop the Russians before it's too late.'

His voice sounded urgent, thought Porter. 'Where's the compound?'

Tully said, 'North of the mining field.'

'Is it guarded?'

'Same deal as the mine. There's a metal fence, security lights. Normally we post a few guards outside the entrance. But them fellas were relieved of duty at the same time as the rest of us. Soon as the shit hit the fan with the rebels, everyone was recalled from the mine.'

'So there's no one to stop the Russians from getting inside the compound?'

'No.'

Bald said, 'Won't they see us coming?'

Tully shook his head. 'There's a drainage ditch that runs from the mine to the north-west corner of the compound. We can crawl through it and get inside without anyone spotting us.'

'What kind of military intelligence?' Porter asked.

'There's no time,' Soames replied. 'We've got to stop the Russians.' He forced a smile. 'I'll make it worth your while. There's a job for you both if you do this.'

Bald nodded. 'Let's go.'

TWENTY-FOUR

2017 hours.

They hurried out of the Portakabin. The fluorescent lighting had degraded their natural night vision and Porter struggled to pick out much detail beyond the illuminated patches of ground immediately in front of him. As they moved north he heard movement. He turned and saw a pair of dark shapes approaching from the direction of the guard hut. Porter stopped in his tracks and reached for his weapon. Tannon and Solomon moved into the reflected glow from the Portakabin window, then stepped tentatively forward from the darkness. Tannon glanced at the cabin. Then at the four men in front of her.

'What's going on?' she asked. 'Where are the Russians?'

Porter told her about the diamonds they had found. 'We think they're at another compound, on the other side of the mine.'

'What's in there that the Russians want?'

Soames sighed irritably. 'We're wasting time. We need to go, right this bloody second.'

Tannon said, 'I'll come with you.'

Porter shook his head. 'Not until we've taken care of the Russians.'

She went to reply, but Soames interrupted her.

'Porter's right, for once in his damn life. It's too dangerous. I'm the authority here. If you know what's good for you, young lady, you'll stay put.'

Tannon stared pointedly at the ex-Rupert but didn't respond. Porter dug out the dead sat phone from the back pocket of his combats and handed it to her.

'You want to make yourself useful, search the buildings for a charger. We need to get the sat phone up and running so we can make contact with our handler. Tell him the Russians have reached the mine and we're going after them.'

'Try the accommodation blocks,' Tully said. 'There's no phone lines in these parts. Most of the guards used sat phones to call home on the job. You should find a charger lying around somewhere.'

'What about me?' Solomon interrupted.

'Guard the entrance,' Bald said. 'Look out for any approaching enemies. We think the Russians have called for reinforcements.'

Solomon nodded eagerly. 'Anything you say, boss.'

The man-mountain turned and padded towards the front of the compound. At the same time Tannon made for the concrete buildings opposite the Portakabin. Porter watched them depart. Then he about-turned, hurried north past the buildings and joined Tully, Soames and Bald by the edge of the mining field.

'This way,' Tully said.

They set off through the mine, following a rough track that ran down from the buildings. For the quick transportation of excavated diamonds, presumably. Tully led the way. Porter and Bald fell into step behind him, with Soames pulling up the rear. The four moved at a brisk pace, picking their way past the open-air bell pits that covered the length and breadth of the field. Mounds of excavated soil were heaped next to each pit. Shallow streams bisected the field, snaking between the piles of loose dirt. There were a few pieces of machinery lying around the field, but most of the work here was done by hand. Hour upon hour toiling at the earth, sifting through mud and gravel deposits, searching for the stones that would eventually end up in the jewellery shops of Hatton Garden and Fifth Avenue. A process that hadn't changed much in centuries.

Every so often Porter glanced up at the security lights to the north. They were five hundred metres from the lights. Was Soames lying when he'd claimed the Russians were after military intelligence? Porter couldn't be sure. But whatever is inside that compound, we'll soon find out, he thoughts.

They pushed on, weaving past the bell-pits and the stacks of sifting pans dumped beside each hole. Pools of water glistened in several of the deeper craters and Porter had to scramble for purchase as he followed Tully along the soft, muddy ground. Tully upped the pace as they drew closer to the security lights, chopping his stride. They were three hundred metres from the compound now. Porter could feel his calf muscles burning. A powerful stitch speared his right side. Every muscle in his body ached with tiredness. The years of hard drinking, taking its heavy toll. His body screamed at him to rest. You made it this far, Porter told himself. You can't give up now. Keep going.

Stop the Russians, and then it'll be over.

They were a hundred and fifty metres from the compound now. To the north Porter could see a wide one-storey concrete building with a shingle-tiled roof, partially obscured by a line of ironwood trees. A farmhouse, he thought. It looked older than the mine. Perhaps the farm had been here first. Then the geologists had arrived, and the mine had opened but the farmer stubbornly refused to sell. Hence the present arrangement. Several outlying structures were situated to the west of the main building, backing onto a densely forested slope. An additional two-metre-high metal fence surrounded the farmhouse, with a gated entrance visible between the security lights. Porter scanned the area around the house. A pair of torchlights cut through the darkness, moving from the outlying buildings to the farmhouse.

'The Russians,' Bald said. 'Must be them.'

'Looks like they're searching for something,' Porter observed. He looked over at Tully and frowned.

'What the fuck is this place, Bob?'

'Keep moving,' Soames urged.

They hurried on. When they were a hundred metres from the fence Tully tacked to the left and manoeuvred towards the north-west corner of the compound, avoiding the stark glare of the security lights arranged along the perimeter. Porter understood now why they couldn't make a frontal approach to the compound. There were no dark areas they could use to sneak forward. All the security lights at the front of the compound were in perfect working order. Unlike the lights guarding the approach to the mine itself, Porter thought. Which made him wonder. *Why is this place better protected than the diamond mine?*

Tully hit the north-western corner and stopped. Porter halted alongside him. A gentle slope led down to a deep drainage channel that backed directly onto the perimeter fence. There was about an inch of standing water at the bottom of the ditch. The ground this side of the fence was slightly downhill from the compound, Porter realised. Which made it a natural flow point for excess water. The ditch extended south for half a mile from the edge of the compound, emptying out into the river west of the mining field. At the mouth of the channel was a water-flow outlet mounted on a concrete base, with a metal grating fastened across the opening.

The outlet looked just about wide enough for someone to crawl through. Large rocks and logs had been piled high on the slopes either side of the outlet. To prevent soil erosion, probably. On the far side of the perimeter fence Porter spied a manhole cover, twenty metres west of the farmhouse. The outlet tunnel led underground from the ditch up to the manhole cover on the opposite side of the fence. From the manhole to the bottom of the drainage ditch was a drop of about six feet, he estimated.

Tully picked his way down the slope and waded towards the outlet, motioning for the others to follow. Porter and Bald dropped down into the ditch, with Soames awkwardly lowering himself into the channel after them. All four waited for a moment beside the outlet, stilling their breath and listening for movement on the far side of the fence. Above the trickle of water, Porter heard a pair of faint voices. Like tuning into a radio station at the edge of the signal range. They sounded guttural, harsh. Foreign.

The Russians.

Five seconds passed. The voices faded. Porter and the others waited another ten seconds, in case the Russians returned. Then

Bald grabbed hold of the metal grate and tried wrenching it open. The grate rattled. Tully set down his pistol, stepped forward and grabbed the other end. The two of them tried again.

'No good,' Bald muttered. 'Bastard's fastened tight.'

Porter reached for a log from the pile of rocks and timber to the left of the outlet. The tip of the log was splintered from where the other end had broken off. He shoved the split end of the log into the narrow gap between the outlet mouth and the grating. Then he started prising the grate open, using the timber as a lever. The metal resisted at first, groaning on its hinges.

'Hurry, man!' Soames hissed, his voice straining with anxiety.

Porter pushed harder against the log. The grating buckled but held firm. Porter dug his boots into the slippery ground and leaned in again, applying his full weight to the log. There was a pause, and then the grate sprang loose from the outlet mouth and clattered to the rocks piled up against the concrete base. Porter froze. He listened and waited to see if the noise had alerted the Russians on the other side of the fence. He heard nothing. After several moments he stepped back from the tunnel and nodded at Soames.

'Wait here. Don't fucking move.'

Then he turned to Bald and gestured to the outlet.

'Ladies first, Jock.'

'Fuck off,' Bald whispered.

He dropped to his elbows and knees and crawled into the drainage tunnel, clutching his AK-47 close to his chest. Porter went second. Then Tully. It was darker then night inside the tunnel. A dense, solid blackness that made it impossible to see more than two inches in front of his face. Dank water slicked along the bottom, and there was a putrid smell in the air that made Porter want to gag. He crept on behind Bald, his elbows grazing against the sides of the tunnel. The pipe extended horizontally for eight metres and stopped directly beneath the manhole cover on the far side of the fence. A shaft of artificial light pierced the darkness through a gap in the manhole. Ahead of him, Bald stooped low beneath the cover. He placed both palms on the underside of the manhole and pushed up. There was a dull scraping noise as the cover lifted, then slid across. Then Bald stood fully upright, spread his arms up through the opening and hoisted himself out of the drainage tunnel.

Porter waited for a couple of beats while Bald checked the surrounding area. He had emerged five metres north of the fence and twenty west of the farmhouse. When he was sure the coast was clear, Bald signalled down to Porter. The latter climbed out of the opening and joined his mucker next to a dense thicket of bushes. A few moments later Tully crawled out of the drainage tunnel and crouched down beside the two operators. Then Porter crept forward and looked out across the compound.

The farmhouse was set back at the end of a wide yard. There was a generator shed to the left of the building, with a small timber-framed structure further west, at Porter's twelve o'clock. What looked like some sort of shed. Further back, to the rear of the property, Porter could just about see a one-storey concrete annexe to the farmhouse. Another larger outlying building to the left of it.

In front of the farmhouse there was a playground, fitted out with brand-new equipment. There was a wooden climbing frame with a plastic green slide attached, a metal swing set and a see-saw. A swingball to the right with a couple of bats lying next to the pole. Five-a-side football pitch to the left, next to a wooden club-house. A sandbox. Everything looked immaculate. The grass was freshly clipped, the toy dolls neatly arranged in colourful boxes. The lines on the football pitch looked freshly painted. A light beamed in one of the windows at the front of the building. There was a sign fixed to the front of the building that said KONO ORPHAN PROJECT.

Not a farmhouse, Porter realised.

An orphanage.

'Who the fuck builds an orphanage right next to a mine?' Bald whispered.

Tully said nothing.

Porter scanned the compound again. Above the whir of the generator, he heard two voices.

The Russians.

Coming from inside the shed at their twelve o'clock, twenty metres away.

Porter observed the shed for a few moments. He caught the flicker of torch-light slanting across the window. The Russians sounded angry, he thought. As if they were shouting at one another. He heard the distinct crash and clatter of equipment inside the shed. *They're tearing the place up*, Porter realised. They're definitely looking for something. Something more valuable than a safe-load of rough diamonds.

He turned to Tully and lowered his voice. 'What's in there?'

'Nothing, fella,' Tully said. 'Just a storage facility.'

Porter nodded. 'Wait here. Me and Jock will drop those fuckers while they're still inside. Cover us.'

'Roger that, fellas.'

Porter said, 'Let's move, Jock.'

They crept forward across the open ground, advancing cautiously towards the storage shed directly ahead of them, parallel to the farmhouse. Porter trapped his breath in his throat and pushed the fire selector up to the middle setting. Full auto. He kept his weapon raised, the heel of the AK-47's mahogany stock tucked against the pocket of his right shoulder. Bald moved forward at his three o'clock. The Russians were still talking with raised voices inside the shed. Whatever they're looking for, they haven't found it yet, Porter thought. He edged closer. They were fifteen metres from the shed door. Now fourteen metres. Thirteen.

The crashing noises suddenly stopped. So did the voices.

The door flew open.

Spray-Tan stepped outside first. Nilis was a step behind him. Both men were gripping their SLR assault rifles. Spray-Tan clutched a Maglite torch in his left hand. Nilis was holding a satellite phone, similar to the one that Porter and Bald had been given. They were both following the arc of the torch beams as they moved outside the shed and pivoted towards the rear of the compound. The Maglite killed their natural night vision. Which meant they didn't see Porter and Bald twelve metres to the south. Not until it was too late.

Bald dropped to a kneeling stance and fired first. His AK-47 barked twice. Two rounds thudded into Spray-Tan's upper back. He jerked wildly as the bullets punched through his body. In the next half-second Bald fired another two-round burst at the Russian. The bullets caught him on the half-turn, ripping into his torso. Spray-Tan grunted and dropped.

In the same motion, Nilis spun towards Bald and Porter, firing a three-round burst in their general direction. Two bullets missed Porter, zipping past his neck. The third round smashed into his left shoulder. He felt a hot pain explode inside the joint. Like someone sinking their teeth into the bone. Nilis shaped to let off another burst. Porter buried the pain, placed the iron sights on Nilis's torso and depressed the trigger. The muzzle flash lit up the ground, like the flash of a million paparazzi cameras. Two rounds thumped into the Russian's intestines. The third struck lower, nailing him in the groin. Nilis gasped, stumbled backwards, and landed on the ground next to Spray-Tan. Howling in agony as he cupped a hand to his shredded balls.

Porter sprinted forward. He stopped in front of Nilis. Pointed the AK-47 at the Russian's forehead. Nilis looked up at him, eyes blinking, his teeth stained with blood. The guy was a fucking mess. His belly was stitched with bullets. Blood stained his safari shorts, slicking out of the gaps between his fingers. His eyes focused on the black mouth of the AK-47. He started shaking his head at Porter.

'No,' he gasped. 'Don't—'

Porter fired twice, blasting the Russian at point-blank range. Nilis flinched as the rounds pulverised his skull. Then he went still.

Fuck him, thought Porter.

It's over.

Bald moved forward and nodded at Porter's shoulder. 'You're fucking bleeding.'

'Just a flesh wound,' Porter replied, grinning through the pain. 'Nothing a dressing and a few painkillers won't sort out.' He clamped a hand to his shoulder and pointed to the bodies. 'Grab his sat phone. We can call it in to Hawkridge.'

Bald reached down and picked up the unit Nilis had dropped. It was a Russian-manufactured military handset. Bigger than the slick Motorola device they had been using. A smaller display flashed up a line of Cyrillic characters. Porter stood up, shoved the phone in his back pocket.

Then he heard the moaning.

It came from the east. Porter hadn't heard the noise before. He had been concentrating fully on the Russians. The din they had been making as they turned the storage shed upside down, the constant whir of the generator in the background. But now, in the still quiet of the dark, he heard the moan clearly. He looked across his right shoulder, towards the source of the sound. It was coming from the direction of the orphanage. From inside the main building, Porter realised. Bald heard it too. He frowned.

'The fuck is that?'

Porter didn't reply. He gave his back to the dead Russians and beat a quick path towards the orphanage on the eastern side of the compound. In the periphery of his vision he saw Tully hurrying over to the open manhole to help Soames climb out from the drainage tunnel. Porter ignored them and moved across the playground, Bald hurrying after him.

I don't know what the Russians were after. But it's got something to do with whatever is lurking on the other side of that door, thought Porter.

I'm going to find out what it is.

The moaning sound grew louder as they approached the front porch. From the outside the orphanage looked well-maintained. The salmon-coloured paint on the walls was spotless. The shingle tiles on the roof showed no signs of wear or tear. Probably run on a generous budget, Porter figured. Maybe the orphanage was funded by the diamond mine owners. Maybe that was a condition for doing business in a shithole like Sierra Leone. You could take whatever you liked out of the earth, so long as you fronted the cash for an orphanage or two.

He stepped up onto the sun-bleached planking and approached the front door. Then Porter stopped again. He could hear the diesel-engine burr of the generator, the sound of his own breathing. The sound of the child moaning. It was definitely coming from the other side of that door.

He reached down and tested the handle. Locked. Porter took two steps back and shaped to take a run at the door. Bald manoeuvred to the left, his AK-47 pointed at the entryway, ready to neutralise any threat that might be waiting on the far side. Then Porter strode forward and kicked the door in, slamming the heel of his boot into the mid-section. The door crashed inward and bounced back off the inside wall. Porter spread his palms, stopping the door from rebounding shut. He stood in the entrance for a moment, searching for any movement or threat.

Nothing.

Then he stepped inside.

TWENTY-FIVE

2028 hours.

A corridor extended in front of Bald and Porter for fifteen metres. There were doors on either side of the corridor. Porter counted five in total. Two on each side of the corridor. A fifth at the far end. Office to the left of the entryway, with a dining area to the right. The décor looked like it had been lifted straight out of a seventies sitcom. The walls were fake wood panelling. The carpet was orange, and layered with colourful patterned rugs. Everything was well maintained. Every surface was spotless. The air had the clinical, antiseptic smell of a hospital ward.

Porter kept his AK-47 raised as he swept into the office. There was an oak desk with a chair behind it. Set of keys on the desk. Children's drawings on the wall behind, the kind of primary-coloured scribblings that a proud parent might stick to the front of the fridge. Chintzy sofa pushed up against the wall, the cushions sagging in the middle. The Russians had already cleared the room out. The filing cabinets in one corner of the office had been emptied, the drawers ripped out and the contents tossed onto the floor. Next to the sofa Porter noticed a bank of monitors. Each screen displayed a lumpy black-and-white image with a time and date stamp in the top left corner. Like CCTV cameras, relaying live feeds from the grounds around the orphanage.

What kind of orphanage runs such a tight security operation?

He stepped back from the office. Turned to the right and peered into the dining room. Empty. The moaning sound was coming from further down the corridor, he realised. He beat a path towards the nearest door on the left, the cries increasing in volume and multiplying in number. More than one child. Porter stopped in front of the door. Twisted the knob. The door was locked. He swept past Bald, retraced his steps into the front office and snatched up the set of keys from the desk. Hurried back down the corridor, and tried the first key in the lock. He struck gold with the third key on the chain. The latch clicked. Porter yanked the door open.

The room looked like a dormitory, he thought. *Or a holding cell.* Bunk beds were pushed up against the walls. Linoleum floor. Metal bars on the solitary window. A single fluorescent light overhead.

Then he saw the boys.

They rushed forwards from their bunks as soon as the door cracked open. Porter counted twelve of them. Most of the kids looked roughly the same age as the child soldiers that Porter and Bald had seen in the jungle. Except these children weren't sporting over-developed biceps. They were all painfully thin and dressed in tattered rags or frayed shorts. Some of the kids were whimpering. Others made strange inhuman sounds. There was a bucket in one corner of the room overflowing with piss. Piles of festering shit in another corner.

How long have they been locked up in here?

The kids flooded past the two Blades in the corridor and scurried towards the front door in a mass panic. One of the boys moved slower than the rest. He approached Porter, hugging a frayed teddy bear close to his chest. The boy stared up at him with deadened eyes. He looked to be around nine or ten years old, Porter figured. He had pinkish scars on both ankles and wrists, and his arms covered with burn marks. Like someone had been using him as an ashtray. His ribs protruded above his swollen belly. The boy opened his mouth and spoke in a tongue Porter didn't understand. Some kind of local dialect. Probably from one of the villages, probably spoken by a few hundred people total. The kid saw the look of confusion on Porter's face and tried again, pointing down the corridor. Towards the door at the far end.

'Kid's trying to tell us something,' Bald said.

Porter moved down the corridor, a sick feeling of dread brewing inside his chest. He stopped in front of the next room along and tried the keys in the lock until he found the right one. A dozen more kids flooded out of the girls' dormitory, making the same despairing moans as the boys. Their pink dresses stained with blood and dirt, their lips smeared with bright-red lipstick, eyelids coloured with glittery blue eyeshadow. Like some grotesque parody of a child beauty pageant.

Porter continued to the end of the corridor. He swung open the door at the far end. It led directly through to the annex. Bathroom and bedroom to the right, both modestly furnished. Kitchen to the left. Bright yellow walls, dark wood cabinets. Directly ahead was an open doorway leading into a wide living room, roughly the same size as the dormitories. It was dark inside the room. Porter stopped just inside and fumbled for the light switch. Found it, flipped it up. Three overhead chrome pendant lights switched on, bathing the room in a warm orange glow. The room had the same dated look as the front office. There was a vintage oval teak coffee table in the middle of the room with three chintzy sofas arranged round it in a semi-circle. A couple of armchairs. All the furniture was covered in clear plastic wrap. Bottle of water and paper cups on the coffee table, an ashtray overflowing with cigarette butts. A bottle of expensive vodka.

Half a dozen cocktail glasses, filled to the brim with bright blue pills.

'Viagra,' said Bald.

Porter lifted his eyes from the cocktail glasses. There were dark crusted splodges on the carpet, he noticed with a quickening in his guts. More patches on the walls. Then he realised what the patches were.

Dried blood.

Bald said, 'What happened here?'

Porter said nothing. His mind was reeling. His shoulder wound throbbed. Nausea tickled the back of his throat. He stepped outside the living room. Made his way back to the bedroom and glanced inside. There was a wardrobe with a sliding glass door, a single bed and a bedside cabinet with a lava lamp on it. The floor was bare except for a patchwork wool rug between the wardrobe and the bed. The bed looked newly-made, the pillow unruffled. Like nobody had slept in there for a while. Porter stepped back out of the bedroom and scratched his head. Trying to make sense of it all.

Then he saw the cables.

A big bunch of them ran along the kitchen floor. The cables were black, thick as anacondas. They looped up to the window and fed outside, running through the long grass to the smaller outlying building to the rear of the compound. Bald had noticed them too. He furrowed his brow.

'What's in there?'

Porter shrugged. 'Let's have a look.'

There was a door at the rear of the kitchen leading outside. Porter and Bald stepped out onto a patch of bare ground behind the orphanage. Outlying building at their twelve o'clock, twenty metres north of the annexe. What looked like a building site five metres to the east at their three o'clock. Porter guessed the owners were expanding their operations. The foundations had been laid for a new block, roughly the same size as the existing annex. A load of equipment lay around the kitchen door. A cement mixer, bricks, bags of cement. Porter and Bald moved past the building site and beat a path towards the outlying building. It was about a quarter the size of the orphanage, Porter figured. It looked shabbier than the main building. Like an afterthought. The walls were bare concrete. The corrugated tin roof was coated in about an inch of rust. Power cables trailed from the generator shed to the building.

No windows, Porter noticed.

As he approached the door he remembered something Tannon had told him back at the hotel. Something that had been knocking around inside his head ever since. When she had mentioned the heavy security presence guarding the mine.

Soames is hiding something, Tannon had said.

Something big.

There was a security camera fitted above the door. The door itself was a solid-looking thing secured with a flimsy padlock. Porter took two paces towards the door and hefted up the AK-47. Then he brought down the buttstock of the rifle down against the padlock in a rapid motion, smashing apart the rusted metal bolt and ripping the shackle loose from the latch. Porter planted his hand against the door and shoved it open. He heard footsteps pounding across the open ground at his back. He glanced behind. Soames and Tully were charging across the compound towards Bald and Porter. They were twenty metres from the manhole cover now. Twenty metres from the two Blades. Soames shouted at them to step away from the door, his voice carrying crisply across the darkness.

Porter ignored him and stepped inside.

Bald followed.

They entered a wide, low-ceilinged room dimly illuminated by banks of glowing screens. There were bits of machinery and components everywhere. Keyboards, mice, external disk drives. Like a computer shop selling off its stock. Miles of wire. A spaghetti tangle of cables ran from the backs of dozens of tower units to the power sockets. Computer fans whirred. Screensavers flickered on the monitors. The room was furnace-hot. A result of housing a serious amount of computer equipment in a building with no natural ventilation or windows. This place must be what the Russians were after, Porter told himself.

There was a CD burner on the desk next to one of the computers, plus a stack of discs. Porter browsed through them. All the discs were marked with dates scrawled across the aluminium surface in marker pen. The most recent ones were several weeks old. He picked up one of the CDs, punched the eject button on the tower. Placed the disc on the tray and shut it. The CD drive beeped and whirred. Porter nudged the mouse to make the screensaver disappear. Then a media player panel appeared at the bottom of the screen.

Outside the building he could hear Soames shouting at him, ordering him not to touch anything. Porter blocked out his old

CO's voice, hovered the arrow icon over the Play button and left-clicked the mouse.

A black-and-white image filled the screen.

The guest suite in the annexe. Dated six weeks ago.

Three boys were running around the room. They were naked, and around the same age as the kids Porter had seen in the dorm rooms. They were being chased by two older white men with cobwebbed hair. The old men were also naked. They pursued the boys round and round the sofas, saggy flesh hanging from their outstretched arms, faces grinning. Like they were playing some depraved playground game. The image quality wasn't great, but Porter vaguely recognised one of the guys from Sky News. The Tory MP with the wire-framed glasses.

The other guy was a retired army general.

The general chased one of the boys around the coffee table, caught up with him and then let himself fall on top of the boy, tickling his ribs. The boy wriggled and laughed. Like any normal dad playing with his son. Except the man and the boy were both naked. The Tory MP took no notice. He was focused on the two other boys. Hunting down his prey. Then the general suddenly stopped tickling the kid. He wrapped his arms around the youth's waist and pinned him to the floor. Pressing down on the kid's slender frame with his considerable weight. There was no audio, but Porter could see the kid's mouth widening into a scream, his arms and legs flailing as he kicked out at the old man.

Seconds passed. The boy stopped struggling.

The general kissed the child on the mouth.

'Jesus Christ,' said Bald. 'Jesus fucking Christ.'

Porter heard footsteps. He looked up at the entrance. Soames stood in the doorway, exuding a strange calm. Tully stood behind him, watching Porter and Bald steadily. Porter's eyes wandered back to Soames as the latter took a slow step into the room.

'What the fuck is this place?' Porter demanded.

'I like to think of it as a private retreat,' Soames replied. 'Somewhere discreet, where certain individuals are free to indulge their fantasies, free of the moralising constraints of Western society.'

Porter shook his head. His throat tightened with anger. 'You're protecting a bunch of kiddie fiddlers?'

'That's one way of putting it, I suppose. The individuals who frequent this orphanage are pillars of the Establishment. Men who work at the highest levels of Westminster, the civil service and the military. We provide them with a secure, discreet environment where they can do as they please. No questions asked.'

The blunt admission startled Porter. *My old CO is operating a paedophile ring, in the middle of the jungle.* He clenched his fists. His knuckles whitening, the nails digging into the palm of his hand. He wanted to punch Soames so hard his teeth would shatter.

Bald said, 'You told us this was about diamonds.'

Soames stiffened. 'I had no choice. The Russians were threatening my position. There was no time to explain everything. Besides, I didn't know how much you had been told about our operations here in Sierra Leone. It's only when you rescued me from the West Side Boys that I realised you didn't know about the orphanage. Obviously, you've both been kept in the dark by your superiors.'

Anger clamped its fingers around Porter's throat. Like it had him in a chokehold, cutting off the air to his brain. He felt an immense pressure building between his temples.

More than anything, he needed a fucking drink.

'Why here?' he said. 'Why Sierra Leone?'

'Simple,' Soames replied. 'Life here is dirt cheap. No one asks any questions, no one causes trouble. All that civil war, crushing poverty and lack of government infrastructure makes it easy to steal children from the villages without anyone kicking up a fuss. Besides, we had no choice but to shift our operations from the UK. Hosting these sessions in London was increasingly difficult. Too much risk of media exposure. I'm sure you've heard the rumours.'

Porter nodded slowly. There had been the usual tabloid rumours, allegations of a Westminster paedophile ring that

287

sexually abused young boys. Every so often you'd hear something on the news. Some dirty old MP with a fondness for kids. Now he understood why Tannon had been so curious about the VIPs making unannounced visits to Sierra Leone. *Because they were visiting this place.*

Nausea tickled the back of his throat.

Bald shot Tully a screw-face. 'You knew about this place?'

Tully grinned. 'Of course I knew, you dense cunt. I'm the day manager.'

Soames saw the look of confusion playing out on Bald and Porter's faces and stepped in.

'Bob's in charge of the day-to-day operations at the orphanage. He's been doing a fine job since he started working here, I must say. Keeps the children in check. Makes sure they do their best to entertain our guests. Brings in more kids from the surrounding villages whenever we need them.'

Porter stared at Tully and felt sick.

Dozens of children have gone missing, Tannon had said.

'You took the kids,' he said.

Tully grinned again. 'Like I said, fellas. This is the best job I've ever had. Top pay, good hours, and the kids are dead easy to find. If anyone of them step out of line, you cut them up and get another one. Simple.'

There was a note of pride in Tully's voice, and a sadistic gleam in his eyes. Porter looked away from him. Nodded at Soames.

'You're the one running the network?'

'Running is rather a strong word, I think. I merely provide the location, the transport and the children. What my Westminster friends get up to behind closed doors is entirely up to them.'

Porter glanced over at the monitor. On the screen, the retired general had moved over to the sofa, helping himself to a joint while the boy lay in a foetal position on the carpet, weeping. The Tory MP with the wire-framed glasses sat on the other sofa, tugging on his flaccid penis while another boy sucked on his toes. Porter looked away with a wave of revulsion. He glowered at Soames.

'You're fucking sick. Once the Firm hears about this, you're finished. Both of you.'

Soames smiled faintly. 'I sincerely doubt it.'

'The fuck are you talking about?'

A quick smile flashed like a knife at the corner of Soames's mouth. 'Your handler really didn't tell you *anything*, did he?'

Porter said nothing. The pounding between his temples grew louder. Soames took another step towards him. His smile broadened.

'What do you mean?' Bald said.

'MI5 knows about this place already, you fool. They know what goes on here.'

Porter felt a slash of cold air on the back of his neck. A shiver spider-crawled down his spine. Turning the blood inside his veins to ice.

'Bullshit.'

'It's the truth,' Soames insisted. 'I work for them. I run the orphanage on their behalf.'

Porter shook his head furiously. 'Why the fuck would the Firm get involved in running a paedo network?'

Soames waved a hand at the stacks of CD and the computer monitors. 'Look around you. This place is an intelligence gold mine. Everything that goes on here is recorded with secret cameras rigged up inside the building. Every buggering session is filmed. Every individual who abuses an African boy or girl is captured on camera, the footage copied onto disc and handed over to Five for safekeeping.'

'This place is a honey trap for paedos?' Bald said.

'One of several, actually. There are other sites similar to this one in South Africa, Canada and Belize. Among others. Not every diplomat feels safe travelling to Sierra Leone, naturally.'

Porter shook his head. 'The Firm would never allow that.'

'Oh, really?' Soames chuckled easily. 'Think again, John. There are paedophiles in every corner of government. More than you might imagine. Senior civil servants, army chiefs, cabinet members . . . the list is endless. Thames House decided long ago that it was infinitely more profitable to blackmail these men rather than report them. They provide us with intelligence, spying on colleagues, that sort of thing. The individuals concerned are in no position to refuse Five's demands, of course. If the footage was released, it would ruin them.' He smiled. 'Why on earth do you think the Russians were so desperate to find this place?'

'The footage,' Bald said.

'Correct.'

'How did they find out about the orphanage to begin with?' Porter asked.

'One of the children escaped a few months ago. He ran off to the West Side Boys and told them what was going on at the orphanage. The Russians got word through their rebel contacts and decided to rob me. They were going to kill me, take the footage and use it to strong-arm our government. I couldn't let that happen. So I killed their agent. The man you found in my office.'

'Why would the Russians be so keen to get their hands on footage of a few dodgy old British paedos?'

'If the Russians stole this material, they would have cast-iron proof that MI5 was actively involved in running a top-secret paedophile network, using war children. The fallout would be politically toxic. Five and Six would be instantly discredited, perhaps even dismantled. The knives would be out inside Westminster. Our national security would be put at risk, along with the hundreds of operations and thousands of field agents we're running around the world. It would be nothing short of a disaster.' Soames paused. 'Which is why we must remove the CDs at once. Everything that is stored at this site has to be taken away.'

'What the fuck for?' Bald said.

'The orphanage has been compromised. No doubt the Russians have already notified their superiors at the FSB as to the where- abouts of the orphanage. This facility is no longer secure for our purposes. We'll have to relocate, before reinforcements show up.'

'Where to?'

'Guinea. I own a ranch in the countryside. If we move now, we can make it across the border by first light. Once we're out of Sierra Leone the footage will be secure.'

Porter shook his head. 'That's not part of our mission.'

'I agree with Soames,' Bald said. 'We can't let the Russians get their hands on this stuff, mate. If word got out, the press would have a fucking field day.'

'Why don't we just torch the material?'

'Out of the question,' Soames replied. 'The Firm has invested a lot of time and effort in running this place. The footage is too valuable to destroy.'

Porter gritted his teeth. The pain in his shoulder had dialled down to a dull, constant ache, the blood sticky against his skin. I don't mind being sent halfway round the world to a bloody war zone, he thought. I don't even mind having to protect the life of the guy who shafted my career. *But I draw the line at putting my balls on the line to save a bunch of Westminster paedophiles.*

Soames saw the look of uncertainty on his face. He made a sidelong glance at Tully, then looked back to Porter. 'Call your handler if you don't believe me. He'll tell you the same thing.'

There was a challenge in his eyes as he spoke. Porter hesitated and glanced at his mucker. Bald shrugged as if to say, 'Your call.' Porter set down his assault rifle on the desk. Fished out the Russian satellite phone from his back pocket.

'Sod it,' he said. 'I'll make the call.'

Soames looked relieved. He looked at the piles of CDs and wrinkled his features in thought. 'Someone should head back down to the main road. Bring up one of the wagons so we can load up all the material and computers. There's too much here for us to carry down by hand.'

'I'll go,' Tully volunteered.

'Good man, Bob.'

Tully hesitated by the doorway. 'I'll need a weapon.'

Porter frowned at him. 'What happened to your collector's item?'

The guy held out the M1911 pistol. He had the grip and receiver in one hand. The rust-coated slider mechanism nestled in the palm of the other.

'Slider's fucked. I checked to make sure there was a round in the snout, when you asked me to cover you both. Bastard snapped clean off. It's useless.'

'Bob makes a good point,' Soames added. 'If the Russians have sent for reinforcements, he might run into them on the main road.'

'What about your secondary weapon?' Porter asked.

'Left it in the wagon,' Tully replied dismissively. He turned to Bald, nodded at the AK-47. 'Come on, Jock. I thought we were friends. Do us a solid, mate. I saved your arse back at the hotel. The least you can do is sort me out with a piece.'

Bald wavered, then handed over the rifle. 'Here, mate. Take it. There's more than half a clip in there. Should be enough to send any more Russians packing.'

Tully gratefully accepted the weapon and smiled at Bald. 'Cheers, fella. You're a good mate, you know.'

Tully grabbed the rifle and stepped out of the building. Porter couldn't get a signal inside in an enclosed space, so he ducked out of the room too. Bald followed, then Soames. Porter flipped up the antenna and paced east towards the building site, pointing the phone skywards until he found reception. After eight paces two bars flashed up on the display. He punched in the number for Vauxhall that he'd committed to memory. Although the display characters were in Cyrillic, the numerical layout and graphics were broadly the same as the Motorola, and Porter had little trouble operating the handset. He hit the green icon for Dial, then waited for the call to patch through.

The phone rang and rang.

No one picked up.

They don't recognise the number, Porter thought. They're not going to answer.

He was about to terminate the call when a voice on the other end of the line said, 'Who is this? How did you get—'

'It's me,' Porter interrupted.

'Porter?' Hawkridge spluttered. In the background Porter heard the tap-tap of keyboards, the chorus bleeps of ringing phones. He imagined the agent sitting behind a desk in a climate-controlled office somewhere inside Vauxhall.

'Where the hell have you been?' Hawkridge continued. 'We've been trying to contact you for hours.'

'Battery died,' said Porter. 'We're at the mine. We've got Soames.'

A long pause played out on the other end of the line. 'Whose phone are you calling us from?'

'The Russians. One of them had a sat phone on him.'

Another pause. 'You fucking idiot. This isn't a secure line. The FSB is probably listening in on us right now.'

'What did you want us to do?' Porter said. 'Our phone's dead. We had no other way of reaching out to you.'

Hawkridge said, 'Make it quick, then. What's the situation? Have you secured the mine? If you're using a Russian sat phone, then I presume you've taken care of our friends.'

'Aye,' he said. 'The Russians are dead. We're at the orphanage now.'

'I . . . see,' Hawkridge said. Slowly.

Porter said, 'Soames told us about the paedo network.'

'I see.'

'He reckons the Firm is helping him run this place.'

Silence.

The guilty kind.

Porter looked across his shoulder at the front of the compound. He could see the security lights glowing in the distance, the dark oblivion beyond. He briefly wondered where the kids had gone. Perhaps Tannon and Solomon had seen them running out of the compound and come to their aid, he thought.

'John? Are you there?'

'You fucking lied to us,' he said.

'There's no time for any of that now. Listen to me carefully. I'll make this very quick. Is Soames there with you now?'

Porter looked back towards the outlying building. Soames and Bald were standing four metres away, at the edge of the building site. Bald at his two o'clock, Soames at his twelve. The ex-Rupert had his arms folded across his broad chest, a smile trembling on his lips. Tully was still there too, standing at Porter's ten o'clock and clutching the assault rifle he'd borrowed from Bald. Porter briefly wondered why Bob Tully was still hanging around the compound.

'Well?' Hawkridge snapped. 'Answer me, man.'

'Yeah,' Porter said. 'He's here. Why?'

'I need you to kill him. Soames. He has to go.'

TWENTY-SIX

2047 hours.

Porter said nothing for a beat. He just stood rooted to the spot, gripping the sat phone and staring dead ahead at Soames. The ex-CO of 22 SAS was looking at Porter with a face so blank it could have been packaged and sold as paint canvas.

'Did you hear me, John?' Hawkridge said, his voice burning in Porter's ear. 'Soames knows too much. The man is a threat. You have to get rid of him and destroy everything related to the orphanage. Torch every scrap of evidence. We can't let these materials fall into the wrong hands. Do you understand?'

He still said nothing. The same thought repeated inside Porter's head on a loop. *Why would the Firm want to burn Soames? They've gone to great bloody lengths to protect him, and now they want him dead.*

It doesn't make any sense.

'I'll make sure there's a reward for you and Jock at the end of it all,' Hawkridge continued. 'A big reward. You have my word. Say yes if you understand my instructions.'

'Yes,' Porter said at last.

A sigh of relief shivered down the line.

'Good man,' said Hawkridge. 'Now finish the job.'

Click.

Porter kept the sat phone pressed to his ear for a few seconds for effect, listening to the dead line. He made a sidelong glance at Bald and pointed with his eyes at Soames. Bald flashed a quizzical look at his mucker. Soames just stood there, uncomprehending. *My AK-47 is out of reach in the building,* Porter told himself. *But I've still got the Makarov.* He could feel the pistol stuffed down the back of his combats, the Bakelite grip pressing against the small of his back. He had eight rounds in the clip, Porter knew. More than enough to get the job done.

A hot thrill ran through his veins as he lowered the sat phone and reached around to retrieve the Makarov. He visualised blowing Soames's brains out. How good it would make him feel.

Then a voice said, 'Lose the piece, fella. Nice and fucking slow.'

Porter froze.

Looked up.

Tully stood five metres away, pointing the AK-47 at Porter. The muzzle eye-fucked him. Tully's index finger curled around the trigger.

Ready to blow my brains out.

'Drop it,' Tully repeated.

Porter stayed very still. His mind rapidly processed the situation. There's no play here, he thought. *There's no way out.* I can't put the drop on Tully. He's already got his weapon raised. By the time I've retrieved the Makarov and lined up to shoot, he'll have pulled the trigger. At a distance of five metres, it was impossible to miss a target. Especially for a Regiment-trained shooter. *All you can do is try to buy yourself a few moments.*

'What the fuck are you doing, Bob?' he said. 'We're on the same side.'

'Not any more, fella.'

'What do you mean?'

Soames stepped closer and smiled. 'You really should work on your poker face, John. Honestly, you're far too easy to read. I knew as soon as I saw you speaking to your handler that Five has turned against me.'

'Don't know what you're talking about.'

Soames chuckled to himself. 'Oh, come on. Do you really think I'm that naïve? I always suspected Five might try to get rid of me eventually. It's in their nature, after all. The only thing Thames House loves more than a secret is making sure they have exclusive ownership of it. That's why I cut a deal with Bob.'

'What deal?'

'To keep an eye on you two. And to stop you from making a move against me.'

Porter gritted his teeth and glared at Tully. The guy showed no reaction. He still had the assault rifle raised, the barrel trained on a spot between Porter's eyes.

'Last chance. Put down the fucking gun.'

'Do as he says, John,' Soames urged.

All eyes were on Porter as he slowly withdrew the Makarov from the back of his waistband. He bent down, placing the pistol flat on the ground next to the Russian sat phone. Then he stretched to his full height and side-footed the gun across the ground towards Tully. Soames grinned triumphantly. Porter could feel the muscles on his neck pulling tight with rage.

Then he heard a deadly click at his two o'clock.

The sound of a pistol hammer being cocked.

Porter looked across. He saw Bald holding the PSM in a firm two-handed grip, aiming directly at Tully. The pistol Bald had taken from the dirty old German back at the hotel. Porter had almost forgotten about it. So had Tully, judging from the look of complete surprise plastered across his face.

'Drop the fucking tool,' Bald said.

Tully didn't move.

Soames stood between the two men. His eyes shifted cautiously from Tully to Bald. 'Think about what you're doing,' he said, nerves creeping into his voice. 'It doesn't have to go down like this. You can join us. We'll cut you in on the profits from our arrangement.'

Bald frowned. 'What arrangement?'

'When you two came looking for me at the hotel, it confirmed my suspicions that Five were looking to bury me,' Soames explained. 'So I made alternative plans. Bob and myself are leaving Sierra Leone. We're going to seize the discs, relocate to Guinea and use the footage to blackmail HMG. Those fools in Westminster will pay whatever it takes to keep this material away from the public eye. Along with the revelation that senior figures in British intelligence were helping to run this place.' He smiled at Bald. 'We'll ransom the government and live like kings.'

Bald's eyes narrowed in thought. Porter bristled with anger and frustration. 'The Firm won't let you get away with this.'

That prompted a hearty chuckle from Soames. 'I hardly think they'll have much choice. If they kill me, I'll see to it that the footage from this orphanage is released to the editor of every major newspaper in Britain.' He shrugged. 'Although if you're the best operator Five can rustle up, I shouldn't have too many sleepless nights. It says something about our intelligence agencies that they're relying on a washed-up old drunk to do their dirty work, don't you think?'

'Piss off.'

Soames hardened his gaze. 'You always were a fool, Porter. Straight as a bat, but you never had any guile. Unlike your friend,' he added, gesturing to Bald. 'You're obviously a smart fellow, Jock. You're not going to pass up the opportunity of a lifetime just so you can be pushed around by some overpaid fool at Thames House, are you? Put down the gun, and join us. I'll make you filthy rich. You have my word.'

Bald said, 'How much wonga are we talking about here?'

'Millions,' Soames responded, his voice growing steadily more confident. He took a half-step closer to Bald. 'You'll have enough money to keep you in women and drink for the rest of your days.'

He's actually considering it, thought Porter.

Bald clamped his eyes shut for a moment, as if wrestling with his conscience. His finger tensed on the pistol trigger. Porter looked on helplessly at Bald, his skin pricked with fear. He imagined the 5.45x18mm round exploding out of the PSM's snout. The nugget of hot lead boring through his frontal lobe, mashing up his brain matter before exiting through the back of his neck. Soames looked on, grinning expectantly.

Porter said, 'Think about what you're doing, for fuck's sake. You're not gonna kill me to protect some dodgy ex-Rupert, are you?'

'Don't listen to him!' Soames thundered. 'Porter's a dead man either way. The only choice is whether you want to be rich, or end up in a mine pit next to this drunken fool.'

Bald kept the PSM trained on Tully. But his finger paused on the trigger. There was the slightest flicker of hesitation in his eyes, Porter noticed. A barely perceptible twitch of his facial muscles.

He's wavering.

'Soames is lying,' Porter said. 'As soon as your back is turned, he'll drop you.'

'Bullshit,' said Tully, making his appeal directly to Bald. 'Ronald's telling the truth. You can trust me, Jock. We're friends.'

Bald clenched his jaws. He's going to do it, thought Porter. He's going to turn on me and put a bullet in my head. *You've got to keep trying to get through to him. That's your only chance.*

'If you kill me, you'll have the Firm on your back,' he said. 'The Regiment will hear about it too. You know how word gets around. You'll make an instant enemy of every bloke who's ever walked through the gates at Hereford. You'll be fucking marked. You'll spend the rest of your days looking over your shoulder.'

'Ignore him!' Soames yelled. 'Kill Porter, man!'

And then it happened. Bald slanted the PSM away from Tully and rested the weapon on Porter. Specifically, at a point between his eyes. Porter could hardly believe what was happening. The cold, hard look of certainty calcified in Bald's eyes, and the grim realisation seized Porter that there was nothing he could say to sway Bald's mind. *Nothing I can do to stop that Jock bastard from pulling the trigger.*

Bald relaxed his shoulder muscles. A cruel smile formed on his lips. He took a deep breath. Tensed his trigger finger. The pistol hammer poised to spring forward and eject the round nestled in the chamber. To the left, Soames looked on, grinning from ear to ear. Tully lowered his rifle.

It's over, Porter thought.

He closed his eyes and waited to die.

In the next instant he heard the booming crack of a round discharging.

It took half a second for Porter to register that he hadn't been shot. Then he opened his eyes and saw Bald standing in front of him, pointing his gun at Tully. Smoke wisping out of the barrel. Five metres to the left, Tully let out a sclerotic hiss of pain and staggered backwards. Blood spurted out of a wound to his abdomen, staining the seat of his trousers. He lifted his eyes to Bald, a look of dumb shock playing out on his face.

Bald fired again. The second round thumped into Tully's upper chest. Tully grunted and fell backwards, releasing his grip on the AK-47. Bald fired again as Tully landed on his back, his mouth sagging open in agony, his left hand pawing at the wound to his guts.

Porter glimpsed a flicker of movement at his twelve o'clock. He looked up and saw Soames diving for the AK-47 that Tully had dropped. Bald hadn't yet noticed the new threat. He was still emptying rounds into Tully, his features twisted with inhuman rage. The PSM only had a mag capacity of eight rounds, Porter knew. *If Soames gets his hands on that rifle, we're both fucked*.

Soames bent down to scoop up the rifle. Porter lunged forward. He had a second or two before Soames grabbed the AK. The guy was moving fast. But he was slower than Porter. Soames had spent his later years enjoying the good life, and it showed. Porter slammed shoulder-first into the guy before he could pick up the weapon, knocking him off his feet. Momentum carried Soames backwards a couple of paces. He let out a pained cry as he fell to the ground next to the building site, the impact driving the air from his lungs. Porter landed on top of him and snatched up a spare brick lying next to the cement mixer.

'No, man!' Soames pleaded. 'Don't! I can make you rich!'

Porter raised the brick over his head then brought it crashing down, battering Soames's face and shattering his front teeth. Soames let out a gasping groan of pain as Porter hit him again, battering the triangle of his face. Porter kept pounding away until there was nothing left of his face except a crater of flesh and blood and broken teeth. Soames gasped in pain between each ragged blow. At his six o'clock Porter could hear Bald getting the dead man's click as he emptied the last round from the PSM clip into Tully.

Soames begged him to stop.

Porter raised his arm to strike again.

Then he heard a second metallic click.

Soames noticed something to his right. Coming from the annexe. Porter stopped and looked in the same direction.

He saw the kitchen door at the rear of the annexe hanging open.

Tannon stood a few metres beyond the doorway. A Makarov pistol snug in her two-handed grip.

At first Porter wondered where she'd got the pistol. Then he remembered. *The hotel rooftop.* The lull before the second wave of rebels had attacked. He recalled handing Tannon one of the pistols. Telling her to turn the gun on herself if the hotel fell to the enemy.

There's one round in that chamber, Porter reminded himself.

Tannon took two steps forward. Weapon raised. Her right arm fully extended, her support arm bent at a forty-five degree at the elbow. There was something about her firing stance that told Porter this wasn't the first time she had handled a weapon. She had the Makarov pointed broadly in the direction of Porter and Soames, but from the angle it was impossible to tell who she was aiming at.

Me or my old CO.

By now Bald had also become aware of Tannon's presence. He stood over Tully's limp body, his hands clasped around the grip of the empty PSM, watching the deputy commissioner as she edged forward. Porter cast an eye around the immediate area, evaluating the scene. *Tully's AK-47 and the spare Makarov were out of arm's reach. The only one who's got a gun right now is Tannon.*

'Help me,' Soames rasped at Tannon in a nasal tone of voice. Blood trickled out of the corners of his mouth. 'Kill this bastard.'

Tannon took another step forward. Porter still couldn't tell who she was aiming at.

'I said kill him!' Soames thundered. 'This man is a traitor to his country. He's threatening to jeopardise a vital MI5 operation. Call your boss if you don't believe me. I'm a good friend of his.'

Tannon stopped four metres away from Porter and Soames. She held the gun steady in her grip. Nobody moved.

'If you know which side your bread is buttered, you'll kill this scumbag and help me get out of the country,' Soames went on. 'I can make it worth your while. Whatever you want. Diamonds. Money. Promotion. Name it.'

Tannon lowered the weapon.

'This is for the kids,' she said.

Then she moved towards Soames and shoved the Makarov pistol into his mouth. Soames's eyes bulged with fear. He made a muffled screaming noise deep in his throat as she pulled the trigger.

The Makarov boomed. Soames jolted, as if a team of paramedics were trying to revive him with a defibrillator. His brains blasted out of the roof of his skull, splattering bits of cranium and brain matter across the red earth.

Fuck him, Porter thought.

He stood up. Tannon did too. She slid the Makarov out of Soames's gaping mouth. The tip of the barrel was slick with blood. She let the pistol hang by her side. Stared down at his contorted, limp body.

'Feel any better?' Porter said.

'You know that feeling when you step on a cockroach?'

Porter nodded.

'Like that,' Tannon said.

'Where's Solomon?' Porter asked, casting his eyes across the compound.

Tannon pointed towards the front of the compound.

'Watching over the children. I told him to stay put and guard them, no matter what.'

Porter nodded. 'We should tell the authorities.'

'Solomon's already on the case. We found a spare charger for the sat phone. I told him to call my contact at the Mothers of the Lost foundation. Let them know we found the kids.'

She closed her eyes, as if trying to wipe the memory from the hard drive of her brain. *But you don't forget images like that*, Porter thought. *What me and Bald saw in that orphanage tonight, we won't forget that in a hurry.*

'When I saw those poor kids streaming out of the orphanage, I knew something was wrong,' Tannon continued. 'So I ran over to investigate. That's when I saw you and Soames struggling on the ground.'

Porter stared at her for several seconds. 'I thought you said you were no good with guns.'

'A white lie. It was part of my cover.'

'Cover?' Porter repeated.

Tannon nodded. 'I work for Six. Angela is my boss.'

A whole bunch of stuff clicked into place inside Porter's head. Stuff that had been bugging him throughout the op. Like why Tannon had transferred from military intelligence to a backwater posting with the Foreign Office. Her interest in Soames. Why Angela March had been present at the mission briefing to begin with.

Tannon is MI6.

'Why did Angela send you here? To kill Soames?'

Tannon shook her head. 'Not initially.'

'Why, then?'

'I was brought in to look into his business affairs. Angela set me up with diplomatic cover at the High Commission. She'd heard rumours about rogue elements at Thames House helping to orchestrate a high-profile overseas network for Westminster paedophiles. She thought Soames might be involved and wanted someone on the ground to have eyes on him.'

'Wait a minute,' Bald said, shaking his head. He'd tossed the PSM aside and stepped away from Tully. 'You're telling me MI5 was running this operation, and no one at MI6 had a fucking clue?'

Tannon stared at him. 'Contrary to what you might believe, the spirit of cooperation between the intelligence services isn't exactly strong. We share only what we need to share. Which isn't much. We knew Soames had to be involved somehow. He was connected to a lot of the suspects. He had access to the Firm, he was part of the old boys' network that operates at the heart of the establishment. He was in the perfect position, really.' She slanted her gaze back to Soames. To the hole in the roof of his skull. 'But we never expected this.'

'Who else was involved at the Firm?' Porter asked.

'Hawkridge,' Tannon replied. 'But you probably figured that out already. Along with one or two others. We're talking a small number of people. To limit exposure. The people at the very top will deny any knowledge, of course.'

'Those bastards always do,' Bald muttered.

Porter said, 'Why did Hawkridge agree to the op in the first place? If he knew Six was investigating Soames and the paedo network?'

'He didn't have a choice,' said Tannon. 'Hawkridge doesn't have the clout to kill a live investigation. So his best bet was to stonewall it for long enough to get rid of the evidence, along with any witnesses. As far as we can tell, he planned to kill Soames and then dispose of you two quietly once you returned to the UK. That would have put him in the clear.'

Porter clenched his teeth and dug his fingers into his palms. *That's why Hawkridge ordered us to kill Soames and destroy the evidence. The bastard was covering his tracks.*

'Why didn't you tell us earlier? That you were working for Six?'

Tannon pursed her lips. 'There were question marks about your loyalty.'

'From you?'

'From Angela. You both had a pre-existing relationship with Hawkridge. You were both working on secondment for Five. There was every chance you might have been on the inside on this whole thing.'

'What now?' Bald said.

'We clear this place up,' Tannon said. 'Burn everything. Make it look like an attack from the West Side Boys.'

'There's one problem,' Porter cut in. 'We put in a call to Hawkridge on the Russians' sat phone. They'll know about this location by now. They'll be sending more assets. If they're not on the way already.'

Tannon nodded thoughtfully. 'Then we'll need to move quick. The nearest Russian training camp to here is across the border in Liberia. That's a two-hour drive from here. Three, max. We'll have to get to work now. Remove any evidence of our involvement here.'

'Then what?'

'We get out of the country. There's an extraction team with a plane waiting for us at an airfield east of here, on the border with Guinea.'

'How far?'

'Sixty miles, give or take. Which means we can be back on a plane by one o'clock in the morning and back in London by lunchtime. We'll need a thorough debrief from you both, of course. Help expose Hawkridge and the others at Thames House.'

Bald grinned at her. 'You can debrief me any time you want, lass.'

Tannon stared back at him. Said nothing.

The anger welled up inside Porter again. Clawing at his vitals.

'We shouldn't be torching this place,' he said. 'We didn't risk our necks just so a load of old paedos could be let off the hook. We should be taking all this footage and putting it out there.'

'We can't. My bosses won't allow it. Believe me, I tried.'

'Why not?'

'It's too close to the top. The people in these files. They're not middle managers at Intel. They're some of the most prominent names in politics and the military. People from the cabinet down would be tainted by association.'

'That's bullshit.'

'It's not my call to make. This place has to be wiped from the map.'

'She's right,' Bald said. 'We need to burn this place, mate. There's too much at stake.'

Tannon said, 'This is a win for us, John.'

'Yeah? It doesn't fucking feel like one.'

'Soames is dead. The orphanage is out of business. The kids here are safe now. We'll have enough evidence to take down Hawkridge and the rest of the conspirators inside MI5. The old boys' network will inevitably close ranks, but by then it'll be too late.'

Porter looked away. Towards the orphanage. The playground, the slotted Russians. The evening air was hot with the stink of lead and warm blood. Everything stood empty and still and terribly quiet. Like visiting the site of an old battlefield. He thought again about the footage he'd seen, the Tory MP pinning that boy to the ground, and he needed a drink. *Like I've never needed one before in my life.*

'Fine,' he said, returning his gaze to Tannon and Bald. 'Let's scrub this fucking place out of existence.'

Tannon moved off to investigate the outlying building. She wanted to see for herself, despite Porter's warnings about the content on the discs. He watched her walk away, then turned to Bald.

'What was all that about back there? Pointing that fucking gun at me.'

Bald grinned. 'You didn't think I was serious, did you?'

Porter said nothing. He just stared at Bald.

'I needed to get Tully to drop his guard,' Bald went on. 'He wasn't going to lower his weapon until he was convinced I was about to pop you. That's why I did it.' He burst out into a full-throated laugh. 'After all the shite we've been through today, you honestly thought I was going to put a bullet in your head?'

'No,' said Porter, inwardly breathing a sigh of relief.

'I should fucking hope not, mate. You and me, we're like brothers.'

Porter grinned. 'Careful, Jock. You're getting emotional. You sure you're not on the Bell's again?'

'Twat.' Bald mock-scowled at Porter. Then his face relaxed into a smile. 'Speaking of which, let's finish up and get the fuck out of here. I don't know about you, but I could murder a bloody pint.'

TWENTY-SEVEN

2138 hours.

It took them almost an hour to prep the blaze. While Tannon made arrangements with Médecins sans Frontières volunteers based in a nearby village to take the children into protective custody, Bald and Porter organised the fire. They dragged the bodies into the main orphanage building, because they figured it would be easier to start one big fire instead of several smaller ones. Solomon helped out too. The three carted the dead guys into the guest suite and dumped them on the floor. Tully first, then Soames. Then Nilis and Spray-Tan. The three men were soon sweating hard from the strain of lifting all that dead weight. Then they retrieved several of the worn car tyres and wooden pallets from the front of the compound and lugged them over to the orphanage, along with one of the jerry cans taken from the back of the Range Rover. They dumped everything in the guest suite, then doused the tyres and pallets. Tannon emptied the computers from the outlying building and added them to the pile in the annexe. She found a toolbox in the Portakabin and took a power drill to the hard drives. The only way to make sure the data was fully corrupted, she explained. Then she took the drives and the CDs and the backup tapes, and threw everything onto the pile.

When they had finished building the fire, Bald and Porter stripped the bodies of anything that might identify them to the authorities. Wallets, watches, jewellery. They wanted it to look as if the Russians were security guards working for Soames, Tannon said. MI6 would create false identities and add them to the list of personnel employed by Soames's PMC. It was unlikely that the

FSB would publicly claim the dead Russians as their own. And it was important to make the story look convincing, she added. So no one tried digging too deep, asking too many questions.

Then they lit the fire.

The flames spread quickly, consuming the annexe, then the rest of the orphanage. They watched the fire from a safe distance to the south. Black smoke gushing into the blacker sky. They all agreed they felt better after setting fire to the building. Not great, but better. It was a start, Tannon said. A case as wide-reaching as this, nothing was going to be straightforward. Hawkridge would pay, along with anyone else at Five who helped run the orphanage. She had already contacted Angela March. Her handler was hinting that Hawkridge wouldn't be going to prison. That people higher up the food chain had already decided it would be better if he simply disappeared.

Porter said he was okay with that.

They watched the fire burn for a while. Then Tannon collected the diamonds that had been emptied from the floor safe in the Portakabin and bagged them as evidence, to Bald's obvious disappointment. Tannon said the diamonds were potentially compromising. They could provoke an international scandal, particularly if it was proven that Soames had been stealing diamonds from the mine owners with the complicit knowledge of Whitehall. She didn't say what would happen to the diamonds, and Porter didn't ask.

Shortly after ten o'clock four aid vehicles arrived at the mine. Eight MSF volunteers debussed and began tending to the children. The kids were hesitant at first. Then the volunteers started dishing out sweets and bottles of Coke, and they were soon smiling as they were each given a brief medical examination before being ushered into one of the wagons. Solomon joined them. He gave Bald a bear hug before he left and promised Jock that one day he would come visit him in London. Bald didn't look too happy, but said nothing. Three minutes later the aid convoy rolled out of the compound, headlamps shrinking to pinpricks in the solid black mass of the night.

Then Porter, Bald and Tannon left. They took the Discovery, because the Range Rover was almost out of petrol. Porter drove, with Tannon riding shotgun and Bald in the rear passenger seat. It was a forty-mile drive east to the border with Guinea, along a bumpy and desolate track. Pitch-black, so Porter took it slow. They didn't run into any trouble. He figured the local rebels were probably busy partying in their camps. They crossed the border around midnight and hit the airfield thirty minutes later.

The airfield was a single-lane runway set in the middle of a barren field, with a low-rise concrete building to one side. There was a light cargo aircraft at the end of the runway. A Cessna 208 Cargomaster, with EVERGREEN CARGO splashed down the side in the same big gold lettering Porter had seen back at Lungi airport. He steered the Discovery to a halt next to the building. Cut the gas.

Three guys were waiting outside the office. Two guards, and Shoemaker. The guy who had greeted Bald and Porter at Lungi airport two days ago. Two days, but it feels like a lifetime ago, thought Porter. *Me and Jock have been through hell and back since then*.

He said, 'The CIA were helping you out?'

'They're an interested party,' Tannon replied. 'They were worried about Soames, but for very different reasons.'

'How'd you mean?'

'The Russian angle. The Agency's playing a bigger game. They're worried about Russia trying to increase its sphere of influence in Africa. The new president's looking to flex his muscles, buying power wherever he can and propping up dictators to do business with. Washington's keen to clip his wings. Anything that could give the Russians leverage in Sierra Leone was a threat.'

They debussed. Shoemaker acknowledged Porter and Bald with a tip of his baseball cap. Tannon headed for the office.

'I'm going to put in a call to Angela,' she said. 'You guys go on ahead.'

Porter nodded, then started towards the Cessna. There'd better be some booze on that plane, he thought. I don't care what. I'd knock back a Babycham right now.

'One more thing,' said Tannon.

Porter and Bald simultaneously stopped in their tracks and looked back at the deputy commissioner. Porter said, 'What's that?'

'A couple of weeks from now, you'll read about the deaths of two British heroes in the obituaries section. The report will state that Bob Tully and Ronald Soames died defending the mine against a rebel attack. They'll be cited, I expect.'

Bald almost choked on the warm air. 'You've got to be fucking kidding.'

'We don't have a choice. This cover story has to be watertight, to make sure the truth never gets out. Their families are less likely to investigate if Tully and Soames died as heroes. It makes them look less suspicious. In fact, don't be surprised if there's a posthumous investiture at Buckingham Palace.'

'So Bob and Soames get a medal each. What the fuck do we get?'

Tannon shifted awkwardly on the spot. 'We can't acknowledge your role in this operation, for obvious reasons. But we can offer you something else.'

'Like what? A pat on the back?'

'A job.'

'Working for who?'

'Us,' Tannon said. 'You're at a loose end with Five, and we could use a couple of guys like you at Vauxhall. We've got plenty of experts and middle managers, but not many people who are good at the dark stuff.'

Bald shook his head angrily. 'Not for me, lass. I'm going back to Hereford. I've had enough of the grey-man crap.'

'It's not a choice,' Tannon said. 'It's an order. Angela's already requested your transfer from Five, as a matter of fact. You'll start working for us immediately after the mission debrief.'

'So that's our reward?' Porter said. 'A job working at Legoland?'

'It's better than nothing.' Tannon smiled at him. 'And that's ma'am to you, John. You can address me properly now I'm your new boss. Now, if you'll excuse me. I'll see you on the plane.'

She turned and strode towards the office, nodding a greeting at Shoemaker. Porter watched her go, shaking his head in disbelief.

'Looks like we're going home empty-handed.'

'Not quite, mate.'

Porter glanced at his mucker.

'What's that supposed to mean?'

Bald didn't reply. He watched Shoemaker and Tannon and the two guards disappear into the building. Waited until the door had closed behind them. Then he reached down into his side pocket, took something out. Whatever it was, Bald had clasped his fist tightly around it. He glanced around the airfield, making sure no one else was around. Then he extended his arm towards Porter and unclenched his fist.

'I grabbed it while no one was looking back at the compound. Just before we left the manager's office,' he said. 'And I know a bloke in Amsterdam who can fence it for us . . .'

Nestling in the palm of his hand was a rough diamond the size of a golf ball.

THE END

You have to **survive it**
To **write it**

NEVER MISS OUT AGAIN
ON ALL THE LATEST NEWS FROM

CHRIS
RYAN

Be the first to find out
about new releases

Find out about events with
Chris near you

Exclusive competitions

And much, much more …

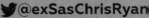

RIDE THE WILD TRAIL